DAUGHTERS

of

TEUTOBOD

DAUGHTERS

of

TEUTOBOD

KURT HANSEN

RESOURCE *Publications* · Eugene, Oregon

DAUGHTERS OF TEUTOBOD

Resource Publications
An Imprint of Wipf and Stock Publishers
199 W. 8th Ave., Suite 3
Eugene, OR 97401

www.wipfandstock.com

PAPERBACK ISBN: 978-1-6667-4985-4
HARDCOVER ISBN: 978-1-6667-4986-1
EBOOK ISBN: 978-1-6667-4987-8

JULY 15, 2022 1:40 PM

Dedicated to all the women who persisted.

CONTENTS

Preface

— IX —

Prologue: The Teutonic People

— XI —

SECTION I

GUDRUN'S STORY, C. 104-102 B.C.E.

— I —

SECTION II

SUSANNA'S STORY, 1941

— 53 —

SECTION III

GRETEL'S STORY, 2019

— 201 —

PREFACE

THE IMPETUS FOR THIS BOOK stems from two observations and a resultant question. The first observation is that throughout my working life, the best managers I have worked with or for have nearly always been women. Whether in the field of mental health, the business world, education, or ministry, I have continually found myself appreciative of the leadership style and capabilities of the women I have encountered. This is not to say every woman I have known is a great manager. Nor is it to dismiss the excellence of all the men I have worked with. But overall, the preponderance of those managers and leaders I have encountered for whom I have had the most respect were women.

The second observation derives from the knowledge of my own family system, specifically the distaff side. My maternal grandfather was a traditional German American, born on a farm in Wisconsin and raised in the traditional way. He grew up to be dogmatic, misogynistic, inflexible, authoritarian and at times, even abusive. Awareness of the struggles experienced by my mother throughout her life, her many accomplishments despite the emotional baggage she carried, and my later study of mental health and family systems theory form the background for the plot structure of this book.

The question which emerged from these observations is this: how did they do it? Women, once powerless, stolen by domineering, warlike men and used for their childbearing and labor value, somehow moved from being chattel to owning roles of mystics and seers and consultants. Women became the models for angels with major roles to play in the mythical stories of Valhalle. And they did this in a few generations. How did they do that?

Prologue

The Teutonic Peoples

THE TRIBES WHICH BECAME KNOWN as the Teutonic peoples began their incursions into what is now Germany in the second century before the common era. They were hunters and fishermen, and they earned a reputation for being fierce warriors as they moved south from the Nordic states, plundering other tribes for treasure and slaves. Over the many years of their migration, they learned the skills of farming and gathering plants for consumption as they moved from place to place. Patriarchal and pagan, Teutonic cultural practices toward women were initially barbaric, although (with some exceptions) they practiced a strict monogamy. Endogamic marriage was rarely practiced, and only with a significant bride purchase. The far more common practice was to "take" women for marriage via raiding of other tribes they encountered.

Teutonic tribes bore a great many names, peoples who eventually combined to form several major nationalities including the Franks, the Saxons, the Alemanni, the Goths, the Slavs, and the Vandals, as well as a number of minor tribal leagues. As these various Germanic and Nordic peoples clashed first with one another, and then for six centuries with the styles, customs, language and religious beliefs of the Roman Empire (including those of the emerging Christian religion), the eventual amalgamation of blood and culture engendered the creation of Europe and its various nation states.

This book begins, however, with a focus on those earliest times of migration, resulting in an all-out battle with Rome carried out by two of the largest groups, the Cimbri and the Teutons. Though the entire hoard was defeated by the Roman general Marius (the Teutons in 102 B.C.E., followed by the annihilation of the Cimbri a year later), the absolute de-votion of these peoples – and especially of their women – so impressed the Romans that their heroism and fierce resistance to subjugation was recorded in detail by some of the earliest Roman historians, Tacitus and Julius Caesar, as well as by Plutarch, Valerius Maximus and others. The historians even coined a phrase to describe the character of these peoples in battle: *furor Teutonicus,* or the "Teutonic Fury," as a testimony to what the Roman generals had observed.

The events recounted in the culmination of Gudrun's story are based on these early historical records and can be presumed to have happened much as described, although some license has been necessarily taken regarding their presentation.

KURT HANSEN

Section I

Gudrun's Story

c. 104-102 B.C.E.

CHAPTER ONE

THE smoke of the grist fires rose incessantly, grey black against the cloudy blue sky as the day meandered toward its middle hours. It was the season of harvest, and those konas who were able were out among the plantings, gleaning grain or digging turnips, carrots, or beets out of the black, loamy soil. Some ground grain into flour and some baked bread, while others tended the fires and the fleshpots. Still others were about the business of tanning hides, mostly of deer, raccoons, rabbits, or fox, occasionally from a bear. The smells of death intermingled with the breathing life and beating heart of the sveit.

Gudrun liked this time of day best. She grabbed another handful of golden wheatstalks, slicing off the grain heads with a strong whisking motion and dropping the grain into her tightly woven flaxen gathering bag. She paused for a moment, wiping the sweat from her brow with the back of her hand. The sun was bright today, making the air steamy. Gudrun looked out across the hills, down the valley, past the wooded glades where she could see dozens of other kǫngulls like her own, and she knew there were even more beyond the reach of her eyes. Most of the kǫngulls contained about 100 persons, but some had more. As she fixed her gaze closer, to the kǫngull where she lived, she could see the jungen, chasing one another, some wielding sticks or branches, others seeking to escape the assaults of their aggressors. The jungmädchen were variously helping their mothers with cooking or cleaning vegetables or sewing hides; the kinder simply hid in corners or clung to their mothers' legs.

Several hours passed, and now the sun was receding, thankfully, because its blazing, yellow glare kept breaking through the billowing clouds all day, intensifying the laborers' fatigue. Gudrun emptied her grain bag into the large, woven basket at the edge of the planting. The basket was filled to the brim, and as she plunged both hands into the basket, letting the harvested grain sift between her fingers, a smile of satisfaction soft-ened her face. Filling up her basket all the way to the top was for her, a measure of the goodness of the day. She hoisted the heavy basket, glad for the leather strap she had fashioned to carry it. Before she designed the strap, two women were needed to carry the woven baskets—one on either side—especially when full. But Gudrun decided to cut a long strip from the edge of a tanned deer hide and, with a sharp bone needle she affixed the strap to her basket, allowing her to shoulder the entire weight by herself.

When she first showed her invention, one of the men—Torolf—chastised her for taking the piece of deer hide. He pushed her to the ground and threatened worse, but Teutobod intervened, bashing Torolf on the head with his club and sending him reeling. Teutobod, Gudrun's mann, was the undisputed leader of their sveit, and he had been their leader long before he took her for his wife, ever since the sveit's earliest days in Jutland. He ordered that all the grain baskets be fashioned with straps for carrying, and Gudrun won the admiration of all the konas (and even some men). Torolf avoided her from then on.

As evening approached, it was time to prepare for the return of the männer. Most hunting excursions were a one-day affair, bringing in meat for perhaps a few days at best. But as the harvest season proceeded, the männer would leave for days at a time, seeking to increase supplies for the long winter to come. This foray had lasted nearly a week, but Gudrun was told by Teutobod to expect their return before seven suns had passed, and she shared this information with the some of the other konas. By now all the kongulls were preparing for the männer coming home.

As the sun began to set, the konas started pulling out skins from their bærs, unfolding them and laying them on the ground about the fire pits. The flesh pots were stirred and stoked, and a hearty stew was prepared with deer meats, mushrooms, yellow beans, potatoes, turnips and carrots, seasoned with salt and fennel and black peppercorns. Flasks of beer that had been cooling in the stream all day were brought to each firepit and hung on a stake which had been plunged in the ground for that purpose. Various dinner ware made from carved bone or fashioned out of wood or clay were laid out. All was in readiness.

An aura of anticipation and anxiety tumbled around the kongull, shortening tempers as the waiting lengthened. Finally, about an hour af-ter the sun had fully set, the sound of the ram's horn distantly blasted out its announcement: *Die männer komme!* The jungen were hustled away to the kinderbærs. One never knew the mood that might accompany the hunters when they returned, and things could and often did get ugly. The konas sat or knelt respectfully beside the firepits, twitching, nervously swatting insects away from the food, inhaling excitement and breathing out fear. Soon the rustling of leaves and the snap of twigs underfoot grew louder and closer until the shadows brought forth the whole troop of men, bustling in to the kǫngull, carrying or dragging the meat they had procured, pounding their chests, howling, pulling on their scraggly hair or beards, banging the ground with clubs or spears and smelling of the hunt and of the forest. Similar sounds of triumph and dominion could be heard resonating throughout all the kǫngulls below as the männer clamored in across the entire sveit.

Here in Gudrun's kǫngull, the konas kept their gaze to the ground, their eyes fixed on the fire, and as the hunters' swagger slowly abated, one by one the konas silently lifted their plates above their heads, each looking up to her mann as they all found their respective places. Once the providers were all reclining on skins beside the firepits, the konas stood and began to prepare plates of food for them. The men ate loudly, hungrily, slurping the stew from the lips of the bowls and using hunks of bread to grasp chunks of meat and vegetables.

The food having been consumed, skinflasks of beer soon followed, and before long the sated belches and grunts of the eaters gave way to boisterous banter, the proud providers reliving the thrill of killing a stag or the bravery of facing a bear. The konas scraped up the leftovers to take to the huts for themselves and the children, after which the cleanup tasks commenced. The women worked in groups of three or four, tending two large boiling pots to soak the dinnerware until all remnants of the food floated up to the top and were skimmed off. A little more soaking, then all the dinnerware was stacked and stored for the next use. Gudrun, along with two other konas, took the job of drying the cleaned dishes, swinging a dish in each hand to move the air. They playfully swung the wet plates or cups at one another, spritzing each other in the process and giggling like little meyas.

This being the end of a prolonged hunting venture, the children were tucked in early in the kinderhäusen, and the konas prepared to receive their husbands. For those unlucky enough to have brutish men, their wifely duties were not at all pleasant. Others were more fortunate. Gudrun was happy to be among the latter, hoping only that the beer ran out before Teutobod's love lust. She retreated to the bær she shared with her husband, glad for the privacy his role as leader provided. This entire kǫngull was comprised of the sveit's leadership and their skuldaliðs, and as such it claimed luxuries not generally known throughout the sveit by underlings. The leaders camped furthest upstream, and therefore got the cleanest water for drinking, cooking, and bathing. The leaders claimed individual space for themselves and their vifs, while others down below had to share living space with two or three other skuldaliðs.

Gudrun removed her garments and lay nude on the soft deerskins in her bær to prepare herself for her husband. Covering herself with another skin, she began to move her hands over her thighs and abdomen, softly, back and forth, her rough-skinned fingertips adapting to their more delicate uses. She moved a hand upward, swirling around her breasts and throat, teasing each nipple at the edges, holding back from contacting the most delicate flesh.

Her stroking and probing continued, a bit more urgently as she felt her breath rise and grow more heated. The muscles in her abdomen began to pulse, and as her hands found the sensitive spot between her legs, she felt the moisture beginning to flow inside her. When she was young Gudrun had learned from the older konas how to help her husband in this way, to ease his entrance and hasten his joy. Along the way, over the years, she also learned to enjoy herself more in the process. As the instinctive rocking motion in her pelvis began, she eased her manipulations, not wanting to be prematurely excited. Breathlessly, she looked toward the bær's entrance, hoping Teutobod would hurry.

CHAPTER TWO

GUDRUN was running. Her feet, wing-like, seemed barely to touch the forest floor as she ran away from the great scourge behind her. The strangers had come in the early morning hours when all was quiet and many of her clan were still sleeping comfortably in their thick, turf-covered huts. Gudrun was startled awake by a muffled cry which at first seemed surreal, perhaps part of a dream. But she woke and moved from her bed of straw and hides, feeling the musty coolness of the night mist on her bare feet as she peeked out the entryway into the dark haze.

She saw movement. She thought it was just one of her clan out relieving himself. But then more movement, and even more. Many dark figures were stealing through the little village, and suddenly it was clear: these were marauders! Gudrun turned quickly to her father Berndt's bed to wake him. "Vater!" she whispered urgently, shaking his shoulder. "Vater, waket!"

Berndt woke with an irritated grunt, not used to his sleep being interrupted. "Was ist's?" he snarled, his eyes not even fully focusing as he rousted up like a disturbed bear. At that very moment the entryway broke down, kicked in by three invaders. They rushed in, one carrying a torch and the other two armed with clubs and blades. One of them went quickly to the berth nearest the front and clubbed Gudrun's father to death. Blood came spurting and splashing from his head and face, hitting the top and sides of the hut. Gudrun knew he was instantly dead, and her eyes widened with fear as she saw the invaders move to the next bed, that of her father's first wife, Estrild. Gudrun screamed in fear and rage as they pulled Estrild out of her bed and stripped her, looking her up and down as if considering a purchase. The one holding the torch said, "Drepa inn kerling." It was a language Gudrun didn't know. But as the man closest to her slit her throat, the meaning of the words became terrifyingly clear.

They moved quickly to the next bed, grabbing Berndt's second wife Amalia by her hair and lifting her nightclothes. Amalia was younger than Estrild and was with child. Apparently, her pregnancy made her valuable enough to keep, so they grabbed her along with Gudrun, tying the hands of each securely before moving them out to the center of the village.

As the raid continued, Gudrun heard babies crying and small children screaming in fear, and the terrifyingly sudden silence of their cries as they were systematically clubbed to death. She looked around, seeing nothing but young women like herself, each with hands tied, bound at the waist to another both front and behind, a human chain of misery. As the sun's rays began to illuminate the horror, Gudrun could see piles of tools and weaponry, gathered up from among the huts. She could also see a smaller gathering of boys, none younger than about seven and none older than about twelve winters, similarly shackled and lashed together.

Gudrun was at the end of a line of about fifteen women. Her hands and wrists were slender, and she worked the leather straps against themselves until she was able to feel a bit of freedom. Back and forth, twisting and twisting, she worked the bindings, careful not to be too energetic. But finally, one of her small hands slipped free and she quickly untied the fetter from her waist. Slowly, quietly, step by agonizing step backward, Gudrun moved gingerly into the forest and dropped into the underbrush. She crept away on her belly for what seemed like forever until she felt safe enough to stand and run.

And run she did! Like the wind! She sweated out great drops of fear as she moved through the woods. She imagined that an elk could not have moved any faster. She ran until her lungs were near to bursting and her sides ached with a pulsing fury. When she finally stopped and bent over, her hands on her thighs, pulling in every bit of air she could, she dared to think that she might be safe. But no sooner had the thought entered her head than she heard the crackling of someone approaching. "They followed me! They are coming!" she cried to herself. Terrified, she took off again, running wildly, with the image of Estrild, naked and her neck spurting blood, driving her onward. But before long her legs melted beneath her, the muscles of her thighs and calves quivering and cramping. She dropped to the ground, her chest heaving. She closed her eyes, hoping her pursuers would not see her. But the crackling continued, closer and closer, and when she looked up, there was only one man. His strong shoulders loomed above her like the forest, and in his right hand was a battle club that seemed bigger than her whole body. As she considered her fate, she steeled herself to accept it. Her *mien waxed defiant. She would not cower before him. She was completely exhausted, but she forced herself to her knees. She stared defiantly into the man's eyes.*

But the look which he returned was not that of an assassin or a marauding invader; rather, his eyes held a kindness, even admiration. She hated that kind look. She would have killed him where he stood if only she was able. He spoke some words which Gudrun did not understand, but when he bent down and scooped her up like so much kindling, it was with a tenderness that disarmed her a bit. Her anger rose again, and she began to struggle against him. But she could do nothing. At that moment, she realized she had done all she could, and she simply had no power to resist him further. She would come to know later that his name was Teutobod.

❋❋❋

Gudrun softened in her bed, stirred by the dream and its vividness. That raid, and her subsequent initiation into Teutobod's sveit had been twelve winters ago, so long ago that she could barely remember her life before. She remembered it best like this—in dreams and reverie, either at night or during quiet daytime musings. And despite the horrific way in which she and most of the other konas had entered the sveit, Gudrun had become accustomed to this life of wandering and work. She had grown to be esteemed by her husband, so much so that he chose no other. And since he was the clear leader, his example was being emulated by other leaders as monogamy began filtering its way through the entire sveit. Certainly, there were männer who had more than one vif, but less and less each year. And while Teutobod's role as head of his hus was unassailable, Gudrun knew that he valued and appreciated her standing beside him. In that knowledge, Gudrun took some satisfaction.

She slipped quietly out of bed, trying not to disturb her husband prematurely. Her rough feet padded softly on the skin floor of the hus, her naked body shivering as it met the cold dampness of the early morning air. Quickly, Gudrun slipped on a cloth garment reserved for her morning cleansing routines, and moving toward the doorway, she picked up a piece of hard lye. She paused, looking back at Teutobod as he slept. His long, brown hair was surprisingly neatened, she thought, for someone just back from the hunt and still in bed. Even his thick beard looked trimmed and even. She looked at his shoulders, so broad and muscular that even now, even in the early hours of the day and after a night of passionate lovemaking, looking at him there brought a sudden stirring to her belly.

And then, just as suddenly and for a reason she could not understand, Gudrun felt a disturbing urge to kill Teutobod in his bed. She let the scene play out in her mind: She saw herself espying his broad axe, standing against the wall of the hus. She saw herself walk calmly over to that weapon, stepping not timidly but with intrepid silence. She felt her hands on the rough wood handle, hefting the weight of the blade end easily. She felt the air on her cheek as she swung the blade full force. She heard the crack of the impact like the butchering of a hog as it split his head nearly in two, and she felt the blood gushing forth, spurting its warm power onto her face and hands and feet. Just for a moment—a bit longer than was comfortable for her—Gudrun stood fixed in place, immersed in her husband's blood in her mind, no longer shivering from cold but from the tension of her strange imaginings.

Regaining her senses, Gudrun looked again toward her husband's bed, but lowered her gaze to avoid actually seeing him there. Slowly, she turned to take her leave of him, pulling back the thick skins covering the doorway to reveal the growing glow of morning. Happy for the light and the safety the early sunlight provided from her dark thoughts and fears, she headed out for a badly needed cleansing.

CHAPTER THREE

MORNING snuck into the kǫngull like a soft-footed invader, its shafts of misty light meandering through the cracks and crannies of Teutobod's hus and rousing him from his deep snoring. He saw that Gudrun was already awake, as expected. He knew that she and many of the other konas could be found standing in the river, washing off the sweat and smells of the prior day and night. Some of the men would be there as well, mostly those who had less tolerance for beer. It was common for männer and konas to share the river in the morning, though the groupings formed gender-specific circles that faced inward and kept a respectful distance one from the other.

Teutobod rose and headed down to the river to bathe. The aroma of beer brewing was pervasive. It was early, but the process of making beer was involved and took time. Those konas who brewed beer were called braufraus, maybe as a taunt originally, but the name stuck and became a title of some prestige over time. It was a highly valued and important position, a daily responsibility involving several steps. Their work began early, cooking the barley and soaking the bitter hops. After cooking down the grain, they mashed it into a paste, adding fresh water and hops and sealing the mixture in skin bags, which were then hung on bone hooks or wooden pegs on the walls of a brauhus. As the bags began to swell from the yeasts growing inside them, each was opened briefly to relieve the pressure. Occasionally, an old skin would give way under the expanding gasses, and the exploding *Bang!* could be heard everywhere, resulting in shrieks of startled laughter from the jungen. The yeasty, loamy smell of the brauhus wafting in the breeze was constant, like the rising smoke from the campfires. And like the demand for more beer from the men.

At the river, Teutobod found a group of his lieutenants and joined their circle. All the others feared and respected Teutobod, but he knew leadership was always subject to challenge. Teutobod trusted no one. That's why his bone knife, razor sharp and stained with blood, was in its customary place, sheathed in a deerskin holster suspended from a sash around his midriff. Still, he knew from experience that while respect may be born out of fear, it is solidified in fair treatment. So, he took interest in the well-being of all the men of the sveit, and especially in the lives of those leaders and their skuldaliðs with whom he shared the close community of his kǫngull.

"You all had good reunion with your vifs last night?" Teutobod said with a lusty smile as he glanced around at the other men, temporarily interrupting their lathering and splashing. The nodding heads and smiling, bearded faces gave the answer. "You deserve it!" Teutobod said. "It was a good hunt!"

Torolf kept his gaze downward, saying nothing. "No success in your hus, Torolf?" Teutobod taunted him. Torolf was the one most likely to replace Teutobod as leader of the sveit, or at least to want to try. He was among the fiercest in battle and the most competitive in games of chance and hunting skill. His face was emotionless, his eyes focused on washing his loins as he responded, "My vif did not please me. I killed her. I'll find another."

The bathing stopped. All eyes in the circle of men were on Torolf, then on Teutobod. Torolf finally could no longer avoid the strong gaze of Teutobod, and he slowly met Teutobod's blue eyes with his own steely stare. Everyone knew it was a man's right to divest himself of a vif if she did not please him. But to kill her was not allowed, except perhaps in cases of adultery.

"What had she done deserving death?" Teutobod demanded. Torolf continued with the challenge of his eyes locked on Teutobod. "As I said, she did not please me."

Teutobod had long known of Torolf's penchant for aggression, especially towards women. He took his first vif, Sunga, during a raid on a tribe in the Moravian hills, and after the sveit got settled in that area, she regularly appeared bruised and bloodied, sometimes so much so that she was unable to do her work. The other konas had come to Gudrun to ask that she intervene with Teutobod on Sunga's behalf, but Teutobod would not interfere in the affairs of another man's hus. Sometime later Sunga bore Torolf a female child, and Torolf killed the baby in a rage, smashing its head on a rock and tossing it into the woods. Sunga was so horrified she stood in the midst of the kǫngull and slit her own throat with Torolf's knife.

Torolf soon took a new vif from a raid on another, smaller tribe. Her name was Vilma, and for a time, he seemed to treat her with less violence. Luckily, Vilma had borne a son for him, and Torolf continued his generally benign treatment of her. What had happened last night to cause this sudden murderous behavior toward her, no one could surmise.

Teutobod responded, "Torolf, you are a strong warrior and a great hunter, but I think an evil spirit lives in you. I will have to decide which is more important. For now, you must bring Vilma's body out to the place of preparation." With that, Teutobod left the circle. All the rest of the men followed, leaving Torolf standing alone.

✳✳✳

The place of preparation, called the hegjahus, was set off beyond the end of the sveit, about five flights of an arrow downstream from the last kǫngull. There, in an open area, cleared of all brush and saplings, was a large, flat rock leading out to the riverbank, raised up a bit in appearance due to the ground having been dug away around it, and with stone trenches on either side leading down to the river below. On this rock the bodies of those who had died were laid for burial preparation. Adjacent to this cleared area was a small bær with a single occupant: Brunhild.

Brunhild was a mystic, a seer and caster of runes. All feared her, but with a different fear than Teutobod commanded. Brunhild was seen as dangerously odd, even otherworldly. To approach her brought a sense of possible doom, as though the wrath and promise of the gods were wrapped in the mantle around her shoulders, and she might unleash either at any moment.

Brunhild's visage was off-putting. She decorated her head with a jumble of peacock feathers held in place by a netting fashioned from spider silk and beeswax. Her face was always painted in a variety of bright colors, none of which was sufficient to shift one's focus away from her huge, deep-black eyes. Those eyes seemed never to blink, and when one had the misfortune to fall under her gaze, the first instinct was to turn and run. A mantle of furs usually draped over her shoulders and hung down below her waist. In warmer months she sometimes wore nothing but that fur mantle, eschewing the usual modesty of public life. Around her waist she carried a variety of leather pouches, each carrying mysterious concoctions she employed to treat various ailments or to administer charms and spells. In general, the männer of the sveit tended to avoid contact with Brunhild, although she had visits from a steady stream of konas seeking counsel about issues related to sex or illness or other family matters.

Brunhild was also undoubtedly the oldest person in the entire sveit, which in itself made her odd. People did not ordinarily live to an old age. When the vitality of elders was gone and their usefulness exhausted, it was common for the younger members of their skuldalið to hold a ceremony, praising their elders' accomplishments before mercifully ending their lives.

But Brunhild was different. She had set herself apart from the other konas in the sveit. Even the oldest members could barely remember when her strange ascendency began, but Teutobod knew; it started with a battle. The women were preparing to accompany the men into battle as usual, to tend to their men's wounds and urge their bravery, and if need be, even to join in the fighting. But prior to the battle, Brunhild, who had not been taken as a vif (probably due to her peculiar looks and disposition), approached the hus of Teutobod's father and walked right in with neither invitation nor permission. She looked directly into the eyes of Teutobod's father, Olav, and produced a small pouch. She opened it and emptied its contents onto the deerskin floor of the hus. She circled the scatterings three times, holding her hands over them while she rhythmically raised and lowered her upper body like a snake. Then, suddenly, she dropped to her knees, hovering closely above the bits of bone and teeth and claws, closely considering each in relation to the others. With her face still fixed on her runes, she began to prophesy in a hollow monotone: "This battle must not begin before the new moon. If you attack before the new moon, you will suffer great losses. If you wait, you will suffer only two losses. So say the gods. Be warned."

Brunhild then gathered her runes, replaced them in her pouch and departed without another word.

Teutobod, then only a junge, had seen this strange event. He had heard stories told around the fire, stories of special women who had foretold futures and who could intercede with the gods, but he never really understood them. As he grew to manhood, he learned to trust most in his weapons, his instincts and his strong body. But Olav later reminisced about Brunhild, recalling how he had decided after her visit to wait till the new moon to attack, and how after the battle, when only two men were lost, he had been convinced. He consulted Brunhild in every major decision from that time on. That had been some thirty winters ago and now, a leader in his own right, Teutobod carried on the tradition; he consulted Brunhild on a regular basis. She had never steered him wrong.

***

Torolf brought the cart reserved for carrying the dead and placed it outside his hus. Everyone knew what the appearance of that cart meant. They began to gather as the word passed quickly that someone had died. When Torolf brought out Vilma's lifeless body and laid it on the cart, it was plain to see what had happened. The purple finger marks on her neck and her bulging, pinkish eyes bore undeniable testimony to the fact that she had been strangled. Ordinarily when someone died, some of the konas and perhaps some of the männer would gather to help push the cart to the place of preparation. But not one person stepped forward. Torolf looked around expecting some help, but seeing none was forthcoming, he finally uttered a disgusted grunt, picked up the handles of the cart and pushed its heavy weight forward by himself. It took him the better part of an hour to maneuver the gruesome load past all the kongulls to the place of preparation, and word of what happened began to spread quickly throughout the sveit.

When he arrived at the hegjahus, Torolf was surprised to see Brunhild standing there, waiting for him. Her staring eyes seemed to look through him to a place he did not want to acknowledge existed. Standing a good distance away, Brunhild raised her hand toward the body, moving it such as one might if offering a caress. Torolf backed away as though accused. Brunhild quickly moved her hand to a stopping gesture, palm out, halting Torolf in his tracks. Looking directly into his eyes, she pointed a gnarled finger at him, then toward Vilma's body, then toward the rock. Torolf lifted the body off the cart and carried it to the place of preparation. He then grabbed and turned the cart, glad for the lessened weight, and hurriedly departed. He could feel the eyes of Brunhild boring holes in his skull as he hurried to escape the reach of her mystical vision.

A short time later, a group of konas, Gudrun among them, arrived bearing buckets, a variety of wildflowers, and some spices, as well as a sharp knife. They filled the buckets with water and carried them up to the preparation place. Sigrid, the oldest of the konas and a close friend of Gudrun's, removed the clothing from Vilma's body and washed her thoroughly. She made two small slits in Vilma's neck to drain out most of her blood. As the blood mingled with the water into the trenches along-side the rock and drained into the river, Gudrun made a wreath of flowers and placed it on Vilma's head. She pushed Vilma's eyes gently back into their sockets, pulling the eyelids down and weighting them with some rocks.

Finally, the konas dressed Vilma's body in a clean burial gown and strewed the remaining flowers over and around her. The group looked up to see the approving eyes of Brunhild before they dismissed themselves to their kongulls. Gudrun and Sigrid lingered a bit longer, kneeling be-side Vilma's lifeless body. No words were exchanged, but when Gudrun's green-gray eyes met the dark brown eyes of her older companion, they brimmed like sego lilies after a dark rain. As they considered the injustice and senseless brutality Vilma had endured, the feeling of sadness and rage needed no words; it was as clear as the sound of the ram's horn. When they finally rose to follow the others, they stopped to look back at Brunhild. Brunhild raised her hand and brought it slowly down, as though bridging the distance between them, perhaps a sort of blessing. Gudrun felt an endearing sense of inclusion, and she looked up at Brun-hild with an appreciative smile. Then she and her older friend turned and slowly made their way back to the kongull.

✳✳✳

That evening, just before sunset, the people gathered for the brenna. Some brought flowers or small tokens of food or stone or clay and laid them on the body. Torolf did not, of course, attend. As the sun fully departed the sky, the body was lifted onto a pile of dried sticks and branches reaching up taller than a mann's head and out from the center as far around as two männer's outstretched arms. Brunhild raised her hands to the sky, calling out to the gods to receive Vilma and conduct her to the river of life and peace. When she gave the signal, the brenna was lit and the flames quickly rose to an immense conflagration. Some stayed to watch, but most simply turned away in sadness, unwilling to witness the awesome, ugly truth of death and its aftermath. Seeing the looks of abhorrence on their faces as they left, Brunhild simply smiled. She would tend the fire until its holy task was fully accomplished.

CHAPTER FOUR

THE days of harvest piled themselves into stores of grain and salted meat stocks as members of the sveit prepared for the coming winter. Brunhild had informed Teutobod of her visions of a particularly harsh winter ahead, and while he was not fully convinced of her accuracy in weather forecasting, neither was he willing to test it. He and the other leaders met with the männer of the other kongulls to plan two more extended hunting trips, the results of which brought hundreds of pounds of meat for use throughout the sveit. It was after returning from the second of these forays that the situation with Torolf reached a point of crisis.

As the männer reunited with their vifs, Torolf remained alone in his hus. That night he drank too much beer and wandered down to one of the lower kongulls in search of female company. He saw a young woman, not yet of age to be married, as she walked out into the forest to relieve herself. Torolf secreted himself along her path and seized her, clamping his muscled arm around her neck from behind and covering her mouth with a massive fist. He held her that way, squeezing tighter and tighter, until he could feel the fight go out of her. Then he let her go and she slumped down to the forest floor. As she lay there helpless and dazed, Torolf lifted her garments and drove into her with the dark fury of lust and hatred, and after releasing his seed, he stood up, hovering over his conquest as if it was a mighty thing he had done. He looked down to see blood on his loins; apparently, she had been untouched before. The sight of her blood further fueled his sense of conquest, and as she started to stir, weeping softly, Torolf began to laugh. He relieved himself on her, mixing his urine with her tears and blood and anguish. And then he grabbed a nearby rock and moved to the place above where her head was laying. He knelt on the ground, raising the heavy rock high above his head, and just as her blurry, confused eyes found his face, he brought the rock down on her head, crushing her skull with one furious blow. Her extremities violently jerked three times, and then she lay motionless. He stood up, adjusted his clothing, and made his way back up the hill, meandering around the outskirts of the encampments until he reached his own kǫngull. What Torolf did not know, was that he was being watched.

A pair of jungmädchen had also come out to relieve themselves just a few minutes after their older kinswoman. By the time they reached that part of the forest, Torolf was lost in his bloodlust, raping the young woman (whose name happened to be Ada). The two shocked observers hid behind a thick pile of brush, fearful of making any noise that might indicate their presence. The girls saw every detail of what Torolf did to Ada, and when they saw him kneel down with that big rock in his hands, the girls instinctively covered each other's mouths tightly, choking back the terrified screams that were bursting in their throats.

After Torolf had finally moved far enough away, the two girls ran back to their mother and told her what they had seen. Their father went with them to the place to see for himself, and then he went immediately up to see Teutobod, bringing the two young witnesses with him. Teutobod questioned the girls. No, they had not seen where the man went; they were too scared. All they knew was that he was moving uphill. Yes, they saw his face; they knew he was not an outsider. Yes, they would recognize him if they saw him again. Teutobod sent word to all the leaders to gather in the center of the kǫngull. He asked the man to stay so that he and his daughters could tell all the leaders of the sveit what happened.

Within a few minutes, all the leaders were gathered around Teutobod and his visitors from the kǫngull below. All, that is, except for Torolf, whose absence was instantly noticed by Teutobod, and whose face had been in Teutobod's mind almost immediately after hearing this horrible story.

"Where is Torolf?" Teutobod questioned. No one could say where he might be. Teutobod picked out three men, "You and you and you, go to his hus and find him. Bring him here." The three left, stopping by to get weapons before confronting the inimitable Torolf. A few minutes later, Torolf strode confidently into the group, feigning ignorance of the situation. As he walked up, the eyes of the girls widened in terror, and they hid behind their father. Teutobod saw their reaction, and he called them out. "Meyas, komme." At first, they refused, shivering in fright. But Teutobod, sensing their fear, knelt on one knee and softened his voice, and he again said, "Meyas, dáð. Komme hér." Slowly, the two emerged, holding tightly onto their father's cloak until he gently pushed them forward to face Teutobod.

Gudrun was watching from the gathering, which was growing as more and more people joined from the kǫngulls below. She admired Teutobod's ability to dispel fear among the weaker members of his community. She could see that look in his eye, that same look she had seen when he stood over her those years ago, a look she initially refused to acknowledge but had grown to accept and even to admire. Maybe the little girls could see it too, because they came forward to stand close to Teutobod.

"Why were you hiding?" Teutobod whispered to them. He watched their eyes, as both girls looked past Teutobod to the man standing directly behind him. Teutobod whispered again, "Do you see the man you saw out in the woods? The man who hurt Ada?" Both girls looked back to Teutobod as their heads slowly nodded.

Still whispering, Teutobod told them, "Now I want you to be very brave. There are many here to protect you. I am here to protect you. But I want you both to walk over to the man who did this, and I want you to look at his face, and I want you to point your finger at him. If you will be that brave, I promise he will never hurt anyone ever again."

The girls looked at each other, then back at Teutobod. The older girl, Acca, looked around the gathering, seeing the eyes of all the konas encouraging her, as though a huge responsibility was being conveyed on her little shoulders. Teutobod stood up as the young girls moved forward, hand in hand, to stand directly in front of Torolf. They looked up at his glowering, rage-filled eyes, and as though guided by one mind and spirit, both girls pointed at him. Acca became even bolder, and she poked Torolf in the belly, hard. "He is the one! He is the one who we saw kill Ada!"

Torolf emitted an animal-like growl, an erupting volcano sound emerging from the bowels of hell itself. The two little meyas shrieked and recoiled in fear as Torolf began to lash out in all directions, trying to run, trying to escape. But there was no escaping from the growing crowd of the gathered sveit, no escaping the consequences of his actions. He was subdued by several of those around him, männer and konas alike. Teutobod said, "Bring him here to me." They brought the struggling, howling monster to stand before their leader.

"Torolf," Teutobod began, looking him in the eye, "I once told you I would have to decide which was more important: your strength in the hunt and in battle, or the evil spirit in you. You have answered that question for me." Looking among the other leaders in his kǫngull, Teutobod said, "Bind him tightly, hand and foot, and secure him to a strong tree, away from all. No one is to have contact with him. Tomorrow I will decide his punishment." They took their prisoner away and did as they were commanded. Teutobod dismissed the crowd to their bærs, and he returned to his, as well.

As they entered the hus, Gudrun could see the strain of leadership on him, the tired sadness of responsibility, the weight of his impending judgment. Teutobod was incredibly strong, but over the years Gudrun had seen another side of him. He hated violence and meanness. He certainly continued to lead and participate in all the battles and raids on other tribes, but it was something he never enjoyed, and it seemed to get harder on him with every passing year. Sensing an opportunity, Gudrun broke the silence.

"Do you know what you will do with Torolf?" The rivulets of tension stiffened on his face. "Not yet. I know he can no longer live among us here. Beyond that, I have not decided."

"May I speak?" Gudrun offered, cautiously. Teutobod opened his eyes, turning to look at her. "Speak," he said.

"Torolf's violence was against konas. Two vifs. Even the baby he killed was a meya. Why not let his hatred return to him? Why not let justice be given by the konas?"

Teutobod looked down, pondering Gudrun's words. The idea appealed to him. There was a fitting logic, sort of the closing of a circle in what she had said. "Gudrun, you have spoken very wisely," he said. "It will be as you have said, but the decision must be mine. No one must hear of this conversation between us." He looked deeply into her eyes, seeking her assent. It was a look both gratifying and dangerous. Gudrun realized she was making a pact here, any breech of which would have dire consequences for her life.

"Our words will remain with me, minn mann. I will not betray you."

Teutobod pulled her close in a genuine show of affection. She snuggled into his chest, feeling satisfied and safe. It was then she chose to tell him: she was with child.

✼ ✼ ✼

In the morning there was an uneasy buzz throughout the sveit. Everyone had heard what happened, and everyone awaited Teutobod's decision about Torolf. Many thought Torolf was possessed by an evil spirit. Even the more brutal of the männer in the sveit who sympathized with Torolf's dominating posture toward konas, even they knew he had crossed a line and needed to be dealt with. Most everyone was hoping for the severest punishment.

When Teutobod emerged to stand at the center of the leaders' kǫngull, a throng of people surrounded him. He raised his hands, turning around slowly in every direction, motioning for silence. He motioned to three of his strongest leaders as he said, "Bring Torolf here." They went immediately, and a few minutes later they returned with the bound man, who was hissing and growling like a furious badger. Torolf stood before Teutobod, filthy, bound at the wrists, glaring with hatred, as the peoples' murmurs of contempt for him rose to a cacophonous pique. Teutobod again raised his hands for silence, and when order was restored, he began to speak.

"This man has committed violence not once, but many times. He has no further right to live among us, nor shall his name be spoken. This evil must be punished. My judgment is this: He is to be taken immediately to a place far outside the sveit and bound to a thick tree. There he shall be killed, and his corpse will be left to rot. And because this man's evil and violence has in every case been directed at konas, even his own vifs, and even against jungmädchen and his own offspring, it shall fall to the konas to carry out the punishment."

A full ten seconds passed with no one speaking. So shocked was the crowd at what they had heard from their leader, so unprecedented were his words, no one knew quite what to say or do. Gudrun, standing near her husband, nearly bit a hole right through her lip. But finally, when the entirety of Teutobod's pronouncement had sunk in, there rose such a roar of approval and appreciation from all who were gathered there, the gods must certainly have heard it. With one voice the community of the sveit praised Teutobod's judgment. And for the first time, the voices of the konas were heard above the others.

The konas moved forward, surrounding the doomed murderer, and the crowd separated to allow the death march to proceed. Initially, the prisoner pushed back as the throng forced him along, but his fury and resistance gave way to a sort of desperate acquiescence. He began to weep, a thing which no mann was ever seen to do, and seeing his weakness, some of the konas began to taunt him, making loud, mock sobbing sounds and jabbing at him with their fists or fingers or sticks.

The crowd came to a clearing about an hour's walk through the forest, where they bound him tightly across his chest, his midriff, his thighs and his ankles. Someone exposed his genitals which soon became bloody after suffering assaults from rough sticks and even from clawing fingernails. He howled in pain. But Gudrun stood in front of the man and raised her voice. "Enough! Will you become the evil you wish to destroy?"

A hush fell over the group as their raucous, liquid rage was thinned by a measure of virtue. Gudrun spoke again. "This man must be killed. But his evil must not live on in us. He will be killed and left to die, as Teutobod commanded. But we do not dare enjoy our task. One blow will end him. Who will deliver it?"

The eyes of all the konas were moving around, back and forth, searching out who among them should be the executioner. Finally, a voice spoke up. It was Disa, a neighbor to the family of Ada. Looking directly at Gudrun, she said, "You do it." All the others immediately agreed, and Gudrun looked down at the ground. She had not anticipated being the one to carry out such a thing as this. But she knew it must be done. She looked upward toward the heavens, as if hoping to find an approving glance from the gods, and then she turned slowly, fixing her gaze on the bleary, bloody, yellowing eyes of the convict. With her eyes locked on his, she stretched out her hand behind her. "*Brandr. Þurfa brandr.*" Someone brought forth a knife, and she felt the handle in her hand. A quick slice across his neck and it was over. As his blood gushed out, riding the trail of her blade on its merciful task, it splashed its warm, dark thickness on her hands and neck and feet. Instantly Gudrun remembered her daydream, when she stood beside the sleeping body of her husband, enrapt by her murderous fantasy. But this reality was nothing like it. Nothing like it at all. She choked back the bile of revulsion that was climbing up from her gut. She dropped the knife, turned, and walked through the sea of konas, her eyes fixed on the ground in front of her. The others followed without another word. Disa, whose knife had been proffered for the task, retrieved it. As she stood up, her eyes looked deep into the dead emptiness of Torolf's eyes. Justice had been served. And for once, serving had been an honor.

Chapter Five

THE winter came bullying its way through the sveit, indifferent, relentless. The weeks passed by slowly as the energies of the people were spent neither producing nor seeking produce, but merely surviving. Gudrun's belly grew, and Sigrid and the other konas began to take special interest in helping her. This was not Gudrun's first pregnancy, or even her second. She had lost her first child when only four moons had passed in her third year with Teutobod. Six years later she carried a second baby to full term—a little girl—but the infant died from some illness less than a month later. It was not unusual for newborns to die; it was simply part of the ongoing life of the sveit. There had even been a third time when she thought she was pregnant, and she might have been, since her menstrual blood had stopped for nearly two moons, but nothing came of it. For some time, Gudrun had thought herself cursed, though she could not imagine for what offense. She had even consulted Brunhild, who offered a spell which had no effect. But now, Gudrun was determined. She would raise this child to be healthy and strong. All she had to do was make it through this awful, killing winter.

Life amidst the gruff assaults of winter yielded fertile time for teaching. Männer met with the jungen, telling stories of hunting and battle, and demonstrating techniques useful to such pursuits. In all but the most intolerable weather, the jungen's lessons took place outdoors, to allow room for throwing axes and blades, shooting arrows, and practicing fighting skills, but also to acclimate the boys to the harsher temperatures. "A true warrior will battle any opponent, on any battlefield, at any time," Teutobod was fond of saying. His father had taught him and the other boys his age this same lesson, and Teutobod always took it to heart more than anyone else. He became known early on for his prowess and stamina after he volunteered to stay out all day and night in a blizzard just because another junge had said it was impossible. When they went to find him the next morning, he was standing, tethered to a tree and leaning on his club, with icicles hanging like stalactites from his scraggly hair and stiffened deerskin clothing. When they tried to help him, he pushed them away and issued a growling refusal, "I am a warrior! I walk my own way!" He then staggered, stiff-legged and unassisted, back to his father's hus, where he shortly collapsed. He could still remember the look of pride in his father's eyes.

As for the konas, winter was a time of preservation. Foodstuffs, of course, were preserved, as were the precious pieces of clothing and foot-wear, so important to the ongoing life of the sveit. Cracks and holes in the bærs were patched and covered over, as well. But beyond the need for physical things was the need to preserve history. And this was done chiefly through the telling of tales, an activity which was, for many, a favorite part of life together in the sveit.

On a typical, freezing, inhospitable day, Gudrun and several other konas had gathered about twenty jungmadchen in one of the kinderbærs for *Singt und Sagt*. Many of the tales were told through songs, songs with many verses, verses which recounted age-old ancestral sagas of heroism and triumph. There were stories of battle and bravery, of struggle and sacrifice, of interaction with the gods, of conflict and trial. There were stories of angels, beauty-bright creatures, colorfully adorned and aglow with shimmering light, who would fly above the struggles of männer, providing encouragement and urging warriors forward in battle.

It was always these last types of stories the little meyas most loved to hear. And today it was Sigrid's turn to sing a tale. Being one of the oldest konas in the entire sveit, Sigrid's teaching had special importance. The tale she chose to sing was entitled, "The Tale of Noble Skeya," and all the fidgeting ceased, and all the eyes looked up in eager anticipation as Sigrid began to sing her tale:

Skeya was the most beautiful of the angels in all the heavens.
Odin favored her more than all the others,
For Skeya inspired all who saw her to do their very best.

Skeya had long, golden hair, with waves like the sea
And eyes of azure blue like the clear summer sky.
Her arms were strong, and she could run like a deer.

A battle was coming, and Odin summoned Skeya.

Skeya came rapidly, and with her eyes lowered in respect,
Skeya asked Odin, "how may I serve?"

"A battle is coming! A time of great struggle is nearing!
The warriors will face a furious foe, and many will die.
Will you go with them to give them courage?"

"I will go willingly, great Odin," Skeya replied.
"I will gladly give comfort and help to our men in battle.
I will do whatever you believe I am able to do.

"And who shall go with me in this glorious task?"

At she sang this last line, Sigrid looked up and around at all the little
meyas and jungmädchen in the circle, and all the little hands went up and
their voices clamored as one: "I will go! Let me! Let me!"

The song-story continued with details of how strong, lovely Skeya
and her brave sisters supported and encouraged the men, and how after
the battle those who had died valiantly were honored in the heavens, and
how Skeya and the other angels served them at table in the presence of
the gods and of Odin himself.

The Singt und Sagt dismissed for miteßen, and as the young girls
walked out hand in hand with one another or with their mothers, their
excited chatter filled the air with images of heavenly glory. The group split
into two halves of about fifteen persons, and the konas prepared a quick
lunch of bread and salted fish which they ate with the young ones. As they
ate there were nearby sounds of the jungen outside. They heard sounds
of grunting and straining as some engaged in fighting practice. They also
heard sounds of cheering and encouragement as others practiced with
bows or other weapons. Some of the older jungmädchen pulled back the
deerskin doorway coverings to catch a glimpse of the jungen, giggling
and pointing at whomever each favored.

It began to snow, softly at first but then much harder, and some of
the girls went outside to play, spinning and sliding, catching snowflakes
on their tongues. One small group began packing snow into shapes
which they then fashioned like pieces of art on the ground. One created
a fish, another a deer, and one older girl named Gria even created a small
hus out of the frozen medium. A group of jungen came running by, being chased by another group in some sort of battle game. They ran right

through the place where the jungmädchen were sculpting the snow, and all their creations were stomped into a muddy, unrecognizable mess. One of the younger girls began to cry, and Gria stood up angrily. She yelled after the group of jungen, calling them "stupid hogs." Just then, one of the männer showed up, following the jungen. He heard Gria's shouts, and he stopped, towering over her. "Know your place, mädchen!" he said, as he pushed her hard and she fell backward, hitting the frozen ground behind her with a thud. She glared back up at the mann, who began to laugh before he took off again after his group of trainees. Gria stood up again, taking up a posture of resistance, but the other girls were already leaving, their heads bowed in sadness and resignation.

Gria called after them, "Where are you going? There is more snow! They don't have to win!" But nobody came back, and Gria was left alone. She looked around at the sloppy mess and plopped herself down right in the middle of it, exactly where her sculpted snowhus had been, and there she sat, sulking.

Gudrun had been observing the entire scene from outside her hus across the kongull. It was snowing even harder now, and soon she could see Gria begin scooping and piling new snow all around her. Gudrun went back into her hus, and she soon emerged carrying a bundle. She walked across the clearing to where Gria was on her knees, gathering in the snow. Gria looked up to see her visitor, defiantly at first because the sun was behind Gudrun, making it difficult to see her. But Gria's visage softened when she recognized Gudrun. "Stand up, daughter," Gudrun said, and Gria stood. Gudrun unfurled her bundle of deer skins and laid them on the ground. "Every hus needs a floor," Gudrun said with a sly smile. Gria's face broke into a full grin, and Gudrun helped her lay the skins where she wanted them. Then the two set to work.

They scooped up and carried snow, using their coverings as baskets, and dumped the snow all around the periphery of the deer skin floor. Before long they had built a small fortress with snow walls the thickness of Gria's thigh. They fashioned an entryway big enough to crawl through, and then gathered brush and sticks for a roof. They criss-crossed the branches until a substantial ceiling was created, and then they both crawled back inside their creation. They each sat with their backs up against one of the walls, and Gria pulled her knees up against her chest. She looked around her little castle, feeling satisfied and proud.

"Now let us close our eyes and dream," said Gudrun. They closed their eyes, imagining this new house they had built, and as they spoke of it, it grew in their visions to be much bigger than the small snowhus it was. They spoke back and forth of the various rooms it might contain, and how there would be a place to cook and eat, and another place to sleep, and another place to gather and visit with others. They imagined two or even three fire pits to keep warm in the winter, with vents to let all the smoke escape, and how there would be piles of skins on which to rest.

The wind had picked up outside, and the cold was disturbing the daydreams of the little hus. Gudrun suggested it might be time to leave. Gria's eyes were still closed in reverie, but she opened them, looking at Gudrun with appreciation. She crawled over and snuggled up to Gudrun, embracing her warmly. "Thank you," she said. She laid her hand gently on Gudrun's belly, allowing herself to share—just for a moment—in the wondrous mystery of the growing life within her. "This baby will be very lucky to have such a good mother," Gria said, looking up at Gudrun with a smile. She moved toward the entryway and then looked back, "And I hope it is a little meya."

Gudrun smiled at the thought as they emerged from their shelter to walk through the storm back to their bærs.

❋ ❋ ❋

While the winter doldrums provided opportunity for education and for preserving history, they also allowed for another important function in the life of the sveit, namely, planning. Teutobod called gatherings of his leaders, usually three or four times during a typical winter, when issues of training, resources, and management of the sveit were discussed.

But Gudrun began to suspect something important was happening when she noticed these meetings were occurring more frequently than usual. The männer were meeting as often as one or even two times per week in the former hus of Torolf, which had been converted for the purpose. One evening as they reclined before sleeping, Gudrun asked Teutobod about the increased frequency of their meetings. "Is there anything I should know?" she queried. "Are we moving?"

"No need to worry about that yet," he replied. There may be changes coming, but nothing has been decided. When that happens, I will let you know." His response frustrated her. She turned roughly over in their bed and pulled away from him, pulling the deerskin cover down to wedge between them.

The next morning the konas gathered around the washing cauldron where river water was heated for bathing. There was the usual chatter, and Magda offered her customary plaint about being sore from her husband's thrustings (which everyone knew was a barely veiled attempt to brag about her husband's voracious appetite for her and the size of his penis). Sigrid looked at Gudrun and rolled her eyes and they both quietly snickered. As she washed herself, Gudrun said, "Our husbands have been meeting quite a lot this winter." All responded immediately in assent, and while Gudrun was hoping to hear some bit of explanation from some of the others, it was to her that all the eyes turned expectantly. Sensing this, and not wishing to show her own frustration, she said, "I'm sure the männer will let us know when they come to any conclusions."

Gudrun knew the importance of her role as Teutobod's vif. But inside, she was as full of anxious wondering as all the others.

CHAPTER SIX

WINTER drudged onward, and the hours of sunlight lengthened bit by bit, though not enough to lighten the season-darkened mood of the sveit. By mid-winter, everyone was suffering with one degree or another of hopelessness. Gudrun, however, was focused on her belly. She began to feel her baby moving inside her, relishing those moments of incomparable connection. Teutobod, for his part, seemed to take little notice of Gudrun or her baby as his planning meetings—sometimes all-day affairs—continued. It was perhaps in response to his distance that Gudrun began to feel an increasing closeness to the other konas, who cared for her and shared in the excitement of the coming new life. This was especially true in her relationship with Sigrid.

The wisdom of Sigrid's many winters shone in her patient demeanor and in her grey-blue eyes and silvering hair. Sigrid had always spent more time with Brunhild than did anyone else, which lent even more mystery and authenticity to her matronly image among the konas. It was Sigrid who led efforts to teach the younger vifs about married life and about childbearing, and many konas turned to her for counsel. But for Gudrun, Sigrid had become more than a symbol. She had become a sort of mother figure, and even more so now that Gudrun was with child. And for her part, Sigrid returned Gudrun's tender affection, treating her like the daughter she never had.

Sigrid visited Gudrun often in her hus, and during one particular morning visit Gudrun said, "You bore three sons who lived and grew into männer. Were there more?"

Sigrid looked away for a moment, seeing a memory she did not relish. "Yes, there were three more. One died in my womb. That was the hardest. Another died from illness about six moons after I gave birth to him. And a third—a little meya—died in the raid that brought me here. She lived just over four winters."

Gudrun considered these painful truths. "Why do the gods give us children only to take them away?" she said, her eyes showing the fear behind her words as she clasped both hands protectively over her midriff.

Sigrid shook her head slightly as she responded, "The gods . . ." There was a note of disdain, even vehemence, in her tone. "If the gods are here at all, they seem to take little notice of the lives of konas and kinder."

"But Brunhild . . ." Gudrun stuttered.

"Brunhild?!" Sigrid said, chuckling. "I knew Brunhild when she was younger than you. She was crazy then and she's crazy now." Sigrid's chuckle grew into a full-throated laugh. "When I first came to this sveit, I was only fourteen winters old. Brunhild was a bit older, but she was so different from all the others. She never showed any interest in the ways of the konas. She never joined any of the other jungmädchen in work or play. She would go missing for hours or even days, and then she would show up again, looking like one of the männer returned from a hunt, all mud-streaked and her hair full of thistles and briars. And those eyes! The older she got, the wider and darker her eyes became. I used to be able to look at her. I even teased her; sort of felt sorry for her in a way. But by and by, I also distanced myself from her."

"But you go to see her all the time!" Gudrun said, quizzically. "I thought—we all thought . . ."

Sigrid interrupted Gudrun's sentence before she finished it for her. "You thought I was seeking counsel from her and favor from the gods. You thought I was being wise." She smiled softly. "Do you want to know the truth?" Gudrun nodded eagerly. "Why I spent so much time with Brunhild is mostly because I had less and less to talk about with my husband, and I had fewer and fewer other konas my age to talk to. Brunhild and I could be ourselves with one another. I knew her secrets and she knew that I knew. We would talk of long-ago things. We would make fun of the männer and all the lusty jungen. And we would speak of the konas, how eager and how sad they were. We would imagine together a time when life would not be so harsh. When konas could help their children and their husbands in more than just physical ways. And more than once we would speak of you, Gudrun, and how you were a spark of hope for the future."

Gudrun was taking all this in, fascinated by this new way of seeing the mystical Brunhild. Sigrid continued. "I still have to respect her," she said. "She didn't fit in the world of konas, and she found a way for herself in the world of männer. She's crazy, but she's smart. As for the gods, I don't say the gods don't exist. How could I know? How could anyone know? I say it's fine to ask the gods to favor our kinder with safety and food, but it is we who bring them out of danger. It is our breasts that provide the milk and our hands that prepare the stewing pots. I learned many winters ago to hope for favor from the gods, but to depend on myself and my husband to provide it." As she finished her moderately heretical retort, Sigrid could see that her words had shaken Gudrun a bit. She was about to soften her tone when she heard the voice of her son, Arn, outside the hus.

"Gudrun, may I enter?" the voice said. "Come in, please," Gudrun replied. Both women stood as Arn emerged past the deer and bear skins. The look on his face was grim as he addressed Sigrid. "Your husband— my father, Alrek, was found dead in the forest. He suffered no violence. He apparently died of old age." Arn offered an embrace to his mother, and she briefly accepted it, and Arn quickly departed, leaving Gudrun to console his mother.

Sigrid was devastated. She had truly loved her husband. Their marriage was seen as exemplary, much as that of Gudrun and Teutobod. After embracing and consoling her friend, Gudrun walked arm in arm with her back to her hus. "I will come back after I see to his preparation," Gudrun said, and then she left to help move Alrek's body to the hegjahus, where she took charge. She directed that his body be treated with special care and respect as she and the other konas prepared it for the brenna.

On returning to the kongull, Gudrun returned straightaway to Sigrid's hus, where Sigrid was sitting quietly, trancelike, in the place where she and Alrek had slept together. Gudrun knelt beside her and said, "He was a good mann and a brave warrior, and we prepared him with great respect. He will be received and honored by the gods; I know it."

Sigrid did not respond in words, but her apparent absence spoke loudly. Her eyes were hollow windows into an empty place. Her face was motionless, blank as frozen river water. Time passed, and Gudrun sat there beside her quietly. Finally, Sigrid spoke. "I am alone now. I am no one. I have no place but with my husband."

Gudrun worried at Sigrid's words. Sigrid was of the Chatti tribe, and she had told Gudrun about the tradition among her people of vifs being burned with their dead husbands. Gudrun knew of this practice among other tribes, as well, but the tradition had been especially strong among the Chatti. Gudrun knew the practice had diminished over the years but hearing Sigrid's words now and seeing her distant look was frightening. Gudrun said, "You have a place with me and with the other konas. The little meyas need your stories." Sigrid did not respond at all. Then Gudrun said "Sigrid," and she paused until Sigrid looked up. Gudrun looked deep into her eyes and said, "*I* need you." It may have been Gudrun's emphasis on the "I" in her statement that broke through—just momentarily—to the dark place behind Sigrid's empty eyes because those eyes moistened a bit, connecting with Gudrun's own tear-filled eyes. "You have been like a daughter to me," she responded, "and you make me proud. Things will be better because of you. But my time is accomplished." She looked away again, a look that said she had already left for a long journey. Gudrun knew there was no point to further words. She bent forward, caressing Sigrid's face, tucking some strands of gray-blonde hair behind her ears. She kissed her forehead softly, and then she stood. She paused, focusing on this woman she respected so very much, framing her face and fixing the image of her in her memory. And then she departed. She told no one.

Later that evening when people gathered for the brenna, Sigrid appeared as expected. The männer had assembled a bier and placed Alrek's body on it, along with his battle club and shield. They were about to place the bier atop the brushpile when Sigrid stepped forward. She took off her covering of skins and fur, revealing a light-colored burial gown. She placed a wreath of flowers on her head. All were aghast, and many konas screamed out their protest as they realized Sigrid's intention. But Gudrun stepped forward, offering Sigrid a single flower. Their eyes met and Sigrid mouthed the words, "Thank you." Gudrun clasped the flower into Sigrid's hand and tearfully turned away.

Sigrid addressed the gathering, "My dear ones. I am of the Chatti, as was my husband. This was the way of our ancestors, and I choose it. I think it will not be this way for you in the future, and that will be better. But I choose to die as I have lived." With that, Sigrid lay down beside her husband and, pulling out a blade, she punctured her throat. Her lifeblood pumped forth in powerful gushes, draining out over her husband's body. The process was over quickly, though it seemed to take forever. When it was sure that Sigrid was dead, a visibly shaken Teutobod ordered the brenna to proceed. Brunhild stepped forward, her face like stone but for a single tear on her right cheek. She intoned her blessing, and the männer moved in to lift the bier. But this time Gudrun and several other konas stood up to help. After the pyre took hold, it seemed to carry a heavier burden than usual. The flames always joined the hopes of the living with the bodies of the dead. But this time the hope felt somehow grander, more intense. At least it seemed that way to Gudrun. She looked up to see the very tips of the reaching fires, crackling forth their sparks as they melded with the stars in the vast sky. "*Better,*" she thought to herself. Sigrid's dying word echoed in Gudrun's ears as the image of Sigrid, sitting on her husband's empty bed, blazed in her memory.

CHAPTER SEVEN

THE Spring plantings asserted an unstoppable potency until summer was simply lush with vitality. It was the season of life and hope, and Gudrun loved it. Her belly was now quite large, and she could feel her baby moving inside of her, as though the little thing wanted to come out and revel in the joy of summer. In the late afternoon Gudrun went for a walk alone in the forest to escape the warmth of the summer sun, and growing weary in her legs and back, she found a mossy spot next to a white birch tree and sat down there. The baby inside her seemed to rouse in response to her inactivity and began to explore her rib cage, with a foot, she thought. She drew her knees up and pulled her feet toward her as she placed her hands on her bulging womb, imagining this little child into the cradle of her lap. But lacking that possibility, she focused instead on its watery, internal world. What was he—or she—thinking? Can she hear my voice?

But her quiet musing was suddenly interrupted. She was startled by an eerie feeling that she was being watched. Without moving from her spot on the ground, her hand subtly moved inside her garment to find the handle of the knife she secreted there. Slowly, her eyes rose to look out into the forest, scanning the brush and greenery for any danger. She looked straight ahead, and then moved only her eyes left and then right. Nothing there. She allowed her head to turn a bit to the right, and when her eyes moved even further right, she saw it. It was a grey wolf, standing beside a spruce tree, its blue eyes watching her intently. Gudrun felt the fear rise up in her and she instinctively crossed her arms over her child as she considered what she might do.

"I could stand, but I should not run." That was her first thought. No way to outrun a wolf.

"If I stand, I could climb a tree." Wolves cannot climb trees, she thought. She looked back and forth for trees she might reach quickly enough that she could climb to safety. Every tree looked either huge or like a sapling. And the wolf could easily cover the distance with a few quick leaps anyway.

"I could simply stay here and hope the wolf will go away. I'm not any threat to it. And I have my knife if I have to use it." She chose this last option as making the most sense, but the fear she felt in her chest and her lower back did not appreciate her choice. The fear wanted action, and right now!

As she sat, looking in the direction of the wolf, the wolf sat down. She had never seen a wolf sit before. She had seen many wolves, sometimes in a group but usually alone like this one, and they had always been standing off in the distance or moving. Something about seeing this wolf sit seemed to calm her fears a bit. Sitting is not an aggressive thing to do. Gudrun felt the tension in her muscles begin to rescind a bit, and she allowed first one and then the other leg to slowly extend out from her. The wolf laid down. Its grey fur was intermixed with a variety of brown shades, and the hair around its large ears was nearly black. Its eyes were almost icy blue, and they continued their fixation on Gudrun.

For some reason, Gudrun began to feel she was safe, that this wolf meant her no harm. She took her hand off the hilt of her knife, and slowly let her arm fall beside her toward the wolf, with her hand landing in a welcoming posture. The wolf considered her another moment or two, and then slowly stood up. It began walking, ever so slowly, over to where Gudrun sat motionless by the birch tree. Its head was down in a posture of non-aggression, and it very slowly walked until it stood right next to Gudrun. Gudrun fought the urge to grab her knife, but something inside her knew she was in no danger. The wolf carefully sniffed all around Gudrun's belly and the area between her legs. And then she (by then Gudrun could see that it was a she wolf) laid down and put her head on Gudrun's lap as though she were guarding the baby. Gudrun moved her hand to stroke the fur of this amazing creature, but then, startled by the touch, the wolf suddenly stood and moved away. Having retreated a safe distance, she turned and looked right at Gudrun. Their eyes—bright blue grey wolf eyes and grey blue human eyes—met in a wordless communication, a wondrous understanding that made Gudrun convinced this wolf was also with child. The wolf headed back into the woods, and as the sun's light was beginning to fade, Gudrun stood and returned to her hus.

***

With the growing season came a growth also in skirmishes and all-out battles. Teutobod's sveit joined with männer from the Ambrone and Cimbri peoples, first in planning meetings and then in mutual forays against the Roman outpost at a place called Aquae Sextiae. This was only the most recent of a several years successful history of violent encounters with the Romans, and the männer had become emboldened by each victory. There had been two major battles, both taking place along the Rhone River. The first was five summers hence at a place called Agen, a Roman defeat in which about 10,000 soldiers fell. The second and most severe battle was fought at Arausio three harvests back. In that battle the Cimbri took the lead, and the Romans were so badly outnumbered that virtually no Roman soldier was left alive. About 80,000 were killed. The battlefield was so gory with severed limbs and blood-soaked soil that many of the männer refused to speak of it on returning home to their kongulls.

Rome would not, of course, allow this defeat to go unanswered. Legion after legion of troops marched out to defend the ever-expanding territory of the empire, fortifying Rome's outpost at Aquae Sextiae downstream from Arausio. It was only a matter of time before another major clash was inevitable, and when Teutobod called the sveit together for a major announcement, Gudrun knew what it meant. They were going to war.

Preparing for battle involved the entire sveit . Weapons were fortified and sharpened, and new weapons were fashioned. The sveit owned many pack animals, asses and mules, mostly, and a few dozen horses, all of which had to be tended and prepared for travel. Männer engaged in sparring matches and practiced archery and the throwing of hatchets for maximum effect. Jüngen served as gatherers and retrievers of arrows and hatchets, and they also gathered stones the right size for throwing, piling them up on over three dozen wood wagons.

As for the konas, war meant preparation for them, as well. Some— the young and fit—would accompany the männer into battle. Others, those who were either too old or too young or, those like Gudrun who were with child, oversaw preparations. Some made poultices and tore strips of cloth into the many bandages which would certainly be needed. Some groups of konas packed a variety of dried fish and game in containers of salt to stock the battle camp. They all took turns watching the kinder and cooking a communal lunch for their respective kongulls.

One group of konas worked as seamstresses. Some concentrated on sewing bright white garments for the konas to wear in battle, and others fashioned leather sheaths which they would strap around their necks and shoulders to carry swords. Gudrun used her skills in leather working to good effect, sewing strong battle garments to protect her kinswomen, the männer, and even the horses. As they worked, someone began to sing a battle song, and soon all the voices joined in:

> Oh, look upon the fighting fields,
> Our strong and mighty, warriors all,
> And joining from Valhalle's hall
> The Valkyrie will touch their swords
> And bless the bravest with a holy kiss.
>
> The Valkyrie! The Valkyrie!
> Those golden angels from on high,
> May we become like those bright lights
> To guide and urge our warriors on.

✳✳✳

Days piled upon one another as the growing season began to shift toward harvest time. The many tasks of preparing for battle were now added to the labor-intensive work of harvesting and storing the various fruits of the harvest. The sveit was abuzz with activity each day. Wheat, rye, and barley had already been cut and stocked, but the root vegetables and other garden stocks all had to be variously picked, cut or unearthed, and then dried and stored for the coming winter. War might demand attention in the short term, but even victorious people would need to live through the winter. And running in, under and through the sveit was the undercurrent of the coming battle. When would it happen? Rumors collided with fears as a general anxiety broke into skirmishes between konas and männer with increasing regularity.

Of course, the resources for war were also piling up. Gudrun didn't travel to other parts of the sveit, but if the preparations in other areas were anything like those amassed in Teutobod's kongull, there would be enough to sustain a very long battle indeed. Gudrun had so adjusted to the daily routine that she nearly forgot the reason for the work. And then, one day in early September, the ram's horn sounded the gathering call. Gudrun looked around at her sisters, and the fear rose in her throat. She could see the fear in all the eyes of those around her, too. They arose as one body, moving to the place of gathering. Not a word was spoken among them. They all knew what they were about to hear: The day of the battle had come.

CHAPTER EIGHT

THE Roman General Marius was a seasoned, battle-tested and famous defender of Rome. Julius Caesar had appointed him to this post at some cost to himself. Marius was several years away from qualifying for another proconsulate, having won battles for Rome only three years before. The Senate had a policy of spacing out the honor of leading a garrison so that no man might amass too much power nor gain too much loyalty for himself. This policy also enabled each leader the opportunity to prove his loyalty and his leadership ability to the Senate. But after suffering terrible defeats in recent years and facing a crisis of losing arable land in northern Italy, Caesar was convinced that a decisive blow must be delivered to the barbarians. He was further convinced that the greatest likelihood of delivering that blow would come from Marius. And he was so convinced of these things he was willing to override Senate protocol and appoint Marius as imperial proconsul.

In the Roman court at Aquae Sextiae, Marius was meeting with his commanders and lieutenants to plan battle strategy. "I have seen for myself the way these barbarians fight," he said, "and so have many of you. They attack like animals, like jackals or a pack of wild boars. They will send out groups of ten or twenty to harass us. They will try to engage us in skirmishes that draw us into the trap they have set. And if we respond, they will pick away at us as they have done to other garrisons in the past. So, my first order is this: Do nothing. Do not respond to their attempts to goad us into battle on their terms."

Marcellus, Marius' most experienced commander, frowned. "I understand you, Proconsul, and I will obey. But it will be hard to restrain my troops. They are hard-trained and thirsty for barbarian blood. Many of our men lost fathers or brothers or friends to these pigs. They want revenge."

Marius nodded his understanding. "I am fully aware of the feelings of our soldiers, and I certainly share them. But if we are to win this battle—and win we must—it will be because we have learned the lessons those soldiers died to teach us. We must dictate the terms of the battle. And keep in mind: we are in a fortified position; the enemy is in the field. By lengthening his time in the field, we force him to deplete his resources. We must be smart.

"Another thing," he continued, "as some of you have seen for yourselves these barbarians even employ their women in battle, which can be confusing at first. And these are not the dark-haired, olive-skinned, genteel women of our usual acquaintance. These barbarian women are white in skin and garment, with red or golden hair and fierce blue eyes. And they stand ready to fight alongside their men in a manner most Roman soldiers have never seen. Remember the first time you saw these women? Remember the sounds of their high-pitched voices in battle? It can be disarming to young Roman soldiers. And after so many losses in recent years, most of your men are indeed young. Many have yet to see battle. This is another reason we will restrain our forces from engaging with the Teutons and their cohorts. A week or so of skirmishes will help the men get used to the look and feel of the enemy. Then when it comes time for the true fight, they will be ready."

❄ ❄ ❄

Nearly all the members of the sveit, some 80,000 in all, crowded into the gathering place, a broad field which had been kept fallow for this very purpose and for pasturing the animals. Teutobod stood on a high point in front of a cliff edge made of limestone. He was dressed for battle. The thick leather bodice sewn for him by Gudrun encircled his bodice, and the metal helmet he once removed from the severed head of a roman centurion was strapped to his head; its pointed pinnacle enlarged his presence even more than usual. He raised his arms and extended his hands in a gesture of silence, to which the throng quickly responded. He spoke out with a thundering authority. "The time has come for battle with the Roman invaders. This will be a major battle in which we will be joined with peoples of the Cimbri and the Ambrone. You have prepared for this day. You have done well. Those not able to fight must continue the preparation and stockpiling of supplies, as our plan is to draw the enemy out from his encampment at Aquae Sextiae in a series of attacks which may take days or weeks.

"After we have destroyed the Romans, we will move onward to Italy and set up a major dwelling place there. There are fertile lands in the north of Italy, lands which will provide for all our peoples abundantly. But first we must be victorious. We must win the battle!" Teutobod drew his sword and raised it high, and all those bearing arms, konas and männer alike, raised their weaponry in response. "We depart tomorrow at first light." he continued. "Be ready to fight like a true warrior! The gods be with you all!"

A loud cheer arose from the people as Teutobod stood, sword brandished, larger than life, a seemingly god-like presence in physical form. He was their warrior king. He would lead them, and they would follow him anywhere. Victory was a presumption, an expectation like the rising of the sun in the morning. Not one among them even considered otherwise.

❊❊❊

Sleep was fitful that night for Gudrun. Between the demands of her bladder, the incessant kicking of the infant in her womb and her worries about the coming dawn and what it would require from her husband and her people, Gudrun merely dozed. Teutobod had been in late meetings with his leaders and chose to sleep there instead of in his own bed. It was barely dawn when Gudrun was roused by her husband. He was dressed for battle, as he was yesterday at the gathering. He held a candle, and in its flickering light Gudrun recognized her leatherwork with some pride.

"My vif, I must take my leave of you. Be strong. And give me a son!"

Gudrun smiled up at him and said, "Jünge or meya, I just want to raise our child. I want to raise our child . . ." Her hand reached to touch his above the hilt of his sword as she finished her words, "with you." Their eyes met in a deep communication. No words were needed.

Teutobod responded, "I will make sure that you do just that." He bent forward to kiss her forehead, cradling her face in his gnarled hands. He then stood and departed.

By the time Teutobod made his way to the gathering place, the commotion and excitement were palpable. All the combatants were clamoring into the field. Soldiers queued in groups of about one hundred. Mules were fitted with bit and bridle and mated with wagons full of various supplies. Horses were similarly attached to pull larger vehicles, many of them sporting skins or woven material stretched over wooden or bone ribbing as a protective covering.

Teutobod issued the order to depart just as the sun was peeking above the eastern horizon. The entire battle force began to move south along the Rhone River, a trek which would take two days before nearing their target at Aquae Sextiae.

Along the journey riders from the Cimbri and Amarones approached. Teutobod and several of his leaders pulled aside, issuing orders for the march to continue while they met with their visitors. Together, they solidified a plan made months ago in which the Teutons would serve as instigators, goading and harassing the Romans with skirmishes and insults until they would pursue the Teutons east toward the foothills of the Alps. The Cimbri would be lying in wait in the foothills and would attack the Roman force from a superior position. Anticipating a Roman tactic of division and circling behind their enemies, the Amarones would be camped to the south, ready to meet the Roman divisions when they came.

It seemed a good plan to all, and no changes were thought needed. The riders departed to carry the message of assent to their leaders, and Teutobod and his men rode fast to rejoin their own troops.

When the city of Aquae Sextiae began to be visible on the southern horizon, Teutobod ordered the party to bivouac there beside the river. It was nearing the end of the second day, and initiating battle without food and proper rest was deemed senseless. Temporary dwellings were set up, and Teutobod gave the order to place the dwellings so that they would hide the campfires as much as possible. If they could conceal their presence through the night, they could gain the element of surprise in the morning. After all orders had been obeyed and the encampment was secure, sentries were posted, and all the exhausted fighters retired to a deep sleep.

CHAPTER NINE

GUDRUN was at her usual post, working a sharp needle into two pieces of leather to stitch them together. She had just started another small hole with an awl made from bone when she felt a sudden jolt in her belly. The feeling was as though she were cramping from a stomach illness. It was a strong seizure, and it was in her lower abdomen muscles. She had felt this before. The baby was no longer willing to remain in the safety of her womb. The birth pangs had begun.

One of her coworkers, Carla, noticed Gudrun doubled over and came to help. She was soon joined by another kona whose name was Ballee. Together, they helped Gudrun to sit. They worked quickly to get a small pile of cloths and two buckets before they helped Gudrun to her feet and walked with her down toward the river. A place had been established there for the purpose of childbirth. A uniquely shaped, smooth river rock served as a sort of birthing chair in which the expectant mother would sit while her legs were supported by konas on either side. By the time they arrived, Gudrun was more than ready to sit down. Carla took the two buckets to the river and filled them with water before lugging them back up the embankment to the birthing place. One bucket would be used for cooling and cleansing and the other she placed between and beneath Gudrun's legs to catch the newborn baby once delivered.

Gudrun looked at Carla and Ballee with appreciation. Most of the konas were kind to one another, but at a time like this such kindness was even more welcomed. Her mind briefly flashed back to Sigrid, who had been like a mother to Gudrun. She missed Sigrid terribly right now. Still, Ballee and Carla were here. She was not alone in her labors. She looked at her belly, distended and with pinkish-white streaks at its periphery, and the wonder of it all came over her so suddenly it felt like a waterfall. She sat there, lost in the awe and mystery of bringing life into the world, when she realized the waterfall was her own womb gushing forth its contents. There was no turning back now. This baby was going to come.

***

The first assault was an hour after first light. Wagonloads of stones were carted forward to the northernmost bounds of the Roman outpost. Swords and broadaxes were brought as well, but arrows and spears were reserved for the later, larger conflict. It started at two spots simultaneously, with shouts like, "Hey, you Roman pigdogs!" and, "Here is some hail from Odin!" followed by dozens of rocks, mostly smooth, river stones, being hurled down on the Romans by their opponents. Many of the stones found their mark and several of the soldiers went immediately to the ground. Others got their metal shields up to block the assault and some were able to fly off a few arrows in response, none of which had any effect. The whole affair lasted less than 15 minutes.

As the first group retreated, a second group was readied and within a short time continued the harassment of the Romans. This went on all day; one assault followed another unceasingly in hopes they could goad the Romans into sending out a cohort or two to chase the Teutons. It had worked before. But it was not working this time.

Teutobod was not deterred. He ordered his men to carry out the same plan the next day, and the next. For several days the Teutons attacked and hassled the Romans, injuring many and even killing some. But the Romans would not give chase. Although Teutobod's leaders were beginning to lose patience with the plan, they kept up their assaults. After the fifth day Allard, one of Teutobod's eldest leaders, questioned him, "When are these Romans going to come out and fight?" Teutobod responded, "When they are ready. We will have to wait them out."

***

Gudrun's contractions were increasing both in intensity and frequency. At one point the pain was severe enough she began to react irrationally, as if suffering an unreasonable assault. The anger welled up in her, the sort of feeling she was accustomed to directing at some bully or accuser. Then, suddenly, she realized it was her baby she was angry at. Tears of guilt and frustration welled up in her eyes as she forced herself to love this little creature who now exacted such tortures on her.

Carla dunked a cloth into the bucket and, squeezing out the excess, cooled Gudrun's face and forehead, gently smoothing away the beads of sweat and strain. "Don't give up," she said. "This might go on for a while yet. But we are with you." Ballee nodded her assent. Gudrun managed a smile of appreciation, just before the next contraction grabbed her like a giant, horribly powerful fist, and squeezed. Gudrun felt the strong urge to push, to expel this ricking demon from her body, and she shouted, "I want to push now!" but Carla said, "Wait." She checked Gudrun's birth canal and said, "I do not see the head yet. You must give the baby the time it needs. If you push too early you might harm the baby or yourself. I know it's frustrating, but you must wait."

Gudrun trusted Carla. Besides, she knew it was too soon. She had been through this before when Sigrid was the one helping her. That baby did not live through even one winter. What if this will be the same? The fear rose like a huge wave inside her. "What if this baby dies, too?" her thoughts became words. "What if my mann dies in the battle? What if this is all for nothing?" Hearing herself speak these words, hearing the panic she was feeling spoken in the real world, it made the fear even more actual and terrifying. Her eyes became wide and wild, searching around desperately for answers to the questions she had never wanted to ask.

Ballee encircled Gudrun's shoulders with her long arms, pulling her head against her chest and stroking back her sweat-soaked blonde hair. "It will be good," she said softly. "I know it will be good. Shhh . . ."

The contraction finally relented, and Gudrun almost slept, nestled against the warm breasts of her sister kona. The baby was coming, but not yet.

❄ ❄ ❄

The Teuton stockpiles were beginning to dwindle as the Romans stubbornly maintained their posture of non-engagement. It was on the sixth day, after yet another unsuccessful onslaught of harassing attacks, that Teutobod was forced to withdraw. He met with his leaders in the evening, and it was decided they would send out the wagons to procure supplies in the morning. The troops would simultaneously march along the way to the foothills of the Alps and settle in there to await restocking and, eventually, the Roman soldiers. The Cimbri would be encamped another two days march east, on the other side of Aix, and they could join in the battle if needed. "Now *we* will play the waiting game," he said. "Let's see how they like it." All were in agreement, especially Marcellus and Allard, both of whom had plenty of stomach for battle but little for patience and strategy.

Meanwhile, Marius was also planning. He had anticipated just this scenario, and three days earlier he had dispatched two entire Roman legions—one marching a day behind the other—south and then east to take up a position ahead of the Teutons in the foothills of the Alps, near Aix. When the Teutons inevitably arrived there, it would be they and not the Romans who would be surprised. The feeling of battle was in the air, and the Romans breathed it in deeply as they settled in.

✼✼✼

The pulsing thrusts of her abdomen were much stronger now as Gudrun had begun to push out her new baby. Carla was positioned between Gudrun's legs, ready to assist with the baby's delivery. While Gudrun supported her right leg on Ballee's hip, her left leg she kept aloft by placing her foot on Carla's right shoulder. With every contraction—coming now so closely to one another there was little time between them—Carla adjured Gudrun to PUSH! And Gudrun gathered her strength to do just that. She thought she might pass out at one point after pushing so hard she had virtually no air left in her lungs. She gasped for breath and fought the urge to push almost immediately again, because she was quite sure if she pushed again at that moment she might die.

But finally, some strength churned up inside her like a wind from Valhalle, and all her fear and anger and pain gave way to an enormous and overwhelming power, welling up from someplace deep inside her, so deep Gudrun would later think it must have been from Odin himself, and Gudrun bore down in a final push that finally, ever so slowly, bit by agonizing, mesmerizing, incredible bit, presented the new life she had carried inside her. Young Gria (Gudrun's snowhus friend) had gotten her wish: it was a little meya. Carla caught the pinkish-grayish thing, waxy and elongated at its crown, and eased it down into the water long enough to wash off some of the blood and birth fluids. She covered the nostrils with her mouth and sucked out the little plugs of mucus, spitting them on the ground. She turned the baby upside-down to help drain any remaining fluids from her airways, at which point the baby screamed forth its announcement: I am here. I am free. I am alive.

Carla handed the new creation, umbilicus still attached, to her exhausted mother who received her with pure joy. All three women cried tears of happiness, relief, and amazement as the two caretakers continued to fuss over newborn and mother, wiping here and cleaning there. Carla pinched and cut the umbilicus, tying it into a simple knot before guiding the afterbirth out and cleaning Gudrun up.

They remained there at the birthing place for perhaps an hour, happy to dwell—just for the moment—in a world of hope that knew only of life and new birth. Then, slowly, they rose to return to their preparations for battle.

Chapter Ten

THE ultimate battle was a two-day affair. The Romans, inferior in number but superior in weaponry, tactics, strategy and field position, drove down on the advancing barbarians with a fury. The Ambrones, who had come up to join Teutobod, were the first to be destroyed. After some 10,000 lay dead in the fields, the remainder fled back to their base camp, only to be assaulted by many of their own women, who attacked them with hatchets and accused them of cowardice.

That night, Marius dispatched Marcellus with a force of 3,000 men in a familiar tactic of circling around behind the approaching enemy. The infantrymen secreted themselves among the foothills overnight and awaited the opportune moment. Marius also issued orders that the leader of the Teutons was to be taken alive and brought before him.

On the morning of the second day, October 5th, Teutobod led his troops eastward toward Aix, not realizing what awaited them. The Romans, having fortified an encampment at Porrières about 4 miles west of Aix, attacked the Teutons from the slopes of Mt. Sainte Victoire, raining down arrows and fire and heavy pila upon them. The hills became slippery with blood as the heat of the day and the intensity of the climb took their toll on the Teutons. Eventually they were driven back. Marius then ordered a general advance, and hand-to-hand combat ensued, which lasted much of the day until Marcellus and his legionnaires appeared from the rearward position and confused the Teutons. By the end of the day, some 70,000 männer lay dead or dying, and along with several of his lieutenants, Teutobod was led away in chains.

***

Word of the battle had not yet reached the sveit. The ongoing work of preparing supplies for battle continued unabated. Except for Gudrun. Gudrun was totally enraptured with this new creature she had created. She said to her, "I will ask your father, but I think he will agree that your name should be Ulfa. When he hears about my visitor in the forest not long ago, he will understand. The baby began to struggle, looking for nourishment, so Gudrun slid off her garment to one side and helped her find the breast. She sucked strongly, hungrily. "You, my little meya, shall not die. You shall live and grow and be strong. You will be beautiful and powerful like the creature whose name you bear." Gudrun settled back on the skins of her bed, warm and secure, holding her little one close and feeling as powerful as life itself.

Suddenly, she heard a commotion outside. Konas screaming! Children crying out! Gudrun arose and peered out from the skins covering the doorway to her hus, her child still nursing vigorously at her left breast. The site which met her eyes was surreal. Roman soldiers on horseback, dozens of them, riding in to the kǫngull like they owned it. "Where is Teutobod?" she gasped. "How can this be?" And then she saw it. Amidst the phalanx of soldiers was a wagon drawn by two horses which carried prisoners, all of whom were in metal clamps and chains. And standing among them was her mann, Teutobod. He was bloody about his head and left ear, which appeared to be hanging to one side. The blood had caked in his beard and ran down his shoulders onto the leather battlement she had sewn for him. He looked differently than she had ever seen him. He looked . . . defeated.

Gudrun emerged warily from her hus, hoping to gain Teutobod's attention. Just then a Roman centurion called out to the members of the kǫngull in a loud, lordly voice: "You members of the Teutons, hear me! Your husbands are dead. You are a defeated people, now subject to the authority of Rome. Your leaders are here with me in chains, and they will attest to the terms of your surrender. All your livestock, all your grains and foodstuffs, and all your weapons now belong to Rome. You will begin gathering these things when I am finished speaking. In addition, 300 of your married women will be taken to Rome to become servants in the house of Vespa, where you will service our Roman senators and legionnaires. Prepare yourselves for travel, for tomorrow we depart for Rome. Roman guards will now gather the women, who will be brought to temporary shelters for the night. Any resistance will be met with immediate death. That is all. Long live the emperor!"

Gudrun could hardly believe her ears. Teutobod would never have agreed to these terms. Shock and disbelief could be seen on the face of every kona throughout the kǫngull as shouts and screams of protest rose in response. Gudrun moved closer to the prisoner wagon, weaving her way between the Roman horsemen, her little meya still snuggled and concealed under her blouse. "Teutobod!" she cried out. He did not respond. She moved even closer and shouted out again, "Teutobod!" Still, the man's focus was on his manacled hands. He didn't acknowledge her at all. Gudrun, determined to hear her sentence confirmed from her husband's own lips, moved right next to the Roman wagon and its awful cargo until she stood directly below her mann.

"Teutobod! Look at me!" She reached inside her garment to reveal the infant at her breast and said, "Look! You have a daughter. Tell me you never agreed to these terms of surrender. Tell me you did not betray me. Tell me you would not turn me into a temple whore. Tell me! Tell me!!" Gudrun's cries grew more insistent, angrier, more accusing with each passing moment of Teutobod's unresponsiveness. But he never spoke a word. He never even looked up, not even to see his child. And finally, Gudrun had to believe what the Roman centurion had said. She and the other konas were again chattle for capture and use. They had been discarded.

Gudrun's mind flashed back to Sigrid, to that empty, soulless look in her eyes after Alrek died when she said, "I am no one. I have no place but with my husband." Gudrun turned away angrily from the wagonload of broken promises, and as she made her way back to her hus a monstrous rage roiled deep within her. She could see the Roman soldiers, grabbing konas on all sides, choosing the fairest to be included in satisfying Teutobod's treachery. Many, like Gudrun, had small children with them, either infants in their arms or small kinder clinging to their skirts. And Gudrun's rage erupted into a loud, thunderous scream as if from the pit of hell itself. She screamed so loudly and at such a pitch that the sound of her voice even terrified some of the Roman legionnaires. Suddenly the scream became a declaration. "YOU WILL NOT HAVE MY CHILD!" And with that, Gudrun reached inside her shirt covering, grabbed her little meya by the feet, pulled her from her dripping breast, and smashed the infant's head onto the ground. The blood from her split open skull splashed up onto Gudrun's feet as she screamed even louder. It was as if all the powers of life and goodness she had so recently known in giving birth had been inverted, transformed into their opposites. She had become death.

Many other konas, seeing the horrible scene, did similarly with their own children. The shout was repeated over and over again, "YOU WILL NOT HAVE MY CHILDREN," as one after another, the blood and brain matter of dead children splashed over the feet of the Romans and their horses. The horses began to rear and startle at the sight and smell of the blood and at the terrified sounds of screaming women and children. Some of the Roman infantrymen vomited, unprepared as they were for such debauchery. The cohort commander, sensing the impending loss of order, realized the presence of the prisoners was feeding the frenzy of the women, so he ordered the prisoners to be taken away immediately. As the wagon moved forward, many of the konas threw their children under the wagon wheels, shouting out accusations at the prisoners, and especially at Teutobod, "You killed my child! This is your doing! Traitors! Weaklings! Cowards! The blood of my children be on your head! May the gods damn you forever!"

A guard grabbed Gudrun by the arm to take her to one of several hussa which were now converted to temporary prison cells. As she was being led away, Gudrun could be heard shouting, "They will not have us! We will not be taken!" Her words began to be repeated throughout the kongull until they became a sort of mantra: "They will not have us! We will not be taken!" The Roman guards laughed at the irony of it: a bunch of captured women being herded off and imprisoned, claiming loudly that they will not be taken. They laughed again and again as they guarded the hussa throughout that night. In the morning, one guard joked to another, "These barbarian women can yell about not being taken while they are being taken to Rome." They both laughed.

When morning came sneaking in on the devastated kongull there was an eerie silence. The guard outside the first hus unblocked the doorway to rouse the prisoners. What he saw was unlike anything he could have imagined. Thirty women had been imprisoned in that hus overnight, and all thirty were dead. He could tell by their bulging eyes and by the marks on their necks they had apparently strangled one another. All but for one, apparently the last one, who was hanging from a makeshift hook with a noose of hemp rope around her neck.

The young infantryman, obviously shaken, emerged from the hus and reported his grisly discovery to the cohort commander. Soon similar reports began to come in of other hus prisoners having similarly throttled themselves. Three hundred women had been imprisoned. Three hundred women were found strangled, many in each other's arms. The young guard who last night had joked about these women cast his gaze to a far-off place as he said, "They really weren't going to be taken."

General Gaius Marius, unwilling to believe what his men were telling him, came to see for himself. As he moved from hus to hus, the sight of bulging, accusing eyes coupled with the stench of death and released bodily fluids filled his nostrils made him want to retch, but he forced back the urge. He ordered the bodies to be burned in the dwellings in which they were found.

❋ ❋ ❋

The Roman garrison marched back to Rome, victorious but strangely quiet. The soldiers were so shaken by what they had experienced that the victory seemed somehow less triumphant. Many of the soldiers, usually lusty with tales of battle and weaponry, simply marched for long periods in silence. When they finally arrived in Rome, the usual fanfare awaited them, but most of the men just wanted to go home.

Marius and Marcellus met with Caesar to report on the victory. As they recounted their experience against the Teutons, Caesar was astounded. When Marcellus rose to depart their meeting he said, "I have encountered many enemies in battle, but none whose people fought so fiercely. I have decided to remember it as the *furor Teutonicus.*"

Section II

Susanna's Story

1941

CHAPTER ELEVEN

I T was time for the washing again, a time made readily evident by the odors of sweat and barnyard emanating from the house's bedrooms. "Phew!" Susanna said aloud as she deposited the variously strewn sources of her repugnance into the thatched laundry basket she balanced on her hip. The socks were the worst, she thought, holding back her breath as she tweezed a pair between thumb and fingertip that Karl had recently worn. She buried them under some less malodorous pieces. But a momentary sadness overtook her, and she stuck her hand back into the pile to feel those socks again. She recalled the lovely, clean smell of the strands of wool she had spun into yarn for the making of those socks, how the yarn slid through her fingers back then, how it spindled onto the spool, how the spool grew and grew, how she had shaped the cone of it. And she recalled her sense of connection to the sheep and to the land and to the later uses to which the yarn would be put. Handling the socks now, even soiled and disgusting, her fingers still remembered. She lingered, just for a moment, her bent back galvanized by the reverie.

Straightening herself, Susanna finished gathering the clothing as she moved from room to room. She headed to the new wringer washing machine Karl had procured for her after their fourth child was on the way. But looking through the curtains at the sunshine of this unseasonably warm late-May morning, she decided instead to head to the back yard and her old wash tub. "Let's just do it the old-fashioned way," she said to no one in particular, although Gretel cooed happily in response. Gretel, her youngest child now aged 8 months, smiled up at her mother from the confines of her makeshift playpen (a couple of planks hemmed in by two chairs against the kitchen wall). She was holding the little wooden rattle Oompa made her for at Juletide. Susanna smiled back at her and said, "Meine kleine Schatz, let's go do our work outside today, shall we?" As if in anticipation, Gretel reached up for her mother and Susanna lifted her high in the air, eliciting a shriek of joy as she was guided down and whooshed right on top of the clothes in the basket. And out they went giggling to the back porch.

Susanna set the basket down in the grass and removed her daughter from the stinky-soft bed. Still grasping her rattle, Gretel happily sat in the cool, shaded greenness beneath the giant elm tree, one of seven which towered over the small farmhouse owned by the Neuenschwander family for three generations. Those seven trees engendered the name, Seven Elms Farm, which had identified the homestead to the residents of Schuylkill County for the last two of those three generations. Susanna pumped water for the washing and carried two large pails over from the well to dump into the washtub she had placed on the workbench Karl had built for just that purpose some years back. She added two capfuls of Dr. Bronner's Magic Soap, agitating the water into a luxuriant foam. After retrieving her old washboard from its hanging hook on the back porch, she began the arduous task of civilizing her family's rags.

Before Gretel, Susanna had borne two daughters and a son for her husband: Karla, Johann, and Marta, now aged 17, 16, and 11 years, respectively. Karla saw her name as a lifelong reminder of her father's disappointment in her gender. Marta inherited the name of her maternal grandmother, and Gretel was named—at Karl's insistence—after his mother (although in Susanna's mind, it was after the Grimm's fairy tale character). Johann, on achieving school age (and over his father's objections), had quickly adopted the Americanized moniker, Johnny. His was a somewhat schizoid world, in that nobody at school ever called him anything but Johnny, and at home, he was always called Johann. He longed for the day his father would finally call him by his real name, but he doubted that day would ever come. One dare not cross Karl Neuenschwander on his family farm, especially when you are an only son who is of no particular use and who is not particularly interested in farming.

Of course, being disinterested did not excuse anyone from contributing to the ongoing work of the farm. All the Neuenschwander family members were required to do their part. Ten cows had to be milked morning and night, the barn had to be cleaned daily, and feed had to be distributed to the cows and to the calves and heifers, as well. The calves had to be bottle-fed until they were old enough to chew. There was a substantial chicken coop which needed cleaning at least every other day, and eggs had to be gathered and meal distributed each day. The pasture animals also needed tending. Sheep and hogs needed food and water. Eggs were taken to market weekly, and butchered pullets monthly. Fences had to be regularly inspected and sometimes refashioned.

It was a year-round, non-stop cycle of working. In the spring, rocks pushed up by the melting permafrost had to be picked up out of the fields to prevent damaging the implements used for plowing and planting. In the harvest time the wheat had to be shocked, the corn picked and stored, and the fields prepared for the fallow months. And in Winter, all the live-stock work continued without a break, much of it rendered more difficult and time-consuming by the rages of ice and snow. And then, of course, there was the rest of the work to do. Like the gardening. And the canning. And the meal preparation and cleanup. And the mending. And . . . the laundry. Always more laundry.

Susanna finished wringing out the last of the now clean clothing and set about the task of hanging it on the clotheslines. She looked down to see little Gretel, busily inspecting the grass and twigs near her spot in the yard. She had a furrow in her little brow, inspecting each leaf or pebble as though solving a complex puzzle. Susanna smiled at the scene. So serious! And so curious! It made her wonder if Gretel would keep this intense curiosity, and what the future might hold for her if she did. No use worrying about that, she mused, and she turned back to the task at hand. One piece at a time, shaken out, hung up and pinned to the line. One at a time. Do your work, and all will be well. That's what her mother used to tell her.

She moved her way down the line, away from the house and to-ward the edge of the cornfield, then back toward the house with the next clothesline. She couldn't see Gretel for a few minutes, and when the last piece of laundry had been hung up, she grabbed up her basket and headed back, ducking and weaving through the maze of wet clothing along the way. There was Gretel, slumped over and snoozing in the grass. "Meine kleine Engel," Susanna whispered with a smile. She lay down beside her, carefully, and watched her breathing. Not a care in the world, she thought to herself. She began again to think about Gretel's future, and before long mother and daughter were softly soaring together, winging above the toil and worry, adrift on the dreams of a summer morning.

CHAPTER TWELVE

KARL and Johann came rumbling down the dusty road in Karl's old Ford. Susanna heard them as soon as they turned in to the end drive. She popped up from her morning slumber like a startled partridge. Gretel also stirred and squawked her irritation at being disturbed. She always woke with a bit of crank. But Susanna picked her up and snuggled her, moving her back and forth with an exaggerated sway of her hips and murmuring a singsong lilt into her ear as she moved into the kitchen. Soon, Gretel's attention was fixed on the bottle Susanna was warming on the stove, and soon after that she was hungrily drawing in the milky protein before her next adventure.

The truck clabbered and screeched to a halt beside the barn, and Susanna heard Karl's voice from across the yard, putting to an end the calm serenity that had been her morning. It was not going to be a good day.

"You just don't care!" Karl shouted angrily. "About anything! I built this farm up with my own hands. Everything you see here my father and I created, and I have kept it going. Through the Depression, through storms and droughts and floods, this farm stands. And you are my son! My only son! This should all be yours someday. And you don't give a shit about any of it.! You are worthless as tits on a bull!"

Susanna heard the truck door slam like a weapon. She looked out and saw Karl stomping off into the barn. She also saw Johann sitting in the passenger side of the truck looking sullen. His hollow-eyed stare reminded her of a runt calf that had refused to suck. She fought the urge to go to him, to nurture him in some way. Maybe take him a cookie and a glass of milk. It was probably the same maternal instinct she had just followed with Gretel. But she thought better of it. After all, Johann wasn't eight months old. He was growing into manhood. And men must work out these things their own way. Besides, she felt a deep sense of trepidation at the thought of interfering in her husband's frustrations.

"Get your arsch out of that truck and get in here! There's work to do!" Karl's tone left no room for interpretation. And Johann knew that tone all too well. He may have wanted to do something else, but the painful memories of various blows and cuffs from his father motivated him to immediate response. "I'm coming!" he yelled out as he quickly exited the vehicle.

"Ja, ja, you're coming," his father replied. "But unless I tell you, you would do nothing! You are like a big rock on a hillside. You would sit there forever until someone pushes you down the hill. And when you get to the bottom, there you would sit until someone picked you up and moved you out of the way. Useless!" Johann gave no response.

"Ach!" Karl threw up his arms wildly in disgust. Johann instinctively cringed a little in response, and when Karl saw it, he barely resisted the urge to knock him to the ground. "Weakling! Go clean out the calf pens and lay out fresh straw, and then clean out the cow stanchions. You can handle that much, can't you?"

Johnny was playing baseball. He was playing for the Phillies in a game against the Boston Bees. It was the bottom of the ninth inning with two men on. The game was tied and there were two outs, and Carl Wilson had put Johnny in as a pinch hitter. Heimie Mueller, Johnny's favorite player, was cheering him on from the dugout. But just as the pitcher was about to throw his first pitch, Johnny stepped back from the plate and responded, "Yes, Papa, I can handle that much." Karl turned irritably and trampled out the door and into the tool shed. Soon the sound of wood sawing and nails being pounded replaced the angry shouting.

※※※

Lunchtime was fast approaching, so Susanna began the preparations. Liverwurst, onions, bread for sandwiches, pickled beets and dills, butter and milk were laid out on the kitchen table. A fresh custard pie also found its way to the table, as did two glass pitchers, one full of milk and the other filled with cold water. She set places for Karl and herself and for Johann. Karla and Marta were at the Bielfeldts up the road, helping Helen Bielfeldt with laundry and chores due to her broken leg. The girls weren't expected home until suppertime. Finally, Susanna moved the highchair Karl had made for their first child from its place against the wall over to the table. "My, but this chair seems to get heavier with every baby!" she said aloud. She looked over at Gretel looking up at her quizzically. Gretel smiled a baby smile, and Susanna's heart melted. "Such a sweet, special little Kind you are!" and she went over to pick her up. No sooner had she placed the highchair and the baby in it than in came the men, Karl first, followed at a safe distance by Johann. They took turns at the washbowl before sitting down in their respective places at the table. No words were spoken. Karl looked grumpy like usual. Johann sat waiting for his turn at the food. Karl always ate first.

"So, how goes your work today?" Susanna asked her husband, hoping to sound cheerful.

"Es geht," came the cheerless response. "One thing follows another. It might go better if I had some help," he grumped, offering a sidelong glance at Johann. Johann was lost in his liverwurst. "When are Karla and Marta going to be done with this free labor over at the Bielfeldts? I need them here."

Susanna replied, "They are going every other day. Helen has no children to help her, and her leg will take another month to mend."

"Ja, ja. And my work gets another month behind." Susanna was about to remind her husband of the times the Bielfeldts had helped him in the past, but seeing his glare and sensing his general demeanor, she thought it best not to challenge him, not even with the truth.

"We'll be all right. Is there something I could do to help you? What can I do?" Susanna offered.

"You have your own work to do. You, on the other hand," his burning stare turned directly at Johann, "you will need to work harder. All day long I give you things to do, and I come and find you daydreaming. Yesterday you were even sleeping! When are you going to take some responsibility? When are you going to care about something? Look at me when I'm talking to you!"

Susanna felt the blow coming before it happened. As the volume and anger rose with the rhetoric, the backhand smack was inevitable. It was like a thunderstorm: first the lightning, and then the thunder. Johann knew it too. He instinctively recoiled at the very moment Karl drew his hand back to strike, thus avoiding the brunt of it. But Karl's anger would not be slaked by a glancing blow. He rose from his chair and landed a solid punch to his son's right ear, knocking him off his kitchen chair onto the shiny wood floor.

Gretel shrieked in fear as Susanna grabbed her up from the high-chair like a she-bear with her cub. "Karl! Stop!" she cried as she cradled Gretel against her chest and backed away. "He has to learn!" Karl responded, angrily. He began to look for some sort of utensil with which he might continue his assault, but Johann scrambled to his feet and ran out the door. Fearing he might direct his angry attention her way, Susanna turned quickly and took Gretel to her crib, sitting there with her in the rocking chair in which she lulled her to sleep every night. She sat down and rocked, but Gretel would not be comforted. Susanna suddenly realized she was holding the child very tightly, and her rocking had been almost violent. She fought back tears at the thought she had carried her husband's mood so intensely into her daughter's bedroom, and she took a couple of deep breaths. She began to rock her baby gently, cooing a soft lullaby for her. Presently, things calmed down, baby and all.

Susanna eventually heard the door slam followed by the sound of Karl's truck heading back out to his fieldwork. She carefully laid Gretel down for a nap and went in to tend to the lunch dishes and begin the preparations for supper. She gathered up the plates and food and picked up the chair on which Johann had been sitting. She felt glad for the tedium of the chores and the resulting distraction from the volatility that still seemed to fill the room. "Just do your work and everything will be fine," she said aloud.

⁂

It was about 4 o'clock when Karla and Marta came home. "Hi, Mutti!" came Marta's cheerful greeting as she ran across the kitchen to hug her mother around the waist. Seeing the supper her mother was preparing, she said, "Mmmm, potatoes and roast beef!" Susanna welcomed the interruption, turning and hugging her daughter warmly and long. Seeing the look on her mother's face and her tear-streaked cheeks, Karla knew at once what this long hug meant. Her father had been at it again. "I'll gather the laundry," she said, and exited to the yard.

Karla looked out over the farmyard and to the fields beyond. She had always loved being outdoors. Unlike her younger brother, Karla loved farming. She shared her father's pride in the heritage of this place, and in the produce that was created there. Karla always felt happiest when she was working the ground. The Spring disking and planting, even spreading the manure; she loved it all. But harvest time was her favorite. She loved gathering in the wheat and then the corn, seeing the cribs and bins grow full with the results of their hard work. She once tried to broach the subject with her father, whether she might take on the work of the farm alongside him and maybe she could be the one to keep it going into the next generation. But he laughed at her. He said, "Just be a good woman and raise a crop of grandchildren for me. Leave the farming to the men." She never brought it up again.

She grabbed the laundry basket and began to unpin the clean clothing, folding each piece as she laid it in the basket. Before long the basket was full, and she was returning to the house when Johann approached her from the side yard. His appearance was disheveled, and he seemed nervous. "Karla, have you been in the house? Is Papa here?"

"No, he is out working. Was iβt los? You look scared."

"I'm afraid of Papa. He is always angry at me. He punched me and hurt my ear. It was bleeding." Karla turned her brother's face to expose the injury and she could see the dried blood.

"Are you okay?" she said, genuinely alarmed.

"Ja, it stopped bleeding. But this ringing is so loud I can hardly stand it. I don't know what to do. Nothing is ever good enough. I try to help him, but I really don't care about the farm, and he knows it. I'm not the son he wanted, and I never will be. I think some day he might kill me."

Karla contemplated Johann's words, and for a moment she considered the possibility he might be right. Her father really could get that angry. "He can be such a monster! But what can we do?" she said. "We must live here, all of us." She pondered the situation and said, "Let's think of something you can do right now that would at least satisfy him a little. What would he want you to do?"

Johann looked at the ground, defeatedly. He took in Karla's words but found little inspiration in them. Karla lifted his chin until his eyes met hers. She wanted to cuddle him like the small boy he seemed at this moment to be, but instead she concocted a stronger stance. "Think! What would he want you to do right now?"

Johann began to think of things that needed doing. The first thing that came to mind was the hog pen. "I think he would want the fence mended, over by the hog pen." Karla brightened her eyes as she said, "Well? Macht schnell!" Johann went to the tool shed and got busy. Soon he was sawing fence planks and Karla carried the laundry basket into the house.

Susanna was sitting at the table with Marta, chopping onions and carrots. Gretel was in her makeshift playpen, throwing her wood blocks and then scolding them for abandoning her. Just as Karla entered, Marta got up and gathered the blocks, placing them back in the playpen, which had become something of a ritual. Karla walked through to the bedrooms with the laundry and proceeded to put it all away. She came back in, placed the empty basket out on the porch, and then sat down at the table. "What happened?" she said to her mother. Susanna gave her a look of warning, shaking her head briefly with a glance over at Marta. Karla covered neatly, "Today, I mean? What happened today? How was your day?"

Susanna looked at Karla with appreciation as she responded, "Well, Gretel and I did our laundry the old-fashioned way. It was such a beautiful day that we spent all morning out in the yard. Didn't we, Gretel?" The little girl smiled up at her mother as if in agreement. The sounds of hammering broke through from outside. "Sounds like your father must have come back, but I never heard his truck."

"No," Karla responded, "That is Johann. He decided to fix the hog pen fence." Susanna looked over at Karla with a knowing smile. She really was growing into a wise young woman.

As for Johann, he was finding a bit of peace in the rhythm of the saw's motion. Each direction, out, in, out, in . . . he matched to a phrase in German. Then he would repeat the game using a phrase in French. He had always excelled at languages, so much so that his teachers had difficulty knowing how to challenge him. He had learnt enough German at home to get by, so learning the more academic uses of his father's native tongue came easily. In response, his language teacher offered him French lessons, which he quickly accepted and quickly mastered. Now it was a see-saw language game, one word or syllable per motion. *Si mon père rentrait maintenant, je verrais sa tête!* Before long, Johann was done sawing in French, and was hammering away in German. Soon enough, the gate was fixed.

✳✳✳

The sun was finding its bed in the western sky by the time Karl came rumbling down the end drive. He observed Johann working on the hog pen with a sense of satisfaction. "That cuff on the ear did him some good," he said aloud as he parked the truck. He shouted over to his son, "Nice to see you finally getting something done!" Johann waved in response, but he took in the left-handed compliment with no pleasure. In fact, at that moment he hated his father more than ever. Just then Susanna emerged from the porch door with the announcement, "Supper's ready!"

The Neuenschwander family gathered around the kitchen table and ate their meal just like a normal family. Regarding the earlier violent events of the day, not a word was spoken.

Chapter Thirteen

Samuel Boehm drove up the Neuenschwander drive in his '38 Plymouth as he did every Thursday. Samuel was the local mailman, and except for a rare special package, the route on which Karl and Susanna lived was scheduled for weekly deliveries. He beeped the horn and waved at Susanna and her daughters, who were working in the vegetable garden. "Guten Tag, Samuel!" Susanna smiled and waved.

Karl heard the horn and rose immediately from his morning coffee. He always looked forward to receiving his mail, especially when it brought news from his father's family back in Germany. These days, the news was increasingly intense and prolific. Karl greeted Samuel just as he was about to knock on the door.

"Wie geht's, Samuel?" Karl offered, opening the door. "Komme!" he said, motioning him inside. Samuel had his heavy leather mail pouch slung over his right shoulder with the weight hefted on his left hip. "Lots of mail today, ja?" Karl said. "Yes, indeed!" came the reply. "I sometimes wish people would just call on the phone more!" The men chuckled. "Can you sit for a minute? A cup of coffee, maybe?" Karl said.

"Ach, I wish I could," Samuel responded, "but this mail won't deliver itself." He reached into his pouch and pulled out several pieces addressed to Karl, two of which were from Munich.

"News from the Old Country," he said, knowingly. "It is getting very scary over there. The rumors are flying around. It's hard to know what to believe." He handed the bundle of mail to Karl. "You let me know what you learn, huh?"

Karl nodded his assent. "We will talk soon. When you have some time."

Samuel headed back out the door. "Wiedersehen!" he said over his shoulder.

The porch door had barely slammed shut before Karl was already seated at the kitchen table, tearing open the earlier of the two postings from Munich. It was from his uncle Horst. Horst was serving in the SS as a Gruppen führer. He worked under Heinrich Himmler, helping to build a new generation of Aryan German people. Horst had risen high in the ranks of the National Socialist Party and was highly regarded, even by Hitler himself, with whom Horst had met on several occasions. Karl nearly worshiped his uncle, so when he opened the two-page, hand-written letter, it was with a sense of reverent pride.

> *My dearest nephew, I hope this letter finds you and your family well. I trust your farm is the envy of Pennsylvania and would make your father proud.*
>
> *As for me, my important work continues. There is much I cannot tell you due to national security concerns, which I am sure you will understand. What I can say is what the rest of the world already knows, namely, that our German heroes have conquered France and are well-established there. The battle for Britain is commencing even as our victories mount to the east. What comes next, I am not able to say. But our Reich is indomitable. Europe will once again prosper once the good German people are in charge.*
>
> *My work with the Lebensborn program occupies a good deal of my attention. Your cousin Helga (who makes me very proud indeed!) has devoted her own life to this important work. We are building a new and strong Germany, a fountain of decent German blood to serve our glorious Fatherland!*
>
> *Please give my very best to Susanna and to your children. Tell them of our great mission and of the many sacrifices their people are making on behalf of the whole world. May God guide our glorious Führer as he leads us to victory!*
>
> *Your loving uncle, Horst*

Karl read through Horst's letter three times, trying to imagine his uncle in his uniform and wondering what it must be like to be part of such a great and important work. *All I do is dig in the dirt,* he thought to himself. He wondered if his father would truly be proud of the way he kept the farm up. His father was always the consummate German farmer. A true perfectionist.

Karl shifted his attention to the second letter from Germany. It was from his cousin Helga, Horst's oldest daughter. Karl ripped open the letter and read it eagerly.

> *Greetings, Karl! It's me, your cousin Helga writing you from Munich while I am home for a visit with my family. My father told me he had written you, so I thought before I return to the place where I am working, I would take a few minutes to let you know I am also thinking about you.*
>
> *How is your lovely wife? And now it is four children? My goodness! And Karla is already a young lady! I almost said I can hardly imagine all those children, but that is no longer true. I spend my entire day helping young women of pure Aryan blood. Some are expecting and others are new mothers. And so many babies! We have thirty beds and another 35 bassinets, and all are full most of the time. And ours is only one of many such places! We are all doing this wonderful, important work to help raise good German children for the new Reich.*
>
> *I am so proud of my father for his leadership in this work, and for recommending me for such an important job. German men all can serve as soldiers, and many German women contribute to the war effort in supportive ways. They work in factories making everything the men need. It is all important. But for me, this work is a way to make a real, lasting contribution to Germany. I am very happy.*
>
> *I hope you also are happy, Karl. You deserve to be. Please write me back at my parents' home address, which is where I receive my mail. God be with you and your family! And Heil, Hitler!*
>
> *Love and hugs, Helga*

Karl stood as he finished Helga's letter and carried it with him over to his bedroom, where he stood in front of the full-length dressing mirror. He came to attention, clicking his heels together as he had seen in the newsreels, and stiffened his right arm in the Nazi salute. "Heil, Hitler!" he said, longingly. *If only I could be there,* he thought to himself. He considered his image in the mirror. Strong, blondish hair with grey eyes and a well-muscled physique. He imagined himself in the uniform of a German officer, helping to reestablish the noble history of his people and his family.

But no. Karl went to the bed and sat down there. His lot was this farm. His father Johann's farm. Johann established the farm after fleeing with his family to America in 1892. Kaiser Wilhelm had ousted Otto von Bismarck in 1890 and assumed complete power over all domestic and international policies. Karl recalled his father referring to Wilhelm as a "spoiled cripple", and that he knew Wilhelm's ineptitude would lead the country into ruin. There was a steady stream of Germans and others heading for the promise of fresh opportunities in the new world, so Johann decided to join the throng. Karl's mother, Renate, was pregnant with him before they left Germany, and Karl took special pride in knowing he had been conceived in Germany. In his mind, this meant he was a true German.

Still holding his cousin's letter in his hands, Karl looked up at the portrait of his parents in its oval walnut frame on the wall. They were both dead, of course, his mother of consumption when Karl was only twelve, and his father in a threshing machine accident six years later. As he sat there remembering them, Karl hoped he had made his father proud, like his uncle Horst wrote. Karl honestly believed he had done his duty by keeping the farm productive and well-maintained after his father died. But a piece of him hated the place. He was only eighteen years old when he took over the responsibility of running the farm, so he missed out on the usual fun of late teenage years. He never had time for much social life, which was why he was so late in marrying. He met Susanna at the local Oktoberfest when he was 24 years old. Most of his contemporaries already had two or even three children by age twenty-four. Karl had begun to actively seek a bride, which was why he made time for the Oktoberfest. Susanna, five years his junior, had recently moved to the area, and when they met at the festival it was almost automatic. A year later they were married, and 18 months after that, Karla was born.

Karl looked one more time at Helga's letter. "You deserve to be happy," he spoke the words out loud. *What does happiness have to do with it?* he thought, glumly. He stood and went back to the kitchen table, laying the letter beside its companion there, and then he headed out to his father's farm to do his duty.

❋ ❋ ❋

The day took its course and suppertime arrived. Susanna prepared briny pork hocks and sauerkraut along with some roasted carrots and rutabagas. Slices of pumpernickel rye bread and seasoned butter completed the menu, and all were quite satisfied, especially little Gretel, who was cooing happily and giggling while Johann played peek-a-boo with her behind his hands. Even Karl seemed in an uncharacteristically salubrious mood. Susanna said, "A pleasant meal and a pleasant day. Papa, I saw you got some letters from Munich?"

"Ja, from my uncle Horst and one from my cousin Helga."

"It goes well with them, I hope?"

"Very well. Uncle Horst is very highly placed in the Nazi party. He has even met with Hitler himself. He talked about the Lebensborn program which he oversees. Helga is now also working in this program. They are helping to ensure the birth of healthy, pure-blooded German children for the future of the Reich. I am very proud of them."

"It sounds like very important work, indeed. And something positive. Not killing anyone. There is so much killing. The news is full of it all the time."

"Well, it is war. In war people get killed. What do you expect?"

Sensing the general openness of the moment, Johann paused his peek-a-boo game to ask a question. "I don't really understand it all. Why is the war necessary?"

Karl said, "The so-called 'Great War' was a complete disaster for Germany. My father was right: Kaiser Wilhelm was a blithering idiot, and he led the country into ruin. We Germans lost our honor, our pride, and our industry. Your grandparents moved here to America just in time to escape all that misery.

"But now a strong leader has emerged. Hitler has taken bold steps to reestablish the great name and rightful place of Germany in the world. I often wish I could be there to be a part of the effort. How wonderful it must be to help rebuild our country!"

Little Marta, who had been arranging the crusts of her rye bread into various shapes on her plate, suddenly looked up, "But Papa, I thought this was our country?" Susanna offered a bemused glance at her husband as she reached over to stroke Marta's hair behind her ears. Karl was caught up short by such an innocently pointed question, but he responded, "Yes, Marta, America is our country. But we are also Germans by blood. It is hard to explain. When you are older you will understand."

Karla had been helping her mother clear away the supper dishes and listening to the discussion. She said, "Well, I am older. And I don't understand. I really don't. I know I am no scholar, but I did complete my high school studies with high honors. And I still don't understand how invading and taking over other countries will bring back German honor."

At this, Karl began to bristle, and his tone was no longer fatherly, but abrupt and increasing in volume. "Listen, young lady, all those other countries collaborated to defeat Germany and robbed her of her lifeblood after the first world war. If you don't understand what that is like, try working without food. Try growing up with no possibility of a way to make a living. Try having children who have no future. Then tell me what you would do."

Karla wanted to interject further. She was inclined to point out that Germany's warring tendency started the whole problem but knowing her father, she decided to relent. "I guess I see what you mean, Papa. It is just such a waste. All those young men. All that money. I just wish it would stop."

Karl backed down a bit but reasserted his patriarchy. "You want to be a farmer with the men. You want to decide world affairs like a man. Just be who you are. Find a husband, have his babies and leave the affairs of men to the men."

Karla did not respond, but helped her mother finish the washing up and headed out to the side yard without another word. She sat down on the bench beneath one of the elm trees and looked off into the distance. Johnny soon came wandering out and sat down beside her. "I think you were right, you know," he said. "But I just didn't dare say anything. I wish I would have."

Karla said, "No, I'm glad you didn't. But I think you are a very smart young man. Especially when you agree with me." They both laughed, and a jab in the ribs resulted in a shoulder bump in return, and soon the two siblings were wrestling around on the lawn, laughing and taunting one another like a true German family.

Chapter Fourteen

IT was Saturday and the Neuenschwander women were out tending the garden. Karla leaned on her hoe and looked at the sun's position in the early afternoon sky. "Mutti, I hate to leave you while there is so much to do, but I have to get ready for my lesson with Professor Schutte." Karla had been nurturing a natural talent for music since she was a child. Her mother saw her giftedness early and encouraged her. Over the years Karla began to sing often for her family, especially during winter evenings or on long rainy days. Her father first disparaged the idea of lessons, calling it an extravagance; but after she learned to sing Schubert lieder and then an aria from Wagner, he stopped complaining. Once, after Sunday dinner, he even requested a song from her. That was a proud memory for Karla.

"No, no, meine Süsse, I'm glad for you to go," Susanna responded. "Your voice is a gift to the world from God, and you must nurture it." Karla responded to her mother's praise with a smile and a brief embrace before heading to the house. What her mother did not know was that Karla was just as interested in nurturing her relationship with Hans Schutte as she was in nurturing her voice. It was Hans she was thinking of as she headed to the washroom to clean up. She splashed her face and arranged her hair in an attractive bun. She looked at her face in the mirror, considering her eyes, her cheeks, her lips, trying to imagine her face from his perspective, wanting to be attractive to him. This was a brand-new affectation for Karla, and it was exhilarating and not a little daunting.

Heading out to the farmyard, Karla thought about asking her father for permission to use his truck, but decided against it, opting instead to ride her bike for the two-mile trip into Shenandoah. She disliked the image of riding a bike like a girl when she wanted so badly to be regarded as a woman, but the prospect of a confrontation with her father made the bike ride somehow less repulsive.

She headed down the end drive to the road. The image issue aside, Karla truly was an outdoors person and loved every minute of the trip. All of nature seemed to her to be fairly crying out for connection. She noticed the smell of hay and fresh manure perfuming her senses. It was for Karla the smell of growing, of life. A cardinal sang out a whistling overture and its mate responded. Tree frogs were sending out their raucous signals, each to another. Crickets and grasshoppers were similarly engaged in the musical back and forth of seeking mates. And along the way into town, Karla was warming up her voice, too.

As she approached the Schutte home, the size of the place impressed her yet again. It was a very old Victorian structure with an immense front door—at least ten feet tall with a dormer window above—and an old bell pull which, amazingly, still functioned. This was the home of Hans' mother, Hannah, the widow of the Rev. Dr. Adolf Schutte, a local Methodist pastor who had died of cancer 18 months ago. Hans' father had been deeply loved by his congregation, and after he died, the elders voted to allow Hannah to remain in the manse for as long as she wished. Hans had just received his position as assistant professor at Albright College in Reading that same year, so he adopted the routine of coming home weekly to look after his mother; he taught a few private voice and piano students while in town.

Karla pulled up to the yard of the Schutte house and quickly discarded her bike outside the bushes that lined the fencerow. She straightened her dress and patted her cheeks on the way up the front porch stairs. She pulled the antique doorbell just as Professor Hans Schutte was opening the door.

"Come in, come in," he said, "it's so nice to see you again! I want to hear your lovely voice. Come in!" He stood to the side, ingratiating himself a bit and motioning her in with his left hand, ever the gentleman. His right hand found its way to the middle of her back to guide her gently to the parlor. Karla felt an electric shock shoot up her spine at his touch. She hoped she wasn't blushing.

"So how is the voice today?" the professor asked as he sat down at the Baldwin baby grand piano. "Let me hear, gently at first. We don't want to damage the instrument. Let's start with a nice, round ah," he said, as he pounded out an E major chord. The sound of the chord brought an automatic response from Karla, and she sang out a perfectly rounded "ah" to the first five notes of the scale, holding the fifth tone for two beats before descending once again. *Do re mi fa soool, fa mi re do.* "Good!" came the professor's response as he moved up one half-step to F major, with Karla following. As the routine of warming up continued, higher and higher and then back down again by half-steps, Karla could feel her throat muscles beginning to relax and the vibrancy and resonance of her tone became more obvious and natural. She was glad for the music and its focus away from the professor's strong shoulders. "Now," the professor said, "you are all warmed up, yes?" Karla thought to herself, "*If you only knew,*" but she simply responded, "Yes, Professor Schutte." He said, "Very good. Now sing the Schubert Nacht und Träume for me." There was nothing she wanted to do more.

✱✱✱

Johnny was preparing to head down to Reading for what he looked most forward to every Saturday afternoon. The Bijou held a weekly feature movie, which this week happened to star his idol, John Wayne. Johnny was getting dressed, trying to look his best in case a young Fraülein caught his fancy. He stood in front of his dresser, staring himself down in the mirror. He gave himself his most steely, tough hombre look as he imagined his gun duel face-off in the old West. His hands were at the ready, elbows cocked for the draw. Suddenly, quicker than lightning itself, he drew both his imaginary six-guns. "Bang! Bang!" he exploded. "Not quick enough, dude," he said, blowing the smoke off his smoking finger barrels. That's when he looked past his own image in the mirror and saw his father standing in the hall behind him.

"Always with your head in the clouds," Karl said with that familiar tone of disapproval. Johann's victory was as illusory as the smoke of his pistols. "I guess you are heading all the way to Reading to spend your money on your fantasy world again, eh? Over an hour each way! Such a waste!"

"Yes, Papa. It's only 25 cents. David and Thom will be here soon to pick me up. We always split the gas cost. And today we are seeing that new John Wayne movie, 'The Shepherd of the Hills.'"

"A waste of time and money as far as I am concerned. But you do what you want. I have chores to do." With that, Karl Neuenschwander removed himself from the presence of his son. After he heard the porch door slam, Johnny returned his gaze to the mirror. He found that place in the mirror where his father had stood behind him. Suddenly, he whipped around to face his enemy and he snarled, "Sneaking up on me again, eh you son of a bitch! Bang! Bang! B-b-b-b-bang!" He emptied both his guns into the dirty bastard, dropping him where he stood. As he walked over to the spot, envisioning the bullet-ridden body of his father on the hallway floor he said, "You really hadn't oughta mess with Johnny Wayne." Just then the sound of Thom's Ford driving into the yard jolted Johnny back to reality, and he ran out to escape his father one more time.

"Come on, Johnny! Move your arsch!" Thom shouted. "We don't want to miss the newsreels! We have to get the latest on Hitler and the war." Thom and David were Mennonite cousins, but they had moved away from their parents' farms to test life outside their strict religious community. They shared a sleeping room at a boarding house in town to save money, and they split the cost of an old '32 coupe which they shared to get to their job building houses. Johnny met them while standing in line at the Bijou a year ago, and they just sort of hit it off over their love of movies.

"I'm coming, I'm coming!" He scooted into the passenger's seat next to David, scrunching him into the center of the Ford's bench seat. "Okay, let's go!"

In forty-five minutes the threesome arrived at the Bijou. They each bought their tickets, a box of popcorn and a cold bottle of coke, and then they got settled into three seats smack in the middle of the theater. They were just in time for the newsreel to begin. The newsreels tended to be fluffy promotional pieces about this or that movie star, or sometimes travelogues showing various foreign or distantly domestic locations. Johnny was sometimes intrigued, but not often. Most of the time he only tolerated them in order to get to the movie. But recently the newsreels had been focusing more and more on the situation in Europe and the fight against the Nazis. The entire situation was confusing, but riveting.

Today's newsreel was entitled, "1940, the Year in Review." It was from England and focused on the German attacks on Britain by sea and by air. All three of the young men were fascinated by the scenes of British ships destroying a host of German warships, followed by the valiant attempts to defend their homeland from something they called a blitzkrieg. "A hundred thousand people dead . . ." Johnny saw images of bodies piled together in London's underground, and he leaned over to Thom and repeated the words he had heard, "A hundred thousand dead? Why are the

Germans bombing people in the city?" Thom responded, "I don't know. Doesn't seem right, does it?"

David chimed in, "It isn't right. I know our families come from Germany and all, but this is not right. Makes a guy want to do something." Thom and Johnny looked at each other. Each could see in the other's eyes what neither wished to acknowledge. They were thinking thoughts not of boys, but of men. Men willing to fight. Both looked over at David and the same look was there on his face, too. No one said a word. Words weren't needed.

The newsreel finished with images of men and women in various uniforms, all joined in the effort to repel the Nazi threat. It was inspiring and challenging. All three young men were very happy for the beginning of the movie. But as John Wayne strode confidently onto the screen, Johnny couldn't help thinking about those scenes in London. *A hundred thousand dead,* he kept saying to himself. By the time the movie was over, he wasn't sure he could recall much of it at all.

They piled back into the car and at first, they just sat there. After a few minutes Thom spoke up first. "Do you think it's real?" David answered immediately, "Of course, it's real! Did you see those poor people?" Johnny spoke aloud what he had been repeating in his mind, "A hundred dead. Men, women and children." Thom looked at David. "What are you thinking about doing?" David said, "I'm signing up. I'm joining the Army."

Thom was the older of the two cousins by almost a year. He had been in the protector role when they were growing up. But now David was leading the way. Thom said, "I suppose I'll have to go with you. Somebody has to look after your dumb arsch." The cousins looked at each other and grinned. Suddenly they both looked at Johnny. Thom said, "You coming with us?"

Johnny looked out at the dimly lit evening sky. He thought about what he had seen in the newsreel, and in all the other newsreels and newspaper articles he had seen in the past year. He thought about all those people in London. And he thought about the rest, too. The people in France and Belgium and Denmark and all the Eastern countries. He thought about all of them. He thought about his father, of how proud he was of being a native-born German and of his connections to the Nazi leadership. *I wonder what Papa will say when I tell him. IF I tell him . . . He will probably forbid me to go. But I am eighteen years old in three weeks. I do not need his permission.*

"My father . . ." Johnny said out loud. "Thom and David both knew the whole situation with Johnny's father and his German pride. "Yeah, I know," Thom said. But if it's up to you, what do you think? As an American with your own mind, what do you think is the right thing to do?"

Johnny needed no time to respond. "I will go with you." He extended his hand, palm down, to the space between them. Thom placed his hand on Johnny's, and David followed suit. The three hands clasped together in a bond of unity. Thom cranked up the Ford and they headed out of town, making plans for heading to the recruiting office there in Reading. "So, Johnny, what are you going to tell your Papa?"

Johnny thought for a minute before responding, "I don't know. I might not tell him anything. I know he won't like it. But I am going. I have to."

✻✻✻

Supper that evening was unusually quiet. Susanna wondered about the movie, but knowing it was a bone of contention between Karl and his son, she declined to bring up the subject. Johnny mostly picked at his food, eating a bite here and there. "Eat, Johann, your food will get cold," Susanna said. Karl, not missing an opportunity to berate his son, jumped in as well. "If you don't want to eat what your mother worked hard to prepare for you, then just leave the table. You can go to bed hungry."

Johnny looked at his mother and said, "Mutti, it is very good, but I am not very hungry right now. I don't feel well. May I be excused?" His mother, sensing something more than an upset stomach might be involved here, said, "Of course, Johann. I will save some in the icebox for you if you want it later."

At this, Johnny stood and picked up his plate to take it to the kitchen. Karl snarled at him, "Leave that! You are not a woman even if you act like one." Karla looked up at her father with a seething anger as Susanna stood to take Johnny's plate to the kitchen. But Johnny kept his plate and walked past his father into the kitchen to place it on the counter. Karl growled at him, "I said leave it!" And he stood up gruffly, expecting his son to run out the door. But Johnny squared around to meet his father's challenge. He looked him in the eye and said, "Papa, I am leaving soon. I am joining the Army to fight the Nazis. Excuse me." And he walked past his father, brushing shoulders with him in a deliberate and unyielding gesture.

Karl was so stunned at first that he made no response at all. But soon the impact of his son's words hit him like a solid right cross, and he followed him quickly down the hall to his bedroom in a manner that left little doubt as to his intentions. Susanna grabbed Gretel, who was already sensing the anger and beginning to whimper, and she motioned to Karla to take Marta, and all the women headed out to the barn. "Let's go check on the chickens, shall we? Maybe we have some eggs to gather."

They entered the chicken coop just before Karl's first thundering tirade rang out, which they could hear despite Susanna's attempts to shield them from it. "Mother?" Karla said. "Yes, meine Tochter," Susanna replied. "Do you think Johann would have decided to fight the Germans if it weren't for the way Papa treats him?" Susanna did not respond, but when Karla looked over at her, her face displayed a deeply sad and vacant look, as if she were suddenly recognizing the absence of a necessary puzzle piece. Karla moved next to her mother and placed a hand on her shoulder. She said, "I'm sorry, Mutti. I shouldn't have asked you that." Susanna did not look up, but she patted her daughter's hand. "Come on," she said, let's see if there are a few more eggs here."

Back in the house, Johnny was in the corner of his bedroom, but he was no longer cringing. He stood up to face his father's anger. "Who do you think you are? You think you are a man now?" Karl shouted. His face was now boiling red, beginning from his neck and fanning out like some hideous, spiked plant upward to his ears and cheeks. "Answer me!!" The demand was accompanied by a backhand slap across his son's face. But Johnny did not back down or try to avoid the blow. He took it full force, never breaking his stare directly into his father's eyes.

"Papa, I am going. What they are doing over there is not right. It is not German. It is terribly wrong. And it must be resisted and defeated. I must go to do what I can."

"You will not go! I forbid it!!" He brought the backhand again, this time with even fuller force and from the opposite direction. Johnny's lip was cut. and he tasted his own blood. Still, he stood toe to toe with his father. Karl shouted out, "America is not even in this war! You think you know more than the government about what ought to be done?"

"It won't be long, and we will be in it. And when we are, I want to be ready to do my part. I am going," Johnny said defiantly.

"You are not going!" Karl said, this time balling up his right fist and raring back to let fly. But something in Johnny stood up tall at that moment, and ducking inside the coming roundhouse, he delivered a solid blow of his own to his father's solar plexus. Karl doubled over and fell into a ball on the ground, unable to breathe. And, suddenly, unable to bark any more orders to anyone. Johnny looked down at the image of his father, writhing and rolling about like some gasping fish on the riverbank, and he felt no pity for him. No love, no empathy. Nothing.

Johnny said, "I am going. I'll walk to town and find a room for the night. I'll get my things later." He threw together a few necessary items in a rucksack and exited his room. As Johnny headed down the end drive, he turned his back on his father for good. He remembered the earlier scene in his bedroom before the movie that afternoon, how embarrassed he felt at his father's disapproval and snide remarks. As he made his way toward the road Johnny said out loud, "Well, Papa, I am trading in my six-guns for the real thing. Like I said, you really oughtn't mess with Johnny Wayne."

Susanna and her daughters emerged from the henhouse with their basket of eggs just in time to see Johann heading down the end drive. Karla started to run after him, but Susanna held her back. "Best to let things calm down a bit, I think. Perhaps tomorrow things may look different, ja?" Karla looked into her mother's eyes and saw a wisdom there which she sometimes forgot existed. "You are right, Mutti. Of course, you are right. Let's get ready for bed."

When they entered the house, they found Karl sitting in his chair by the fireplace, holding his bottle of beer and staring sullenly at the fire. No words were exchanged, and before long all the Neuenschwander womenfolk were nestled in bed. Karl remained by the fire, alone.

As for Johnny, he found his way to the same boarding house where Thom and David stayed, and it occurred to him that his walk to town had seemed quicker than usual. He rented a two-dollar room and within fifteen minutes he was fast asleep.

CHAPTER FIFTEEN

SUSANNA awakened to her husband's absence. She had suffered a restless night, but near morning she had been dreaming of a pleasant scenario, a picnic back in New York when she was a girl. She was with her parents and her brothers, Berthold and Hans, who were running and chasing after one another in an open, grassy lea near their farmhouse. Susanna and her mother and father were seated on the wooden chairs her father had made. A brightly checkered cloth table lay on the ground with a round stone at each corner and a woven picnic basket in the center. Her father was reading a book by Goethe (she didn't know which one), and all was serene and uncomplicated. Peaceful.

But as she moved from dreaming to awareness, alone in her bed, the memories of the previous evening came flooding back in her mind, dissipating her peaceful mood on waves of anxiety and fear. *Where is Johann? Did Karl go after him? Was there a fight? Or worse?* The sound of Gretel stirring and fussing propelled Susanna into action, but a feeling of foreboding went with her as she donned her housecoat and headed to Gretel's room.

Before long the morning routines asserted themselves and the baby was changed, the bottle was warmed, the coffee was cooking, and the porches were swept. *Just do your work and all will be well.* Karl came in from his morning chores. He sat at the kitchen table without a word. "Only biscuits and coffee this morning," Susanna said. "Church meeting begins in an hour."

"Ja, ja, I know," Karl said resignedly. "We go and we pray. Then we come home and do the work like every day." Susanna poured him a cup of coffee and set it down before him.

Marta came shuffling into the kitchen, rubbing her eyes with both her little fists. She crawled up into her mother's lap and snuggled into her chest. "Mutti, must we go to church meeting today? I'm still sleepy." Karl didn't wait for Susanna to answer. "We go to church meeting every Sunday. Sleepy or not."

Karla came in from the barn. "The stalls are clean, and I fed the calves. Mutti, I gathered the eggs for you." She placed a small wicker basket filled with white and brown eggs on the counter beside the icebox. "Thank you, Karla! You are such a help to me," Susanna said with a smile.

"Just practicing to be a good hausfrau," Karla responded, the sneer toward her father obvious in her tone. Karl never noticed. Karla headed to the bathroom to clean up for church.

❊❊❊

The Neuenschwander family arrived at the Shenandoah Evangelische Kirche as usual, minus one member. The Pfarrer greeted them at the door, shaking Karl's hand and nodding toward Susanna and the children. "And where is young Johann this morning? It goes well with him? Not sick, I hope."

Karl was about to respond when the Pfarrer looked past them and said, "Ahh! Here comes the son and heir, bringing up the rear." The family turned around and were stunned to see Johann standing right behind them. Susanna could not help giving him a spontaneous, relieved hug, which he accepted only briefly. The cut on his lower lip was closed but still obvious. Karl turned and led the way to their usual pew with the family following him in. Johann usually sat next to his father, but today he sat on the end beside the main aisle.

The church meeting proceeded as usual, with admonitions and corporate confession followed by the proclaiming of absolution, Biblical readings and a 45-minute sermon, all interspersed with various congregational hymns. Karla always loved the singing, and Karl could not help being proud of her voice ringing out above the gathered faithful. The worship culminated in the sharing of the Holy meal, after which the congregants were dismissed. By the time the meeting ended, all were more than ready to head home for a hearty Sunday dinner. But first came the "meeting after the meeting." The men all gathered on the church lawn, many enjoying a cigarette or pipe as they exchanged the news of the day and their respective opinions thereof. The women similarly gathered under the shade trees, exchanging pleasantries and discussing their children, their men, and the local affairs and scandals of recent times.

But man or woman, the first subject of discussion these days was always the war. Samuel Boehm, the postman, approached Karl and said, "Have you any news to share from your family in the Old Country?" Several others overheard the overture and turned their attention to Karl.

"Ja, my uncle Horst and cousin Helga wrote to me from Munich. They both are involved in a program to develop healthy, true German children for the Reich. Horst even works right under Himmler! He wants us all to know how hard the German people are working to restore honor and pride to Germany. He couldn't say too much, but he assured me that the German Reich is unstoppable. I am very proud of him!"

Unbeknownst to Karl, Johann had joined the gathering of the men just as Karl began his response to Samuel. "Did he say anything about the 100,000 civilians killed in London last year from the German air raids?" The voice was unmistakably Johann's voice, and the tone was obviously challenging. The sudden hush of those gathered there was brimful with tension.

Karl responded with a fiery stare at his son. "And you know this to be true? How? You who know more than our own government! How do you know?"

"It is in the newsreels and in the newspapers. It is reported by eye-witnesses in radio broadcasts. Why do you doubt what is reported by so many who have seen with their own eyes? How are you so sure it is not true? And if it is true—which it is—what is the responsible thing to do? 100,000 civilians—men, women and children—dead! If you are a man, a true man, a man who is a Christian and does what is right, what do you do?" The rhetoric was pointed and unyielding, and those gathered had increased in number. They reacted like observers at a tennis match, their heads swiveling from one forehand volley to its response from across the net.

Karl Neuenschwander was not accustomed to being publicly challenged by anyone, let alone by his own son. The heat was rising in his neck, and had he been at home he would have lashed out with his customary backhand. But here he was in the churchyard, surrounded by other men, with his wife and the other women looking on, being openly defied by his 18-year-old son.

The Pfarrer had heard the exchange and was reluctant to get involved but, sensing the possible eruption of violence, he could not stay silent. "Johann," he called out, approaching the group. "Come with me." Without breaking eye contact with his father, Johann responded, "Yes,

Pfarrer." And he pulled away to follow the man of God into the church building.

"Johann, you must not talk that way to your father at any time, but especially in public. You put him in an impossible position. A man must have his honor, and if you disrespect him like that, he will not soon forget it."

"Yes, Pfarrer, but with all respect, you do not know my father as well as you think. He is like a growling bear at home, and nothing pleases him. And he refuses to see the truth about what his precious home country has become. I have become convinced that this Nazi regime is evil and must be stopped. I told him last night that I am joining the Army to fight them. He became violent, and I left. I joined my family for worship this morning for the sake of my mother and my sisters and for my own faith, but when I heard him out in the yard giving praise to the Nazis and his relatives who work for them, I could not remain silent."

The Pfarrer listened carefully before responding. "I understand. And you may be right about the Nazis. It begins to look like war is inevitable. If they are guilty of the things you and others believe about them, they must be stopped. But listen to me carefully. "It might be right to oppose the Nazis. But if you will take just a few minutes to walk in your father's shoes—the shoes he wore out in that churchyard—you might at least begin to understand the sort of human misery that caused Nazi followers to be what they have become."

Johann considered his pastor's words. "I'm going to think a lot about what you have said to me. Thank you, Pfarrer." The Pfarrer responded with a blessing, after which Johann left the church via the front door.

Meanwhile, the Pfarrer made his way back to where the men were gathered. A lively discussion had ensued, evincing strongly held opinions both in support of and against Hitler and the Nazis. "Pfarrer, gut!" one man said. "Tell us! What do you think? What is the faithful thing?"

This was precisely why the Pfarrer had not wanted to enter this discussion in the first place. He had to be pastor to all these men and their families; taking a strong position on either side risked splitting the church into factions. But there was no avoiding it now. "You ask me what I think, and you ask me what is the faithful thing. I hope what I think is always the faithful thing, but how can anyone know? I have studied the Scriptures and books of theology for many years, because I believe that is the route to a faithful life. So, all I can do is say what the Scriptures have taught me. The Holy Bible is full of examples of war and claims of

God's involvement in one conflict or another. But taken as a whole, God opposes those who dominate or abuse others, always taking the side of the oppressed, the widow, and the orphan. Those who support Germany see the German people as having been dominated and oppressed after the Great War. So, one could see Scriptural support for God taking their side as an oppressed people."

Karl Neuenschwander spoke up, "You see! Just like I said! The German cause is a righteous one!"

"However," the Pfarrer continued, "If the oppressed then become oppressors of others, whose side should God take then?" Karl was again caught up short. He did not know what to say.

"If Germany is attacking innocent civilians—people of any nation or creed or religion—then God will not hold her blameless. To God all life is precious, and in the end God's son suffered and died to make it clear for all who will listen: abuse and domination are not faithful ways to live, and ultimately, God will overpower and defeat them. You asked me what is faithful. That is my answer. You must each decide what action your faith requires."

The men were pensive, taking in the words of their pastor, who then continued. "Now I think it is time to go home to dinner with your families. Perhaps you will give this matter some prayerful consideration. If you want to talk further about it, come and see me. God bless you all." The gathering dispersed quietly.

While the men were talking, Karla had noticed Johann heading out the front of the church. She ran to catch up with him, calling out to him, "Johnny! Johnny, wait!" He heard her and turned around, waiting for her.

"Where are you going? Where are you staying?" she said, breathless.

"I got a room at the boarding house on Front Street in town. It's where Thom and David are staying. I'll be all right. Let Mutti know not to worry."

"I wish you didn't have to go. And I wish I could go with you. I wish . . ." Tears began to well up in her eyes and he gave her a warm hug. She sunk into his chest and let her tears flow. "You are suddenly a man," she said," pulling back and grinning an embarrassed grin. Johnny looked down at her, aware at that moment that he was, in fact, seven inches taller than his older sister. "Ja, well at least I am trying to be. Take care, Sis. I'll keep in touch." They hugged once more and then went their separate ways.

Chapter Sixteen

S PRING morphed into Summer, and the sun's heat was an analog to the growing rancor throughout the German American community in and around Schuylkill County. The morning coffee klatches in the local cafes, traditionally filled with friendly banter among neighbors and retirees, had become bogged down with strong opinions and refutations. So also, with the afternoon and evening gatherings in the local pubs, which sometimes broke into fistfights requiring police intervention. Nearly every week brought another strained relationship, and Karl was chief among the antagonists. As the weeks passed by into the harvest season, he had become more and more isolated. He had his adherents, but more and more people were being appalled by the continuing barrage of reports from Europe, chronicling what seemed to be a pattern of increasing cruelty wielded by the Nazi forces.

Johnny, Thom and David were in basic training at Ft. Leonard Wood in Missouri, and now it was not only Karl who looked forward to the Thursday mail. Susanna often intercepted Samuel Boehm in the yard, anxiously searching through the bundle of postings for news from Johann. She wouldn't admit it if asked, but she had a sad suspicion that if Karl got to the mail first. he might intercept and discard any letter from his son. There wasn't a letter every week, but most weeks there was one and sometimes two. Today's delivery brought only the one letter, which Susanna opened eagerly. It was dated October 28th.

Dear Mother: I am happy to report that basic training is going well. I am getting stronger every week, and I am surprised to learn that I am quite a good shot. I have earned a special designation for my marksmanship, and there is a possibility I may be selected for special training in the infantry as a Ranger. It is quite an honor, and by no means a guarantee, but I am hopeful. If I am selected it will mean another 8 weeks of specialized training at another facility. I will keep you posted.

Susanna paused here to say a little prayer that Johann would be chosen for the special training, partly out of pride in his accomplishments, but also because she knew while he was in training he could not be in harm's way. She read on.

I am so glad Thom and David are here with me, although we are all three assigned to different units. They don't give us much time off, but two weeks ago on our first weekend pass we got together and went into town. It is very different here from home. So many soldiers! I couldn't begin to guess how many! There are some spats here and there between the units, but everyone is here for the same reason. We all get along.

Well, another two weeks until I finish basic. I'll let you know what's happening when I can. Give my best to Karla and the girls.

Love, Johnny (Johann)

Susanna clasped the letter to her chest for a moment before secreting it inside her apron. She went back to her kitchen to find Karl sitting at the table. "I am not used to waiting for my mail," he said with irritation. "Another letter from your son, I imagine?"

"From *our* son, you mean," she said with an unusual stiffness. "Ja, he wrote me. He is doing very well. Two more weeks of basic training, but he has excelled in shooting. They may select him for further training to become what they call a ranger. He said it is a high honor and very competitive. If they select him, he will have eight weeks more training."

"He is not my son any longer if he goes to fight against his own people," Karl said. He rifled through the bundle of mail Susanna placed on the table and found a letter from Munich, which he eagerly tore open. Susanna bristled at Karl's continued rejection of Johann and she very nearly retorted; but, looking over at Gretel sitting happily in her highchair, she decided to hold her tongue. Instead, she said, "Well, I have laundry to do," and she grabbed her laundry basket from the back porch and began to gather up the clothing. Karl never heard her; his attention was completely on the letter, which this time was from his cousin, Helga.

> My Dear Karl:
>
> Gegrüssung! It is me, Helga. I write with a full heart as I continue in my good work here in Germany. It still makes me laugh to write that word! 'Germany' is such a funny-sounding way for the English to say Deutschland! But I write in English, so there we are.

Oh, Karl! My father and I attended the Bayreuth Festival. We were able to stay for the entire festival. All four operas in Wagner's Ring cycle! I can hardly begin to tell you how wonderful it was. The epic stories of the interaction of the gods and human beings, and of the beautiful and blessed Walkyrie, angels of Valhalle, inspiring and honoring the bravery of our German (there is that word again!) warriors, all gloriously displayed and enacted, and accompanied by the most thrilling music ever written! It was almost too beautiful to bear!

And as if the opera were not enough, we were in the company of so many great leaders of National Socialism. Herr Himmler sat in the box seat with us, and Field Marshall Goering sat in the next box to ours, along with Herr Goebels and his family! There was a rumor that the Fuhrer himself might show up for at least a part of the festival, but alas, he never did.

Karl, I hope you know these great, foundational stories from our history, and if you do not, you owe it to yourself and to our heritage to learn them. These mythical heroes continue to be a great inspiration to all Germans. Yes, even to me! In my work with the Lebensborn program I feel a strong kinship with those angels of Valhalle, serving the glory of our God-like Fuhrer, giving support and encouragement to our men in battle and ensuring the rebirth of a new, thousand-year Reich! I am so very proud to be a part of this noble and honorable mission!

I hope it goes well with you and Susanna and your children. I look forward to the time when the struggle is won, and I will finally be able to meet your family. One day we will all be together. Until then, go with God, and Heil, Hitler!

Your affectionate cousin,
Helga

Karl looked up from Helga's letter, dysphoric. It was the same whenever he read news from Munich, as though that were his real calling, the place he really should be. Reading these letters from Helga or from his Uncle Horst always seemed to include him—if only temporarily—in the great work of rebuilding Germany's rightful place of leadership in Europe and the world. But every time he read one of his family's letters, the instant he lifted his eyes from the page, his mood plummeted into an abyss of mud and manure and misery.

He read through the letter once more, aware that he had no idea of the great stories to which Helga had referred. *I wonder why my father never taught us those stories? Maybe he never knew them either.* The thought motivated him. As he rose from his kitchen table Karl resolved to find some way to learn these stories. *For myself and my heritage,* Helga's words echoed in his mind. "I can at least do that much," he said aloud as he headed back out to his farm work.

***

Karla and Marta were at the Bielfeldts. Nellie Bielfeldt was only beginning to bear some weight on her leg, so the young neighbors still helped with the laundry and cooking and cleaning. Alfred Bielfeldt was working on his machinery in preparation for the harvest.

"We so appreciate your willingness to come and help us," Nellie said. "You be sure and tell your parents for me, won't you?" she said.

"We don't mind, do we Marta?" Karla said. Marta's bright smile showed her agreement. "Well, you certainly do your parents proud. Some wouldn't be so neighborly. But your mother is raising you right. I believe we are put on this earth to help one another, and I think we all need to remember that even more these days."

Karla was quite aware that her father and Alfred Bielfeldt held opposing views about German aggression, and particularly the reported Nazi pogroms against the Jewish people. The Bielfeldts were members of the Moravian church and were against the taking up of arms. They also had relatives from the old country in Swabia, and Nellie's side of the family were Jews. "I agree, Mrs. Bielfeld, and so does my brother. He is nearly done with basic training in the Army."

"I truly hate war. I believe it is against the will of God. I am sorry young Johann is going to fight, and we will pray every day for his safe return."

"Thank you very much, Mrs. Bielfeldt. I will tell him when I write him next."

'I imagine your father is not happy about his son joining the Army either, but not for the same reasons," Nellie said. "No, he is not happy about it," Karla said, shortly. "His reasons are his own. I had better head out to hang up this laundry now."

She headed out to the yard, and as she pinned up one piece of the clean, damp laundry at a time, she was brooding about her family's troubles. She had no wish either to express or to apologize for her father's views. It was hard enough to live with the man, let alone having anyone think she might be aligned with his nationalistic German stance. As for Johann joining the Army, Karla blamed her father, just like she said in the chicken coop, although she would never again talk about it with her mother.

With the laundry hung up, Karla went out to the henhouse to find Marta, who had swept out the floor, gathered the eggs, and was just beginning to scatter feed for the hens. "My, aren't you the good little worker!" Karla said, stroking her sister's pig-tailed hair. "Let's take these eggs into the kitchen. You can finish tidying up and dusting, and I will put together some hot dish suppers for tonight and tomorrow. The bread should be about done by now."

The two of them went back into the Bielfeldt house, and after another 90 minutes their work was finished. "Thank you again, girls. And please greet your mother for me," Nellie said. "You are very welcome, Mrs. Bielfeldt. We will say hi to our mother for you. See you in a couple of days. Wiedersehen!" And the two of them headed back home.

Chapter Seventeen

I T was the last Saturday of November, and Susanna was excited to get her morning work done and the evening meal started, because the women's quilting group would be meeting at 2:00 that afternoon. Karla used to help her on this day, but with Johann gone she was out helping Karl with the farm work.

Susanna loved this day each month. She loved it because of the work itself; she was an expert seamstress, and she had enjoyed sewing all her life. She loved the time away from the daily humdrum on the farm. She loved the usefulness of the work; over a year's time, about two hundred quilts were assembled and sent off to orphanages and nursing homes. And finally, she loved the opportunity to be with other women to share stories about life and family.

The appointed time arrived, and Susanna said to Marta, "I am leaving now. There are two bottles in the icebox for Gretel. Remember to heat them and test the temperature like I taught you." Marta smiled up at her mother, excited to be placed in charge. "I remember, Mutti. Don't worry." Susanna considered her little girl, so happy and willing to please. "You are getting to be a big girl!" she said, kissing her on the top of her head. Marta snuggled into her mother's abdomen in response. Then Susanna waved good-bye and headed off to borrow her husband's truck as usual (the one time he never complained about her using it), for the drive into town.

Susanna was the second to arrive at the church, pulling into the parking lot just as Frieda Koehn was walking in the door to the church hall. Frieda was the one who headed up the women's group at the Evangelische Kirch, and she usually arrived early to get things set up. One never knew how many to expect due to varying farm and family demands, but if everyone showed up there might be as many as twenty-five women gathered to sew and tie quilts and share coffee klatsch.

Before long the cars and bicycles began arriving, and that day a total of twelve quilters participated. Four groups of three workers organized themselves, mostly by affinity. Some women sat and sewed quilt tops together while others worked at one of two large quilt frames, assembling or tying the quilts together with colorful yarn. Susanna joined Frieda Koehn and Marietta Schmidt at one of the sewing tables.

"I look forward so very much to these Saturdays!" Susanna said gleefully.

"Ja, me too," Frieda responded. "It gets me away from my husband!" And all three women laughed. "All this talk about the war. Germany this and America that. Sometimes I just can't take it anymore."

Susanna responded immediately, "Oh, I know! And now my son Johann is training to go fight. Karl is furious about it. I don't know what to think. I am glad Johann is finding his way, but I wish it weren't *this* way." The doleful look in her eyes was unavoidable. Marietta reached over to pat Susanna's arm, and Susanna quickly forced back a tear and changed the subject as she threaded her needle. "How was Thanksgiving with your families?"

Frieda responded first. "Everyone from both sides of the family came, of course, to our house. I cooked for two days just to prepare. But everyone brought something, so it worked out." She pushed her needle through and pulled it back again mechanically. "Everything was great until the men gathered to smoke and babble afterward. The war. Always the war. And of course, the women did all the cleaning up as usual. We have no time for the war."

Marietta nodded her assent. "We went to Max's sister Dierdre's for dinner. It was pretty quiet. Only eight of us. And when we were done eating the kids ran out to play while the rest of us gathered around the radio to listen to Bob Hope's Pepsodent Show. I just love Bob Hope! Such a wag! Then, after the show, Dierdre played the piano for us, and we sang and sang. It was wonderful. No talk of the war at all."

"That does sound wonderful," Susanna said. "We only had our family. Minus one, of course," and the sadness in her eyes returned. "The dinner was fine; turkey and everything. But it was so quiet and tense. It's always so tense. Karl is so . . ." she didn't know what word to use to describe her husband accurately and faithfully. One word wouldn't do him justice. Every word that crossed her mind needed an ancillary, mostly opposite descriptor. He was strong, but inflexible. He was dutiful, but bitter. He was her husband and the father of her children, but also their tormentor, and especially so with Johann. She began again, "He's so . . ."

"German!" Frieda finished the sentence for her. "And a man! And a bully! And you won't change him. He is who he is. And we are finished with this quilt top." Frieda always had a way of getting to the point. And along with Marietta, Susanna sighed and nodded in agreement. "You are right, Frieda," Susanna responded. "I can't change him. But I can raise my children. That's what I can do. Maybe for them it will be better." Her eyes looked off to a fleeting vision of family Thanksgiving gatherings with Karla and Marta and their husbands and kids, of Gretel maybe working as a nurse or even a doctor, of grandchildren happily playing and with no talk of war or Germany or Nazis or anger. She was startled when she realized that in her vision, Karl was nowhere to be found.

"Yes, you can, Susanna. You can raise your children, and you can make a difference. And you can certainly sew a perfect seam!" Frieda said as she inspected Susanna's work. "I swear, I've been sewing for many years, and not even my mother-in-law, who would be quick to tell you or anyone else what was wrong with your sewing—and anything else about you, for that matter," she said, pausing for effect. "Not even Elvira Koehn could sew any more evenly or straighter than you do."

Susanna blushed in response, "Oh you! Let's start another top." Marietta brought over another bunch of fabrics and the three women began the process of assembling yet another quilt to send out into the world.

CHAPTER EIGHTEEN

I T was Sunday evening, and the Neuenschwander family was gathered around the radio like most Sunday evenings. Suddenly, the usual variety hour show was interrupted by news of a surprise attack on the US Pacific Fleet stationed at Pearl Harbor, Hawaii. Nobody said a word. Marta was coloring a picture and seemed not to grasp the situation at all. Karl got up and left the kitchen, heading out to his workshop. Karla's and Susanna's eyes met in a wordless, terrible communication, and then they both spoke it at the same time: "Johann!" *What would this mean for him?* Susanna had a sudden instinct to pick up Gretel and hold her close, and a cold shiver ran through her. She felt the urge to run, to run anywhere. *But where should I run?* she thought.

When Monday came, lunch was accompanied by the sound of the radio, which was not unusual. But today brought the promise of a first-ever live broadcast of the President addressing a joint session of Congress. At 12:30 the broadcast began. "Yesterday, December 7th, 1941, a date which will live in infamy . . ." President Roosevelt's stern, somber tone carried the weight of his words. His message concluded with a request for Congress to declare war against the empire of Japan, and the sound of the unanimous applause by all the members of Congress seemed to presage a complete unification of the American citizenry. Even Karl Neuenschwander could not deny the need to answer such an unprovoked and deliberate attack by the Japanese. He was fine with the declaration of war against Japan. It came, in fact, as a sort of relief for him. He told Susanna, "Now *there's* somebody worth fighting! If Johann wants to shoot the bad guys, let him go and kill Japanese instead of his own blood! That I can agree with!" But all Susanna could think of was the image of her little boy loading up a rifle, aiming it at another human being, and firing. The mere thought of it very nearly made her retch.

Instead, Susanna did what she always did. She got busy. She and Karla finished up the kitchen work, and then she said to Karla, "How about if we take your sisters for a nice walk. I can hardly believe this is December. It's such a beautiful day!"

Karla responded, "I would love to, but I am meeting Hans . . . I mean, Professor Schutte this afternoon." Susanna looked up and a coy smile crept across her lips as she said, "Hans, is it? And this is not Saturday, or am I confused?" She was toying with her daughter and enjoying it. "Oh, Mother!" Karla said, obviously embarrassed. "He doesn't go back to the college until tomorrow, and he asked me over for tea with his mother and their friends. I might sing for them."

"For them? Or for him . . ." Susanna's smile broadened as the cat and mouse episode continued. Finally, Karla couldn't stand it anymore. She pulled her mother into a corner of the kitchen and her voice dropped to an excited whisper, as if telling a sacred secret. "Oh, Mother, I wish I could tell you how he makes me feel inside," she whispered. "It is like nothing I've ever known. When I go for our lesson, I can hardly stand the wait. And when I see him, he is so welcoming and charming. And he plays so beautifully. I know I sing better just because of his accompaniment."

Susanna got caught up in her daughter's youthful, brimming joy. Just for a moment, she was carried off by the memory of what it was like for her when Karl came across the dance floor and extended his big hand, taking her small one so gently. She remembered how her hand disappeared in his. Completely disappeared! It had made her feel somehow safe. He was an awful dancer, but it hadn't mattered. She recalled how he looked at her as if she were the only girl in the place. It wasn't on that first time they met, but it didn't take too long before she was feeling just what her daughter was feeling now.

"Isn't he a bit too old for you?" Susanna wondered.

"He is older, I know he is. In fact, I don't know how old he really is," Karla said, her brow furrowing quizzically. "I think about ten years or so older than me. But I don't care. I think I am in love." The joy on her face was irresistible to Susanna and she embraced her warmly.

The lovely moment was interrupted by a loud snort from the living room. Susanna looked over at Karl and she could see he had fallen asleep in the big chair with his bottle of beer still in his hand. She tiptoed in to take it from him so it wouldn't spill, but he roused just as she pulled the bottle away. "Was ist's?" he roared, startled into a quick rage. Susanna recoiled from his anger and said, "Your beer. You were sleeping," He answered her gruffly, "Ja, ja. Just leave it," he said, settling back into his nap.

Susanna moved the beer to the lamp table beside his fireside chair and headed back into the kitchen. She turned to look at the sleeping hulk, already snoring again. A sadness came over her which she tucked under the cloak of her daughter's budding romance. Cupping Karla's face in her hands, she smiled at her and said, "You go on and get ready for your visit with the Schuttes. Marta will help me take Gretel for a little walk, won't you Marta?" Marta looked up from her coloring book at the table with her usual smile, "Ja, Mutti."

❀❀❀

Since the weather was so unseasonably warm, Karla chose to walk the two miles into town, arriving at the Schutte home at 2:00 on the dot. Hans met her at the door, chivalrous and accommodating as usual. "Karla, meine Süsse, come in! Come into the parlor. We will have some tea." Karla stirred inside when she heard the word, 'meine', and she felt herself walking a bit lighter as she followed him in.

They entered the familiar parlor and Karla saw three elderly women, all attired primly and with precision, as though they had been dressed for a tin-type portrait sometime in the last century. Mrs. Schutte smiled broadly and welcomed her. "Karla! I am so glad to see you again! Thank you so much for coming." She extended her hand, which Karla accepted gently. "I am happy to see you, too, Mrs. Schutte. And who is with you?"

"May I introduce my sisters, Mrs. Greenbaum and Mrs. Gutknecht. They are visiting me this week from Pittsburgh." Karla smiled and greeted each of the matrons with deference. Mrs. Schutte motioned toward a nearby wing chair, "Please, Karla, sit with us. Hans will pour us some tea."

Karla sat with them there in the parlor, which suddenly felt like home to her. The visitors spoke of their children and of their grandchildren, of life in Pittsburgh and of the exploits of their husbands, both of which had died in the past three years. Eventually the conversation turned toward Karla and her family. She told them about her mother and father, about the farm and her love for it, about her sisters, and about her brother Johann in the Army.

"Where is your brother serving?" Mrs. Greenbaum asked.

"I really don't know," Karla responded. "His last letter said he is training to be a Ranger, and he thinks his facility in German may be put to use somewhere in Europe, but he can't say more."

"I thank God for him and all the brave young men who are fighting those awful Nazis and that devil, Hitler," said Mrs. Greenbaum. "We have family in Duesseldorf, and we have heard nothing from them in months. The news is nothing but rumors, and the rumors are terrifying. Concentration camps and murders, businesses and synagogues burned, children taken from their parents. I want to do something. But what can I do?" The tears welled up in her eyes, and soon all the eyes were dampened by the visions which now floated through the room like a ghastly presence.

Karla didn't know what to say or do, but she very suddenly understood in a new way her brother's need to join up and fight. She was surprised at the urge she felt to go and join him. Hoping to provide some measure of comfort, she said, "Maybe it is just a problem with communications. Surely your family members aren't in danger. I have read that mostly they are targeting Jews."

Mrs. Gutknecht's gaze became steely as she looked Karla in the eye and said, "Our family name was Steinmetz. We were all raised to be observant Jews." Reaching out to take Mrs. Greenbaum's hand, she said, "Ursula and I still go to synagogue every Sabbath in Pittsburgh." The careful avoidance of eye contact with Mrs. Schutte hinted at a conflict among the sisters, sitting as they were in a Methodist manse.

Karla was truly shocked at this news. "I am so very sorry!" she said, as tears began to form. "I have never met a Jewish person before. I've never been more than a few miles from our farm. I am so ashamed . . ."

Mrs. Schutte reached over and placed her hand on Karla's hand. "My dear, you have met a Jewish person. In fact, you have met two: me and my son. And now you have met two more. You just didn't know it. And that really is the point, is it not?" Karla looked up and gazed in turn at each of these genteel women, who seemed to respond as a unit with the same gentle, knowing smile. "Thank you," Karla said. "Thank you all." It was all she could think of to say. A light had just shone into Karla's soul, and she welcomed that light, even though she was embarrassed by what the light was revealing.

Hans, who had been quiet to this point, sensed it might be just the right time to inject some levity into the gathering. "Karla has the most beautiful voice of all my students," he said with a glance of admiration (which Karla could easily have taken for affection). "Shall we have some music?"

All brightened immediately at the idea, and Hans and Karla chose two of Schubert's Lieder. Karla became immediately immersed in the music, forgetting all else, and her hearers were similarly enrapt. The music carried them all off to another place, a place of beauty and joy, a place beyond sectarianism and devoid of violent power schemes. The experience was, in a word, heavenly. And after the musical performance was finished, the power of its mystical, unifying grace remained. Just for that afternoon, all was right and good.

The afternoon came to its conclusion, and after the exchange of more pleasantries and expressions of appreciation for the wonderful music, Hans offered to drive Karla home. They headed out of town toward the farm, and Hans suddenly pulled over to the side of the road and killed the engine. "Is something wrong?" Karla asked, quizzically.

"Karla, I need to say something to you. I hope I'm not . . . I mean, I want to tell you . . . I hope you won't misunderstand . . ." Karla could see he was troubled about something because he was stammering, obviously upset and not his usual confident self. "Just say it. It's okay," she said. "I'm listening."

He turned to look at her directly. Somehow, looking directly at her face seemed to calm him down and the words just flowed. "I have developed deep feelings for you, and I think I have seen, or I hope I'm not imagining . . ." Karla interrupted him, "You are not imagining. I feel it, too."

At this, Hans brightened like a little boy on Christmas morning, and he said, "I'm sure I am in love with you, and I wonder if you would consider becoming engaged to be my wife." He reached into the vest pocket of his suit jacket and retrieved a simple gold band. "This belonged to my mother's mother, and I would be honored if you would accept it as a pledge of my love."

Karla was so dumbfounded by all that had just happened, she at first said nothing at all. As she gathered herself, it suddenly occurred to her that she must have looked like a wild animal caught in the headlights. Seeing her reaction, Hans assumed he must have spoken too soon, that he should have waited longer. "I'm sorry, Karla. I can see you are startled. I should have . . ."

"Yes," Karla said, interrupting him.

"I am so sorry." His gaze was cast down at his feet on the pedals. "I should have waited. I am so clumsy sometimes . . ."

"Yes," Karla said, again.

With a glum resignation, Hans reached for the ignition to start up the car again. "I hope you can forgive me. I will take you home now."

Karla reached over to place her hand on Hans' hand, and he looked over at her. Her face was beaming with the most beautiful smile he had ever seen. She said, "I meant, yes, Hans!"

"Yes?" he said, the joy returning to his face. "Yes?!"

"Yes, Hans. I love you, too, and if we can take a year or so to be sure, I would be so happy to be your wife."

At that, Hans got out of his car and walked (ran!) around to the passenger door, which Karla had already opened, and the two of them embraced like there had never been any other possible outcome. He placed the ring on her finger, and it fit perfectly. They both beamed with joy and kissed passionately. And once again, just for the moment, all was right and good.

They got back into the car and continued the journey to Karla's home. "I cannot wait to tell our families!" Hans said, excitedly. Karla's face showed a frown of concern, and Hans noticed it instantly. "You look sad," he said. "Did I say something wrong?"

"No, no, Hans. It's not you. It's just that . . ." She paused, not sure how to introduce her father into this joyful time without ruining everything.

"Go ahead, I'm listening," he said with a kind smile, mimicking her earlier response to him.

"It's my father," she said. Her gaze followed her mood, focusing on the ground. "He can be . . . well, difficult."

"I will be very proper and respectful. I will declare my love for you and ask him to give me your hand in marriage." Hans supposed that would satisfy a traditional German American farmer.

"I think you had better let me be the one to decide when is the right time to do that," Karla replied. "Will you trust me on this?"

They had arrived at the end drive to the Neuenschwander farm and as he turned in, Hans once again stopped the car. He looked at Karla, her face still looking down and so sad. He reached over and cupped her face in his hands, gently lifting her vision upward until their eyes met. "I will most certainly trust you on this, and on every other matter."

Karla fairly jumped into his arms, hugging him tightly around his neck and kissing him warmly under his ear. Warm tears of happiness welled up in her eyes and she said, "Thank you, Hans." The two embraced for another several minutes before he delivered her to her family.

As Hans waved goodbye and headed back down the drive, Karla looked at the ring on her finger. It really did fit perfectly. But she removed it and carefully placed it in the pocket of her coat. *I will wait for the right time. I will not let Papa ruin this for me.*

Karla headed into the house and, seeing her mother in the living room she hugged her very warmly, so warmly in fact that Susanna wondered just what sort of greeting this might be. Then Karla even hugged her father, who was sitting in his usual chair by the fireplace, and who was so totally surprised that he stiffened in response. And then, without another word, she headed up to bed, lighter than a zephyr wind.

CHAPTER NINETEEN

T HE U.S.S. Wasp was making good headway eastward on the choppy waters of the frigid North Atlantic Ocean. The Wasp was a carrier class vessel, currently tasked with transporting about 3,000 men, mostly from Canada, and various military supplies to a place called Carrickfergus in Northern Ireland where they would receive further training and await future deployment. With Hitler having declared war on the United States after Pearl Harbor and America responding in kind, the conflict with Nazi Germany was no longer avoidable, and everyone was on edge.

Johnny Neuenschwander was on the main deck, bundled head to foot in his winter gear against the January wind. He had been in his berth below, but he decided to take advantage of the temporary calming of the sea swells and get some air. As he braved the cold, his hands draped over the railing, he was lost in the vastness of the ocean. Soon Johnny's bunkmates, Tim Hays from Denver and Alan McComb from Macon, Georgia, were standing there with him, and they were similarly enrapt. The threesome was part of a group of only 50 American soldiers, all elite trainees, who were hand-picked to undergo advanced combat training in Northern Ireland.

"It's a big, big world, isn't it?" Johnny mused. Tim responded, "It sure is. I used to think the mountains made me feel small, but this . . ." He motioned with a broad sweep of his arm, which seemed to complete his thought.

"What do you think, Bulldog?" Johnny said to Alan. Ever since they began Ranger school Alan had been assigned the moniker of 'Bulldog', due in part to his love of Georgia football and perhaps due even more to his tenaciousness in physical training. Bulldog never broke his gaze on the horizon. He said, "Yeah, it's big all right. Too big. Takes forever to get anywhere." Johnny loved to hear the Bulldog talk. His thick Southern accent lent a certain colloquial appeal to whatever he said.

"I used to be able to get wherever I was going in fifteen or twenty minutes, most times. Even a trip to Atlanta was less than two hours. We've been on this boat for four days!"

"Hey, Johnny," Tim said.

"Yeah?"

"Where do ya suppose they got a name like Carrickfergus? Weird name for a city, eh?"

"Yeah, I s'pose. Somebody said it has something to do with the Gaelic word for rocks. Must be rocky there. I guess we'll find out soon enough."

"Not soon enough for me," Bulldog said. "I just wish we were already there. I want to get this crap done and go home." The others nodded their assent.

Just then the sirens broke through the rhythmic sounds of the sea as they blared out their "Whoop, Whoop, Whoop, Whooooop!" alert, accompanied almost immediately with the order, "General quarters! All crews to battle stations!" A flurry of activity ensued, as men in battle gear and wearing metal helmets raced up and down various stairways to their appointed stations. For their part, Johnny, Alan and Tim joined the other non-Navy personnel below on the galley deck to await instructions from their unit commanders. As the three men formed up with their fellow American Rangers, Colonel James Mattingly of the Royal Canadian Armed Forces entered the room. "Attention!" came the Staff Sergeant's order. All fifty men stood straight and silent.

"All right, men, stand at ease," Col. Mattingly said. Everyone relaxed a bit, but only a bit.

"Men, the reason for assuming battle stations is that we are entering the area near Iceland where two ships were attacked and sunk by German U-Boats in recent months. If you don't know about U-Boats, they are vessels which can travel underwater and deliver explosive missiles called torpedoes in an ambush attack. There is new technology that enables us to detect their presence, and the Navy is ready to respond to any provocation. You are to remain here below and be ready to assist as needed. If a battle ensues, you are to take your orders from the Navy commanders and obey them immediately. Are we clear?"

"Sir, yes, Sir!" came the enthusiastic response. "EX-cellent!" the Colonel replied, after which he said, "Unit leaders, you may dismiss your men." SSgt. Robert Jennings, Johnny's unit leader, addressed his men, "Rangers, Atten-TION!" They stiffened instantly. "All right, you heard the man. Stay loose but stay ready. Dismissed!"

✳✳✳

The hours passed by in agonizing slowness as the men variously smoked, played cards, and talked in small enclaves. Here and there a musical instrument could be heard, sometimes accompanied by singing. The mood was scattered and labile. There was much laughter and horseplay, but everyone felt the underlying tension; it was uncomfortable and inescapable, like the freezing Arctic wind.

Johnny, Alan and Tim found a spot at a table in the mess hall and sat down together. Alan pulled out a pack of Lucky Strikes and lit one, offering the pack to the others. Tim accepted a cigarette, which Alan lit for him. Johnny declined. "What's the matter, Johnny? Too young to smoke?" Alan ribbed him.

"Naah, I tried it once back home. Once was enough for me. I figure anything that can make you cough that hard and that fast can't be good for you."

"Yeah, you Yankee pussy!" Alan took a deep, long pull off the unfiltered cigarette and inhaled it deeply, blowing the smoke out in rings through his pursed lips. He directed the smoke rings at Johnny, and they soon found their mark. Johnny brushed them away and shot Alan a mildly irritated glance. Tim piped in, "I never smoked at all until boot camp. Then it was like everyone was smoking. I just joined the crowd. Now I'm used to it, I guess. It's something to do." He tried to do the smoke ring thing, but he just blew out an amorphous cloud of blue smoke, which he regarded with a frown.

"I was just messin' with you, Johnny-boy," Alan said. "You can't help it if you were born a Yankee." He grinned a mischievous, teasing grin.

"So, what's so special about Macon, Georgia, Mr. Bulldog?" Johnny threw down the gauntlet.

"Oh, man, Macon is a great town!" Alan responded. "Lots of history there. There's even native burial grounds that go back 17,000 years! And museums and music. Lots of Negro jazz. You ever heard of Lena Horne? What a voice! And sexy, too, I mean, for a Negro lady. And you should be there in the Springtime! Everybody always thinks about peaches when they think about Georgia, but I'm here to tell you there is no place like

Macon during cherry blossom time! The air is so sweet with cherry blossoms you don't even want to breathe out! I mean, in April—sometimes it even starts in March—there is no place a body can look in Macon and not see a cherry tree just chock-full of pink blossoms and pretty as you could imagine." Alan's enthusiasm was contagious. He sat forward now; his eyes filled with memories of home.

"And in the summer, my dad and me used to go on a Saturday and get in a little paddle boat?" His pause was inflected like a question, like you were supposed to say, "uh-huh", but nobody did, which didn't stop him. "And we would float down the Ocmulgee River. It was like heaven, I tell you. Toss in a line, maybe pull out a big catfish or a bass. Listen to the bullfrogs croakin' and let the trees shade you from the summer sun. Man, that's livin'! I wish I was there right now." Everyone's thoughts turned to home. Just then, it was impossible not to think of home.

"And what about you, mountain man?" Alan redirected the conversation. "Tell us about Denver."

"Oh, Denver," Tim said. "The mile-high city, they call it. But I wasn't born there. My family moved all over. I was born in Missoula, Montana, or so they tell me. We moved to Wyoming before I was even two years old. I started school there, but in the middle of second grade we moved to Springfield, Illinois. Then in seventh grade we moved to Wichita, Kansas. I almost made it through high school in Wichita, but then we moved to Denver in my junior year. So, I only have about three years of experience with Denver. I guess I never took much notice of what there is to do there. One town is about like another to me."

"Why did you move so much?" Johnny asked.

"Well, my dad was an aeronautics engineer, and his work just kept us moving to different aircraft companies. He made a lot of money, I guess, but we really didn't see him very much. I'm closer to my mom and my little brother. We just learned to hang around together and do stuff at home."

"Okay, your turn, Johnny. Tell us about Pennsylvania," Alan said.

"Oh, there is not a lot to tell. My family is a second-generation German American family, living on the farm my grandfather started before the Great War. My mother is a very loving, very hard-working woman who takes good care of us all. I have an older sister, Karla . . ."

"Ohh now, hold up a minute!" the Bulldog interrupted. "Older sister, huh? Hmmm . . . do you have any pictures?" Alan leered at him. Tim also was not disinterested in this bit of information. Johnny responded, "No, she has no interest in Confederate rebels and vagabonds." Alan threw a wadded-up gum wrapper at him in response, which Johnny caught and threw back.

"So, where was I? Oh yes, Karla, my older sister who is a gorgeous Yankee girl and who sings like an angel . . ." He shot Bulldog a taunting glance before continuing. "And my younger sister Marta, who is now 12 years old and a precocious, sweet girl. And then there is little Gretel, who was a late surprise to my parents and is now just 18 months old. And we all live together, and we all have our chores to do to keep the farm going. It is a hard life, but a good one."

"You didn't mention your father," Tim said, perceptively.

"Ah, yes, my father," Johnny responded with a sigh. "Well, let's just say that my father and I do not see eye to eye." There was a decidedly uncomfortable pause, which was finally interrupted by Alan.

"Well, you can't stop there," Alan said. "What do you mean, you don't see eye to eye?"

"It's not just one thing," Johnny explained. "I suppose it begins with the farm, which to him is the most important thing in the world, next to his German heritage. That farm is his badge of honor. He sees it as a duty he owes to his father and to the integrity of his family's name. And he expects me to take on the farm like he did. The fact that I have no interest in farming is not something he will accept, and that drove a big wedge between us.

"But now with what's happening in Germany, the situation at home has become even worse. My father identifies with the Nazis! He even gets letters from an uncle who is pretty high up in Hitler's regime; I swear he almost worships that man. And I don't understand it. I mean there are probably thousands of German Americans in Pennsylvania, but most of them don't want anything to do with the Nazis. Anyone in their right mind can see the horrible things they are doing over there. But not my father. So, I left. Me and a couple of my friends from high school signed up as soon as we could. I will fight these Nazis. I have to fight them. And not only because it's the right thing to do; I need to fight them to apologize for my father. I am an American. And in this country, we stand up for what is right."

The three were silent for a few moments. Then Alan spoke. "I tell you what, Johnny: you are my kinda people." He reached out his hand, and Johnny took it. Tim added his own hand to create a sort of clunky, three-way handshake. Johnny suddenly laughed. "What?" Alan said.

"Oh, nothing. It's just that my friends and me shook hands this exact same way when we decided to join up. It's just kind of funny. Like a connection or something."

"Well," Alan grinned in response, "Us rebels got to stick together."

CHAPTER TWENTY

THE mild Pennsylvania winter droned on into the approach of Spring until the seasons were melding in a gray sameness. It was a Saturday morning in late March and the Neuenschwander family was gathered at the breakfast table. Karl was his usual, disconnected self, studying his eggs for meaning and finding none. School was over for the year and Marta was in a joyful mood. "Mutti, may I go over to Judi's house this morning? We want to work on a sewing project for church."

Karl broke into the conversation, gruffly. "I need you here this morning. With your brother gone and Karla in town with her music, you are old enough now to help me with the livestock."

Marta, ever the cheerful one, brightened her smile even more at her father's pronouncement. "Oh, Papa, I am proud you want me to help!" she said, and she jumped up and hugged her father around his neck. He received her affection but offered none in return.

"What will we do today?" Marta asked as she returned to her seat. Without looking up he said, "Besides the usual chores we have a hog that is ready for butchering."

The words took her completely by surprise. Images of blood and knives and the sounds of loud, squealing animals leapt forward in her mind. She remembered how after her brother taunted her with lurid descriptions of the process, she had always found a way to be somewhere else whenever such a chore was necessary. The thought of it made her uncomfortable at best, and perhaps even terrified her. But she knew better than to let her father see her fear. Even at twelve years old, Marta had learned the rules of the Neuenschwander family.

"I don't know what to do," she said, trying to mask her trepidation with inadequacy. "Well," Karl responded, "it's time you learned."

Susanna looked at her husband with a concerned frown, but he did not acknowledge it. She looked over and saw Marta, clearly anxious and unsure about this new venture into which she was being thrust. Susanna said, "Well, Marta! You are growing up and your father seems to think you are ready for more responsibility. I am very proud of you!"

Susanna's instinct had been correct. The look on Marta's face softened from worry to a cautious optimism and pride. "Well, Papa, I'm ready when you are!" she said. Her father managed a brief smile as he rose from the table and said, "Then let's get to work!" And off they went.

Little Gretel had begun to fuss, and Susanna hoisted her from her highchair. "My goodness, you are getting to be almost too big for that chair!" she said, swirling the baby around in a thrilling whirl that elicited a shriek of joy from her. But the joy soon gave way to impatience as she began wiggling for freedom. "Down!" came her little voice, loudly asserting what had been one of her first words. She began walking at 10 months of age, which was nearly a year ago, and it was increasingly plain to see that Gretel was innately independent. As Susanna lowered her, Gretel was nearly running before her feet hit the floor. She found her little corner toy box and began pulling one thing after another out of it as Susanna busied herself with her work.

❋❋❋

Out behind the barn Karl and his twelve-year-old butcher's helper were preparing for the task at hand. "First," Karl said, "you must separate the boar away from the others. You must work your way into the pen and gradually move him toward the gate. This is one of the reasons for using two people. You grab a bucket of corn and keep the others interested while I begin to lead him away with my own feed bucket."

Marta was comfortable among the pigs, and she was used to feeding them. So, she did as she was accustomed to doing and her father began to lure the boar away. Before long he swung the gate aside and threw a big handful of corn on the ground in the path outside the pen leading to the slaughterhouse. The boar followed the feed, handful after handful, eating his way to his doom.

Marta was so focused on feeding the other hogs in the pen that she had almost forgotten the specific reason she was there on this day. Her father's voice startled her back to reality. "Marta! Come here now!"

She climbed over the fence, dropped her feed bucket, and headed to the slaughterhouse.

When she got there, the boar was enclosed in a pen just big enough to hold him. He was munching contentedly, his face planted deeply into a bucket of corn. "What happens now, Papa?" Marta asked.

"Now we must act quickly. Once we begin to restrain him, he will be angry and frightened. So, pay attention and do what I tell you, ja?" Marta nodded automatically. Her eyes widened as she focused on the two rubber aprons near the front of the pen. "Are those for the blood?" she asked, motioning toward the garments.

"Ja," he replied. He chose one of them and hung it over her neck, fastening it behind her. It was heavier than anything she had ever worn before, and it smelled awful. "Do you see those two places in the pen where there is a gap in the wood slats?"

"Yes, Papa."

"Those are the two places where we will subdue him. I will insert a strong metal bar under his haunches, in front of his rear legs. Then you and I will both insert metal bars at the same time, one under his neck and the other on the top of his neck behind his ears. It will be tight, but it must be tight, so don't be gentle." Marta was beginning to envision the whole procedure and the idea of it was disturbing her. Her father saw the look on her face, and he said, "Now Marta, you must listen to me. This hog will give his life for our family, and we owe him a quick and merciful death. When he becomes trapped by the bars, he will become very angry and terrified. It is up to you to shorten his fury. You see this big knife?" Marta's eyes widened as she considered the knife her father held out to her. It looked menacing and horrible. "Yes, Papa."

"This knife is extremely sharp, so be careful how you handle it. Once he is subdued, as quickly as you can, you must plunge this knife deep under his neck with the sharp edge up, and then pull it up hard toward the back of his jaw, here." He pointed to the spot on the boar's jaw, which was currently still moving rhythmically as he gorged himself on the feed in front of him. "Don't be timid. It is a violent thing to plunge a knife through hog skin and jowl, but to do so without conviction would be very cruel, indeed. Remember, he will be extremely angry and terrified, but you will be his angel of mercy. Do your job well and there will be no more fear, no more anger. Do you understand?"

Marta had been lost in the fantasy of what she was about to do, and her urge to run away was just below the surface. But when her father called it an act of mercy, when he called her an angel, she began to think she could do this. She said, "Yes, Papa. No more fear, no more anger. Papa, could we pray for him, that he might suffer as little as possible?"

The question took Karl Neuenschwander aback. He softened a bit and he responded, "Ja, Marta, if you wish, we may pray."

Marta folded her hands and closed her eyes and said, "Lieber Gott, please make me strong in what I must do so this hog, who gives us his life, might not suffer. Amen." She looked up to her father, who had begun to move toward the steel bar at the rear of the animal. "Papa?" she said, quizzically. "Ja, Amen," he said.

"Okay, Papa, I'm ready." They took their positions, Karl at the rear and Marta at the front. Karl gently inserted the steel bar under the animal's rear haunches. He then took up his position across from his daughter and said, "Ready?" Marta said, "Ja." They both inserted the bars, one above and one below, trapping the animal tightly. It began to buck and squeal and snort, immediately furious at being restrained. Marta grabbed the knife and did has her father had instructed her. She shoved the knife deep into the boar's throat and violently pulled it upward and backward. She could feel it cutting through sinew and ramming into the spinal column behind the animal's jaw. The blood spurted out and splashed over Marta's hands and face. It felt surprisingly warm and sticky. She was very glad for the rubber apron, which protected her clothing from the mess, but the metallic smell and sticky feel of the blood on her skin sickened her. Almost immediately the boar stiffened, lurched backward and then forward, and then slumped in the pen.

"You did just fine, Marta!" her father said. It was just enough of his approval to suppress the bile which surely was rising in her throat. Karl told her to bend over the pen while he poured some fresh water over her head and face. "Next time, you will remember this, and you will know to stand ahead of the knife and not behind it, ja?" he said, laughing at her.

"I stood where I thought you said I should stand, Papa," she said sharply, her sense of revulsion now changing to anger at being ridiculed. Her normal cheerfulness was gone, and the look on her face was new for her; one might even call it vengeful. When Karl saw the way she looked at him, he felt no longer playful, nor proud. "What do you mean looking at me like that?" he growled, moving toward her menacingly. "You, a mere child and a girl, and you want to challenge me? I am your father! This is my farm! And I brought you out here to be a part of this farm because your brother abandoned his heritage and his family to fight against his own people! Who cares about a little blood? Ungrateful little . . ."

Marta shrank back against the slats of the slaughter pen, feeling suddenly not at all grown up but instead, significantly smaller. "Papa?" she whimpered, a confused plea. She thought at that moment he might kill her just like the hog.

Just then, Karla and Susanna came into the slaughterhouse to see how Marta was faring. They heard Karl's ranting questions, and they saw Marta, weighted down by the apron, covered in blood, her hair dripping and matted, cowering against the pigpen next to the dead boar. She looked terrified.

"Marta, come here to me," Susanna said. Her voice carried an authoritative quality not normally heard in the Neuenschwander household unless Karl was speaking. Marta quickly got up, and Karla helped her remove the blood-spattered apron. Marta ran over to her mother and clutched her as if clinging to life itself. Susanna stared down her husband, daring him to continue his vicious tirade with her. He said nothing, and eventually looked away. Susanna and her daughters turned and headed to the house without another word.

Chapter Twenty-One

ARRICKFERGUS, Northern Ireland, lived up to its Gaelic etymology. Huge boulders of limestone and quartz piled themselves onto the landscape haphazardly, interspersed with ugly clumps of grass that stood defiantly against the constant assaults of the wind. To one side of the village there was a steep hillock with a rough path –better suited to goats than to humans—which lead to the very top and to a marvelous view of the narrow sea channel and the hills of Scotland to the northeast. Many units of soldiers used that narrow path as a challenge, betting pints of ale on who could get to the top and back down again fastest. And more than one ankle was twisted in the attempt.

With the addition of the soldiers on the Wasp, well over 7,000 mostly Canadian and British troops were bivouacked at Carrickfergus, including the small unit of Army rangers who had been hand-picked from America. And from among these 7,000 soldiers, about 750 were chosen to undergo further training under the famed British Commandos in Scotland. The 50 American Army Rangers were there for just this purpose, and within a week Johnny and the others were headed across the choppy sea to the western coast of Scotland, where the 6-week training would consist of open country survival skills, rappelling, riflery, and hand-to-hand combat intermixed with 20-mile hikes in full gear.

The last and most intense portion of the training involved the recruits in what they referred to as CQC or Close Quarters Combat training. The training consisted of a mixture of pugilistic and martial arts training, knife skills, and disarmament and disabling maneuvers aimed at maximizing quickness and stealth. Johnny had distinguished himself in riflery but, to his own surprise, he also became quite adept at hand-to-hand combat. He was gaining a reputation as someone nobody wanted to mess with.

On a particular Saturday in late June, Johnny woke early. The clock above the entrance to the Quonset hut read 0430 as the lights slammed on and the Sgt. Major's voice came screaming through the darkness, rousing all the snoozing trainees to immediate response. "All right, all right! You bunch of sleeping beauties, get your arses out of those bunks and stand to! Up! Up, now! That's right, move it! Smartly now!"

Johnny hopped up and stood beside the foot of his bunk, dressed only in his boxers and dog tags, shoulders back, chin forward, stiff as a fist. "Well, ladies, aren't we looking pretty this morning!" the Sgt. Major taunted. "You ladies have fifteen minutes to get dressed for inspection. Hit it!"

The ensuing flurry of activity reminded Johnny of a flock of hens chasing seed in the barnyard back home. Every single man was moving toward something. Johnny quickly peed, scraped a razor over his stubble, threw on his fatigues and a drab tee shirt, and made sure his locker was neat and orderly. He had just finished tightening the sheet folds on his bunk when the Sgt. Major's voice boomed out once more. "A-ten-TION!" All the men scurried to the prescribed spots beside their respective bunks and stood at attention. "Captain, my men are ready for inspection," he said.

"Thank you, Sgt. Major," came the reply from Capt. Virgil Morgan. He began his slow stroll through the unit's sleeping quarters, stopping here and there for a closer look at one thing or another. Finally, he made his way back to the front of the barracks. "Well done, Sgt. Major. Carry on," he said before departing.

"Right!" The Sgt. Major said. "All right, men, by now you know the routine. Mess in ten minutes, then report to the training field at 0600."

"Yes, Sergeant Major!" came the unified reply. "Dis-MISSED!" he responded.

Johnny met up with Tim and the Bulldog on the way to the mess tent. "Mmm-mmm! Powdered eggs and biscuits! Breakfast of champions!" Alan said with a grin. "Yeah, those tasty, green and yellow powdered eggs, and that great coffee," Tim chimed in. "Battery acid, you mean," Alan responded.

Johnny had remained silent. "What's the matter, Johnny-boy?" Alan poked at him. "Were you expecting bacon and pancakes?"

"Yeah, or maybe a thick, juicy, steak?" Tim added, chuckling.

"Naah, I just . . ." He paused, looking for something meaningful to say, but found nothing. His mind had been wandering back to thoughts of home and the farm. Sometimes—like the current moment—he got an uneasy feeling, as if there were some problem at home. It was the way he used to feel when he knew his father was unhappy about something. Johnny used to use that intuition to avoid his father, but now he was wishing he could be there to shield his mother and sisters from him. It was a change inside him, and one which surprised him.

What he finally said was, "I guess I don't feel real talkative this morning."

The three got to the mess tent and powered their way through the bland protein. Alan said, "I wonder how long before we finally get to go kill some friggin Nat-zis?" His emphasis was on the first syllable which he pronounced like "cat". "I sure am getting tired of this windblown scruff."

"I dunno," Tim said, "but the good thing about this place is, nobody is shooting at you here. I kinda like that, myself." Johnny just sat there, staring into his coffee, trying to think of something to say.

"Well, boys, it's about that time," Alan said. Johnny looked at his watch. 5:50am. Just enough time to get to the field. All three of them got up and headed out.

As they made their way down the rocky path to the training field, the wind bellowed an incessant, irritating message, one which the stiff, stalky grasses seemed hell-bent on ignoring. "I swear: this constant wind could drive a man plum crazy," Alan said with his customary Georgia drawl. Johnny responded, "Well, you don't need to worry then, Bulldog, cuz you can't get driven to where you already are."

Bulldog looked over at Tim and said, "Did that Yankee just say I was crazy?" The grin on Tim's face said it all, but he answered anyway. "Yup. And I agree with him."

Bulldog took off chasing Tim and Johnny with a playful lurch. He caught up with them and all three were rollicking on the gravel path, laughing and wrestling like the boys they still were.

"Knock that shite off!!" It was the unmistakable roar of the Sgt. Major, who they hadn't realized was following them down the path. The three stood immediately at attention. "Good thing you ladies have all that extra energy this morning. You're gonna need it! Now get on down to the training field, double time!"

"Yes, Sgt. Major!" came the tripartite response.

When they arrived at the field, they were ordered to muster with their unit and stand at attention. After all were assembled, the Sgt. Major addressed the group. "All right, gentlemen, stand at ease and listen up.

For the past several weeks you have been engaged in training drills with your instructors. Today is your final evaluation. For those of you who satisfactorily complete this evaluation, today will be your last day of training here in Scotland. Tomorrow will be for packing up and heading back to Carrickfergus, where you will bivouac and await future deployments.

"Whilst you were in training you mainly engaged one-on-one with your instructors. Today you will pair off and demonstrate your fighting skills against one another. Form a large circle now."

The soldiers broke ranks and shuffled about until all formed a circle roughly 60 feet across. There were about 120 men in all. Bulldog looked over at Johnny and said, "Here we go! Finally, we're gettin' outta here!" Johnny looked him right in the eye as he replied, "You have to pass the test first." It was a true statement, of course, but it was more than that. Johnny's steely-eyed look was a nonverbal gauntlet being thrown on the ground between them, and when he realized it, Bulldog picked it right up. Without breaking eye contact, he said, "Well, Yankee, I guess we both knew it was always gonna come down to this one way or another." Johnny saw a slow smile crawl across the Bulldog's lips, easing the mood a bit, and Johnny also smiled. "Yeah, I guess we did. Rebels to the end."

After the circle had been formed and the fighting pairs chosen, the Sgt. Major continued. "This circle will form the boundaries of your field of combat. You will be using rubber knives, of course, but every other aspect of true combat is to be assumed. Make no mistake, it is kill or be killed, and you will be evaluated on both the effectiveness and quickness of your skill at disarming and killing your opponent. When you hear the words, "that's a kill," you will step off and await further instructions. Any questions?" The only sound to be heard was the howling, mocking wind.

"Right!" the Sgt. Major said. "Commence!"

The evaluation proceeded with two fighting pairs engaging simultaneously, each accompanied by a referee and a clerk who recorded the results for each participant. The raucous encouragement from the ranks of the circle was animated and vigorous as the mock combat scenes played out before them. With increasing fervor each man strove to demonstrate his ability to kill another man.

Eventually, it was Johnny and Alan's turn. They stepped to the middle of the circle and received their rubber knives. "All right then, you Yanks," the trainer said in thick Scottish brogue, "Let's see if you bonny lads get to stay in Scotland so we can keep tormentin' you a wee bit longer. Commence fighting!" Johnny extended his hand. He was about to say "good luck" when he felt his hand being jerked forward at the same time as his feet were swept out from under him. He went down, but his instincts kicked in and he was able to roll forward, using the momentum to get his feet on Alan's chest and propel him about ten feet through the air. He landed in a heap as the impressed observers uttered a unified, "OOH!"

Johnny stood up immediately, ready for action. Alan regained his senses quickly, too, and jumped up for more. Johnny said, "I forgot. You rebels always did fight dirty." Alan responded with, "The man said commence!" With that he lunged forward, knife at the ready, slashing across and then back upwards toward Johnny's face. Johnny deftly avoided the maneuver, backpedaling and waiting for an opportunity to use Alan's aggression against him. Which he almost immediately provided as he lunged forward with his knife in a move more apropos of a fencing match than a knife fight. Johnny side-stepped the thrust and turned Alan's right arm downward and outward, grabbing his thumb and bending it severely back. He let out a yowl and dropped his knife just as Johnny was jabbing his own knife deep into his opponent's abdomen.

"Right! That's a kill." The clerk marked down the result. "Well-done, lad," the trainer said, nodding to Johnny. "Okay, collect yourselves, you two, and let's have another go."

The two circled one another like Greek wrestlers, each searching for a vulnerability to exploit. Johnny deked a jab with his knife and Bulldog anticipated it, stepping aside and bringing down his knife on Johnny's knife hand. "That's a wound!" the trainer called out. "Your right hand is disabled, Yank. Tuck it in your pocket and fight on."

Johnny switched the knife to his left hand as he began to move about more, not wanting to provide his opponent with a stationary target. But it was no use. Alan McComb was a formidable opponent for a man with two hands, let alone one. The outcome was inevitable. Alan made a forward lunge followed by another kick sweep, and Johnny went down. He managed to score one more wound on Alan's leg, but then Alan drew his knife across Johnny's throat, and the fight was done.

"All right, all right. Well done, Yanks! Rejoin the circle. Next two!"

The two combatant friends walked across the center of the field, and Alan put his arm around Johnny's shoulders. "Well, do you think we passed?" he said. Johnny looked over at him with a wry smile and said, "I know I did, but I don't know about you. There might be a different code for Bulldogs." Alan grinned back at him and jostled his shoulders as Johnny returned the soldierly embrace.

The evaluation came to its conclusion just in time for noon mess. Tim had drawn a good match and Johnny and Alan cheered him on, shouting their approval when he scored a kill. After the last pair of fighters was finished, the Sgt. Major barked out the order to reform ranks.

"Right!" he said. "Stand easy, men. You will be informed of your grade—pass or fail—by your unit commanders before the day is out. It has been our privilege to serve as your instructors, and we want to wish you all the best of luck, wherever this bloody war might lead you. God Save the Queen!"

"The Queen!" came the loud response from the great majority.

"And as for you Yanks, well, Cheerio!" A general chuckling and good-natured banter ensued as the Canadians and Brits pushed the Americans around like playful brothers.

"Dismissed!"

Johnny, Tim and Alan headed off for the mess tent. "I wonder what we are heading to next." Tim mused. Alan responded, "I'm for anyplace with less wind and rocks."

Johnny said, "I guess it doesn't matter much. But I know one thing: I'm hungry."

They picked up the pace, and before long it became a race to the mess tent, with Bulldog winning the race. The mood in the mess was generally convivial as they ate their fill of chipped beef in white gravy on soggy white bread, a meal that was sardonically referred to as "shit on a shingle," and before long all the men had returned to the barracks to await their grades.

Thankfully, the wait was a short one, and from that moment on time seemed to speed up. Johnny, Alan, and Tim all passed (as did nearly everyone else, they learned), and suddenly it was time to pack up, eat dinner, and hit the racks.

But for Johnny, sleep was elusive. He couldn't stop wondering where and when his first opportunity to fight might come. He tried to imagine himself in combat, aiming his rifle at a German soldier and firing a round into him. Or in hand-to-hand combat, plunging his knife into another man's throat. He felt repulsed by the idea of it, but he no longer wondered if he could do it. He knew he could kill the enemy. *100,000 dead in London, men, women and children.* That is the image that stayed with him. Why his father would continue to support that sort of slaughter by Germany—or by anyone—simply baffled him. It was with thoughts of his father back on the farm that Johnny finally began to drift off to sleep. And at 0500 he woke with those images still in his mind. He sat up and threw his legs over the side of his bunk, shaking his father out of his mind and rubbing his eyes to clear them.

As it turned out, Johnny learned he was not the only one who had slept fitfully that night. Soon he was joined by a cadre of sleepy-eyed soldiers, arising to face the day. Very little was said as all dutifully prepared for departure, and by 1300 hours they were all heading off for England.

Chapter Twenty-Two

L IFE on the Neuenschwander farm changed after the butchering incident with Marta. The days came and went mechanically, but a severe and empty loneliness filled the household, with each person confronting it in different ways. Karl simply absented himself. He came into the house for meals and sleep, and rarely was seen otherwise. For Susanna, the loneliness meant even less congress with her husband. Weeks went by without any intimacy; had Karl initiated it she would have provided sex, but he had become more and more withdrawn and even grumpier, if that were possible. Karla was spending more and more of her weekends in town with Hans, and she felt increasingly detached from her family's life. In an odd way, Karla even noticed feeling a sort of disgust with her mother, something which made her feel ashamed and which she did her best to hide.

But most affected was Marta, who had become odd. She would sit for hours, staring off into the distance. She would respond if her name was called, but her formerly bright-eyed smile had been replaced with something waxen and superficial. The outside Marta appeared cheery and complacent enough, but Susanna knew something was different; the girl inside was becoming increasingly distant and mysterious.

It was early July and Thursday came again. Karl was out spreading manure in preparation for the planting, and Susanna was at the end drive, ready to receive the weekly post from Samuel Boehm. There was another letter from Johann, as well as a letter from Karl's uncle Horst. Susanna headed for the kitchen and quickly opened Johann's letter, eager to learn any news about the Army's plans for him.

> *Dear Mother:*
> *I have completed my training to be an Army Ranger. I am temporarily assigned to the 34th Infantry Division, and*

*I know I am heading to what they are calling the European
Theater of Operations, but beyond that I cannot say.*

*Please don't worry about me. I have become much stron-
ger and more capable than the boy who left your home last
year. And I am surrounded by many others who are just as
capable as me. I would stake my life on them, as I know they
would on me. We are fighting for a terribly important cause,
so please remember, no matter what the future holds, I am
proud to be serving our great country. Nothing I ever do in
life will be more important than the work I am now engaged
in. Pray for our success, and please give my best to Karla,
Marta, and little Gretel, and to my father if he will accept it.*

With much love,

Your Johann

Susanna laid the letter down and closed her eyes, trying to picture
her son when he left, what he was wearing, how he looked, the smell of
him as she embraced him that last time. And then she forced herself to
imagine the man he was now becoming, the trained fighter and committed soldier he described in his letter. She opened her eyes and looked
around her kitchen and dining room table, resting her eyes on the chair
Johann used to occupy next to Karl's place at the table. The chairs were
now empty, of course, but as she considered them, Susanna felt a profound sadness. It was as though the world had become centered on those
two chairs, still connected around her table, but at war with one another.

She looked down to see the other mail that she had dropped on the
table, and her gaze fixed on the letter from Germany with its international striping. Quite suddenly, Susanna grabbed that letter and ripped
it in half. It was an impulse, a need which came from somewhere deep
inside her, a place she had never dared acknowledge, but over which she
now had no control whatsoever. The action of ripping up that letter un-
leashed a fury that erupted in a terrible, visceral scream. It began as one
long, grotesque howl, but as she violently ripped up the letter, first into
strips and then faster and faster into tinier and tinier pieces, every tearing action elicited another guttural screech of revulsion. She had never
known such rage in her life. And as she began considering what she had
just experienced, Gretel's terrified cry startled her back to reality.

"My baby!" she said, bolting up from the table and running to Gretel's room. She had been napping, and the sound of her mother's screams
had jolted her awake and sent her into a state of panic. Susanna ran to
her daughter's crib, where she was standing up, gripping the slats of the

crib gate so tightly that her little knuckles were white. The look of terror on Gretel's face brought Susanna to tears. She reached down to scoop up the crying child, who desperately clung to her mother's neck and sobbed into her shoulder.

Susanna sat down with her in the rocking chair next to the crib and began to soothe her with a lilting coo. Gretel soon eased her grasp and settled into her mother's lap, sticking two fingers into her mouth and quietly sucking on them. "Mommy's here, meine kleine Süsse, Mommy's here. It's okay." The words coming from her mouth were as much for herself as for Gretel. "It's going to be okay." She repeated it like a mantra, over and over, until she began to believe it might be true.

The two of them sat there, rocking rhythmically for a while until Gretel began to fuss. "Time for a bottle, ja?" Susanna smiled at her. The fussing became more animated. Gretel knew the word 'bottle'. Susanna brought her into the dining room and placed her in the highchair. She started warming a bottle of formula and quickly moved to the table where she carefully swept up the refuse of her earlier outburst. She paused there for a moment, wondering how best to dispose of the evidence. She considered the fireplace but discarded that option as insufficient. She settled on the idea of burying the bits of paper in the garden. She knew Karl would never step foot into the garden; to his way of thinking, gardening was work for women and children. She secreted the remains of the letter in her apron pocket.

After Gretel finished her bottle, she was ready for an adventure. Susanna put her little blue jacket on her and carried her out to the garden. She placed Gretel on the soft grass by the edge of the garden and grabbed the shovel which had been left there. Susanna dug out a shovelful of dirt and dumped it on the ground beside Gretel, handing her a small trowel to play with. Gretel went immediately to digging in the soft loam, chattering happily. Then Susanna dug several small holes among the furrows, placing small bits of the torn-up letter in each of them before covering them over again.

When she finished, she couldn't help smiling a naughty smile. She felt as though she were a little girl who had gotten away with some misdeed. But as she surveyed her garden plot, she also felt a distinct sense of unease. Somehow, she knew that although she had successfully buried the letter, the seeds of rage that letter represented would eventually grow. She had no idea what those seeds might produce, but she knew this was not the end of it. It was as certain as death.

CHAPTER TWENTY-THREE

MARTA woke with the sun shining on her face. It was a Saturday, and although she wanted to sleep a bit more, the bright light roused her. She got up and completed her morning routine before wandering downstairs. "Good morning, Marta!" Susanna greeted her. Marta walked past the breakfast table. "Good morning, Mutti," she sighed with a vacant stare. "I'll get the eggs." She grabbed the egg basket like usual and headed out to the henhouse.

As Susanna watched her daughter's slow, plodding gait she was suddenly overwhelmed by a wave of anxiety for her. *She used to be so happy! Now she's just . . .* Susanna could not find the word for what Marta was like these days, but there was no mystery as to what Susanna was feeling for her: it was fear. *What has Karl done to her? She changed almost overnight!* Her thoughts immediately turned to Johann and how quickly his life had also turned a completely different direction. *Can anything last? Must that man poison everything?*

Marta slowly wandered back with her basket of eggs, but no whistling. No singing. No interaction at all. Susanna prepared scrambled eggs and toasted rye bread, which Marta ate only a little of. "Where is Karla?" Marta asked. "She is out already working in the garden. She took Gretel with her. Why don't you go and join them?" Susanna replied.

"Okay" Marta said, abandoning her breakfast. The one thing which still seemed to reincarnate the formerly bright little girl was being with Gretel.

Karla was busy hoeing out the weeds which constantly reappeared in and between the rows of vegetables. Her thoughts, however, were on Hans and on that wonderful ring in her coat pocket. She had had a tough time sleeping the past couple of nights; visions of weddings and of a happy future did battle with worrisome thoughts of her father's potential reaction to the whole idea. The result was a tossing and turning that afforded her only a temporary and unsatisfying escape. She had just driven the hoe deep under a prickly weed when she heard Marta's approach. "Hi Karla. Hi, little Gretel!" Marta said. Gretel heard her sister's voice and got up, running toward her excitedly. Marta stooped down beside the baby and embraced her with a warm hug. She even managed a smile.

Karla said, "That little baby sure loves her big sister!" Marta sat down with Gretel on the soft grass and began making little hills of earth, planting twigs and leaves atop each.

Karla had gotten most of the weeds dislodged and had begun to turn over the soil between the rows. She lifted a shovelful of the black soil and was surprised to see some bits of paper. She bent down and scooped up a handful of the paper scraps, some of which had red and blue coloring on them. She flattened out one of the larger pieces and tried to make out the letters written on it. M u n . . . It suddenly became clear to her. This was a letter from her father's uncle Horst. But what was it doing in the garden? And why was it all ripped up? Karla said, "Marta, will you stay with Gretel for a little while? I need to go into the house." "I will stay with her," Marta responded, as she plopped down another trowelful of dirt beside her sister.

Karla made her way into the kitchen where she found her mother peeling vegetables at the sink. "Mother? Look what I found in the garden," Karla said. Susanna's crestfallen reaction belied any pretense of surprise. Her eyes began to well up with tears. Karla moved closer and placed her hand on her mother's shoulder. "What happened?" Karla asked quietly.

"Remember Johann's last letter?" Karla nodded. "I had just read that letter. I already knew he was heading off to war, of course. But his letter made it real. My son was going to fight the Nazis. My son! Your brother! Our Johann! He might really and truly die fighting the Nazis. And that same day there was a letter from your father's Uncle Horst in Munich. I had your brother's letter in my hand, and I don't know why, but when I looked down at the table and saw that letter from Germany, I got so mad. I've never felt such a terrible anger. I didn't plan it, but something just came over me. I grabbed that letter and ripped it to shreds. I was screaming out loud. I even scared Gretel! And then I knew I had to get rid of it, so I buried it in the garden where I thought your father would never find it."

The tears flowed freely now, and Karla held her mother while she cried. "You know your secret is safe with me, Mutti," Karla said, rocking her back and forth and comforting her like a child. They sat holding each other and gently rocking for a precious few minutes, an island in time, safe from the world of threats and violence. Finally, Karla broke the silence. "There are some secrets that we need to keep for others, and some we need to keep for ourselves. I also have a secret."

Susanna wiped her eyes and nose with her apron and sat up to look her daughter in the eye. "You have a secret?"

Karla looked out at the farmyard, just to be sure her father was not approaching. She reached into the pocket of her coat and pulled out her engagement ring, placed it on her finger and showed her hand—Hans's hand—to her mother. Susanna's face was transformed from a visage of fear and sadness to one of pure joy. The change hurt the muscles of her cheeks; it came so suddenly. She was beaming with a broad smile almost too big for her face. "Karla! You and Hans?! I knew it! When you came in that night and even hugged your father, I knew it! Oh, I am so happy for you!" She grabbed Karla and held her tightly, this time not needing comfort but with a profound, motherly, womanly love. The tears flowed again, tears of joy.

"But I'm not ready to tell Papa yet. I need to wait for the right moment." Susanna nodded her assent. "You are right, my wise girl. Some secrets we need to keep for ourselves. It is your news to share when you wish." Their eyes met in a mutual understanding. And as Karla departed to rebury their now shared secret, Susanna watched her leave with a new perspective. *She really is a woman now,"* Susanna thought to herself. And quite suddenly she realized how alone she had been feeling, and how good it was to feel less so. She returned to her vegetable peeling chores with a welcome sense of peace.

CHAPTER TWENTY-FOUR

WHEN Johnny got back to Carrickfergus, the daily routine was not unlike Army base life in America, consisting of daily exercise regimens, assigned chores to accomplish, and boredom to live through. The people of Ireland were as welcoming and wonderful to the visiting soldiers as anyone could have asked. There were regular stops at local pubs and the occasional pass to head down to Belfast about 20 miles to the south. But as the days turned into weeks, everyone was growing impatient, awaiting orders to deploy. Those orders finally came in early July, but the mission was canceled for reasons the men were not told. Finally, a second mission was ordered in mid-August, and within a week the entire expeditionary force was transported to the South of England.

The Wasp arrived in Newhaven on the southern coast of England, one of five ports from which the operation, code named "Jubilee", was to proceed. After all the waiting, everything now seemed to be moving fast-forward. Along the way the men had been briefed on the operation, which was scheduled to commence the night after arrival. The target was a French port called Dieppe, and the objective was to capture the port, drive back the German forces stationed there, and gather all available intelligence on German naval capabilities. The assault would be divided into four specific locations, each named with a color. Johnny and the other Americans were placed under the command of a British unit known as #4 Commando, and theirs was to be the first landing, at a place code-named Orange Beach. They were to arrive at 0600 at a place called Varengeville, just west of Dieppe. They were to scale a steep cliff from the beachhead and destroy a German battery of six 150 mm guns located along the top of the ridge, and then withdraw and depart for Newhaven at 0730.

At noon mess Tim, Johnny and the Bulldog sat together as usual. "Finally!" Tim said. "Finally, we get to actually do something!"

"It can't come soon enough for me," Bulldog replied. "How about you, Yankee? You ready to get in this war?"

Johnny was slowly stirring his applesauce, thinking about home. Soon it would be time to pick the apples and pears from the trees in the yard. He always looked forward to those times, climbing up into the trees to help his mother and sisters reach the highest fruit. Without looking up Johnny slowly nodded and said, thoughtfully, "It needs doing."

All were encouraged to rest that afternoon to prepare for a very early departure at midnight. But all through the day the ship was abuzz with nervous energy. A couple of spats broke out as the soldiers vented their restlessness and anxiety in anticipation of the coming battle.

Finally, the time came to depart for the three-hour journey to Dieppe. Time had seemed to crawl forward in the time leading up to midnight. But Johnny was amazed how quickly those three hours elapsed. In no time, it seemed, the Orange team was assembled and loaded onto the Higgins boats for the landing. Tim was quiet. His eyes were closed; he may have been praying. Bulldog nudged him, "Are you feeling nervous, buddy?" When Tim looked up, his wide-open eyes showed the answer. Bulldog gave him a brotherly pat on the shoulder. "How about you, Johnny-boy?"

Johnny was amazingly calm. He was able to say, honestly, "Like I said before, it needs doing. I really am ready." Their eyes met and Johnny could see that Alan was feeling scared, too. Something in Johnny's eyes seemed to help. No words, no physical communication, just a solid determination seemed to emanate from him, and as he moved his focus from Alan to Tim and back again, all three seemed to become centered.

The landing craft approached the beach, and the order was given, "Advance!" All the men moved quickly forward, walking onto the lowered ramp and into the cold waters of the English Channel. As they slogged onto the beach they could see before them the 50 ft. cliffs which they were to ascend. Grappling hooks were propelled up and over the top and once secure, the men began scampering up the rocky escarpment. One by one, all the soldiers reached the top and belly-crawled forward to find cover.

Johnny was among the first to scale the slope, and he was surprised to find no resistance from the enemy. He could see their objective—the massive guns arranged like a six-fingered hand, pointing out at the coastal waters. Johnny was soon joined by dozens of other troops, and after about twenty minutes, each of the six attack teams had established positions and the order to proceed was issued.

Since it was so early, the German soldiers were mostly still asleep in their bunkers, save the few who were on guard duty. An advance team crept up and dispatched the unfortunate guards, and the sound of gunfire awakened the German troops. Outlying sniper fire began to pick off a few of the invasion force, including Tim. Johnny saw him fall and couldn't get to him. A rage rose up inside him and he burst in on one of the bunkers, killing the three men still inside. He was surprised to notice that he was feeling nothing at all. No sympathy, no regret. Not even revulsion at the process of shooting another human being, which he anticipated he might be feeling. He simply felt as though he had completed a job.

The entire operation was over in a less than an hour. The guns were dismantled and dumped over the cliff edge into the sea and all the men of Orange team rappelled down to the beach, boarded their LCVPs and headed back to the ship. A general mood of victory and celebration was evident among the men, with hoots and hollering and back-slapping abounding, as well as no small amount of braggadocio. Johnny took part in all these festivities, too, but minimally. He couldn't forget the look on Tim's face when that sniper round ripped open his chest. Suddenly, he was gone. So suddenly.

Once safely back aboard the ship, Johnny's mood was pensive. The Bulldog had been assigned to a different part of the mission and he had not yet returned. As he lay in his bunk alone, Johnny reflected again on his complete lack of emotion after having killed three men. He began to think about Thom and David, the Mennonite brothers who were his friends back home. *"I wonder where they are now. I wish I could talk to them about this. They were raised to be against all forms of killing, even in war. How would they handle this?*

He thought about writing to Thom and David, but how? He had no idea where they might be assigned. And he could not write to their parents, because their parents would not support their sons participating in this war effort. Their family may even be required to shun them for being outside the faith.

Johnny finally decided he would instead write to Karla.

> *Dear Karla;*
>   *I am writing you from my bunk aboard a ship. I wish I could tell you where I am, but I cannot. I just returned from my first actual fight against the enemy. We were the first to*

land, and things went very well for our part of the mission, although there were some casualties including a friend of mine named Tim. There were several other landings in this mission, and I do not yet know how things went for the others.

What I do know is that today I killed three men. I expected to feel, well . . . I don't know what I expected to feel, but something! And except for being sad about Tim, I really am okay. Should I feel guilt for not feeling bad? I can't say anything about the mission, but I can say I am convinced that what we did today was right. I keep saying to myself that it needs doing. Maybe that is all I need to keep me focused. To keep reminding myself of what we are fighting, and that defeating Germany absolutely needs to be done.

I hope and trust you are well. I found myself thinking last night about the apple and pear trees and how we would pick the fruit. Maybe another month, I suppose, before they will be ready. Remember how once I threw a rotten pear at you, and it got all in your hair? Ha Ha! You were so mad at me. And mother was, too.

I miss you. Please pass on my love to Mother and our sisters.

Your brother,
Johnny

Later that day at evening mess Johnny learned that the remainder of the mission's objectives had failed miserably. The entire operation had been a complete debacle. The total numbers were still coming in, but it was known that over 3000 men were either captured or killed by the Germans, among them Pvt. Alan McComb, who was killed in a mortar blast. It was then that the whole thing became real for Johnny. He went back to his bunk, turned to face the wall, buried his head under his pillow and sobbed uncontrollably.

Chapter Twenty-Five

I T was the last Sunday in August and Karla woke early. It was her nineteenth birthday, but that had nothing to do with the butterflies fluttering around in her stomach. This was the day Hans Schutte was coming over for dinner. The two men in her life—one tender and genteel, the other gruff and coarse—were meeting face-to-face. Would this be the day her secret would be revealed? Never had she both wanted and feared something so intensely. She lay in bed, pulling the coverlet back up to her neck, her head reeling. *I must calm down!* she thought to herself. *Better get up and get busy. Just do your work and all will be well.* Her mother had said those words so often over the years that Karla had begun to resent them. Now here she was, taking direction and comfort from those same words. *Dammit, Mutti!* she laughed to herself.

She arose and followed her mother's mantra. She made her bed, bathed, and prepared herself as best as she could to welcome the man she loved into the home of the man she feared.

"Good morning, Mutti," Karla said as she entered the kitchen. Her mother was already peeling carrots and potatoes for the roast beef dinner which would greet them all after worship meeting. "Good morning, daughter. My, but don't we look pretty today! Something special happening? Oh, yes! It is your birthday! And a happy birthday to you, meine Susse." Susanna then feigned a quizzical look, furrowing her brow in mock confusion. "But no, that can't be it. You have had birthdays every year, and I don't remember you ever dressing up for one of them. What else then? Anything unusual about this particular day?" Susanna's coy smile caused a blush on Karla's face as she drew in for a hug. "Oh, Mutti. You do love teasing me!"

Just then Karl came in from his morning chores. After shedding his work garments and washing up, he sat down to the cup of coffee he knew would be there for him and awaited his usual Sunday biscuits. Karla brought in a plate of biscuits and a cup of coffee for herself and sat at the table with her father.

"Another year older, ja?" he said as he shoved half a biscuit into his mouth.

"Yes, Papa. I'm nineteen today. And remember, my voice teacher, Professor Schutte, is coming for dinner after church. I invited him because . . ." Karl interrupted, "Ja, he is a professor of music, nicht wahr?"

"Yes, Papa. He teaches at Albright College and still comes to take care of his mother in town every week. I am fortunate to be one of the few students he teaches here."

"I am looking forward to meeting this professor. I have some questions for him. Music questions."

Karla was taken aback at this. *Music questions?* She had the immediate inclination to probe further about this but decided to let it be. "I'm glad you are looking forward to meeting him," she said. "He will come over right after church meeting."

"Ja," he said. "Church meeting . . ." He growled a throaty sound of disgust and bit off another warm biscuit as he buried himself in the issue of Time magazine that had arrived last Thursday.

Marta came in, looking lethargic and sleepy. She walked directly into Karla's midsection and threw her arms around her as though she were a cuddle doll as she said, "Happy birthday, Karla. I love you." Karla embraced her warmly and thanked her. The embrace lingered until finally her father gruffly interrupted it. "Ja, ja, enough with the hugging. You have eggs to gather, don't you?"

Marta never looked up at him, but Karla could feel the energy drain out of her sister's thin arms as they dropped in resignation. "Ja, Papa." She headed out to the henhouse, grabbing the egg basket along the way. Karla felt the heat rising in her in response to her father's meanness, but she simply went into the kitchen, where her mother's chopping had suddenly grown more intense.

∗∗∗

Church meeting proceeded in normal fashion, and as the Neuenschwander family exited, Frieda Koehn beckoned to Susanna. A small circle of women was gathering in their usual spot under the massive oak tree in the church yard. "Let me just go and see what she wants," Susanna said to Karl. "You head to the truck, and I'll be right there."

Samuel Boehm looked up to see Karl and began to motion him over, but it was plain Karl had his head down and was heading directly for his truck. Someone said, "I wonder what is wrong with Karl?" And Samuel replied, "Who knows? Sometimes he's just a grumpy old bear. Best to leave him be."

Susanna approached the growing circle of women, and Frieda spoke up. "How are things with you? Any news from Johann?"

Susanna's face showed her sadness as she responded. "No, no word for a while now. I worry all the time, but I must entrust him to God."

"Ja, I know," Frieda said, putting a matronly hand on Susanna's shoulder.

"Listen, I really must get home. We have a guest for dinner. Karla's voice professor, Hans Schutte. And it is Karla's nineteenth birthday. I have much to do."

"Well, well! A gentleman caller! Karla is really growing up, isn't she?" Frieda's prying tone and raised eyebrow ignited a flurry of tittering and "knowing" smiles amongst the circle of women. "Yes, I suppose she is," Susanna replied. "But no rumors are necessary if you please. And they might even be harmful." The serious look she delivered directly into Frieda's eyes got the message across.

"Ja, okay ladies, let us keep our noses in place. And we must let Susanna get home to her family celebration. Susanna, you will be at the next quilting circle, ja?"

"I will be there. Wiedersehen!" All the women responded in kind as Susanna made her way back to Karl's truck to find Karla pacing outside. "Come on, Mutti! We must get home!"

"Ja, ja, I'm sorry. I was only there a couple of minutes. We'll be fine." All piled in and headed for the farm.

***

As they walked into the kitchen, the smell of the beef roast was intoxicating. The vegetables were ready to start cooking, and Karla and Marta began to set the table. They set a place for Prof. Schutte in the chair where Johann used to sit, to the right of Karl and to the left of Karla.

After what seemed like forever, Karla heard Hans' car approaching the house. She had to fight back the urge to run out to meet him like a love-sick teenager, bur she managed to restrain herself. When the knock came on the front door, Karla smiled up at Hans and said, "Welcome, Professor Schutte! Please come in." Hans took his cue from the formal greeting and responded in kind. "Thank you so much, Miss Neuenschwander. It is so kind of you to invite me. Please introduce me to your family."

They walked into the living room where Karl was sitting in his usual chair by the fireplace with his usual Sunday bottle of beer. Susanna came in from the kitchen to join them. "Mother, Papa, may I introduce Professor Hans Schutte. Professor, these are my parents, Karl and Susanna Neuenschwander."

Karl stood up as Hans extended his hand to each and bowed respectfully. "Herr Neuenschwander, Frau Neuenschwander, it is so good to meet you both. Thank you for inviting me to your home, and for sharing your daughter's wonderful voice with me."

Karl shook his guest's hand and said, "Wilkommen, Professor. Please, sit here by the fireplace so we can talk before dinner. And please, call me Karl. Would you join me for some beer? A little schnapps?"

"A small glass of beer would be most welcome, thank you. And please, call me Hans." Karla moved toward the kitchen to get the beer as her parents and Hans sat down together.

"My daughter tells me you teach music at a university, is it?" Karl began.

"Not a university, but a college. Albright College in Reading. It is a growing, liberal arts college with a fine music program. I enjoy my students there very much," Hans replied. He looked over at Karla as he added, "Although none of them brings me nearly the pleasure of hearing your daughter's lovely voice." Karla blushed and demurred, "Oh, Han . . . er, I mean, Professor." Susanna caught Karla's eye with a knowing, furtive smile. "I am sure she must make her parents very proud," Hans said.

"Oh yes, indeed," Susanna said. "She has always had such a gift of singing and a love for music!"

"Ja, ja, she is a songbird, certainly," Karl responded, brushing aside the focus on his daughter. He was eager to pursue another matter. "Tell me, do you know of the works of Wagner?"

Hans looked at Karla quizzically. She could see he was a bit taken aback by the question, as was she. "Why, yes, certainly, Karl!" he responded. "I studied him at university. Karla has sung a couple of his Wesendonck Lieder. Why do you ask?"

"I have a cousin, Helga, back in Germany. She and her father, my Uncle Horst, are both working to restore the honor and leadership of Germany. Uncle Horst even works directly under Heinrich Himmler himself!" Here Karl paused, waiting for some sign of adulation which did not appear. He frowned but continued. "Anyway, I received a letter from Helga in which she described having attended the Bayreuth Festival."

Hans jumped in, "Ah, yes! The Ring Cycle. Four solid days with a full opera production on each evening telling the stories of Siegfried and of Valhalle. I am envious! I have never seen the entire production."

"Ja," Karl said, "Helga was so full of excitement and pride in these great stories of the German people. She told me it is part of my heritage to know and appreciate these 'foundations'—as she called them—of our history. But I knew nothing of them. I was hoping you might tell me of these stories."

"Well! Now that is a task which will take more than a short beer's time, I think. And I smell something wonderful in the kitchen. Frau Neuenschwander, when are you planning to serve the meal?"

"Well, it is ready now. And since my husband opened the door, will you please call me Susanna? Perhaps we should gather around the table and have our meal now. After dinner we can hear the stories from Germany. Shall we?" She stood up and motioned everyone to the table, which had been elegantly appointed ahead of time by Karla. "Marta! Bring Gretel, please, and come to dinner!" Marta, who had been attending to Gretel in the bedroom, did not respond, but soon appeared holding the little toddler's hand.

Karla showed Hans to his seat beside hers and bade him sit while she, Marta, and their mother all headed off to fetch plates and bowls and platters of wonderful food. Hans said, "May I help carry anything in?" which brought a polite refusal from the kitchen and a gruff snort from Karl.

In what seemed like an instant, all were happily feasting on roasted brussels sprouts, baked potatoes with butter and parsley, canned corn, pickled beets and dills, freshly baked bread, a variety of cheeses, and a sumptuous rib roast with a rich, brown gravy and mushrooms.

After everyone had eaten their fill, Hans said, "I cannot remember ever feeling so wonderfully satisfied by a meal in many years. Thank you so very much!" Susanna and Karla responded with a unified and blushing, "Thank you."

"Now I insist you allow me to help clean up. I am used to doing so for myself and also for my mother when I visit her. And I would be a terrible boor if I received such a wonderful meal and offered nothing in return. Please, may I help?"

Karla shot a glance at her father and could already see the red streaks at the base of his neck. She quickly said, "Thank you, Hans, but I think my father is anxious to hear you tell the stories of Wagner's Ring cycle. Why don't the two of you get settled by the fireplace and let us take care of the kitchen. We will try to listen in. It won't take long."

"Ja! Leave the kitchen to the women!" Karl said, gruffly. "Susanna! We would have a little schnapps and two bottles of beer." He rose and led the way back to his chair by the fireplace, and Hans took the hint. He followed Karl and said no more about helping. Susanna was there with the drinks just as they sat down, and as she placed the glasses on the coffee table in front of him, Hans said, "Thank you, Susanna." His words stopped her in her tracks, and she looked directly into Hans' eyes. *"So kind! Such kind eyes he has!"* she thought to herself as she responded with a small curtsey, "Bitte." When she walked back to her work in the kitchen, Susanna suddenly hugged her daughter, and she whispered to Karla, "I think he's a keeper." Karla grinned.

"So," Karl said, "tell me about these important stories of the German race."

"Well, to begin with, they are German now, but they did not begin that way. The origin of these old myths is long before Germany even existed. The stories stem from ancient Nordic myths about struggles between man and the gods and between good and evil. These myths were carried down into the lands which would eventually become Germany and Austria and the Balkans and many other areas. The names changed as the stories moved from tribe to tribe over the generations, but the old Nordic names are still recognizable. For example, the Norse God was Odin, but in the Germanic version, his name became Wotan."

"Ja, ok, gods and men. Go on!" Karl was impatient to hear why this mattered so much to Helga. He also did not like to hear that these "foundational" stories were not truly from Germany.

"When Richard Wagner set out to build his Ring cycle, he began with the Nordic mythology brought by the Teutonic peoples, but he significantly changed it. He wanted to put forth a specifically German hero by means of a completely German version of the ancient Greek tragedy. And his saga begins and ends in the river Rhine.

"As we begin, we are greeted by the Rhine maidens—three mystical water sprites—who are owners of a magical gold rock, hidden beneath the surface. The story is that if one will forever forswear love, live a chaste life, and fashion the gold into a ring, the owner of that ring will have mastery over all life, even over the gods. A dwarf named Alberich of the Niebelungens tries to seduce the Rhine maidens in hopes of owning the magical gold. They rebuff his advances and tell him what is required to have the gold. So Alberich promises to meet the requirements. He takes the gold and makes it into the magically powerful ring."

At this point, Susanna and Karla joined the group. Marta was dismissed outside to play with Gretel. "Go on, Hans, we were listening," Karla said, sitting down across from her father. She decided to abandon the 'Professor Schutte' pretense.

"Back in Valhalle a pair of giants—Fasholt and Fafner—designed and built the castle of Valhalle. Wotan initially paid them off by giving them his sister-in-law Freia, but Wotan's wife, Fricka became incensed and demanded Wotan retrieve Freia.

"Wotan demands Freia's return, but the giants still expect to be paid. So, Wotan steals the magic ring to trade for Freia, which makes Alberich so angry that he places a curse on the ring. The giants then fight over the ring and Fafner kills Fasholt and takes possession of it."

Karl was listening intently, trying to make sense of the story. Karla was focused less on the story than on Hans, impressed more by his telling of the story than by the story itself.

"Wotan visits the earth goddess, Erda, who then bears him eight daughters who are called Valkyries. They are strong, lusty women who support all who fight on behalf of the gods. The Valkyries fly over the battlefields, choosing those who fight most nobly and fearlessly and bestowing on them the honor of dying in battle. Those chosen are then escorted to the halls of Valhalle where they are honored by the gods."

Here Hans paused to take a sip of schnaaps before continuing. "It makes sense to remind ourselves that at this point of the story, we are only amid the second of the four operas in Wagner's ring cycle. There is much left to tell, but I don't wish to be tiresome . . ." He waited for permission.

"No, no, Professor, please continue!" Susanna said. Hans looked around and saw all the heads nodding in agreement.

"Well then, we need to talk about two new characters, Siegmund and Sieglinde, illegitimate children of Wotan's whom he fathered with a mortal woman and who were separated at birth. Siegmund is wounded while wandering in the forest and stumbles onto the home of Sieglinde and her husband Hunding. In this home there is a huge tree growing right through the middle of the house, and this tree contains a powerful sword which was placed there by Wotan for Siegmund to find. Sieglinde offers help and comfort to Siegmund and the two, unaware of their true relationship, fall in love. After freeing the magic sword and administering a sleeping potion to Hunding, Siegmund runs off with Sieglinde.

"Back in Valhalle, Wotan's wife Fricka is appalled at these events and insists that Wotan set things right by killing Siegmund. Wotan agrees to send his daughter Brunhilde, the head of the Valkyries, to see to it that Siegmund is killed in his inevitable upcoming battle with Hunding. However, Brunhilde learns that Sieglinde is carrying Siegmund's child, so she disobeys Wotan and tries to protect Siegmund.

"Wotan is furious at this betrayal, so he comes down from Valhalle to take charge of things himself. He kills Siegmund and breaks the magical sword into pieces. In his rage he kills Hunding, as well. Brunhilde gathers up the pieces of the broken sword and runs away into the forest with Sieglinde to escape Wotan's wrath.

"But her safety is short-lived. Wotan finds her and condemns her to remain in a deep sleep atop a high rock, decreeing that she will remain in that state until rescued by a brave warrior who will take her for his bride. At Brunhilde's request, Wotan surrounds the rock with thick rings of fire, so she is assured that she will only submit herself to the bravest and most fearless man."

"It reminds me of Sleeping Beauty, in a way," Susanna said.

"Yes," Hans replied. You can find elements of these stories in the mythology of many peoples. The sword in the tree becomes the sword in the stone in England, for example." He took another sip of his schnaaps and a pull from his beer.

"Okay, ja. So, what happens next?" Karl said, impatiently.

"Sieglinde gives birth to a son she names Siegfried. His story is the subject and title of the third opera in the cycle. Siegfried leads an idyllic life in the forest, living as the ward of a smith called Mime. It was to Mime's home that Brunhilde escaped with Sieglinde and the broken pieces of the sword, and when Sieglinde died shortly after Siegfried was born, Mime took Siegfried in and raised him as his stepson. It turns out that Mime is the brother of the evil dwarf Alberich. Remember, Alberich is the one who made the gold ring in the beginning, and the one from whom Wotan stole it.

"As he grew up, Siegfried became a handsome, strong, noble, and fearless man. He was highly skilled at the art of smithery, even exceeding the skills of his stepfather, Mime. Mime had tried over and over to repair the broken sword, but unsuccessfully. Finally, Siegfried asked to be told the whole story of the sword, and after learning of his heritage Siegfried sets about the task of rebuilding the sword himself, which he eventually does.

"After finally replacing his father's sword with one of his own making, Siegfried sets off on a quest. He finds Fafner, still in possession of the ring but now appearing in the form of a dragon. Siegfried runs the dragon through and takes the ring, although he has no idea of its significance. He also takes a magical helmet that can make him invisible or disguise him as someone else.

"Siegfried then returns to the home of Mime, and after he suspects Mime of trying to poison him, Siegfried kills him. Next, Siegfried confronts Wotan, who is his grandfather. They quarrel and Siegfried cuts Wotan's godly staff in two. With all impediments now removed, Siegfried heads to the giant rock where Brunhilde still lies motionless, surrounded by thick rings of fire. Siegfried, being fearless, goes through the fiery flames and beholds Brunhilde, dressed in Valkyrie armor and metal helmet. Using his sword, he disrobes her and discovers she is a woman. Up to now, Siegfried has never seen a woman. Well, you can guess what happens next." Hans risked a brief glance at Karla, who did not look away.

"Go on! Go on!" Karl said, anxious for an end to this story.

"This scene on the rock is the end of the Siegfried opera and is also the beginning of the fourth and final opera, 'Gotterdammerung'. Siegfried and Brunhilde are passionately in love, but eventually Siegfried tires of her and goes on a journey up the Rhine. He comes to the kingdom of Gunther where he meets and falls in love with the king's sister, Gudrune. Siegfried uses his magic helmet to disguise himself as Gunther to try to lure Brunhilde for the real Gunther. But in the interaction, Brunhilde recognizes Siegfried's magic sword and realizes the ruse. So, she commissions Gunther's half-brother Hagen to kill Siegfried. Hagen happens to be the son of Alberich, who first fashioned and then cursed the ring, and badly wants his son to retrieve it for him.

"So, Hagen goes on a hunting party with Siegfried and shoves a big spear into Siegfried's back. When he tries to remove the ring from the dead Siegfried's hand, Brunhilde gets there first. She takes the ring and throws it back into the Rhine, back to the Rhine maidens who are its true owners. As they take back the ring, they pull Hagen down under the waters, drowning him. Meanwhile, a huge funeral pyre is built, and Brunhilde mounts her horse with the dead body of Siegfried and rides into the fire. The flames grow higher and higher until they reach Valhalle, and as the play comes to an end, everything—on earth and in heaven—is burnt up.

"So, that's the story of Wagner's Ring cycle. Probably more than you wanted to hear, no?" Hans took another long pull on his beer.

Karl looked glum. "Papa, you look sad," Karla said. "Is something troubling you?"

"It is a lot of nonsense!! How is this supposed to be "foundational" to us German people? I don't understand what Helga was talking about."

Sensing an opportunity, Hans said, "Karl, one thing that was missing in telling this story was the music. Wagner wrote some of the most powerful and inspiring music in history. The telling of the story seems a bit empty without it. Do you have a phonograph player?"

Karl looked up. "Ja, we have a phonograph."

"Maybe I should bring over some recordings and you can hear what your cousin heard at the Bayreuth Festival. That might help you understand her enthusiasm a bit more."

Karl brightened a bit at the idea. "That would be nice," he said. "Danke."

"Bitte," Hans responded. "There is quite a lot of study material available on the meaning of Wagner's operas in the history of Germany. The whole thing is quite complex. Perhaps I could also bring some things for you to read if you like."

"Ja. I want to understand. I cannot be there to help, but at least I can understand what we are trying to protect. Bring some things I can read. I will read them."

Karla was aghast at her father's openness and the warm exchange she observed between her father and Hans. She had been so worried about how this day would go, and it could hardly have gone better.

A few more pleasantries were exchanged, and Hans rose to depart. "Well, I must get home to get ready for my trip to Reading tomorrow morning. Thank you once again for your kind invitation and for such wonderful food and hospitality. Karl, I will bring some recordings and some materials for you to read. Next weekend, ja?"

"Next weekend will be fine. Wiedersehen, Herr Professor." Karl extended his hand and Hans shook it warmly. "Again, please, Hans is just fine."

"I'll walk you out to your car," Karla said, leading him toward the back-porch door. As they walked, Hans said, "Your family is delightful. Did I make a good impression? I didn't sound too highbrow or anything, did I?"

"You were perfect," Karla said. "My mother said you are a keeper." She grinned up at him.

"You told her?" Hans said, surprised.

"Yes, but only her," Karla said. "It's our secret."

Hans got into his green Mercury and started the engine. Karla bent her head into the window space and risked a quick peck on his cheek. "Goodbye darling. See you soon."

"I love you, Karla," Hans said. And with that, he drove off.

CHAPTER TWENTY-SIX

I T had been raining almost non-stop for the past 48 hours in central Pennsylvania, which was certainly unusual for late-August. It was Saturday, and Karl was getting restless. Susanna was working in her kitchen as usual. Karl said, "I have done everything I could with all this rain. I'm going to town for a beer." Susanna never looked up. "Supper is at 6:00 as usual," she responded. Her responses to her husband had been terser of late, and they both knew it.

The drive into town was not enough time for brooding, but as he drove past his soggy farmland Karl managed to brood a bit anyway. *This is still my house. My farm!* he thought to himself. *And she is my wife!*

The local watering hole was simply named, "The Bier Stube," and when Karl pulled into town, he had to settle for a parking space halfway up the block. At first, he was irritated. But he was in need of some genial company, and he was glad to see he wasn't the only one who had decided to fight the floodwater with beer.

When Karl opened the door to the Stube he heard an immediately familiar voice. "Karl! Komme hier mit uns!" It was Samuel Boehm sitting with several other local men, all of whom Karl knew. "Komme! Setzt du sich. Was mochtest du trinken, ein Bier, ja?" He motioned over to the bartender who nodded and began to draw a litre of Yuengling, the locally produced German-style lager.

Karl sat down at the table just as the mug of beer arrived, and he raised his stein with a hearty "Prosit!"

The response came back in the traditional German way: a drinking song, begun at their table but soon including everyone in the place. "Ein Prosit, Ein Prosit, Gemutlichkeit! Ein Prosit, Ein Pro-sit Gemuuut-liiiiich-keit!" It brought a rare smile to Karl's face.

"So, Karl, how are things with your farm with all this rain?" Samuel asked.

"Ach, es geht. Good enough. Karla and Marta help me, and of course Susanna keeps the house going. We are doing all right."

"And what news of young Johann? Where is he these days?" It was a question Karl did not want to answer.

"I don't know," he responded curtly. He took a long pull on his stein of bier, slamming the glass down roughly on the table. He wiped off the foam from his upper lip with the back of his hand and flung it onto the floor in a demonstration of disgust. "What I do know is he is not here helping his father with the farm, that's what I know." He stopped short of his usual diatribe about his son fighting his own people, but everyone knew how he felt about it. And Karl knew that they knew. The consternation rose inside him, and he was glad nobody pursued the matter further.

"And what is the news from Munich? How goes it with your Uncle Horst?" Samuel changed the subject.

"I haven't heard anything from him in quite a while now. I imagine it is getting harder to get word out in any reliable way."

"But I just delivered a letter to you from Munich a couple weeks ago. Yes, it was two weeks ago last Thursday. I remember your wife came out to meet me. There was a letter from Johann and one from your Uncle Horst. I know I delivered it!"

Karl knew that Samuel was always eager to hear of news from the old country. He was very unlikely to be mistaken about such a thing as this. "I'll have to check into it," Karl said. It was a benign enough response, but every man there could see that the ramifications of this information were beginning already to boil in Karl's consciousness. He could feel the customary heat rising from his shoulders and neck up into his reddening ears. "Perhaps Susanna just mislaid it and forgot to tell you," Samuel said. "Here, let's have another litre of bier," and he motioned to the bartender.

"No, not for me, Samuel, thank you. I must head home." He bought another round for the table and Samuel's eyes followed him as he headed for the door. "I hope Karl holds his temper when he gets home," Samuel said, and the others nodded.

When Karl got outside it was still pouring, and every raindrop felt like an insult. By the time he got to his truck, Karl was steaming mad. He put the truck in reverse and skidded out into traffic, nearly backing into a passing driver who blared her horn in response. "Ja, Ja, just get out of my way, you stupid woman!" he growled, and he spun gravel behind him as he lurched the truck toward home.

He skidded to a stop in the barnyard and slammed the truck door shut as he headed into the house. There was Susanna, working in the kitchen as usual. "You are home earlier than I thought," she said.

Karl stood in the entry to the kitchen, menacingly. "Wo isst's?" he snarled.

"Where is what?" Susanna replied.

"WO ISST'S?" he shouted, moving closer to her. "My letter! Where is my Uncle Horst's letter?"

The fear jumped suddenly up from her gut to her chest, seizing her lower back muscles on the way. *He knows? But how could he know? Maybe all this rain?* But she feigned ignorance. Turning toward him, she said, "Letter? What letter do you m . . ."

"DON'T LIE TO ME!!"

Susanna watched a spray of sparkling pinpricks of light—or were those little spiders? They shimmered and chased one another as if being swept across the ceiling by some fantastic broom, all whirling and spinning. Her butt hit the floor with a thud and the back of her head banged against the cupboard door, which was when she first realized that Karl had hit her.

She struggled to regain her senses and began to crawl toward the counter, reaching to help herself stand. Her head was pounding, and her jaw seemed no longer to be working. "What did you do with my letter?" Karl demanded, moving toward her again.

Susanna backed away from the kitchen instinctively, putting herself between her husband and her baby, whom she could hear screaming out in fear. "TELL ME!" he shouted again.

Karla came in the back door and could sense the danger in the room. She saw her mother shrinking in fear, her jaw swollen and purple and her father moving toward her aggressively. He screamed, "TELL ME WHERE IS MY LETTER!" and he balled up his fist to hit her again.

"No, Papa!" Karla screamed at him from behind, and she jumped up on his back to prevent the coming blow. Karl roared like a furious bear and spun around violently, knocking her off his back and onto the dining room floor, where her head slammed into one of the claw feet of the dining table. She lay there, dazed.

Karl again turned his attention toward his wife. "How dare you?" he growled. "How dare you keep my letter from me?! This is my farm! My house!" He moved forward to grab Susanna around the throat, and he began to squeeze. She flailed her arms desperately, trying to free herself from his grip, but he had always been so strong, and now he was insanely strong. She could do nothing to dislodge herself. She couldn't scream or even speak. She began to see those little pinprick spider lights again, and she began to backpedal with her feet, hoping he might trip.

But it was as though Karl was in another world of some kind. He was focused on two things: his Uncle Horst's letter, and the fact that Susanna kept it from him. He could see nothing else. Hear nothing else. Think nothing else. His grip tightened as he backed her against the dining room wall. She began to slip down, lower, lower. Her eyes were bulging. The spider stars were spinning and whirling . . .

Karl never felt the blade as it cut his carotid artery and drew back under his right ear. He stood up in shock and disbelief to see Marta, his twelve-year-old daughter, holding a carving knife which dripped with his own blood. "There, there," she said. "No more anger, no more fear." She said it lovingly, like a caress. He started to move toward her, but the blood was spurting out of his neck in huge, pulsing gushes, and with each pulse he felt less real. He tried to look at Marta with rage, but he couldn't do it. His look turned to one of sad resignation. He dropped to his knees, his eyes now level with Marta's. He began to speak but could only whisper, "My . . ." He fell forward onto his face, landing on the floor beside Karla. He was dead.

***

When Karla regained consciousness, she felt a throbbing pain in her head. She did a quick inventory. *I'm on the floor. No broken bones. My head hurts.* She turned her head toward the kitchen and saw her father laying in a large pool of blood which seemed to be creeping toward her. She jolted up off the floor, steadying herself against the dizziness, and surveyed the room. She checked her father for a pulse and found none. She looked over to see her mother, slumped against the dining room wall. She looked terrorized and in shock, gory with Karl's blood, but she was alive. *Where are the girls?*

She headed quickly to the bedrooms to find Marta sitting in the rocking chair, holding Gretel and gently singing a lullaby. Beside her on the floor was a large knife which appeared to be bloody. "Marta, why is that knife here?" Karla asked.

"I was Papa's angel of mercy," she said, matter-of-factly. "No more anger, no more fear." She returned to her singing and rocking, with Gretel snuggled against her chest, sucking her fingers.

Karla did not want to believe what her eyes and ears were telling her had happened. Her mind began to race through a maze of ideas. *Mother needs help, certainly medical help, and maybe legal help. The Police? Yes? No? If no, then what? Marta will need to be protected. How? I can't deal with all this! I have to deal with this!* She decided that the first concern was her mother. "Marta, will you stay in here with Gretel while I go and help Mutti?"

"Yes, I will stay with Gretel. I will keep her safe."

Karla walked over beside the chair and stroked her sister's hair. "You are a brave little girl, Marta," she said. Without taking her gaze from little Gretel, Marta said softly, "I am an angel of mercy." Karla bent over and picked up the knife, carefully keeping it out of Marta and Gretel's field of vision. She left the room and headed out to attend to her mother.

She had only left a minute ago, but when Karla returned to the dining room the scene startled her again. On her left side was her father who lay on the floor unmoving, his skin beginning to mottle and turn gray. A widening pool of blood exuded from him like a red, toxic threat. On her right-side Karla could see her mother, still slumped on the floor and covered in blood. As Karla approached her, Susanna looked down at her blood-soaked clothing and her eyes widened in panic. Instinctively she began to push herself away from what she was seeing, digging her heels in and leaning back, but all she could do was to press herself against the wall behind her.

Seeing the terror in her mother's eyes, Karla rushed to her side and held her close. Susanna groaned in pain as her fractured jaw pushed into Karla's chest. But when Karla tried to ease her grip Susanna pulled her back with a desperate intensity. They stayed like that, death-gripping the painful love that now united them, for what seemed like forever.

But, of course, it was not forever. Forever was out there somewhere, beckoning from a vastly uncertain future. And forever was requiring that some decisions be made. Important decisions. There were things to do.

CHAPTER TWENTY-SEVEN

IT was Friday morning, and Frieda Koehn was the first to arrive at the now empty Neuenschwander home. She brought with her a mop and bucket, two scrub brushes, some hard and soft soap, some rags, and a pair of her husband's rubber gloves. She came prepared to work. But nothing could have prepared her for what she saw when she entered the house.

When she opened the back-porch door, the first assault was to her sense of smell. The metallic smell of blood permeated the dwelling; not intensely, but it was nonetheless unpleasant. Frieda squinted against this foul insult to Susanna's always tidy home. Entering the kitchen, things seemed somewhat disordered. Several cabinet doors were open, and one was broken, hanging on one hinge. Except for the cupboard doors though, the dishes were all put away. The hand and dish towels were neatly folded and hanging in their usual places. *"That's our Susanna,"* Frieda smiled to herself. *"Always kept a good, clean house."* Frieda looked at the counters. Everything was in order except for an empty slot in the butcher's block where the carving knife should be. Seeing its absence there caused Frieda to shudder as she remembered the last use to which that blade had been put.

She gathered herself and walked through to the living area. There was Karl's chair by the fireplace. The sofa and matching easy chair were in place, as were the cushions and throw pillows. It was when Frieda walked past the living room to the adjacent dining area that the next assault stopped her in her tracks. There she saw the source of the vaguely foul odor. A large pool of blood had dried on the floor. Numerous flies were crawling around on the remains, buzzing, chasing one another. *"That's where it happened,"* she thought to herself. *"That's where she did it."*

The picture ran in her mind like a movie someone else had described to her in vivid detail. She could see a blood stain on the wall beside the China hutch, matted with some strands of hair. *"That's where he was choking Susanna."* She shifted her gaze to the dining table. *"That's where Karla was knocked unconscious."* And finally, Frieda allowed her eyes to focus on the sticky, red stain on the floor near the stain on the wall. *"And here is where little Marta sliced open her father's throat."*

As she stood there, mesmerized by the scene playing out in front of her, the normally unflappable Frieda began to feel woozy. She feared she might be sick to her stomach. She walked quickly past the room of dreads and found the bathroom. She splashed some water on her face and sat down. She thought she was ready for this. The stories of what happened at the Neuenschwander place had run rampant through the town of Shenandoah and all of Schuylkill County, thanks to the loud-mouthed deputy sheriff who loved the attention he got for sharing the lurid tale. The tragedy even made State and National news. The headlines read, "Little Girl Saves Mother, Kills Father," and "Twelve-Year-Old Executioner," and other such sensational things. One less scrupulous rag even ran the horrible title, "A Slice of Rural Life: Girl Slits Father's Throat." Frieda had seen and heard all of it. But it was quite a different thing to walk into the house—Susanna's house—and to see with your own eyes the truth of what happened there.

Frieda thought about little Marta and how horrible it must have been for her, and what will undoubtedly lie ahead for her, and for Susanna and the rest of her children. The questions swirled around her head. *Would Marta ever get to come home? And even if she were able to come home, how could she possibly live here after what happened? How could Susanna? Poor Susanna!*

If she would have allowed herself, Frieda would have broken down bawling and fallen into a heap of sadness right there on the bathroom floor. But instead, she resolutely wiped first one eye and then the other in a defiant motion, as if clearing away detritus. She said out loud, "Enough!" She stood up, walked back to the sink, and regarded herself in the mirror. Her hair was pulled tightly into a bun which sat squarely on the back of her head. She touched its edges to be sure all was neat and tidy, regaining her composure. "You have a job to do," she said to her mirror image.

Just then Frieda heard the porch door slam and headed out to meet several of the other women who had ridden together. "Ladies, prepare yourselves," she said. "We are going to be here a while." And soon others arrived, and despite the unavoidable revulsion experienced by everyone, they got down to work.

❋ ❋ ❋

At Locust Mountain Hospital in Shenandoah, Karla arrived as usual. Karla had been there every day since Monday when her mother underwent surgery to reconstruct her jaw and patch up a cracked skull. Gretel was being cared for by Mrs. Bielfeldt, who had graciously taken them in after the events of last Saturday. Each day Karla would arrive at her mother's room early, remain until mid-morning, and then head back to check on Gretel. She would then return later in the day, stay a few hours, and go back to the Bielfeldt's again to be with Gretel. Between visits, Karla attended to meetings with the Pfarrer and the funeral director about services for her father. She also tried to check on Marta, but they would tell her nothing.

This routine continued largely unchanged until this morning, when Karla walked in to find her mother awake and smiling softly. She took Karla's hand. Karla broke into sobs of relief, sitting down on the bed and nestling into her mother's breast. Susanna held her daughter gently, stroking her hair. She tried to say, "It will be okay," but it was very difficult to enunciate because of the stiff wires which held her jaws immobile. After a few minutes, Karla was able to sit up and clear her eyes.

"We will get through this, Mutti," she said. "We will. Gretel is with Mrs. Bielfeldt. She took us in after the police were gone."

"Marta?" Susanna's look of anguish made that word quite distinguishable.

"Oh, mother," Karla's eyes began to well up with tears again. "The district attorney filed a charge of murder, and the judge issued an order of protection. They took Marta away to the State hospital at Norristown for evaluation."

Susanna's look of sadness could hardly have been more profound. No words were needed. She wanted so desperately to be with her little girl, to comfort her and protect her. But that was not possible right now. She could do nothing. She looked away, off in the distance somewhere beyond the walls of her room. She could feel herself withdrawing. She could hear Karla talking, but the words only came through in echoes, jumbled into clumps of sound, bouncing off high walls that seemed to grow higher with each thought. Susanna had the sense she was falling, and she realized she had lost even the instinct to brace herself. She simply let go, sinking backwards, downwards, falling, falling.

Karla could see it happening. She looked at her mother's eyes, watched them become empty. She began calling her, "Mutti! Mutti!" She placed her face directly in front of her mother's, but it soon became apparent that her mother was no longer in the room. Her body was there. Her heart was beating. Her chest rhythmically rose and fell. But Susanna was gone.

Karla ran to get the nurse and told her everything that happened. The nurse came right away to check on her patient, and she called the doctor in. He examined Susanna but he soon realized there was nothing he could do to help. Physically, she was fine and healing well. Looking at Karla, the doctor said, "We will watch her and keep her safe and comfortable for a few days. Perhaps what she needs more than anything now is rest. Keep coming to visit as often as you can. Maybe you're being here can help. But if she's not better in a few days, I want to call in a psychiatrist to consult on next steps." Karla sadly nodded her agreement, and after remaining until there seemed no further point, she headed back to Gretel.

***

The daylight was beginning to fade a bit, and the women of the Evangelishe Kirche gathered outside the Neuenschwander home in the shade of one the big elm trees that surrounded the yard. There they sat down on the cool grass under the clothesline. Frieda had gathered all the rags and washed them out with lye soap, and she began to hang them on the lines to dry.

Each of the women held a glass of iced tea which Georgianna made for them. Georgianna spent her early years in Alabama before marrying a man from Schuylkill County whom she had met when he was an Army trainer at Ft. Mclellan . When he retired from the service, they moved back to Schuylkill County and Georgianna brought along her Southern accent and charm, including her recipe for iced tea. Her secret was that she boiled a goodly amount of sugar in the water before steeping the tea in it. She called it "sweet tea", and when served over ice with a fresh lemon wedge, everyone just loved it.

"I can hardly imagine what poor Susanna is going through. I heard she had surgery Monday to rebuild her jaw. And little Marta taken away? I don't know if I could stand it," Alma Reuter said.

"What will happen to this beautiful farm?" said another.

"And poor little Gretel. She is still so young. I hope she will never remember this when she grows up. It would be a blessing, I think," Anna Brautsch chimed in. "I hear the Beielfeldts took in Karla and little Gretel. That was very good of them."

"Do we know yet when the funeral will be?" Alma asked.

"Ja, I heard it will be this Monday" Anna responded. "So sad. I wonder if Susanna will even be able to attend? And then poor Johann, off fighting God knows where!" There was general, sad murmuring at the thought of a funeral without the wife and son of the deceased attending.

"I wonder what Karl could possibly have done to deserve this. I know he had a temper, but having his throat cut? By his own daughter?" someone introjected.

Rosalinda Jakobs said, "My husband said Karl was a good man and a good farmer. He . . ."

Frieda interrupted her, and assertively so. "Karl Neuenschwander was a brute, a Nazi lover, and a mean bastard!" Frieda said, as she was sitting down. "It is he who brought this beautiful family into this tragedy. His terrified daughter somehow found the courage to do what she had to do so save her mother. Or else we would be planning Susanna's funeral instead of cleaning that monster's blood out of her house. And any man—or woman . . ." she said, pausing and looking around at the women there with her. "Anyone who says differently is either blind or stupid, and willfully so." The others were stunned into silence, some nodding their heads in agreement and others merely lowering their gaze to the ground beneath them.

"Well, meine Damen, our work here is done," Frieda said, and she downed the rest of her sweet tea. "I must go home to prepare supper for my husband." She stood up. "We did a good thing here today. I hope Susanna will be home soon to take her place with us once again. I miss her. Wiedersehen!"

With that, Frieda Koehn left for home. Soon after, the others followed.

***

All the way back from the hospital, the image of her mother lying in that bed, unable to respond, so despondent and lost, kept reasserting itself in Karla's mind. *"Will mother ever be okay again? And Marta? What about sweet little Marta?"* The thoughts eddied in her mind. *"But I must think of Gretel now."* She wiped her eyes and brushed back her hair before getting out of the car.

Mrs. Bielfeldt was standing on the front porch, leaning on a cane with one hand and holding little Gretel with the other. As soon as she saw Karla coming toward her Gretel began squirming and saying, "Down!"

"My goodness, it seems someone is quite anxious to see her big sister!" Mrs. Bielfeldt said with a smile. She put the little girl down, and Gretel ran out to grab Karla's knee. "Up! Up!" she said, and Karla lifted her up. "Oooof! Such a big girl you are getting to be!" Karla said. "I can hardly lift you anymore!" Gretel hugged Karla tightly around her neck and began sucking on her fingers.

"How is your mother doing?" Mrs. Bielfeldt asked.

"She is managing. The surgery was successful, but she is still under sedation," Karla lied. And then she quickly added, "It's best if she has no visitors for a while."

At this Mrs. Bielfeldt frowned, but her face brightened as she changed the subject. "Well, I do have some good news. Frieda Koehn called and asked me to tell you that the women from the church cleaned up your house and it is all ready for your return. You can stay here as long as you like, but anytime you want to go back home, you can."

Karla was very surprised at this information. "I had no idea they were going to go out there. Oh!" She suddenly realized what an awful mess it had been. "I wish they hadn't done that," Karla said, unable to keep her tears from welling up.

"I think they wanted to help," Mrs. Bielfeldt said.

"I'm sure they did. It's just . . ."

Mrs. Bielfeldt limped down from her porch and offered Karla a warm hug, whispering into her ear, "Hiding it wouldn't make it go away, my dear. You must accept their help as an act of love."

Karla returned the embrace and said, "You are right, of course." Then she stepped back and dislodged Gretel from her neck. She held her out at arm's length, looking at her face-to-face. "What about it, little girl? Shall we go home?" Gretel started clapping and giggling.

They went back into the house to pack up. It only took a few minutes to get their things ready, but Gretel became increasingly impatient. "Go home!" she said again and again, and with growing frustration.

Soon they were back on the front porch and Mr. Bielfeldt was loading their bags into the truck. Karla said, "I can't thank you enough, Mrs. Bielfeldt. You really were a lifesaver."

"That's what we are all here for: to help each other," came her reply. "Let me know how your mother is doing, won't you?" Karla said, "I will." Then another quick embrace, followed by a thank you also to Mr. Bielfeldt, and Karla and Gretel were heading down the road toward home.

Chapter Twenty-eight

WALKING through that back-porch door was like time travel for Karla. She instantly recalled the last time she entered the house, how she saw her mother so badly hurt, and how she flew into action to stop her father from hitting her again, and how he cast her off like a bag of seed, and the sound of her head thudding against the table leg. It all came back like the inner workings of a clock, each little piece moving rhythmically, each action inevitably leading to the next in a tightly crafted picture show. She wanted to stop it. But who can stop history?

Gretel ran past Karla into the house, heading straight for her toy box and screeching with glee as she began pulling out one thing and then another until the whole area was strewn with toddler joy. Karla walked in through the growing mess of toys, and it was then that it hit her. No blood. Not a drop anywhere. Everything looked as clean and normal as if nothing had ever happened. She looked at the dining table and on it was a beautiful arrangement of cut flowers. There were stems of lilac and lavender, some bright yellow forsythia branches, zinnia, chrysanthemum, and two white roses which gave off a lovely scent.

Karla turned back to the kitchen. Everything was in place (minus one notable carving knife). The cupboard door was fixed and closed. All the dishes were put away. Karla opened the refrigerator, and it was literally stuffed with food of all kinds. There was a large glass pitcher of iced tea sitting on the top shelf with two whole lemons beside it. There were at least twenty jars of baby food, several jars of canned apples and peaches and even some fresh bananas! In the freezer compartment she found four casseroles, all prepared and ready to be heated. She opened the bread pantry and found two loaves of baked bread and two pans of yeast rolls and another pan of sticky buns.

"Those wonderful, wonderful women!" Karla said aloud. And she suddenly realized how right Mrs. Bielfeldt was. This was all a gift of love. And Karla's heart was brimful with gratitude.

She turned her attention back to the living and dining area, happy to see Gretel completely engaged with her building blocks. And she saw on the living room coffee table a gathering of unopened mail. Yesterday was mail day, and Mr. Boehm had apparently visited. *"He could have just left the mail in the box on the back porch, but I guess everybody wants to see the house of horrors,"* Karla thought to herself, sadly. She noticed an envelope with international striping. It was from her father's Uncle Horst. Karla tossed it aside. She would have to inform him of her father's death, but that could wait. Her eyes settled on another letter. This one was from Johann.

"Oh my God, Johann!" Karla said out loud. She suddenly realized that her brother knew nothing about any of this. The letter was addressed to her mother, but Karla decided under the circumstances, it made no difference if she opened it.

> *Dear Mother:*
>
> *I only have time for a short note. We are getting ready to move out to another location. You will never believe where I am. I am in North Africa! Imagine! Africa! But no jungles or wild animals. Just a lot of sand and scorching heat. I can say truthfully that I will not miss Africa.*
>
> *How are you, Mutti? Well, I hope. And my sisters, how are they doing? And Papa? Has he settled down by now, I hope? Please greet them all from me—yes, even my father—and let them know you are all in my prayers every day, and I hope I also am in yours.*
>
> *Write me soon,*
> *Johann (Johnny)*

Karla finished reading and sat down. *"What should I do? Should I write Johann about everything that happened? He certainly has the right to know. But how would it help? Who would it help? Would he be able to come back? Would he want to come home or would he just feel obligated to come home? He always hated farming and he was never very good at it. He would be miserable. And he is so completely dedicated to what he is doing over there. But if I were to not tell him right now, how would it change anything? I wish I did not have to make this decision by myself! But mother certainly can't help me. Maybe I should call Hans? But he only just became acquainted with my family. No. I need to decide this on my own."*

All these thoughts were running through Karla's mind. Finally, she worked it out this way: *"Even if Johann could come back home, he could do nothing to help anyway. And if he were unable to come home, knowing the truth of what happened would be a horrible weight on his mind. It might even make him distracted and more vulnerable. I will answer his letter. I will tell him that Mother is under the weather and asked me to write for her."*

Karla started to stand up and then she realized she was sitting in her father's chair by the fireplace. She had never sat in that chair. Ever. It was a strict rule in the Neuenschwander home that only Papa could sit in that chair. She had been so caught up in reading Johann's letter that she just sat down without thinking. She almost hopped up in fear, but then she sat back, just for a moment. She placed her arms on the comfy, overstuffed chair arms and looked across the room. It was a view of the house she had not seen before. It occurred to Karla that now, at this moment, she was the head of this house. Her father was dead. Her mother was incapacitated. Her brother was off fighting the Nazis. There were two children who needed to be cared for. It was now her responsibility. The thought brought with it an initial wave of terrible anxiety. But her feeling of dread was quickly overpowered by a sense of duty and confidence. *"I can do this,* the thought crept forward, declaring itself again and again until she stood and spoke it aloud. "I can do this!"

She ran upstairs and went directly to her closet. There she found the jacket which had been hiding her engagement ring. She dug into the pocket hungrily and found the ring, which she then proudly placed on her left ring finger. "I really can do this," she said. And she walked down the stairs confidently, like the woman she always knew she could be.

Chapter Twenty-nine

THE next months rushed by like a fierce windstorm, leaving bits of destruction while also plowing a new path forward. The funeral came and went. Susanna was unable to attend, as she had been transferred for ongoing care to a convalescent hospital in Reading. It was becoming clear that while her physical health had returned, recovering from her deep withdrawal into psychotic depression was going to be protracted if indeed it would happen at all.

Karla opted to forego the usual visitation, and she insisted the casket be kept closed, as much for herself as for anyone else. She began to realize a furious, seething anger was lurking inside her at what her father had done, at the pain he caused her mother and Marta. Karla decided she wanted never to see her father's face again. Even in a casket. She also tactfully but firmly declined an invitation for a visit from the Pfarrer, claiming she was too busy with the farm work and caring for her mother and Gretel, which was all true enough, but that was not the real reason for her refusal. She simply wanted no conversation about her father.

Although Karla never read that last letter from her father's Uncle Horst, she did write a letter to him. It was comprised of two sentences and a postscript:

To my father's uncle and cousin:

Be advised that Karl Neuenschwander is dead. Please do not send any further correspondence.

Karla Neuenschwander

p.s. My brother Johnny is fighting hard to defeat your horrible evil, and I pray every day he and his fellow soldiers will succeed.

Karla managed the farm as well as her father had. She sometimes needed help with the machine work, but all the fieldwork—including the harvest and storage and winter preparation—all went off without a hitch.

Mr. Bielfeldt became a regular visitor, but after a while he told Karla, "You know, I came over here quite often at first, thinking you might need a lot of help. But young lady, you are every bit the farmer I am." Karla beamed in response, and after he left, she thought, *"If I had only heard one word of praise like that from my father . . ."*

Posing as her mother, Karla also wrote letters regularly to Johnny (she decided it was time to refer to her brother by his preferred name). She managed to keep the ruse alive each time, initially claiming her mother had broken her arm as the reason Karla was doing the writing. She was determined to protect her brother from having to deal with all the tragedy in their family, although she almost changed her mind. When notice came from the District Court that Marta's trial date, originally set for December, was being continued until next April, Karla considered telling Johnny everything. April was several months away; he might be able to get leave to come home. She wondered if Johnny being here for the trial might help Marta's case, as he could testify to the abuse he himself had suffered at the hands of their father. But after considering everything, she decided it was best to keep things status quo.

Karla called the state hospital to inquire about Marta. She asked to be able to speak with her sister but was denied; something about patients in the forensic unit not being allowed phone contact. So, she was left with the option of writing to her, which she began to do on a weekly basis. She eagerly awaited Marta's response, which finally came in mid-November.

> *Dear Karla:*
>
> *Thank you sooo much for writing me! I have moved from the place they called the acute unit to what they call Building 12. It is much nicer here and they let me get mail and I can have paper and a pencil.*
>
> *I was very sad at first, and scared, too. There were some mean people in the acute ward. A couple of them tried to do some awful things to me. But an older woman kind of took care of me. It is better now, but I am so homesick! I miss the farm and I miss Mutti and you and little Gretel. I think maybe Gretel will not even remember me anymore.*
>
> *How is Mutti? I hope she is all healed up now. Please tell her to write me, too. I wish you all could come and see me. Now that I am in Building 12, I think I can have visitors.*
>
> *A man came to see me from Pottsville. He said he is my attorney, and he will be helping me when I go to court. He left*

me a little card with his name, Emory Schenck, Esq. I don't
know what Esq. means, but that's what the card says.

I am sorry for what I had to do, but I did not know what
else to do. I had to stop Papa from hurting Mutti. I really do
think I was his angel of mercy, but Mr. Schenck says I should
not say that anymore. He says people will not understand.

I love you, Karla. I hope I can come home soon.

Marta

As soon as Karla finished reading Marta's letter, she phoned the state hospital again and asked for Building 12. She talked with the unit manager; a nurse named Margrit. Margrit told Karla that Marta was settling into her new surroundings well and that she seemed happy enough. She also said that patients in Building 12 could indeed have visitors, and the next visiting day was on December 17th, a Thursday. When she hung up the phone, Karla immediately sat down to write a response to Marta. She told her that their mother was still quite ill and unable to write or visit, but she assured her that she would come to see her on the next visiting day. After sealing the envelope Karla went to the calendar on the wall in the kitchen and boldly circled December 17th.

***

Despite having little time for her music anymore, Karla and Hans did find time to spend together. On a late November Saturday afternoon, Karla arranged for a baby-sitter and the couple attended a matinee at the Bijou. Before the matinee, the newsreel showed gruesome scenes of immense cruelty toward the Jewish people, as well as the horrible aftermath of bombings in London and other places in England. Karla fought back tears. Hans put his arm around her shoulders, and she snuggled into his chest. "I just don't understand how people could treat other human beings like that" Karla whispered. "Our people! German people! We both come from those people. I can hardly stand it." And her tears flowed even more.

"Would you like to go home?" Hans said. "I don't like seeing you so upset. You have enough to deal with."

Quickly drying her eyes, Karla sat up. "No. I am out on a date with my fiancé." Her tone became resolute. "Those Nazis will not control me. We are going to watch a movie, and then I am going to make us dinner."

They settled in to watch a very enjoyable movie with Jack Benny and Ann Sheridan called, "George Washington Slept Here." The zany plot and the problems of the family on the screen provided just the temporary escape Karla needed. Afterward, they drove back to the farm and enjoyed a casserole and bread, after which Hans drove the sitter home and Karla got Gretel put down to bed.

When Hans returned, he built a fire and Karla poured them both a glass of wine, and they sat down together on the couch in the living room. She snuggled back into his chest. "You know, I'm liking this position more and more," she cooed. "It's a nice fit."

"I must agree," Hans said. And he lifted her face up for a kiss. He said, "You know, we should talk about something." Karla sat up and turned to face him. "What?" she said.

"Well, Gretel will need to be raised. I can think of nobody better than you and me to do that. I think we should push our plans to get married forward, and then I should make arrangements to adopt Gretel."

Karla realized quickly that what Hans was suggesting made all the sense in the world. "I agree completely. And I think we don't need a fancy church wedding. Under the circumstances, a church wedding would be awkward anyway. What if we just get a license and go to the justice of the peace?"

Hans nodded, "I think you're right. I don't need to be back in Reading until Tuesday. Let's get the license Monday."

Karla extended her hand—her left-hand bearing Hans' family ring—and said, "Deal." Hans took her hand and kissed it. Karla nestled back into Hans' chest and sighed contentedly. "All of a sudden, I feel quite married," she said. Hans began to pull her in closer for a kiss, but she beat him to it. It was a deep, passionate, hungry kiss, and before long their marriage was consummated. Right there on the couch beside her father's chair.

❅❅❅

The following week Karla and Hans drove up to Pottsville to apply for a marriage license, and they each arranged for the required physical exams. Although he felt a great temptation to stay with Karla out on the farm, for the sake of his mother Hans continued to stay with her in Shenandoah. It took another three weeks to get the necessary arrangements made, but on the third Monday in December the couple finally arrived together at the courthouse. They made their way to the office of the Justice of the Peace, and ten minutes later they were husband and wife.

While they were there at the courthouse, Hans and Karla went to the office pertaining to orphans, and they initiated the process of adopting little Gretel. When they learned the process would take several months, Hans began to protest. But Karla placed her hand soothingly on his arm and said, "That's only the paperwork. She is already with us. She is happy and loved and safe. The formal adoption will just make it legal. Let's go home." Seeing her smiling face calmed him immediately. "Yes!" he said. "We are married! Hello, Mrs. Schutte!"

"Hello, Mr. Schutte," Karla said, and she managed a demure curtsey. Hans took her arm, and they left the Pottsville Courthouse like newly minted coins, all shiny and valuable and proud.

❈ ❈ ❈

They got back to the farm after retrieving Gretel from Mrs. Bielefeldt, and they sat down for a quick bite of lunch. Karla then said, "Now for the other thing we need to talk about: Marta."

"That's right. You haven't even spoken to her since they took her away. What do you want to do?"

"I want to go see her," Karla replied. "I know it is a bit of a trek to Norristown, but the truck is reliable, and I have enough fuel ration tickets to do it. I spoke to the unit manager a couple weeks ago and she let me know the next visiting day. It is this Thursday. I know you can't go with me, but I feel strongly it is something I must do."

The concerned look on his face was obvious. "I don't like the thought of you out on the road by yourself," he said. "Norristown is basically on the outskirts of Philadelphia. Which is a huge city. And not safe like here."

"It is only a little over an hour away. I will be fine. I can take care of myself," Karla said resolutely. "I just can't leave Marta sitting alone with no contact from her family any longer. I must go."

Hans had always respected the strength of the women in his family. His mother and father were a strong partnership, and when they disagreed his father never lorded his authority over her. Still, Hans began to think along those lines, even against his inclinations. He considered saying to Karla something like, "I am the man of this family now and you are my wife, and I forbid you to go." But when he heard himself speaking those words in his mind, they sounded ridiculous.

"If you must go, then you must," he said. "But I will worry about you until you come home. Telephone me if you can, to let me know you arrived safely, yes?" Hans' look was one of genuine concern. Karla could easily see it, and it endeared him to her even more. She took his face in her hands, looked directly into his eyes and said, "I love you very much. I will be sure to be careful, and I will contact you once I get there." And then she kissed him passionately. It was the sort of kiss that would usually have led to much more, but then Gretel offered a shriek.

"What is wrong, Gretel?" Karla asked. Gretel came running over and wanted to be picked up. Karla pulled her onto her lap. "Weren't you playing with your toys?"

"Blocks fall down!" came the toddler's response, followed by the sort of whining cry which usually indicates the need for sleep. Karla snuggled her into her bosom and said, "Those grumpy old blocks. Maybe they are getting tired. Maybe they will be better in the morning. Do you think?"

"NO!" came the instant response as she pushed violently away from Karla's grasp. "Daddy fix it!" and she reached out for Hans. Hans took her onto his lap, and she clung to his neck. He looked at Karla and his eyes began to tear up. This was the first time Gretel had called him Daddy. Karla smiled back at her husband understandingly. She watched him as he got up and carried her over to where she had strewn her toys. As he acquiesced to Gretel's need for Daddy's attention, kneeling with her and her recalcitrant blocks, Karla felt a deep affection for him. "*This is a good man I married. A very good man.*" And as the little girl was playing with her daddy, the big girl was thinking about that last kiss. She went upstairs to prepare for another kind of his attention.

CHAPTER THIRTY

WHEN Thursday finally arrived, Karla gassed up the truck and checked the tires. Everything was in order. Despite a few snow flurries, the weather had thankfully cooperated. The sun was poking through the banks of puffy, gray, wintery clouds, making the day feel warmer than it truly was. Karla put some ginger snaps and Marta's favorite peanut butter cake in a small sack, loaded a thermos with black coffee, and headed for Norristown.

The drive was uneventful, but slow. Karla was so anxious to see Marta that she began to feel more like an impatient little girl than a grown, married woman. *"Good Lord! Am I ever going to get there?"* she thought to herself. *"This 35 mile per hour speed limit might save rubber and fuel, but it sure takes forever to get anyplace!"*

The miles passed, and the reduced pace made the scenery seem unusually pacific. Snow covered the farm ground and hung from the cedar and spruce and jack pines. Karla saw a buck step out on the highway up ahead. He sported quite the impressive rack. *"Ten points, maybe twelve,"* she thought. When he saw her truck, he quickly took off into the woods, followed by four does and a spike buck. Karla's mind ran back to the first time her father took her hunting. He hadn't wanted to. "Hunting is for the men and boys, not for girls!" he said. But she begged and begged, and when Amelia Braun got to go with her father, Karla finally got her father to give in.

He took her and Johann out for gun training in the woods behind the house. She was thirteen years old and eager to participate. Johann was barely twelve and reluctant and unenthusiastic. Karl taught them, gruffly, how to be safe and when and where to shoot. "Don't expect you are going to get a deer," he said. "Not even I get a deer every year." But that year—on her first hunting trip—Karla did get a deer. She shot a nice, stocky six pointer. It was a clean chest shot and he dropped immediately. Neither Karl nor Johann brought home a deer that day. It was a proud memory, even though her father seemed grumpy afterward.

Karla suddenly was surprised to see a sign welcoming her to Norristown. Her thoughts shifted jarringly from her memories as a thirteen-year-old with her father to Marta, who killed him when she was roughly the same age. It was a chilling connection.

Karla followed the directions she had written down for herself and in a few minutes, she was driving onto the expansive campus of Norristown State Hospital. She drove past six or seven brick buildings, each two or three stories, some with ivies crawling up the walls like brown webbing. Eventually she came to the main administration building known as building 17, where she had been told to register on arrival. It was an impressive building of at least four stories, reaching out with two long wings attached to either side of a central rotunda. A set of concrete steps formed a semi-circle at the entrance, flanked by four white, Tuscan pillars supporting the pointed archway above.

Karla parked her car and ascended the steps into the central reception area. She was taken aback by the stark beauty of the place. Terrazzo flooring lent an air of officiality to the space, and all around were railings and crown moldings and high-back washboards made of dark hardwood. Some of the windows were stained glass, and all bore protective wrought iron cross hatching festooned with embossed knuckling. In another era, one might have expected gargoyles looking down, menacingly.

She found a desk marked "Visitors Registration" which seemed as though it had been set up there in the main entryway just for this occasion. A pleasant young woman took Karla's information and offered her some pamphlets about the hospital campus and history, one of which included a map identifying the various buildings. She also handed her a bright yellow visitors tag and instructed her to display it on the lapel of her coat while on hospital grounds. Karla quickly located Building 12 on the map, clipped the yellow tag on her coat, and headed out to see Marta.

It was nearly a quarter mile walk to Building 12, which Karla covered quickly. When she got there, Karla rang a doorbell to seek entrance. The door was unlocked, she was ushered in, and the door was securely locked again behind her. The realization that she was now locked in a mental hospital ward gave her a bit of momentary pause.

A young orderly guided Karla to a reception area containing ten square tables with four chairs each. There was also an array of settees, lounge chairs and prim couches set up along the outer walls, some with oak coffee tables in front and others flanked by end tables. The orderly invited Karla to sit wherever she liked and asked her, "Whom are you here to see?" Karla responded, "My sister, Marta Neuenschwander."

"Ahh, young Marta!" the man said with a hint of affection. "Such a sweet young lady she is! She has only been here a week or so, but she has already become something of a favorite of the staff. Hard to believe . . ." Karla interrupted him, "Will you bring her here to me, please?" Her mien and tone of voice belied any pretense of openness to further conjecture regarding what was believable or not about her sister.

"Yes, ma'am," the young man said. "I will bring her directly." He disappeared down one of the hallways and reappeared a few minutes later with Marta alongside him.

"Marta!" Karla said, leaping to her feet and moving quickly toward her.

"Karla!" came the overjoyed response. And when they met, the embrace that followed could hardly have been defeated. Both were in tears, first of relief, then of remorse and grief and fear of the future, and finally of profound sadness and deep love. The two stood there embracing and rocking gently for several minutes before Marta stepped back and said, "You know, showing too much affection around here can be a sign of mental illness."

Karla laughed out loud. They both sat down on one of the perimeter couches. "Let me look at you," Karla said. Marta stood and pirouetted, flaring out her skirt like a model and genuflecting. "You look so thin!" Karla said.

"The food is not like Mutti's," Marta responded.

"Well, look in this little sack and see if you find anything interesting."

Marta's eyes sparkled at the thought of receiving something from home. She opened the bag carefully and found the ginger snaps wrapped in wax paper. "Oh! I love Mutti's ginger cookies!" she said, and she took a quick bite. "Mmmmm . . . they are so good!"

"Look deeper in the bag," Karla said with a sly smile.

Marta looked in and then smelled the contents. "Peanut butter cake! My favorite thing! Oh, Mutti, thank you! Karla, you make sure to tell her, won't you?"

Karla's eyes became downcast, and although she quickly tried to cover her sadness, Marta had always been so sensitive to the feelings of others. "Maybe you had better tell me, Karla," Marta said. And she sat down beside her. "How is Mutti?"

Holding back tears, Karla told Marta the entire story. How badly injured their mother had been, the required hospitalization and surgery and recuperation time, and how she had drawn into herself afterward. Marta's face showed an uncharacteristic sorrow. "It is my fault," she said. "If I weren't facing all this . . ."

"If you weren't facing all this, our mother would be dead. You saved her life, Marta. There's no two ways about it. She is alive because of what you did."

Marta looked down at her shoes. She only had the one pair with her, a pair of brown loafers. They were beginning to fray around the edges. "My shoes used to be so nice," she said. "I tried to take good care of them. But I guess nothing lasts." Karla reached over and patted her hand. That is when Marta saw the ring. "Karla?!" she said, her face brightening with excitement. "Are you? Did you?"

Karla grinned and nodded. "Yes. Hans and I got married just a few days ago. On Monday. We went to the courthouse and signed some papers and made a promise to love and care for each other until we die. I love him so much!"

Marta grabbed her and pulled her in for a big hug. "Married to a professor!! I liked him right away when he came to the house for dinner. I am so happy for you!" she said.

"He is a good and kind man," Karla said. And he is going to adopt Gretel. We will raise her and make sure she gets everything she needs."

"Wow! You go away to a mental hospital and everything changes . . ." Marta said, pensively.

"And when you come back from the mental hospital, life will go on in a new way," Karla said, lifting her sister's chin till their eyes met. The tears were about to start again, so Karla stood up. "Why don't you show me around? Who knows, I might need this place myself someday."

Marta showed Karla all the elements of her life in Building 12. She showed her where she slept, the refectory, the lavatory facilities and shower room, the crafts room, the music room, the recreation room, and the nurse's station, all of it—even the isolation room for when someone got out of control. It was all relatively cheery and quite well-organized. Karla was impressed.

The two sisters visited for another hour before it was time for Karla to head back home.

"I will come back soon," Karla promised. "And I am going to call your attorney to see if there is anything I can do to help before the trial." She paused before realizing she had never even mentioned Johnny.

"Something else you need to know, Marta," Karla said. Marta looked up. "I have not told Johann about any of this. He doesn't know Papa is dead. He doesn't know you are here. He doesn't yet know about Mother being in the convalescent home. He knows none of it. I decided it would only weigh on his mind and distract him. The time to tell him will come, but not now."

Marta said, "I trust you, Karla. I am so glad you came. Thank you."

The two embraced one more time, and Karla headed out for home.

Chapter Thirty-one

T HE first year of Hans and Karla's marriage was one of adjust-ments. The weekly trips back and forth to Reading became impossible due to increasingly stiff rationing of gas and oil. Being a farmer, Karla was allotted a greater fuel ration, but she needed every bit of it for the fieldwork. So, by the first of March, Hans reduced his trips to once a month. Neither Hans nor Karla liked this arrangement at all. Neither did Hans' mother, whose health was beginning to fail. Karla and Hans both knew it was time to consider their options. So, when Hans came home on a Friday afternoon at the end of the month, they sat at the kitchen table after supper and began to talk.

"We can't go on this way," Karla said. "I'm worried what happens to my mother and to yours if you get stuck without fuel. I know my mother is being cared for, but I need to see her. And your mother is not getting any younger. What happens to her if your car falls apart? They won't sell new cars to anybody but medical doctors and clergymen. Besides that, I miss you! We have not even been married six months yet and you are only here one weekend a month! And Gretel misses you, too. She was just getting used to you being here and then, poof! You were gone. I've seen how it bothers her. She gets cranky and whiny after you leave. What can we do?"

"What if we looked for a place down in Reading? Maybe we could move my mother down there, too, and you could rent out the farm?" Hans asked.

"I could. I mean, we could," Karla said with a smile. "I'm still getting used to thinking in terms of 'we'. But instead of renting it, maybe we could even sell the farm. There is nothing here for us now but awful memories. I mean, there is the land and the livestock. We can grow our own food and butcher our own meat. We will never starve here on the farm. But I am the only member of the family who would want to continue the farm work. And if staying here means our family is split up all the time, maybe it would be better to just be done with it. I think Bielfeldts would probably jump at the chance to add this property to their own."

Hans took in the idea thoughtfully, rubbing his brown hair with both hands and then resting his face in his hands. "I need a shave," he said, running his fingers over an estimable day's stubble. "Maybe I'll grow a beard," he mused. "Very professorial." Karla smiled and responded, "Okay, Herr Professor, but when you grow your beard, who will be there to admire it? Those young and eager college debutantes who surround you in Reading or your adoring wife and almost-daughter?" Karla did have a way of refocusing Hans when he needed it. And he often needed it.

"Listen. I know you are thinking of this as a decision for us to make together, but it doesn't seem right that I should be involved in selling your family's farmstead. You can rent it or sell it, as you see fit. But either way, it looks as though we are making the decision to move to Reading. Yes?"

Karla responded with a nodding of her head. "I think we are doing just that."

Hans said, "Okay then, we have some work to do. You contact a real estate agent in Shenandoah, and I will begin looking for options down in Reading for us and for my mother. What if I can find us a place with a little land so you could continue to grow vegetables? Maybe even raise a cow or two and a hog. And some fruit trees, too. Would that appeal to you?"

Karla's eyes widened. "Oh, yes! I would love that! I will certainly not miss this house with all its memories, but I will miss the land. If you could find us a place just outside of town with maybe a couple acres of land, that would be wonderful."

"Okay, then that's settled." Hans said. I'll go back Monday instead of Tuesday so I can get right on it." Karla agreed.

Chapter Thirty-two

THE date for Marta's trial arrived in mid-April, and Hans arranged to be there with Karla. She had built up such an air of expectation around this date that the accumulated tension strained every muscle in her body. She had spoken with Mr. Schenck on several occasions, giving him all the history she could to help him understand what truly happened and why. He wanted to call her as a witness, which she was eager to do. He also suggested the possibility that, depending on the results of the psychiatric evaluation, Marta might be released into Karla and Hans' supervision with required psychiatric follow-up care. Karla and Hans were, of course, entirely agreeable to this outcome. In fact, Karla began praying daily that God would allow this to happen.

Karla and Hans took seats directly behind the defendant's table, and as they brought Marta out her eyes brightened seeing them there. She was flanked by two large, uniformed officers, making her appear even smaller than she already did. She sat down beside her attorney, and he patted her hand reassuringly, leaning in to advise her quietly.

"Oyez, Oyez, Oyez. "ALL RISE! The Court of Common Pleas, Schuylkill County, Pennsylvania is now in session. The Honorable William Gottschalk is presiding. All having business with this honorable court draw near and give your attention and you will be heard." All in attendance stood as the judge entered and took his place behind the elevated bench. He sat and gaveled the proceedings into motion.

Opening statements were invited, beginning with the prosecution. The District Attorney stood and addressed the jury. "Your honor, if it please the court, the Commonwealth's case is simple: Karl Neuenschwander was killed by having his throat cut by his 12-year-old daughter. Period. We will present testimony which will establish these facts as undeniable. Gentlemen of the jury, your duly sworn responsibility is to protect the public from any possibility of further harm by finding Marta Neuenschwander guilty of murder in the second degree. Thank you, your honor."

The judge said, "All right, now we'll hear from the defense."

"Thank you, your honor," Mr. Schenck said as he rose to face the jury. "Gentlemen of the jury, my client, Marta Neuenschwander, is a twelve-year-old girl who was faced with an impossible and immediate choice none of us would want to face. She could watch her mother die at the hands of her father, or she could intervene. There was no time to call for help. Her mother was within minutes of dying. So, being roughly 85 pounds, and her father being 200 pounds, my client chose to do the only thing she knew how to do. Her father himself had shown her some weeks earlier when he taught her how to kill a hog. She took a carving knife from her mother's butcher block set on the kitchen counter, and she cut her father's throat. We do not deny these facts. But what we intend to establish is that in making that horrible decision, this twelve-year-old girl saved her mother's life. You will hear testimony from Marta's 19-year-old sister, Karla, as to the imminent danger she witnessed to Susanna Neuenschwander, wife of the deceased, and to the concussion Karla herself suffered when she tried to intervene in her father's assaults. You will also hear testimony from the physicians and surgeons who treated Susanna Neuenschwander's extensive injuries. Susanna continues to be so traumatized by what she suffered at the hands of her husband that she cannot be here today. She requires continued convalescent care.

"Gentlemen of the jury, you will be convinced of these facts and the mitigating nature of these facts as they bear on the actions my client took. And once you have seen and heard all the evidence, including the evaluations of the psychiatric team who has evaluated Marta these past six months, you will see that Marta Neuenschwander poses no danger to anyone. Rather than being further punished, she should be pitied for the terrible situation her father's brutish behavior placed her in. She should be praised for her courage in ending the threat to her mother's life. And she should be released to the care of her family, namely her older sister and her husband, where she may have the chance to heal from this horrible ordeal and grow into a fine young lady. Thank you."

The judge said, Mr. District Attorney, you may call your first witness."

"Thank you, your honor." And one by one, the prosecution called for testimony and submitted evidence showing all the gruesome elements of the case. Karla had to look away on one occasion as the images of her family's tragedy were displayed, showing the blood and hair on the wall, the large pool of blood on the floor, a closeup of her father's dead body and his gashed throat, and one of the bloody knife. The Sheriff and a deputy testified, followed by the coroner. Finally, the medical examiner presented the findings of the autopsy. Throughout the entire case presented by the Commonwealth, Mr. Schenck declined to cross-examine any of the witnesses, nor did he challenge any of the evidentiary submissions. The prosecution rested.

The judge ordered a break for lunch, and when all returned at 1pm, the judge said, "Mr. Schenck, are you ready to answer the charges of the Commonwealth?"

"We are, your honor, if it please the court." The judge responded by saying, "You may call your first witness."

"The defense calls Karla Neuenschwander Schutte." After being sworn in, Karla sat in the witness box just beside and below the bench. As she responded to Mr. Schenck's questions, Karla painted a vivid picture of life on the Neuenschwander farm. She told of the abuse she witnessed her father repeatedly direct at Johnny, and about how she and her mother had interrupted his violence against Marta on the day of the hog butchering incident. She recounted how enraged her father was when she walked into the house on the evening he was killed, how disfigured her mother's face was, and how she jumped on her father's back to keep him from hitting her mother again. She described being thrown through the air by her father and banging her head on the floor, resulting in her becoming unconscious for a time. She recounted the horror of regaining consciousness, finding her father dead in a pool of blood, and finding her mother in shock and with her jaw badly broken and her eyes bulging from being throttled. Finally, Karla recalled how she found Marta in the bedroom with little Gretel, rocking her in the rocking chair and sitting calmly. "Your witness," Mr. Schenck said, motioning to the DA.

Karla responded calmly to each question posed to her by the prosecution. His intent was clearly to try to show some history of bad behavior or angry outbursts in Marta's past. He obviously had found none on his own, and his cross-examination of Karla yielded nothing to further his cause.

Finally, the judge said to Karla, "Miss Neuenschwander, you may return to your seat. Mr. Schenck, call your next witness."

"The defense calls Dr. Harley Simpson."

Dr. Simpson was sworn in, and his credentials were read into the court record. He reported on his findings after six months observation of Marta at Norristown. Karla almost leapt from her seat when she heard the words, "Other than the normal sadness attendant to this terrible event in her life, I found absolutely no psychiatric disorder present in this young girl."

Next up was the testimony of those physicians and nurses who had treated Susanna at Locust Mountain Hospital in Shenandoah, as well as those who were now caring for her at the convalescent home in Reading. Gasps could be heard from the jury as they saw photos taken in the emergency room of Susanna's injuries, and as reports of the surgeon and of the post-surgical care team were read and offered into evidence.

After the jury heard character testimony from the Pfarrer at the Evangelishe Kirche, from Mrs. Bielfeldt, and from Marta's sixth grade teacher, the defense rested, and the case was handed over to the jury. It was 4:15 pm when Karla and Hans walked out, arm in arm, and when they got to the hallway Karla said, "If there is any justice in this world, that little girl is coming home with us." Hans nodded in agreement. They sat there on a dark wooden bench together, reflecting on the trial. Karla said, "Do you think I did okay? Did I say enough? Did I say too much?" Hans could see the signs of worry on her face. He said, "I think you told the truth. You answered every question thoroughly. You gave them a good picture of your family's experience. Which, by the way, I never really understood until today. I am so very sorry for what your father put you through."

Karla looked away. She had no stomach for being pitied. She looked out the window at the building clouds. "Looks like rain coming. I won't be getting any fieldwork done tomorrow."

Hans stayed quiet for a while. Finally, after about ten more minutes, he said, "I guess these things can take quite a while. It is almost time for supper. We may as well . . ."

Hans was interrupted mid-sentence by the announcement that the jury had reached its verdict. Karla looked at Hans in disbelief. "Already? Has it even been fifteen minutes?" she asked. "Barely," came the reply. They quickly rose and moved back to their places behind Marta.

It took another fifteen minutes for the observers to return to the court before the bailiff called for order and Judge Gottschalk re-entered the courtroom, still adjusting his black robe and wiping the corner of his mouth with a napkin. Clearly, he had not expected so quick a verdict. The judge sat down and ordered the jury to be brought in.

The judge said, "Mr. foreman, is it my understanding that you all have come to agreement on a verdict already?" The foreman stood and responded, "We have, your honor."

"Hand it to the bailiff," the judge said. The bailiff brought the verdict to the judge, who read it quickly. Karla thought she picked up a hint of a smile on his face. The judge handed the piece of paper back to the bailiff, and the bailiff returned it to the jury foreman. The judge said, "You may read the verdict."

The foreman said, "In the case of the Commonwealth vs. Marta Neuenschwander on the charge of murder in the second degree, we find the defendant not guilty." A cheer rose from the courtroom and Karla almost jumped over the railing separating her from her sister. They hugged joyously over the railing. The judge banged his gavel loudly several times. "Order! ORDER!! THIS COURT WILL COME TO ORDER!!"

The people quieted down and regained their composure as the judge said, "Mr. foreman, you may continue." The foreman continued, "We further find that a judgment of justifiable homicide is warranted in this case."

"I want to commend the jury on their swift work in this case. Mr. and Mrs. Schutte, are you willing to accept responsibility for the care of the minor, Marta Neuenschwander?"

Karla and Hans rose and spoke with one voice, "We are, your honor."

"Let the court record so indicate. Then this case is dismissed, and the jury is released with the court's thanks. Court is adjourned." The gavel came down one last time, just as the roar rose again from those in the gallery. Karla stepped right over the railing and grabbed onto Marta in a wave of tears and joy and laughter. They both hugged Mr. Schenck and thanked him profusely before clamping tightly onto one another again. Finally, Marta said, "Karla . . . maybe you should introduce me to your husband."

Karla turned to see Hans standing behind them on the other side of the rail, his face beaming with a wide grin. Karla said, "Marta, this is my husband, Professor Hans Schutte." Hans reached out his hand politely, and Marta fully leaped into his arms. "I am so happy! Thank you for loving my sister. And thank you for being here today for me." Hans returned her embrace, looking through happy tears over her shoulder at Karla. Suddenly, Karla said, "Hey! Let's go home!" And they did.

Chapter Thirty-three

G RETEL was now a busy and precocious three-year-old, and when she first saw Marta, she was a bit wary. It was as Marta had feared: Gretel did not remember her at first. When they picked her up from Mrs. Bielfeldt on the way home, Gretel insisted on sitting on Karla's lap in the front seat. But Marta began talking from the back seat, and before long Gretel stood on the front seat and studied her. By the time they arrived back at the farmhouse, Gretel was elatedly chattering and very animated. She remembered her sister. When they got out of the car, she grabbed Marta by the hand and dragged her into the house and directly to her toybox. Before long they were sitting on the floor and coloring pictures together.

Marta tried not to, but she couldn't help looking past Gretel's play area to the place where her mother had been attacked. She looked at the place on the floor where her father had fallen after she cut his throat. The memories came roaring back like floodwater, filled with dangerous debris and swirling eddies, and for a moment she was back there. The sound of her name startled her back to the present. "Marta!" It was Gretel, adamantly calling her. "*She never called me by my name before,*" Marta thought to herself. The awareness brought a smile and a sense of relief from her acerbic musings on things best left behind. She turned her attention to the place it now belonged—to being home with her little sister, and to resuming the process of growing up. And right then, that meant sitting on the floor and coloring. It was perfect.

***

1943 became a year of significant changes for all the remaining members of the Neuenschwander family. Karla approached Mr. Bielfeldt about him buying the farm, and as she expected, he was eager to pursue the idea. In advance of the sale, Karla contacted Mr. Schenck in Pottsville to help her gain legal right to dispose of the property which, because of her age, did involve Hans. Meanwhile, Hans looked at several properties in Reading before finding what he thought were two good possibilities. Karla went along to see both, and Hans knew instantly by her reaction which she preferred. She became as animated as a little girl as soon as they drove onto the property, and her excitement only grew as they moved from touring the house to the outbuildings and the 2 ½ acres of arable land. They made an offer which was accepted in late May, and they arranged a move-in date over the July 4th weekend.

But certainly, the most significant change involved Susanna. Karla planned with her mother's caregivers how best to reintroduce Marta and Gretel into Susanna's world. It promised to be confusing for everyone, especially Gretel, and no one knew quite what to expect. But if they were going to be able to move Susanna into their new home, this was the first step.

It was on a Thursday when Karla loaded her sisters into the truck and headed for Reading. When they got to the convalescent care home, they found Susanna sitting at a table out in the sunroom, looking va-cantly toward the window but seemingly without focus. Karla sat beside her mother and pulled Gretel up onto her lap. Gretel looked at Susanna quizzically and said nothing at first. Marta sat down on the other side, pulling her chair up close. "Mutti," she said.

Susanna winced at the sound of Marta's voice, and then closed her eyes tightly, as if to keep out some awful assault on her awareness. Marta spoke again, softly. "Mutti, it's me. I'm here."

Susanna, her eyes still closed, shook her head intensely from side to side, trying to escape them, but the memories overwhelmed her, chasing her, pressing down on her like an avalanche. "*His eyes! Blood red eyes! His hands choking, choking, tighter, tighter. Can't breathe! Can't talk! The knife!! No, Marta! No!! Not you! The blood spurting! It's on my face! I can taste it! Oh my God!!*"

Marta looked at the anguish so obvious on her mother's face and she began to cry. "Mutti! I am so sorry, Mutti! I am so, so sorry! I didn't know what else to do!" And she broke down completely into uncontrollable, racking sobs. Karla was also crying, and Gretel began to whimper. She placed three fingers in her mouth and began to suck on them, something she had not done in quite a while.

Marta was doubled over. Her tears were so effluent they were making tiny pools on the floor. She felt a hand on her shoulder, followed by a familiar voice. "Marta. Meine Süsse. Don't cry. It will be okay."

Marta looked up and saw her mother looking at her lovingly, a soft smile on her tired face. And she threw herself around her mother's shoulders, her tears continuing but with a changed focus. "Oh, Mutti, I'm so glad you woke up! I missed you so much!" Susanna held her daughter tightly and said, "I missed you too, my brave, brave girl."

Karla's grin broke right through her tears, and she moved closer to join in the reunion embrace. Gretel snuggled into Susanna's neck, and she began to make a sort of cooing sound. The Neuenschwander women were reunited.

Susanna began to make steady, slow progress. Her daughters visited nearly every day. Karla decided to wait to discuss Johann until her mother asked, and after a week or so, Susanna asked, "Karla, what have you heard from Johann? He's okay, isn't he?"

"He's fine, Mutti, as far as I know. Last we heard he was in Italy. He had even been in North Africa!"

"Africa! Oh, my word! Just think of it! How did he take all this terrible news?"

"I have kept it from him. I made up an excuse that you broke your arm, so I wrote as though I was taking down dictation from you. It was a hard decision to make, but there was truly nothing he could have done even if he were able to come home, and I didn't want to burden him with it. We can talk about how you want to handle it going forward."

"I think you made the right decision, Karla. You are such a capable and wise woman. You make me proud."

"I had a fine role model," Karla said with a smile.

***

The year progressed in a series of adjustments. Karla and her sisters adjusted to a new home and the presence of a new man in it. By mid-July Susanna was well enough to go on a visit to her daughter's home, and by Labor Day she was moved in. Susanna and Karla talked it over and decided it would be easier for Gretel to call Susanna "Grandma" and to refer to Karla as her mother. Gretel had grown very attached to Hans as her daddy, so the connections just seemed simpler. Susanna was very pleased with the arrangement. It seemed she was growing stronger and more hopeful by the day.

Hans' mother, Hannah, was now residing in the same convalescent home where Susanna had received care. Susanna and Karla began to visit her there regularly, and a friendship was struck up between the mothers-in-law.

Karla had gotten the crops planted back in May before the sale, but when the sale took place, she agreed to come back and help Mr. Bielfeldt with the harvest. So, Karla decided to stay at their old house on the last weekend in October. As the family ate supper together one evening, Karla reminded them of her plans.

"Remember I will be gone next weekend," she said to the gathering.

"Where are you going?" Marta asked.

"I agreed to help Mr. Bielfeldt harvest the crops on the farm this year. So, I am going on Friday. I will stay in our old house and work over the weekend. Nobody is living there and there is still a bed there." She and Marta got up to clear the table, and Karla dished up some vanilla ice cream. When they brought in the dessert Susanna said, "Would you mind if I came along?"

Karla looked up, startled by the thought. She looked over at Hans who remained intently focused on his ice cream. "Do you think that would be wise, Mother?" Karla asked.

"I don't know," Susanna responded. "But it is probably time for me to face it all. And this being the last Saturday of the month, the ladies will be meeting at the church for quilting. I want to see them. And I should visit your father's grave. He gave me four children. I owe him that much."

Karla studied her mother's face. She really had made remarkable progress. Despite a sort of perpetual sadness that was not so evident prior to Karl's death, there seemed to be no remnant of the deep withdrawal which held her in its throes these past months. "Well, Mother, if you don't mind sharing a bed, I guess it's a road trip! Marta, will you be okay staying here to look after Gretel until Hans gets home Friday?"

"We'll be fine, won't we Gretel?" she smiled at her sister. Without looking up from her bowl of ice cream Gretel responded, "We fine."

✾ ✾ ✾

Friday arrived, and after they packed up the truck with some food and a few other necessities, they headed out to the farm before sunup. "I'm glad you sold the farm," Susanna said.

"It seemed the best option at the time, and I suppose it still is," Karla responded. The gas rationing was really making it impossible for Hans to continue driving back and forth every week, and his mother was needing attention, and I wanted to be closer to you. If Johann had any interest in the farm, I would have consulted him. But you know he doesn't."

Susanna looked out the window at the landscape slowly moving by. "Why are we going so slowly?" she asked.

"The national speed limit is now 35 miles per hour. Saves on fuel and tires, they say. But it does turn a 45-minute trip into an hour and a half. I must admit, though, I've sort of grown accustomed to the slower pace. Kind of peaceful, in a way."

When they drove through Shenandoah, it was still early. The town seemed to be still asleep, but Susanna's memories were wide awake. There was the church with its tall, white steeple and huge brown doors. And the shade trees in the church yard where the women would gather after worship. "I really am anxious to see Frieda Koehn and the others tomorrow," she said. Moving past the church, she could see the cemetery. There was one obviously newer grave, still slightly humped up with brown dirt. She assumed that was where Karl was buried. A small tear formed as she considered the sadness of it all, but she wiped it away quickly.

They proceeded through the small downtown area and headed towards what had been their farm. Turning onto the end drive, Karla paused and put the truck in neutral. "Are you okay?" she asked. "I am okay," came the response. "Let's go."

Karla pulled the truck into the yard. Nothing seemed out of place. They got out and began to carry things into the house. As they moved past the porch and into the kitchen, Susanna was surprised. "Everything looks the same," she said. "Except it is so empty . . ."

They walked through to the living room, now devoid of the usual furnishings except for Karl's chair, which Karla chose to leave there. Susanna looked over to the dining area and hallway. All looked pristine and tidy. "Do you remember everything?" Karla asked, putting her arm around her mother's shoulders.

"It is strange, but I really don't. I must have been in shock, I guess. I remember the fear. I remember him choking me. And Marta . . ." She suddenly shuddered and closed her eyes and turned in to the safety of Karla's embrace. Karla held her there quietly for a moment. But Susanna pulled back and straightened herself, wiping her eyes with her sleeve. "But as for the rest of it, I have no memory at all."

"That is really a blessing," Karla said. "The photos we had to see during the trial were terrible. And hearing them refer to our home as a "crime scene" was awful. But the Bielfeldts took me and Gretel in right after, and a week or so later the women of the church just came in one day and totally cleaned it up. They left fresh fruit and cut flowers. They stocked the pantry and refrigerator chock full. I never asked them to, but when we walked back into this house for the first time, I was so grateful that I actually cried," Karla said, pausing to enjoy the memory. "Maybe you want to go freshen up while I get things put away?"

Susanna said, "I'm fine. I think I want to take a look outside." She headed back out the porch door and took in the scene. Her washing lines were still there, looking forlorn without any clean laundry hanging from them. And there was her old hand washing tub and washboard in its place near the porch. The trees were turning their characteristic reds and rusts and golds. *"It really is a pretty farm,"* she thought.

She walked over to her garden, now overgrown with thick weeds and tall thistles. The traditionally well-tended furrows were still visible, but the formerly productive space was a mess. She remembered the letter she buried there, and the uneasy feeling she had had about it. *"That's how this all started,"* she thought, sadly. "That stupid, awful letter," she said aloud. Suddenly, a Bible verse from Galatians shouted itself into her awareness: *Be not deceived; God is not mocked: for whatsoever a man soweth, that shall he also reap.* "Oh!!" She threw her head back in despair as the enormity of all that had happened overtook her. She dropped to her knees beside her garden and sobbed until she was too weak to continue.

Exhausted, she fell back on the grass beside her garden and sat there hugging her knees, contemplating it. For some reason, her gaze began to focus on some various vegetable plants that she could see were valiantly trying to produce something, defiant against the choking weeds. She looked more carefully, and barely visible under the tangle of thistles and milkweed and tall grass and wild mustard she could see several tomato plants bearing at least a dozen fruit, some zucchini squash ready for harvesting, and some bell peppers. All at once. Susanna sprang up. She knew what she must do. But harvesting those vegetables was going to be virtually impossible with all the weeds and brush. She headed over to the garden shed and was pleased to find a hoe and a spade there. She grabbed those tools and a pair of garden gloves from the drawer of a workbench and got to work.

Soon Karla came out to get the tractor and corn picker hooked up, and she saw her mother vigorously chopping at the weeds. "Mother!" she called over. Susanna stopped and looked up. "Why are you bothering with that? It's not our garden anymore."

Susanna wiped some sweat from her brow. She called out in response, "It might not be mine anymore, but I won't leave it like this for somebody else to deal with. And there are good vegetables in here. Go ahead with your work. I'll be fine."

Karla smiled to herself. *"Just do your work and everything will be fine."* She waved and turned toward the harvest. Susanna turned also to her own harvest.

CHAPTER THIRTY-FOUR

SUSANNA decided to walk the two miles into town on Saturday morning. She carried with her the vegetables she gleaned from her garden. It took the entire day, but she cleared away all the weeds and stacked them into a large brush pile. She discovered even more healthy plants than she thought. All in all, she collected 20 tomatoes, 22 zucchinis, 28 bell peppers, thirty-or-so carrots, almost 5 pounds of onions and a few handfuls of radishes, all of which she loaded into Johann's old rucksack which she found still hanging on the porch. She loaded the greenish-brown bundle on her back and headed down the road like a hiker.

When she got to the church, she saw Frieda's car. *"Always the first one here,"* Susanna mused. She walked in through the side entrance and headed downstairs to the church hall. Frieda was busily setting up one of the quilt frames and had already hauled out some boxes of fabric. She heard someone enter and without looking up, she said, "There are two more frames to be set up."

"Hello, Frieda," Susanna said.

Frieda looked up. "Ach! Mein Gott in Himmel! Susanna!" And the normally undemonstrative Frieda ran directly to Susanna, knocking over her quilt frame in the process. She hugged Susanna with a giant bear hug and did not even try to restrain her tears of joy and relief. The women held each other and cried together. No other words were spoken.

Eventually, Frieda regained her composure and released Susanna from her embrace. She stepped back, wiped her eyes and her nose, and reassumed her traditional, all-business posture. "You look good. A little skinny, perhaps, ja? Sit! Sit down and tell me how you are."

The two friends had about fifteen minutes together before the others began to arrive. Susanna tried to sum up what she had experienced, where she had been, where she was now living, and why she was here. Frieda listened intently, interposing nothing.

"I am so glad you are here. I am even more glad to know you are coming through all of this so well. I miss you here. But life goes on, no?"

Susanna nodded. "Thank you so very much for coming out to clean up that awful mess. And for bringing all the food and the flowers. Karla told me it made her cry when she walked in to see what you had done. I know you had help, but I also know you were behind it." Frieda tried to hide a blush, unsuccessfully. "You are a wonderful friend, Frieda. I have missed you, too. And I will come back when I can to see you and everyone."

"But now we are here! Just like old times!" Frieda said, brightly. "Help me get the frames set up." The two women stood and embraced again, briefly this time, as the others began to arrive. Some twenty women came to quilt that day, but only a little quilting got done. They all chatted and laughed and cried and cared for one another—especially for Susanna—for nearly four hours. When it was time to leave, Susanna expressed her thanks to everyone who helped clean her house, and she distributed her produce, making sure everyone took something with them when they left.

Afterward, Susanna walked out to the cemetery on the other side of the church. She found her way over to Karl's grave and stood there alone. The chilling gusts of October wind blew her dress and her greying blonde hair around. As she stared at the grave, she was surprised that she shed no tears. She had anticipated that she would, but to her surprise, she felt no need to cry over him. She felt no sadness or grief. What came over her like thunder and lightning was rage. "Look what you've done!" she said aloud to her husband's dead ears. "Just look!" It came out loud and scolding and accusing.

She stood not to the side or at the foot of the grave, but directly over it, staring down, imagining his body as though he were right there in front of her, cowering at her feet. "I have something to say to you, mein Mann. I must thank you for our four, wonderful children. But you need to know that your hatred and stubborn German male pride has not destroyed them or me. And I want to tell you I no longer feel anything at all for you. You? You reaped what you sowed. But we? We will continue. Karla is happy and wise beyond her years. Johann is risking his life to oppose the hateful things you so admired. Marta—poor Marta—you almost ruined her. But she is so strong. She will grow up better without you. And

Gretel is so curious and precocious. You will not have the chance to hold her back. That is all. Good-bye, Karl. I am done with you." She turned away and walked back to the farm, swinging her empty rucksack like a young girl might as she walked home on the last day of school. She never looked back. Not even once.

***

Since they got started so early Friday morning, and since Mother Nature saw fit to be cooperative, Karla and Mr. Bielfeldt were able to get all the remaining crops on the Neuenschwander land harvested and into storage by Saturday night. By the time Karla came into the kitchen the daylight had long vanished into the western sky. She was full of corn dust and grit, and her hair was as sandy as a day at the beach. Susanna had made a nice casserole that she could heat up as needed. She also sliced open a loaf of wheat bread and opened a jar of pickled watermelon. "Why don't you have a bath and then we'll sit and eat a bite before bedtime," she said.

"Good idea," Karla said, scratching her head.

Rejuvenated by the bath, Karla emerged with her hair in wet ringlets that dripped onto her shoulders. She was covered in just a towel, drawn and secured in a tuck-knot under her armpit. Susanna looked at her, amused. "What?" Karla said, defensively. "Who's going to care if we sit here half naked and eat?" They both laughed. There was only one place to sit: Karl's chair. Karla chose to leave the chair for her mother. She sat on the floor, using the brick hearth of the fireplace as an ersatz table. Susanna sat in the chair and got a funny look on her face. "I know," Karla said. "I felt it, too, when I accidentally sat in his chair after Gretel and me first came back here."

"He really did exercise a lot of control over us all, didn't he?" Susanna said.

"He did, indeed."

"Well, not anymore," Susanna said, resolutely. She took a forkful of casserole, raised the fork toward her daughter and said, "Here's to sitting wherever we damn please!" Karla almost choked on her watermelon pickle. She had never once heard a curse word come out of her mother's mouth. She burst out laughing, barely keeping her food in her mouth, and rolled over onto her side in a full-out belly laugh. Susanna smiled and ate her casserole.

CHAPTER THIRTY-FIVE

THE first Christmas and New Year's Day in their new home was a bit surreal for Hans. He and Karla were truly still newlyweds, but for Hans it felt like the Neuenschwander family plus one. Hans was spending more and more time visiting his mother at the care home or working late. On one such evening, Karla was reading in bed, waiting for Hans to come home.

"So, you decided to come home to me after all?" Karla said as her husband crept into their bedroom.

"I was trying not to wake you," he said.

"Trying not to wake me or hoping to avoid me?" she said, her tone obviously challenging.

Hans knew she was right. He had, in fact, been trying to avoid facing the rift that was building between them. But he said, "No, Karla, I'm not avoiding you. I was just trying to be considerate. I had to grade some papers."

"It is still the Christmas break," Karla said. "What papers?"

Hans knew his excuse was an obvious dodge, so he sat down on the edge of the bed and stared a hole in the carpet between his feet. Karla waited for him to say something, but he offered nothing further. "Are you seeing someone else?" Karla asked, sadly. "Do you not love me anymore?"

Hans replied instantly. "No, there is no one else, and yes, I love you very much. It's just . . ."

"It's just what?" she said. "Talk to me! What is bothering you so much that you stay away for hours? Gretel keeps asking, 'Where is Daddy?' And I keep telling her, 'Daddy is working,' and she says, 'I want Daddy!' What should I say to her?"

He sat there, unmoving, for several more minutes. Karla decided to wait him out. Finally, he said, "You know, I didn't sign up for all this."

"All what?" Karla said, sitting up straighter.

"I fell in love with a lovely young girl with a lovely voice. We would talk and spend quiet afternoons and evenings together. It was wonderful. But after what happened, I was suddenly the father of a three-year-old girl. And that was fine. I loved the idea of being a daddy to Gretel. But then came the trial, and now Marta is here. And then your mother. And who am I now? I am not Hans Schutte any longer. I feel like a stranger in my own home. I am . . ." he paused. "Well, I am not sure who I am. Or who we are."

His words took Karla by complete surprise. She thought to answer right away that he was her husband and to reassure him that she needed him. All the things that were right and easy to say in response. But she instead said, "I had no idea. I don't know what to say."

"I don't know what to say either, or what to do about it," he said. "I know none of this is anyone's fault, except your father's. But I certainly don't blame you. You have done the best you could to deal with an impossible situation. I admire your strength. I just sort of feel lost in the process, I guess."

Karla swung her legs around to sit on the side of the bed beside her husband. She held onto his arm with both of her hands and laid her head over onto his shoulder. He didn't respond at all. She picked up his arm and put it over her shoulders, snuggling into the side of his chest. "I still like this position, she said with a smile. It's still a good fit."

He stayed in that position for a minute or so before he said, "Maybe we should talk more tomorrow. I am so tired." He stood up and moved to his side of the bed, disrobed, donned his pajamas, and lay down on his side, facing the other direction. He turned out the lamp beside the bed and said, "Good-night, Karla."

Karla turned off her lamp and returned to her bed, near tears. Her mind began to race through everything that happened in the past year. Her exciting, secret engagement. Her father's vicious assault on her mother and his death. Marta taken away. Her mother withdrawing. Trying to run the farm and care for Gretel on her own. Then the quick marriage and trying to make things as normal as possible for Gretel. Then the trial, Marta coming home, the farm sale, moving to Reading, and her mother recovering and moving in with them. It was like a whirlwind! *I did the best I could!*" she thought to herself. Quite suddenly, she sat up. She turned the lamp back on and turned to face her husband's back. "You did too sign up for this!" she said, more loudly than she wanted to.

Hans turned over to face Karla. He was not asleep, but he was a bit groggy. He squinted at the light and said, "What?"

"It was your idea to get married sooner and to adopt Gretel. When we didn't have enough fuel, it was you who suggested buying a place in Reading with the idea that my mother could move in with us. When the trial judge asked, you agreed to accept responsibility for Marta. You did sign up for this! But now that it has all happened, now it is no longer just a concept but a day-in, day-out reality, now that my mother is no longer a passive vegetable and Marta is not a distant fantasy and I am no longer a quiet little songbird, now you are feeling left out? Well, here we are, Professor Schutte. This is life! Real life! And if it is too much life for you, then just roll over on your side and feel sorry for yourself. But I am still here, and so are my mother and sister. And you are a father, whether you like it or not. Either accept your responsibility or don't. But this half here and half somewhere else stuff is going to end. You are either with me in this or you are not. Do you hear me?? So, sleep on that!" She turned roughly over, snapped off the lamp, and threw herself angrily into her pillow.

Neither of them got much sleep that night.

* * *

The radio was playing beside the kitchen table in the morning. The news centered on the war in Italy. The newscast reported a successful campaign had resulted in the Axis forces being driven back. The speculation was that the Allies would retake Rome in short order. Susanna was cooking bacon and eggs, and the aroma of coffee and breakfast permeated the house.

Karla stumbled to the table and flopped into her chair there, pouring herself a cup of coffee. She looked like she slept: rough. Without looking up from her stove, Susanna said, "It is unwise to let the sun set on your anger," waxing proverbial.

"Did you hear us?" Karla asked, alarmedly.

"Not your words," she lied, "but there was no mistaking your tone. You were very angry."

Relieved that her mother had not overheard the subject of their dispute, Karla responded, "Yes, I know, I know. But sometimes the setting of the sun is poorly timed."

"There is a letter from your brother on the desk," Susanna said. "It was delayed due to being forwarded from Shenandoah. I waited so we could read it together. Why don't you open it and read it for us?"

Karla quickly found and opened the letter and began to read aloud.

> *Dear Mother:*
>
> *I have been unable to write for some long while, but there is a bit of a break in the action now, so I want to send you a brief update while I can. I have been reassigned. It was an administrative order, based on my Ranger skills and my ability to speak both German and French. I am transferred to the First Special Force. We landed in Italy in December and have had some good success. Costly, but good. This is a group of the highest skilled soldiers. They have never lost an engagement, and I am very proud to be one of them. I can tell you we are in Italy, but I cannot say exactly where I am or where we may go from here.*
>
> *I hope your arm is now healed and you can write me yourself. Karla writes too sloppy. Ha! I can see her sticking her tongue out at me.*

Karla did, in fact, stick out her tongue at him that very moment. Susanna smiled.

> *I will write more when I am able. Love to all,*
> *Johnny (Johann)*

"They were just talking about Italy on the radio," Susanna said. "And Johnny was there. Our Johann! Right there! But so many casualties! They said over 700 of our soldiers were killed . . ." Karla looked up to see the smoke coming from the frypan and her mother gazing out the window. "Mutti," she said gently. "The bacon is burning."

"Ach! What am I doing?" Susanna lamented. She quickly removed the bacon and served up the eggs. Karla set the table and brought in a tray with toast, jam, butter, and a bowl of applesauce her mother had opened. They both sat down just as Marta came in holding Gretel by the hand. "Smells good!" she said, brightly, and she helped Gretel up into her chair.

"Where is Daddy?" Gretel said.

"Daddy is still sleeping," Karla said. "We will have to start without him."

"NO!" Gretel said. And she hopped down to run and get Hans. They began passing and serving the food, and a few minutes later Hans appeared in his bathrobe and slippers, his hair tousled, and his face indented with the wrinkles imposed by his pillow. He was being pulled forward by his left pinkie finger which was firmly in the grasp of little Gretel. "Here he is!" she said, a look of satisfaction on her face. "Now we can eat breakfast."

Karla did not look up. Susanna said, "Herr Schutte, this is your home. I believe it is your privilege to lead us in the table grace." Karla looked at her mother with a deep sense of appreciation.

Hans held out his hands on either side, and Karla took his right hand with her left. It was then she looked up to see him, looking sheepishly at her. She smiled and squeezed his hand. The grace was spoken. And the Schutte family breakfasted together.

Chapter Thirty-six

As the Spring of 1944 began to proclaim its green hopefulness, Karla was feeling increasingly restless, though not with life at home. She had adapted well enough to living in the larger city of Reading. She got Marta enrolled in the local junior high, and Gretel had begun kindergarten mid-year. This was never done, but when Karla brought Gretel in to be interviewed by the principle, Mr. Gustafson, he was so impressed with her that he agreed to start her in the second half of Miss Gutknecht's kindergarten class. Gretel would be five years old in the first week of February, which helped make his decision easier, but the real reason he acquiesced was that she walked into his office and read his calendar to him. It surely helped that Marta had been teaching her how to read, and "Grandma" had been reading books to her every single day. But beyond that, Gretel was simply and obviously precocious.

Nor was Karla troubled by her relationship with Hans, which had improved substantially as life settled into new patterns. He had even thanked her for "bringing me to my senses," as he put it, and Karla could see by his greatly increased time at home that he was beginning to enjoy his role as father and head of the household. He even talked about legally adopting Marta.

No, what was troubling Karla was the season itself. She was still, in her heart, a farmer. And for farmers, Spring is a season of busy preparation. Implements need to be re-tooled and sharpened, the tractor's clutch and breaks and chain and belt drives need to be inspected and secured, as do the hydraulics. The engine and transmission both require draining and re-oiling and greasing, too. Fields require plowing and fertilizing, seed must be purchased, and all this just to be ready to get those crops in the ground. Plus, there were the regular chores of tending to the livestock and the fencing and the various outbuildings. Always some winter damage to take care of. Always a gate needing repairing or a fence need-ing to be restrung or a post reset, or some dry-rotted wood to be replaced.

But not this season. Not for Karla. The energy of it was all wind-ing around inside her with nowhere to direct it. It helped that she and her mother worked together to plow up and prepare a huge garden spot. And Karla was able to purchase a hog and a few chickens for Marta to tend. All they lacked was a couple of milk cows and they could be largely self-sufficient.

However, beyond those few, small remnants of farming, Karla had little to do. One day her mother found her sitting out on the front porch, rocking and daydreaming. She brought out a couple glasses of sweet tea (Georgianna's recipe) and sat down beside her.

"Penny for your thoughts?" Susanna said.

"Oh, nothing. I just miss the farm work," Karla replied. "I really loved it. Papa never could understand that a girl could want to be a farm-er, but I really wanted to. Of course, when I told him, he just laughed at me." Karla paused, lost for a few moments in her memories. Susanna sat with her quietly. "You know," Karla continued, "they are all talking about 'victory gardens' now. We always had a huge garden and having this nice big garden does help. But for me, it feels not like victory, but defeat."

"I am so sorry for what he cost you. For what he cost all of us, yes, but especially what he cost you and Johann."

"If he comes through it alive, I think Johnny is going to be better than he would have been at home. He learned to stand up for himself and not back down. Papa would knock him down anytime he tried to do anything for himself. He couldn't fight Papa. But he can fight the Nazis." Karla paused thoughtfully and looked at her mother. "Do you think it's time we told him about what happened?"

Susanna thought for a moment. "I think your decision to keep it from him was the right one at the time, and I think it still is. No use clouding his mind with worry about something he can do absolutely nothing about. We can help him deal with it when he gets home."

"We do have to send him the change of address, though. How do we explain that?" Karla asked.

Again, Susanna thought quietly for a bit. "What if we tell him that I left Karl, and that you and Hans took me and the girls in. After all, that is the truth, in a way."

Karla sat up straight and said, "You know, you're right. We really would be telling the truth. It might even be a relief to him. I know he worries about you having to deal with Papa's temper. It's a good idea, Mother. We will tell him the truth. We will just leave out a few small details."

"I am going to write him right now," Susanna said.

❈ ❈ ❈

The spring semester of the school year flew by like a dream, and it was suddenly summertime. Marta made two good friends, both of whom loved to come out to the Schutte farmette, and Gretel had become the leader of her kindergarten class. Whatever game or lesson was being engaged in by the group, Gretel was organizing it. Sometimes Gretel even helped teach the children, especially in reading and in writing their alphabets. Miss Gutknecht told Karla that she had never seen such a bright and intuitive child in all her years of teaching.

Susanna and Karla busied themselves with tending their enormous garden, and in volunteering at the local USO gatherings where they helped to pack and ship care packages to local men who were serving in the war effort around the world.

Marta continued to teach her little sister and to read her more and more books. She also taught Gretel how to feed the chickens and gather eggs. Gretel would not go near the hog, though. She said, "He looks mean at me." If the truth be told, Marta was a little frightened of the hog, too; still, she fed and tended it, and it grew bigger and fatter by the week.

Hans finished the spring semester and was cleaning out his office when he got a call from the care home. His mother had died. There had been no warning signs, no illness detected, no complaint from her. The nurse's aide simply walked into her room and found her slumped in her chair. The administrator said, "The aide reported that your mother looked as though she were smiling."

Per her wishes, Hans arranged for her burial service with the Rabbi at Temple Rodef Shalom in Pittsburgh. Two days later, Karla went with Hans to attend the funeral, and she was pleased to see that Hannah's sisters, though frail, were both still alive and clear of mind. Burial was in the local Jewish cemetery, after which Hans and Karla headed straight back to Reading.

"Are you alright?" Karla asked, placing a supportive hand on Hans' arm.

"I'm okay," he said. "It was time. I have to say I did feel odd in a Jewish temple after having been raised Methodist all my life. But my mother wanted to honor her roots, and I wanted to honor her wishes."

"I'm sure she would have been pleased that you did," Karla said.

"But I draw the line at sitting shiva," he said. "I'm a dutiful son, but I'm a dutiful Gentile son. I don't own a yarmulke. Hell, I'm not even circumcised," he said with a chuckle.

"Yes, I know," Karla said with a wicked little smile. "But it still seems to work okay." Her wicked little smile was becoming extremely alluring as she began to squeeze his thigh and caress his leg while he drove.

"What is it about funerals that makes people feel like making love?" Karl said.

"Oh," she said with mock surprise, "you feel like making love? Whatever for?" She moved her hand a little further up his leg. She could see that he was getting very interested.

"Perhaps you misunderstood my meaning," she said.

"Oh, I'm pretty sure any living man would have no trouble understanding your meaning right about now," he said, swallowing and squirming a bit.

"No, not that," she said. "What I meant when I said it still seems to work."

It took a second, but soon her meaning came driving through the sweaty tunnel of his lust with its bright lights shining right at him. "You mean? Are you? Are we?"

Karla grinned and nodded her head rapidly up and down. "We are going to have a baby!"

Hans pulled the car off the road and threw open the door. But he forgot to set the brake. He jumped out, but then he saw the car was moving! He skipped on one leg, holding on to the top of the door and the top of the car, and he pulled himself back into his seat. He applied the parking brake, jumped out and ran around to open Karla's door. He pulled her right out of the car and off her feet in a huge embrace that might have encircled the entire globe. He kissed her long and deeply, pulling back only long enough to say, "I love you so much," before again covering her mouth with his own.

They drew some obvious attention because a state trooper pulled in behind them. The officer turned on his red lights, got out and said, "Everything all right here? I mean, we have motels and such, you know . . ."

Karla and Hans broke out laughing. "Officer, we're going to have a baby!" Hans said, grinning.

"If you keep carrying on like that, you probably will!" the officer said, "but we discourage doing such things along a public road," he added.

They broke out laughing again. "No," Karla said. "We are on our way back from Pittsburgh to Reading, and I just told him that we are having a baby. We didn't mean to make a scene. We are just so happy!"

"Oh!" the officer said. "Well, that's different! Let me be the first!" He reached out to shake Hans' hand. "Congratulations! I wish you all the best. I've got three of my own." Hans shook his hand and Karla reached up and gave him a little peck on the cheek. "Thank you, officer." She looked over at Hans and said, "Honey, we had better get going."

They got in the car and waved as the officer pulled off. Then Hans said, "Yup. I'm sure glad it still works." Karla laughed and slid over next to him. He put the car in gear, and they headed home.

CHAPTER THIRTY-SEVEN

THE radio was non-stop news in the first week of June. D-Day! The broadcasters gave stunning reports, many from reporters like Ernie Pyle who were there on the ground in Normandy on the west coast of France where the battle commenced. They called it the largest amphibious landing in the history of the world. Susanna and Karla kept the radio on throughout the day on the 6th and for the next several days following. The whole family sat together at lunch that Friday.

"What does the 'D' stand for?" Marta asked. No one knew. "Well, it must mean something!" she said, exasperated. "They keep talking about it and talking about it. Mostly what they talk about is how many soldiers are getting killed. Maybe 'D' stands for dead. And how stupid is that?" she said. Her irritation with the entire topic was eminently clear.

Susanna said, "Marta, maybe after lunch you can sit down and write a letter to Johann. You could even help Gretel to write a few words. What do you think?"

"Good idea, Mutti. Maybe we can call it 'WJ Day' for 'Writing Johann.' At least that would make some sense. May I be excused? I want to go 'WJ' in case he's not 'D.'"

"You are excused," Susanna responded. "Let me know when you are ready to help Gretel write something." Marta tromped away to her room.

"She will be quite the teenager, I think," Karla introjected.

"She does speak her mind," Hans said. "But that seems to be a family trait among Neuenschwander women. And, I might say, not an unwelcome one, at least to my mind."

"Careful, my dear, your words may come back to haunt you," Karla said playfully.

Susanna smiled and nodded. "My girls are going to be strong, independent women. Stronger than I was. And more clear-headed. I gave away too much of myself. I thought I had to. My daughters will know better. They already do."

❊❊❊

That afternoon, Hans and Karla were sitting outside on the covered front porch, avoiding the sun's heat, and enjoying a gentle, cooling breeze. Hans said, "tell me about Johann. I am full of admiration for him, and I haven't even met him."

"Johnny—he likes to be called Johnny—is a strong, intelligent, upright young man who was told by our father that he was worthless. Of course, he wanted Papa's respect. But for Johnny, the only way to get Papa's respect was to lose respect for himself."

"Why was your father so angry with Johann . . . er, I mean Johnny?"

"My father's whole world was his farm. He and his father built it up from nothing, and Papa kept it functioning and prosperous through the Depression and after. He could imagine nothing better than to pass this legacy on to his son. But Johnny had no interest in farming. In fact, he hated it and Papa knew it."

"What is Johnny interested in? What do you think he wants to do with his life?"

"That's a good question. He is still so young. But I know he has a strong affinity for languages. He has already studied both French and German and is capable in both. He reads all the time and on a great variety of subjects. I wonder if he might become a writer or a professor of literature or history. Who knows? What I do know is that he would get no support from our father for anything but staying on the farm and . . ." She stood up, bent over Hans, stuck her right index finger in his face and did her best to mimic her father's Germanic command voice, "Do Your DUTY!" She increased the volume with each word, and she apparently carried it off well enough, because Hans even cringed a bit. They both chuckled.

"So, there were fights between them?" Hans said.

"All the time," Karla said, wandering over to the porch railing. "The battles and accusations and yelling got worse year after year until the anger erupted into full-blown battles. Johnny even told me once that he feared Papa might kill him one day. And he may have been right."

"What drove your father to be the way he was? Do you know?"

"I don't know. But what I do know is that for him, honor and duty were his centering principles. He derived honor from doing his duty, and he raised his children—especially his only son—to adhere to those same principles. What he could not do, I think, is allow others to have their own sets of principles and interests and devotion to duty. For my father, it was his world, and anybody who respected that was included in that world. Everyone else, he simply rejected."

"Including his son?"

"Especially his son," Karla said. "I shudder to think what may have happened to Johnny had he remained here on the farm for much longer. In fact, I've wondered if, in a way, the war with Germany may have saved Johnny's life. At least in the short term. Going to fight Hitler and the Nazis gave Johnny a team to fight on and others to fight beside him. Alone, here at home against Papa, Johnny had no chance. But over there, he could prove himself and stand up tall. I just hope he doesn't end up finding his life only to lose it."

✳✳✳

Marta emerged an hour before supper time with her letter. "Mutti, would you read my letter to Johann?" Marta asked.

Susanna was in the kitchen, cooking supper. "It is your letter, Marta. No one needs to read it except Johann. But if you want me to read it, I will," Susanna answered. Marta said, "I do want you to read it. I'm afraid I might say the wrong things." Her face bore a sadness belonging to another, much later part of life. Susanna wiped her hands and took off her apron. She came in to sit down beside her daughter at the kitchen table. "Let me see," Susanna said.

> *Dear Johann.*
>
> *It is me, Marta. I am now almost thirteen years old. I am going to a different school because we live in Reading now. I have made some new friends and things are good here.*
>
> *I am worried about this awful war. So many soldiers dying. It makes me scared for you. I want you to come home. Sometimes when I close my eyes, I can't even remember your face! I have to go look at your picture on the mantel!*
>
> *Gretel is now five years old, and she just finished kindergarten already! She is like you! She loves to read and to*

have stories read to her. She is so, so smart! You have to come home to meet her!

    Please, please stay safe and come back home to us. I miss you.

    Love, Marta

Below Marta's signature, Gretel had used a crayon to write:

I am Gretel. Please come home and do not die.

Susanna fought back tears as she read Marta's letter. "I think it is a perfect letter, Marta," she said, pulling her over for a warm hug. "You should send it today."

CHAPTER THIRTY-EIGHT

THE summer moved inexorably forward with no new letters from Johnny. As each day passed, Susanna fought a growing sense of foreboding using the only weapons she had—work and routine. By mid-August, her considerable gardening skills were evident in a flourishing plot of ripening vegetables, all planted in straight rows with nary a weed in view. Her daughters all contributed as well and, being mostly free of his college duties for the summer, Hans helped, too. But the garden was most definitely Susanna's domain.

It was a Tuesday, August 15th, when it happened. Susanna was weeding in the garden. The day was muggy and warm, and Karla was tending a brush fire nearby. The sun, although obscured by thick clouds, was discernable moving toward the mid-afternoon. As she stirred the burning stalks, Karla called out, "Mother? We never took time out for lunch. It is getting late."

Hearing no reply, Karla looked up from her burning pile of weeds to see her mother down on her knees, leaning on the handle of her hoe. "Mother!" Karla rushed over to Susanna's side to find her appearing ashen, her face aghast, overwhelmed as if gripped by terror. The last time Karla had seen that look on her mother's face was when her father had her by the throat. "Mother, what's wrong? Are you alright?"

Susanna reached out for her daughter's help as she stood up. She turned and looked directly at Karla. "Something's wrong," she said.

* * *

Operation Dragoon commenced on August 14th. While the invasion at Normandy had been the main thrust of the Allied armies into France, attacking the Germans from the west, Operation Dragoon was mounted to retake the southern ports of Marseilles and Toulon, and sought to drive back the German forces from the south.

Johnny's unit—those who had survived after the battle at Anzio—were reassigned to the First Special Services unit. They were to initiate the operation by attacking German artillery outposts on the Hyères Islands of Port-Cros and Levant. This part of the mission went off with very little resistance, after which time the FSS was attached to the First Airborne Division and moved in to attack the mainland.

It was just 0745 on the 15th when Johnny boarded the plane which would carry him and his fellow parachutists to their drop site south of the French town of Le Muy. As they got seated along the periphery of the plane's cargo hold, Johnny looked across at a young man, obviously nervous, his feet bouncing his knees in a rapid rhythm. "First jump?" Johnny said.

The soldier looked up, seeing Johnny. "Naah, I've jumped dozens of times. But I always hate it."

"I don't mind it," Johnny said. "I sorta feel free up there. At least I feel like I have some control over where I land. I really hate those stupid glider planes."

"True," the man said, extending his hand. "I'm Henry." Johnny reached across to shake the man's hand. "I'm Johnny. Where were you before this?"

"We were in Rome. I got to see the Vatican. I'm Catholic, so . . ."

"Yeah, that's a pretty big deal."

"We also saw some truly gorgeous Italian girls," Henry said, grinning. "Made me think about the Vatican and needing to go to confession," he grinned. "Where were you?"

"Anzio. It was two months of pure hell. A lot of my unit got killed. But then they moved the rest of us over to something they called the First Special Force. We took over a couple of small islands yesterday. Which earned us the prize of going along on this little joy ride!" Both men laughed.

The plane began to taxi, so both men settled back and strapped in. "Good to meet you," Johnny said.

"You, too, Johnny," Henry replied. "Maybe we will get to drink some French wine this evening!" Johnny flashed him a grin and a thumbs up.

The plane ride was a brief twenty minutes, but the clouds were thick, making target zones almost impossible to identify. Their plane circled three times, drawing ineffective artillery fire as the Germans shot blindly into the low-hanging clouds. Finally, about 0820 came the green light and all the paratroopers stood and hooked their chute cords onto the steel cables above their heads. "Get ready!" the sergeant said. The door opened at the rear of the plane to reveal fluffy white clouds. "Go! Go! Go!" the sergeant shouted, each of his words matched by a man jumping out into the cloaking mist.

Johnny stepped out without any hesitation, anxious to land and get formed up with his compatriots. Below him, a 20-year-old German soldier named Helmut aimed his Mauser rifle into the sky and fired at the human targets as they emerged from the clouds, floating slowly down to the French countryside. He fixed his sights on Johnny and pulled the trigger.

The bullet ripped through Johnny's midsection, entering below his ribcage, and traveled upward through his left lung, somehow missing his right lung before exiting and shattering the radius of his right arm. He felt as though he had been kicked in the ribs, and he had trouble catching his breath. He looked down to see blood pouring from the wound in his left side. His right arm, formerly holding the guide strap of his parachute, now hung uselessly. He began to feel dizzy, like he had held his breath too long. He was spinning, round and round, and the ground was coming closer and closer.

Suddenly, Johnny's feet hit the ground heavily. He was so startled by the rifle round that he had not prepared himself to land, so his body weight forced itself right through his ankle joints, fracturing one and badly spraining the other. He lay there in a heap, now feeling every bit of the pain his initial shock had prevented. He could see other paratroopers descending all around. He could hear the gunfire. He instinctively tried to reach for his rifle, but his right arm was unusable. He tried to bring himself to a sitting position, but to no avail. He lay back on the ground, wheezing with the effort of every breath. *Am I going to die here?"* he thought.

Just then, he looked up into the clouds and saw a brightness, an opening as though the sun were breaking through. But he saw something else, too. *"Is that a woman?"* He shook his head and squeezed his eyes shut and open several times, trying to focus, and when he opened them, *"There she is again! What is she doing here? Is she flying? She has no chute!"*

Johnny lay there, mesmerized at the vision he was seeing. *"She's coming closer! She is smiling at me! Oh my God, she is so, so beautiful!*

What is that in her hand? Is it . . . yes! It's a sword! She's pointing it at me! No, no, don't!"

Helmut, a 20-year-old German soldier, stood looking down at Johnny the 20-year-old American soldier. He regarded him with curiosity. *"He looks just like me!"* he thought. He began to feel badly for having shot him. He even had the instinct to help him, maybe get him some medical attention. But the commanding voice of his Leutnant broke through his reverie. "Soldat! Was machst du da?" Helmut snapped to attention, clicking the heels of his boots and saluting. "Herr Leutnant!"

The older man regarded the young soldier with only a little pity which he slathered over with a load of harsh scorn. He looked down on Johnny, who was obviously mortally wounded. "Hast du diesen Mann geschoβen?" Helmut answered immediately, "Jawohl, Herr Leutnant!"

"Ausgezeichnet!" the officer said. "Worauf warst du dann noch? Beende es!" Helmut again responded, smartly, "Jahwohl, Herr Leutnant!" He stepped forward, fixed his bayonet, and pointed it at the base of Johnny's throat.

Johnny's eyes seemed to be fixed on those of his enemy, but they were instead looking through him, beyond him, at the beautiful angel hovering above and around them. She wore a breastplate of burnished bronze, and her golden-blonde hair flowed lavishly to frame her strong visage. Her eyes were so deeply blue that Johnny could hardly help falling instantly in love with her. She smiled the softest smile, and she knelt in mid-air, touching Johnny's shoulder with the tip of her sword.

Helmut stood there for what seemed like an eternity, poised to run his opponent through. Every muscle in his body was saying, "kill him," but every bit of his conscience and his Evangelical upbringing told him it would be wrong to do so.

"Ach! Du Schwächling, du!" the officer snarled in disgust. He stepped behind young Helmut and pushed down hard on the butt of his Mauser, lancing Johnny's throat with a violent, downward push of the bayonet. Johnny jerked violently once and went limp. The Leutnant then grabbed the rifle from young Helmut's hands, spinning him around as he did so, and he thrust the bayonet into the young soldier's abdomen, holding him up with the weapon and watching the life drain out of him. Then he withdrew the weapon and tossed Helmut's dead body down on top of Johnny's dead body, saying, "Jetzt kannst du dich mit deinen schwulen Junge hinlegen!" And he drove the bayonet through both the young men so that the rifle stood over them like a grave harbinger. Then he spat on them and marched off.

✻✻✻

Karla walked back to the house with her mother, staying close to her side the whole way. "Maybe you have had a bit too much sun today and not enough food and water," Karla suggested. Susanna didn't respond.

When they got back to the house, Karla helped Susanna to sit at the kitchen table and poured them both a glass of sweet tea. She sliced some rye bread and some bierkäse and brought them to the table. "Let's have a little mid-afternoon snack, shall we?" she said.

Susanna drank the tea and ate a little of the cheese. The look on her face had not changed. Karla said, "What is it mother? What is wrong?"

Susanna stared out the window to the yard and to the woods beyond. She said, "I don't know what it is, but something is just terribly, terribly wrong. I am going to lay down for a bit." With that, she got up and headed to her bedroom. She stopped and turned back to say, "Don't worry about me. I'm okay. It's something else." And she headed off to her room.

✻✻✻

The telegram came ten days later. "From the Sec'ty of Defense to Karl Neuenschwander family. I regret to inform you that your son, Johann Neuenschwander, was killed in action in Le Muy, France on 15 August 1944. I offer my sincere condolences on your loss."

CHAPTER THIRTY-NINE

DUE to the intensity of the war effort, it was simply impossible to bring Johnny's body back for burial. Susanna decided to ask the Pfarrer to hold a memorial service for him, and she arranged to have a gravestone erected to commemorate his life and to honor his sacrifice.

The memorial service was held in mid-October, and virtually everyone in or near Schuylkill County attended. Susanna and her daughters sat up front in the church, and there was not one unoccupied seat. The Pfarrer gave a moving eulogy, quoting the prophet Isaiah's vision of the peaceable kingdom and Jesus' words about the greatest love being willingness to lay down one's life for one's friends. As there was no body to carry out to the cemetery, it was arranged to deliver the gravestone and to haul it to the gravesite at what would have been the point of interment. The stone contained a flag emblem indicating that Johnny had died in the service of his country. On the stone these words were inscribed:

Johnny Neuenschwander
Born in Shenandoah, Pennsylvania
July 17, 1924
Died in LeMuy, France
August 15th, 1944
He gave his life fighting cruelty

A cadre of WWI veterans formed a rifle brigade and offered a 21-gun salute. They carefully folded a large flag of the United States and offered it to Susanna, followed by a solemn salute. After the final prayers were offered, all began to file out. But the honor guard of veterans remained at attention, saluting the place where Johnny was honored. And standing there with them, saluting the brother she never knew, was four-year-old Gretel.

SECTION III

GRETEL'S STORY

2019

CHAPTER FORTY

IT was the tenth day of August, and the Avenue Gabriel was lush and steamy with the heat of the French summer. The full, green trees lining the grounds of the U.S. Embassy provided shade but no relief from the sauna-like conditions imposed by a 26°C dewpoint. Graduate student Cecilia Drexel pulled a hankie from her backpack and wiped the sweat beads from her forehead as she arrived at the gate.

"Bon jour," she said to the Marine who guarded the entrance.

"Ma'am. What is your business at the embassy today?" he asked.

"I am here for an appointment with Ambassador Eberhart."

"I need to see your passport and identification," he said, matter-of-factly. Cecilia tossed aside a sweaty strand of unruly, brown hair and dug out the necessary papers. The guard examined her identification, looking back and forth between her and her ID photo.

"I need to search your belongings and your person," he said. She handed over her backpack and waited while he examined its contents. "Raise your arms please, remove your footwear, and stand spread-eagle, facing me," he said, and she stepped out of her worn leather flats and spread out. He ran a metal detection wand closely up and down, in and out. "I am sorry for being intrusive, but I must pat you down. If you prefer, I can call for a female Marine." Cecilia said, "No matter. It's the way of the world now, I guess."

"Yes, ma'am," the young man replied. "Please turn away from me and remain in a spread-eagle position." Cecilia complied with his direction. He felt all around her armpits, her breasts and the edges of her brassiere, her sides, the waistband of her slacks, and down the inseams of her legs. He thoroughly examined her shoes before returning them. "You can put these back on now," he said, "and again, I'm sorry for the intrusion. But as you said, it is the way of the world right now." He stepped over to a small guardhouse and pulled out his daily log. "What time is your appointment with the Ambassador," he asked.

"It is scheduled for 2pm," she said. "I am a bit early."

"No problem, ma'am," he said, softening a bit now that he had established her identity and reason for being there. He spoke briefly into a shoulder-mounted mic and received a response. "The Ambassador's aide will be here shortly to escort you." He pointed to a stone bench in the nearby shade, "You may sit here while you wait if you wish."

Cecelia sat down, again pulling out her hankie to clear the moisture from her forehead and eyes. "Is it always this hot here?" she asked the guard. "You must be very uncomfortable in that uniform."

"It has been unusually warm," he said. "You get used to it."

A thin, obsequious-looking young man wearing a tailored suit soon appeared at the gate. "Miss Drexel?"

She looked up. The suit looked maybe one size too large for him. She stood and said, "Cecelia is fine. Yes?"

"Thank you, Cecelia. I am Michel Bertrand, aide to Ambassador Eberhard." His thick, French accent was apparent. "Welcome to the American Embassy," he said. "If you would please follow me."

They walked through the gate and entered through two enormous iron doors into the interior of the impressively columned edifice which housed the Ambassador's offices. It was hard not to be impressed by the structure itself. Cecelia noticed feeling a sense of safety and strength oozing from every direction, beginning with the statue of Benjamin Franklin in the entry garden.

Her guide began reeling off what seemed to be a canned travelogue. "You will find that history is displayed everywhere you look. Here is the famous "witch" mirror in the foyer, dating back to the American Revolution, so nicknamed because of the distorted image its convex surface produces. And these two marble columns in the entryway display sculptures of two great warriors of your country's revolution, General George Washington and the Frenchman Marquis de LaFayette. Both busts were created by Bartholdy, who designed the Statue of Liberty. The large portraits on this wall are of the Comte de Rochambeau and the Marquis de Lafayette."

Looking up, Cecelia could see a grand stairway flanked by ornate balustrades leading to the second floor. "As you can see," the aide's travelogue continued, "hanging on the walls of the staircase are two oil paintings by Gilbert Stuart, the larger is of course George Washington and the lesser is James Monroe, who was the first minister to France from the new republic. You may have also noticed the image of the American eagle, which can be seen in the woodwork, in brass finials, in paintings and sculptures, and in the Great Seal of the U.S.A. everywhere." Cecelia sensed a bit of derisiveness in the way he emphasized the word, 'everywhere'.

They passed under the staircase to a beautiful atrium area, gracefully appointed with eight magnificent chandeliers. "Here is the Wallace library," the aide motioned, which contains many historical volumes from both our countries dating back to Revolutionary times." He motioned for Cecelia to be seated, and he said, "I will inform the Ambassador of your arrival."

Cecelia sat and considered her surroundings. *"The things that have gone on in this place!"* she thought to herself. She considered the intrinsic link between the US and its oldest ally, and the immense role that link had played in world events. *"Two world wars, the interaction in French Indochina, the partnership in dealing with terrorism . . ."* Her musings were interrupted by the return of her guide. "Cecelia, the Ambassador will see you now."

Cecelia was led into a beautifully appointed office of grand dimensions, with a large, antique-looking desk at one end. Behind the desk was a wall of windows looking out across the Place de la Concorde with its many statues and fountains stretching out beyond the Champs Elysees. Framed by this glorious view of Paris stood the person Cecelia had been waiting to meet, the U.S. Ambassador to France. "Ms. Drexel, please come in and make yourself at home. This is your home, in true terms; you are standing on American soil here. But I suppose you know that."

"Madame Ambassador, I am so very glad to finally meet you. Thank you for agreeing to meet with me and for considering my proposal. And please, call me Cecelia."

The Ambassador moved from behind her desk and joined her visitor in a seating area across the room. "It is my namesake you should thank. She is the one who set this up." She took Cecelia's hand and grasped it warmly before she sank into a sumptuous brown leather chair and crossed her legs. "And you, Cecelia, if you truly intend to write my grandmother's life's story for your dissertation, you had better call me Gretel."

Chapter Forty-one

THE Neuenschwander farmstead was ripe with burgeoning crops, as it had been at this time of year for over 100 years. The weather had been especially propitious this year, so the nearly 10-foot-high corn on either side of the end drive created the effect of a tunnel when you drove in.

The lone occupant of the old farmhouse, Senator Gretel Schutte, was hanging out laundry on the line in the warm August breeze, a blue and white checkered kerchief tied around her head to hold her gray, wiry hair together. She had purchased the farm along with what had been the Bielefeldt land when it came available twenty years hence, and she now rented out the crop land and used the house as a retreat whenever the Senate was not in session.

"Senator, would you like some help with that?" It was her new Secret Service detail, Patrick "Truck" Agee, whom she surmised was bored out of his mind. His black Yukon was parked at the edge of the yard, and he alternately sat in it to soak up some a/c and got up to wander around the farmyard.

"Who did you piss off to get this terrible duty assigned to you?" she said. "Seems unfair for your first assignment to be babysitting an old lady. Do you know how to hang laundry on a line? Have you ever actually done such a thing in your young life?"

"Yes, ma'am," he said, walking over to join her. "My grandmother used to hang out the wash in Alabama all the time. 'Most every day, I guess."

"Well, aren't you something!" she said. "Of course, you might run into a pair of old lady's underwear," she grinned.

Agent Agee grinned and looked toward the ground, embarrassed. "Why, I declare, I did not know that a Black man could blush!" Gretel said, teasingly.

"No, ma'am . . . I mean, yes, ma'am," he stammered. He reached down into the woven wicker laundry basket—the very same one Gretel's mother used over 70 years ago—and carefully avoiding anything remotely silky, he picked up a pair of Capri pants and pinned them to the line.

"Senator, how come you do this? You could have someone do all this sort of thing for you. I expect every single Senator on the Hill hires out their laundry or just buys more clothes. Why not you?"

"Well, Patrick, to begin with, you have no real information about what my 99 colleagues in Washington do with their clothing. What you are doing is presuming. And making presumptions is the beginning of all sorts of misery among us humans because we all do it, and many times we presume wrongly, and then we take action or make a judgment based on what we don't know but think we do. Sorry, but I'm an old professor and I can never resist the opportunity to teach." In truth, she really wasn't the least bit sorry. She dearly missed teaching, and she especially relished the opportunity to pass on some tidbit of wisdom to a young, fertile mind.

"But to answer your question," she continued, "the reason I do this is that it grounds me. I was born here. My family farmed this land. The foundation of what unfolded as my life over the next 79 years is right here in this house and on this land. And amidst all the busy, angry, manipulative bullshit in which I am constantly immersed in Washington, I can get kind of . . ." she searched for a word to express how it felt, ". . . asthmatic. Yes, that's the word. I sometimes feel like I'm suffocating. So, I come here to recall my history, to sort of breathe it all in again. Does that make any sense to you?"

"It does for a fact, ma'am," he said, pinning up a blouse by its tails.

"Your grandma really did teach you how to hang out the wash!" Gretel said. "I am impressed!"

The sound of a car engine brought Agent Agee to alert. He checked his watch. "Seventeen fifty," he said. "Right on time."

"Your replacement, I presume," Gretel said.

"Yes, ma'am. I will be back in the morning. Have a good evening, Senator."

"Thank you, Patrick," she said. "And thank you for your excellent assistance with my laundry. And for avoiding my underwear." She smiled, hoping to elicit another embarrassed blush. He turned quickly toward his vehicle so she couldn't see it, but she grinned broadly because she knew that blush was there.

Patrick met briefly with his replacement, Agent Ashleigh Janco. Ashleigh waved to Gretel, "Good evening, Senator. Enjoying this beautiful summer day, I see." Gretel waved back. The agents finished their confab and Patrick departed through the corn tunnel.

***

Gretel woke at first light as usual. She washed her face, donned a robe, and headed out to the kitchen. There she found Agent Janco scrolling through her phone at the table with a cup of coffee. "Good morning, Senator. How did you sleep?"

"Like the proverbial rock," Gretel responded. "And you? That guest bed mattress still in good shape?"

"Yes, indeed. I got my usual six hours."

"You know, you really should get more sleep than that, Ashleigh. You will wear yourself out."

"Naah, I'm good. You know, Senator, the word is that some grad student is going to write your biography. That true?"

"Yes, poor Cecelia. I fear she will become quickly bored. But I guess the Women's Studies crowd finds me inspiring. Cecelia is pursuing her doctorate at Princeton, where I taught for 25 years before running for office. Her dissertation advisor is my old friend and colleague, Letitia Morris; I know it was Letitia who put her onto this project. It all seems a bit overblown to me, but I suppose if what I've been able to accomplish can inspire young women to make a difference somehow, then it will be worth doing."

"Have you met with her yet?"

"Yes, we spent a couple of hours back in Washington sort of setting up the basics. You know, feeling each other out, that sort of thing. I decided I can trust her. Of course, it helped that I had her thoroughly vetted." Gretel smiled, slyly. "Right now, she is in Paris meeting with my granddaughter."

"Ambassador Eberhart."

"Précisement! You are always well informed, aren't you, Ashleigh?"

"The Service makes sure of it, Senator."

"Well, then, I suppose you already know this, but the plan is for me to fly out the day after tomorrow to meet them in Paris. I am to give a lecture on the 12th at the Sorbonne, and then we will get to spend some time together the next day on the train down to Draguignan to commemorate the 75th anniversary of the liberation of southern France."

"I did know you were planning to go to Paris. I didn't know the reason. And I thought the liberation of France came from the D-Day invasion at Normandy."

"The initial push happened on the beaches at Normandy in June of 1944. But Operation Dragoon began on August 14th, when they recaptured the southern ports of Marseilles and Toulon and drove back the German forces northward up the Rhone valley. As it happens, my older brother, Johann, was killed on the second day of the battle there." She was back in her teacher mode and enjoying it.

"I guess you learn something new . . ."

"Whenever you ask good questions," Gretel finished her sentence for her. "Which might be every day, if you are diligent in your search," she said, ever the sage.

The sound of Patrick's vehicle approaching on the gravel road made Ashleigh look down at her watch. "Hmmm. 0653. He's three minutes late. I will have to give him a ration of sh . . ." She interrupted herself out of respect for her elders. "I'll have to razz him about it."

"Good idea," Gretel said. "Like most men, he needs a woman to give him some shit now and then," she said, grinning.

Ashleigh laughed out loud. "Yes, ma'am," she replied, "that he does. I will see you this evening at the usual time." She got up and headed out to her car.

Gretel washed up, ate a bit of breakfast, and headed outside, where she spent the best part of the day digging and weeding in her mother's garden.

CHAPTER FORTY-TWO

THE flight to Orly was smooth. Gretel kept awake most of the previous night and day so she could sleep through almost all the journey, as the arrival was scheduled for 8am. Her granddaughter had arranged for diplomatic passage, so Gretel needed to do nothing but walk to the limousine and head over to the Hôtel de Crillon across the street from the embassy.

After checking in and being escorted to her suite, Gretel phoned her granddaughter.

"I see the plane didn't crash. Which makes me happy," Gretel the younger said. "But then again, it wouldn't dare. How are you feeling?"

"I am fine. I'm used to these European jaunts. I slept nearly all the way here. Have you met with Cecelia?"

"I did, a couple days ago. Nice person. She seems very solicitous and eager."

"Where is she staying, at the Crillon?"

"No, I found her a room at Le Faubourg just up the block. One must cut back where one can. When Cecelia gets to be a ranking Senator, she can stay at the Crillon." Sen. Schutte smiled, "Yes, yes. I get it. Are all the other arrangements made?"

"I think so. Your transport to the lecture hall is scheduled for 2pm on the 12th. I was told the University is hosting a reception after your lecture and they will provide you transportation to the hotel afterward. We will then head down by train to Draguignan on the 13th. Sound okay?"

"It sounds perfect. Thank you, granddaughter."

"You are most welcome, Grandmother. Do you feel up to a nice dinner tonight on me? I arranged a table for three at 7:30 at Sur Mesure."

"Danielle will not be joining us?" Danielle, Gretel's partner, worked as a food critic and writer for *Elle à Table*.

"She is in Hong Kong on business, so no. And I didn't think to ask if you still have your security detail."

"I do. He won't be joining us, but I do have to keep him appraised of my schedule. It is a serious aggravation, but I guess it doesn't pay to piss off the lunatic fringe."

"Yeah, the knuckle draggers don't much like a woman being Chair of the U.S. Senate Foreign Relations Committee. And they really don't like it when a woman calls out their oppressive views against women on the world stage. But hey, your World Women's Initiative got you a Nobel prize, so what's a little security detail, all things considered?"

She laughed, and so did the Senator, but the younger laugh was hiding no small amount of ongoing concern. The folder of death threats directed at her grandmother in the days since she won the Nobel prize made the reality of the situation all too clear.

"So, I guess I will see you and my young admirer at the restaurant. I will get there around 7:00 for drinks. Oh, and thanks for the diplomatic arrangements. You are a peach. Au revoir."

"Bye, Grandma."

✻✻✻

Senator Schutte and her security detail arrived on schedule at the very bright and modern Sur Mesure par Thierry Marx just after 7pm. Gretel would have preferred the six-block walk, but her detail—whom she referred to in his absence as her 'appendage', and whose name was Kirk—insisted on the relative safety of a cab.

Entering the Sur Mesure was like taking a step back one season. Outside, the summer was hot and evident in the sweaty people all moving quickly to get to the next cool place. But inside the restaurant were the vibrant colors of Spring, splashed among the very chic and modern furnishings, and with natural light seeming to come from everywhere and nowhere. Everything about the environment invited guests to pause, to take a deep breath, and to relax. Gretel immediately loved the place, and she took a seat at the bar and ordered an aperitif.

The Maître d' approached and introduced himself. He had been told to expect the Ambassador and her guest, a U.S. Senator and Nobel Prize laureate, so he hastened to ingratiate himself and express his honor at having Gretel in his establishment. He introduced her to the bar attendant, as well, and told him gregariously that "Nobel laureates do not pay for their drinks here."

Gretel thanked the man profusely, although she had never felt comfortable with the special treatment she increasingly received as the years and her accolades piled up. So, she was grateful when she spied Cecelia entering the restaurant. "Pardon," she said, "my friend has arrived." The unctuous man stepped aside and motioned Cecelia over to join Gretel. "I bid you both welcome, and bon Appetit." He bowed in Continental fashion and even backed away a couple of steps before turning to depart.

"I am glad to see you again, Cecelia. I thought that maître d' might ooze French servility all over me. How has your stay been so far? First time in gay Paris?"

"Good evening, Senator," Cecelia extended her hand. "It has been wonderful; I felt very comfortable with your granddaughter. And this is my second time in Paris," she responded, sitting beside her, "but I do not recall it being this hot before. My goodness! It feels like New Orleans! Anyway, thank you so much for arranging this time to spend with me. I plan to make good use of it for both our sakes." She ordered a pleasant Chablis.

Presently, the two were joined by the younger Gretel, and the three went at once to their table, which was set into a private alcove adjacent to the main dining area. They ordered a round of drinks and a tray of cheese and bread, followed by a fabulous set of entrees, which were shared all around. Wine was paired for each course and setting, and by the time the meal was over the three women were prepared for about anything. They decided to retire to the lounge for after dinner drinks.

"So . . . may I ask, Gretel how was it that you came to be named after your grandmother?"

"Well, it was a matter of payback, or so I am told. My father, Grandma's son Norman, was named after his own father, Norman Eberhart. Grandpa Norman was killed in an accident before my father was even born, so Grandma named him after his father. A sort of memorial, I imagine." Gretel the elder smiled and nodded. "However," the Ambassador continued, "my father grew up hating his name. He got taunted. They called him 'Norman Bates,' after the character in 'Psycho'.

"So, when my father and mother married and got pregnant with me, Norman decided to punish his mother by naming his daughter after her. My mother is from France, so for her the idea of her daughter carrying on the name of a grandmother was apropos, no?"

Again, the Senator nodded. "Précis," she said. "Actually, as it happens, I also was named after my birth father's mother."

"Your birth father?" Cecelia asked. Gretel also looked up, confused. "Grandma, I thought Hans Schutte was your father."

"Well, I did not mean to let that slip," she said to her granddaughter, "but since I've let the cat out of the bag, that is why I wanted to include you in this interview. There are things you have not been told about my family history, and it is time that you knew the truth."

Intrigued, Cecelia began to get out her notepad, but Gretel interrupted her. "No, no. There will be plenty of time for that, but not tonight. Right now, let us enjoy our drinks and this lovely place and this salubrious company, and we will live to fight another day." She raised her glass, "À la tienne!" And all responded in kind.

All slept well that night.

Chapter Forty-three

At the Café Rhisa, a young man named Ernst Mahler ordered a double espresso with an extra shot and booted up his laptop. Ernst was from Hanover, and he had made this trip to Paris for one purpose: to kill Gretel Schutte. Ernst was a member of a shadow group of neo-Nazis, most of them skinheads like himself, and all of whom centered themselves around hating all things non-Aryan and all concepts foreign to their goal of restoring power to Aryan men throughout Europe and the world. The empowerment and advancement of women was high on the list of those issues which most inflamed Ernst and his compatriots. And when it was announced that the Nobel Laureate and Senator from the U.S. would lecture at the Paris Sorbonne University, Ernst drew a target on her. He told his friends back home, "I will make it my mission to make an example of this cocky Schweinhund."

Ernst's browser was set to autoload the web page of the group with which he claimed affiliation, Der Wächter (The Guardians). He read through the list of headlines, all gleaned from a variety of liberal blogs and news agencies, mostly from the EU and the U.S., and all chronicling society's preference for promoting everything they hated. One article especially drew his attention: 'International Women's Advocate Gretel Schutte to Lecture at the Sorbonne Aug. 12th'. "There she is," he said. "That's my girl." He clicked on the link to reveal the entire article, including a stock picture of Senator Schutte. Ernst formed his tattooed right hand into a makeshift handgun and pointed it at the photo. He pulled his imaginary trigger and reveled in the thought of her imaginary brains spilt out all over her fancy lectern.

Suddenly, Ernst realized he was being observed. He turned quickly to see a young boy of perhaps nine or ten years of age standing directly behind him. He growled, "Allez-vous en!"

The boy said, "Porquoi veux-tu lui tirer dessus? Est-elle une mauvaise personne?" He was not being rude, he just wanted to know why the man pretended to shoot the lady. Just then, the boy's mother came up and urged him away. "Ne derange pas l'homme, Jojo. Je suis désolé, monsieur." Something in his eyes frightened her, so she grabbed her son's hand and quickly exited.

Ernst stood and closed his laptop. *"Damned liberals! he thought to himself. "That Jojo needs a good cuff in the ear! But he sure won't get it from that fawning little bitch of a mother."* He walked out of the café and immediately became indiscernible amongst all the other hot, sweaty, and irritable people heading in every direction.

❋ ❋ ❋

Ambassador Eberhart blocked off her calendar for August 11th, and she and Cecelia arranged to meet the Senator at her hotel for breakfast at 8am. After enjoying croissants and jam along with freshly squeezed orange juice and a pressed coffee, they relocated to Gretel's spacious suite for some privacy.

After all were settled, Gretel began. "I know I left you both sort of hanging last evening, which wasn't fair. I'm afraid my wine got the best of me, and I let that phrase 'birth father' slip, which I did not mean to do. But we were all so enjoying the evening and I didn't want to introject any serious talk. So here we are, and now I will tell you what I have been told about my family history."

Cecelia pulled out a tape recorder. "Do you mind?" she asked. Gretel shook her head, "No, that's fine." Cecelia placed the device amidst them.

"I did not know of the truth of my birth until I was in college," Gretel said. "As far as I knew, my parents were Karla and Hans Schutte, and we lived with my grandmother, Susanna and my sister, Marta in Reading, Pennsylvania. Karla had a beautiful singing voice, and Hans, who was a professor of music at Albright College, had been her voice teacher. We had a happy, untroubled life together on what they would now call a farmette outside Reading.

"When I grew up, I went away to Lehigh for undergrad. I was in my sophomore year when I got a call to come home because my grandma Susanna was gravely ill. I hurried home and I was able to spend some time with her in the several days before she died. It was during that time when I found myself on the receiving end of the message that I am about to provide to you." The younger women both sat forward a bit in their chairs.

"The long and the short of it is that Susanna was not my grandmother. She was in fact my mother. My birth parents were Karl and Susanna Neuenschwander, and I was born in Shenandoah, Pennsylvania and lived the first years of my life on the farm I now own a couple of miles outside of town. I had been a rather surprising late addition to the Neuenschwander family, having been born ten years after my sister, Marta, sixteen years after my brother Johann, and seventeen years after my sister, Karla."

"Karla was your sister?" the Ambassador asked, amazed. "Why? I mean, why did this happen? Why didn't they tell you? How could Susanna live with you all those years and . . ."

"There is more to tell," the elder Gretel interrupted. "Let me continue." The Ambassador settled back in her chair. Cecelia was sensing the importance of what she had happened into, and she had begun writing furiously in her notebook; the tape be damned.

"My birth father, Karl Neuenschwander was a first-generation German American, and very proud of his German heritage. He was not alone in this. Many German Americans were split on their support for Hitler and for the Allies. My father even had relatives back in the old country who worked under Himmler in the Nazi party. It was a different time.

"The other thing my father was, was a bully. He browbeat everyone in his family, especially his only son, Johann. When Johann went off to fight the Nazis, you can imagine how his father reacted. Things came to a head over some letter that came for my father from Germany that my mother hid from him. He attacked my mother, fractured her jaw, and nearly choked her to death. Karla came in and tried to intervene and he threw her off so violently she was concussed.

"While he was choking my mother, my older sister Marta, who was only twelve at the time, took a carving knife from the kitchen and slit his throat. He died. My mother lived. When Karla came to, she saw what happened, and she found Marta in the bedroom, holding me and rocking in mother's rocking chair."

"Wow," Gretel the younger said. "Holy moly. This is going to take a bit of getting used to."

"I understand," Gretel said. "It sort of knocked me for a loop, too, at first."

Cecelia, who had been quiet to this point, asked, "What happened next?"

The Senator smiled. *"Atta girl. Get on with it. I like this kid,"* she thought to herself. "They sent Marta away for evaluation at the State Hospital. My mother required surgery and an extended period of convalescence, after which she became unable to function for a time. Karla and Hans were planning to be married, so they eloped. Hans and Karla adopted me, and I became Gretel Schutte. There was a murder trial in which Marta was acquitted, and she moved in with us in Reading. Hans and Karla adopted Marta, too. After my mother got better, she moved in with us, Karla sold the farm and our life in Reading as the Schutte family began.

"The way my two mothers explained it to me, they thought it best to not confuse me with the awful truth. 'If Susanna is my mother, where is my papa?' That sort of thing. And I adored Hans. He has always been my father. So, they simply kept the truth from me in favor of employing a kind and loving pretense. After I had a chance to think about it, I came to appreciate Susanna's deep love for me even more. It couldn't have been easy for her to remain in the background. Nor was it easy for Karla to hear me calling her 'Mommy' while her own mother—and mine—was there the whole time. But she never treated me any differently than her own son, my brother Johnny. Yes, Karla and Hans had a son whom they named after my brother, who liked to be called Johnny instead of his given name of Johann. Johnny was killed at Le Muy, not far from the burial site where we will be going for the commemoration on the 14th.

"When you sum it all up, the story of my family history could be called tragic. But I prefer to see it as a triumph of love over hate and of good over evil. I have learned much from these two remarkable women who raised me, and even from my sister Marta, who is now 89 years old and in an assisted living situation in Reading. I have learned that women are strong. I have learned that women will do what is necessary. And I have learned what the definition of love really is. I would never have moved into women's studies at all, and I certainly would never have achieved the things I have achieved without the actions of these three women in my life. I owe them everything."

For a few moments, no one said a word. Cecelia reached over to shut off the tape recorder, and she said, "Holy shit. That is quite an amazing story, Senator. You're okay with all that personal history becoming public knowledge?"

"That is the true story of my life. If the whole story is going to do any good, it must begin with the truth, mustn't it?" Cecelia slowly nodded her agreement, "I suppose so."

The Ambassador was still sitting in shocked silence. "Granddaughter," Gretel said, waiting for her namesake to make eye contact with her. When she did, it was evident that her eyes were moist. Gretel took her hand and looked her lovingly in the eyes. "Every family has secrets in the closet. I think it is high time this particular closet is cleaned out. Besides, like I said, it is a story of triumph. Love wins. Good wins. And it is all due to the strength of those women who came before us. The truth, my dear girl, is that you are made of sterner stuff than you ever imagined. Let that be the frame within which you display this family picture on your internal wall. And display it proudly."

The younger Gretel softened her visage and reached out to grasp her grandmother's hand with both of hers. "I know you are right. Like I said, I just need some time to get used to it. I do thank you for telling me. I'm certainly glad I didn't learn it in some trashy exposé." She looked over at Cecelia with mock regret, "Oh, I mean a biography. Even an excellently written biography." They both laughed.

Cecelia said, "What would be so bad about that? I'd spell your name right and everything." The laughter increased, relieving the intensity in the room like a pressure valve. All agreed it was time for a break to let this all sink in.

The ambassador said to Cecelia, "Since the lecture is at 7pm tomorrow, let's get a bite to eat beforehand. I'll pick someplace fun. I'll pick you up in the lobby at 4pm." Cecelia agreed, and they both left.

Senator Gretel Schutte, now alone with her thoughts after all that had transpired, suddenly broke down and cried. She had no intuition of it. She was in fact stunned by the sudden emotion, and not a little irritated by it. She had never been comfortable with strong emotion. In fact, she was trying to remember the last time she cried. *Was it when Karla died? That was almost ten years ago! No, it can't be that long . . ."* She pressed her memory further, but to no avail. Ordinarily, Gretel took pride in the fact that she was not an emotional person. But realizing now that she had not cried in ten years seemed more like an indictment than an accomplishment. Her spirits sank.

"Pull yourself up out of this," she said aloud. "There must be something useful to be done." Which, of course, there always was. She blew her nose and wiped her eyes before opening her iPad. She spent the rest of the afternoon and evening reading and responding to emails before drinking two glasses of a suitable Chenin Blanc and retiring to bed.

***

It was now almost midnight, and Ernst was on his way to a rendezvous. He had received a text from a Guardian member back home containing a phone number and the name of a local contact who had agreed to meet him at a club called Silencio at midnight. The man's name was Charles, he was bald, and he would be wearing a Harley-Davidson jacket.

Ernst arrived at the club and immediately spotted Charles seated in a booth along the outer wall of the room. He walked up and said, cautiously, "Charles? Est-ce vous?"

"Ernst?" The two men shook hands and sat down. "Is English okay?" Ernst said. "My French is not so good."

"English is fine. I speak a little German, too, but probably less than you speak French. Everybody learns English. Fucking Americans." They both laughed.

"I understand you have something I need for a project," Ernst said.

"I do, indeed. But we can talk about that outside in my car. Let's enjoy a drink first, yes?"

"Sounds good." Ernst ordered a draft Pilsner and a large peppermint schnapps.

"You Germans and your schnapps," Charles said. "You really love that stuff, don't you?"

"Most do, I guess. Why? What do you drink?"

"I am French! I drink wine! And before you ask, yes! All Frenchmen drink wine. It is in our national blood!"

The two men exchanged small talk about the state of the world and their various complaints relating thereto. They finished their drinks and headed out for a two-block walk to Charles' Peugeot. He opened the doors and both men got in. After checking the surroundings to be sure they were not being watched, Charles opened the glovebox, pulled out a Glock 17, checked the chamber, and handed it to Ernst. "This, my friend, is a fully automatic pistol. You see this switch at the back?" pointing it out. "Push it to the left, it is a semi-automatic. Push it to the right, it is fully automatic. Grab the silencer."

Ernst pulled out the black, cylindrical object he saw in the glovebox. Charles affixed the silencer and said, "With this, you can kill a dozen people before anyone hears the sound."

"Impressive!" Ernst said, and he meant it. "This must have cost a fortune! I don't have that kind of money."

"Your friends in Hanover have deep pockets. The weapon has been pre-paid. There is a knapsack in the trunk which contains three boxes of ammo and two magazines. When you leave, I will open the trunk for you. I suggest you put the gun in the knapsack and walk away. Good enough?"

"Perfect," Ernst replied. "Thank you for your kind assistance. Wish me luck."

"You are doing important work, my friend. Be strong! Au revoir!" He extended his hand, which Ernst accepted and shook vigorously. "Auf Wiedersehen!" he said in reply.

Ernst tucked the gun into his waistband, got out of the car and headed to the trunk, which opened with a click. He put the gun and silencer into the knapsack and closed it up. He shouldered the knapsack, closed the trunk, and headed down the street, feeling an exhilaration that he had not felt since his first time with a young girl named Inge when he was seventeen.

CHAPTER FORTY-FOUR

MARTA woke to the smell of coffee. Her small flat was near the community dining room, and she often benefited from the lovely olfactory alarm clock that was the coffee brewing. She sat up slowly. She had learned from hard experience that moving too quickly at her age can be hazardous. And if she forgot it, her stiffened hips and shoulders usually reminded her.

She stood, attended to her morning routine, and sought out a cup of that wonderful alarm clock from the kitchenette, which she brought back to her apartment as she sat at the computer. "Let's see what is happening in the world this morning," she said aloud. "Ah!" An email from Gretel!" She opened it eagerly.

> Dearest Marta, I am happily in Paris. I am to give a lecture tomorrow on the 12th at the Sorbonne, entitled, "Women as Leaders." I am also being interviewed by a grad student named Cecelia who proposes to write my biography for her Ph.D. dissertation at Princeton. I met with her and with your niece Gretel yesterday. And I want you to know that I told them the whole story. Gretel had never been told, so she was a bit shocked, as you can imagine, but it was the right thing to do. I hope you can appreciate that, if a biography is to be published about my life, it needs to be true. And after all, there is nothing shameful in what happened. In fact, I still see you as a hero in this saga. I know I have told you before, but it is important that you remember that: you are one of my heroes.
>
> Cecelia, Gretel, and I will ride the train together to southern France to commemorate the 75th anniversary of Operation Dragoon, the battle in which our brother was killed. I intend to visit his grave at Draguignan where the ceremony

*will be held. It is very strange; I feel like I know him so well
even though I don't remember him at all.*

*I hope you are well and that you are finding things to
keep you active and useful. I will drop another line after the
commemoration.*

Love, Gretel

Marta held her coffee mug with both hands, warming them. Gretel's email elicited so many memories and emotions. Marta rarely thought about those years anymore, or about her father. She had become a different person, after all. She was Marta Schutte, and she grew up not in Shenandoah but in Reading. *"I suppose Gretel is right; the truth is important,"* she thought to herself. Marta really had come to a sense of peace regarding her family's history and her part in it. Still, as she closed the email, she had an uneasy feeling she could not escape.

Marta dressed and set about the tasks for the day. She checked the calendar. August 10th—AM, work in the garden. PM, cut fabric squares. (Marta enjoyed attending a local quilting club at her church.) Her gnawing uneasiness stayed with her, but as she headed out to the garden, she could still hear her mother saying it: *"Just do your work and all will be well."*

***

Gretel arrived on schedule at Le Faubourg to find Cecelia waiting for her in the lobby. "Are you hungry?" Gretel asked.

"Almost always," Cecelia replied. "Something about this wonderful French cuisine simply demands my attention. Where are we heading?"

"I reserved a table at Le Prince Racine, a nice little bistro about 2 blocks from the Sorbonne. I have a driver waiting. Let's go."

In the limo, Cecelia stared wordlessly out the window. Her discomfort was palpable. "It's okay," Gretel said. "I don't know how to start talking about it, either."

"About your grandmother's history?"

"Revisionist history, you mean, and yes, about that."

"We don't have to talk about it if you don't want to. I guess I was worried it might be intrusive if I brought it up, which is why I didn't. After all, what your grandma told you is really between you and her. I came here to write her biography, not to dig into your family's business."

She paused before adding, "But if you want to talk—off the record—I'll listen."

Gretel smiled. "You have a wisdom beyond your years, I think. Let's just enjoy this evening. Maybe we can talk on the train ride to Draguignan."

"Sounds like a plan," Cecelia replied.

The limo slowly made its way through the tangle of cabs, bicyclists, and meandering tourists, finally arriving at the restaurant about fifteen minutes later. "This traffic! We could have walked here quicker," Gretel complained.

"Yes, but then we wouldn't get to pull up in an embassy limo," Cecelia said with a grin. They entered Le Prince and were seated immediately. As they awaited a bottle of wine, Cecelia said, "So, tell me about your life here in Paris. I don't really know what life as an ambassador is like."

"Champagne and caviar, dahling!" Gretel said with her best Bette Davis flourish. They both laughed. "Mostly it is a bunch of daily humdrum like any other job, except my humdrum involves time spent with French dignitaries. I often represent the U.S. at openings and conferences, and occasionally I become involved in matters of diplomacy between America and France, or in international matters where French and American interests are joined. All in all, it's been a great experience. Paris is a wonderful place to live, especially when you get to stay in the luxurious surroundings of the embassy."

"I have to say," Cecelia replied, "being in Paris again is wonderful. I do love it here. Except for this damned heat wave."

"It has been awful. Some folks have even died from the heat. Thank God for the good HVAC system at the embassy. Unlike most of the U.S., not everyone in Paris has a/c."

The steward brought a lovely bottle of Montrachet white Burgundy and poured two glasses. The wine was astoundingly good and filled the conversation with conviviality. After both had dined on seafood that was perfectly seasoned and expertly prepared, they declined dessert and after dinner drinks, wanting to be clear-headed for the lecture.

"You don't mind walking a couple of blocks, do you?" the Ambassador said.

"Not at all," Cecelia said. "We can stand the heat for that long." But she nearly took back her words as they exited to the street, because the heat and humidity smacked her right in the face. It was like trying to breathe through a hot, wet sponge. "Wow!" Cecelia exclaimed. "Good thing it's only two blocks. This is brutal!"

"Yeah, but we're tough," Gretel said. "Let's do this."

They joined the many others who were out on the streets of Paris, many in various stages of undress, and most of whom were moving slowly like dripping wax. Gretel and Cecelia passed stores with familiar names like Lancome, Giorgio, Yves St. Laurent, and Cartier. "So much money here," Cecelia said.

"Only for the few who actually buy something," Gretel replied. "Trust me, most of the people who go in these places just get a kick out of being seen shopping there."

The two long blocks took only about five minutes to walk, but when they arrived, both women's blouses were nearly soaked through with perspiration. "First stop: salle de repos. I need a makeover!" Gretel said. Cecelia agreed, "Yes, the restroom is up the hall. Good thing we have plenty of time to cool off before the lecture."

The Paris Sorbonne University is a stately building befitting its charge, although the current location is not the original. After a significant reorganization in the 1970's, a restructured Academie resulted in a division of colleges across several locations. The original Sorbonne is still intact but stands unused. Still, as they ascended the steps to the main entrance, Cecelia could not help but be impressed with the thought of how many fine minds had been fashioned by this world-class institution of learning.

Refreshed by the cool air that greeted them inside, Gretel and Cecelia found the ladies room and spent some time at the sink splashing cool water on their faces and toweling off with a moist towelette. Cecelia exited, followed by Gretel. They found an unoccupied marble bench and sat down there, drinking bottled water and enjoying the feeling of the cool, smooth stone on their legs. It was 6:25pm.

✳✳✳

In the courtyard along the approach to the main entrance, people were seated or reclining on the grass beneath the trees, utilizing every square meter of shade. Among them, sporting a backpack and reading an essay by Carl Schmitt entitled, "Die Diktatur," was Ernst Mahler. He looked at his watch. Nearly 6:30. *"Where is she?"* he wondered. Ernst had been waiting outside in the heat since 5:45, not wanting to miss his opportunity to see Senator Schutte as she arrived. He wanted to confront her outside rather than in the lecture hall, believing he would have his closest access and easiest egress there on the walkway. Irritated, he thought, *"Maybe she entered through another door."* But he had scoped out the building and it seemed the only logical route was through the main entryway. He was about to abandon his plan and take her in the lecture hall instead, when he saw the large, black diplomatic limo arrive. "There she is," he said quietly. "There's my girl." He reached into his backpack and loaded the magazine into the Glock. He twisted the silencer into place, slung the backpack over his left shoulder, and stood up.

Gretel was moving slowly toward the entryway, accompanied by her "appendage," Kirk. Ernst could see the bodyguard scanning the area for potential threats, so he removed his hand from inside the backpack to avoid drawing unwanted attention. A large group of young people, many of them appearing to be students and many of them young women, began to gather along the colonnade as the Senator proceeded. She was approaching Ernst's position. He moved in closer. The bodyguard was looking away to the left. Ernst saw this as his moment. He reached into the backpack and pulled out the Glock, aiming it directly at Gretel's chest.

Someone screamed, "Il a une arme à feu!" Kirk instinctively placed himself between his charge and the sound of the scream, drawing his weapon and telling Gretel to get down. Pandemonium ensued, with people screaming and running in every direction as the sound of silenced rounds whizzed numerous times through the air. But when the people had dispersed, the only sound remaining was the cries of agony from Ernst Mahler.

Two persons had reacted immediately to the shout about a man with a gun. One, a retired French army officer named Angèle, isolated Ernst's gun hand and aimed it skyward while her daughter, Aimee, who was a martial arts instructor, grabbed him by the scrotum and squeezed. The weapon fired several times into the air as his grip on the Glock tightened, but Aimee's grip on his testicles had the desired effect and he let go of the gun. Angèle tossed the gun a safe distance away before she used the leverage she had on his thumb to bend his arm behind his back and force him to his knees. She placed a knee squarely in the middle of his back and forced him down on his belly, holding him there. She considered whether she should go ahead and dislocate his thumb, since he was already subdued. But she didn't consider it very long. She gave a violent push upward and heard the loud "crack" of the joint being dislodged. The man's loud scream of agony became the only sound remaining.

Kirk, aware of the possibility of other attackers, stayed with the Senator, his gun drawn, looking quickly in every direction. The two-tone, sing-song sirens of the French police cars signaled their immediate arrival. They took the man away and took statements from Angèle, Aimee, and Kirk. The work of the gendarmerie was amazingly efficient. After a short time, other than the sight of a couple of officers left behind for good measure, the entire scene was as though nothing out of the ordinary had occurred there.

Seeing the police departing, those who had been awaiting the lecture began to gather again, and just as Gretel prepared to address the crowd, her granddaughter and Cecelia emerged from the main entrance to see what all the fuss was about. Amazed at the site of all the police cars and the buzzing of the crowd, they joined Gretel alongside the pavement. "What happened!?" Gretel spoke into her grandmother's ear. "Oh, nothing much," the Senator replied. "Just a little botched assassination attempt." The younger Gretel stood with her mouth agape while Cecelia frantically scribbled in her notepad. The Senator moved to the center of the path and raised her hands, asking for calm and quiet.

"Apparently," Gretel said, "my lecture on the notion of women as leaders is not universally welcomed!" The crowd responded with laughter and cries of "boo!" Gretel motioned for the two heroines of the day to join her on the walkway. As they moved forward, all those gathered broke into spontaneous applause, some shouting "Hourrah!" and "Héros!" and "Vive les femmes!"

"Ladies, please accept my profound thanks for coming to my rescue," Gretel said, grasping the hands of each. Again, the applause erupted. "I know my government will want to express its thanks for your brave assistance." She put her arm around Gretel's shoulders, "This is my granddaughter and namesake, Gretel Eberhart, the U.S. Ambassador to France. Please share your contact information with her so we may arrange a time for a fuller expression of our appreciation. But right now, I came to offer a lecture and you all came to hear it. So, let us get out of this terrible heat and gather in the lecture hall. Allons-y!"

With that, the evening proceeded as planned.

CHAPTER FORTY-FIVE

ARTA turned on the morning TV news program and sat with her coffee and yogurt. She was surveying the morning paper when she heard the claim of "Breaking News" announced. *"Yes, yes, always breaking news,"* she thought. Nonplussed, she continued sipping her coffee and looking through the local paper, skimming first through the obituaries, as had increasingly become her custom. But when she heard the words, "assassination" and "Gretel Schutte", Marta nearly dropped her coffee cup.

She grabbed the remote and turned up the volume. *"French police responded to a report of shots fired at the Paris Sorbonne University yesterday evening. Pennsylvania Senator and Nobel Prize winner Gretel Schutte was arriving to deliver a lecture at the University when a man drew an automatic pistol in an apparent attempt to kill the Senator. A retired French police officer and her daughter intervened to prevent the attack, and the lecture continued as planned.*

The man, identified as Ernst Mahler, is reportedly a member of a right-wing neo-Nazi group in Germany. While no motive for the crime has yet been released, Sen. Schutte has been an outspoken critic of groups that seek to restrict the rights of women. We'll have more on this story as updates come in."

One of the nurse's aides, Loretta, knocked on Marta's door and opened it a bit. Miss Schutte? Did you watch the news this just now? Was that your sister they tried to shoot?" Seeing Marta sitting by the table near the television, she walked in.

"Our little Gretel! She was always such a happy, bright little girl. I played with her and read stories to her. And now see what life brings! I am a tottering old woman in a care home, and she is out stirring up hornet's nests! My, Lord, my Lord . . ."

"Oh, Miss Schutte, you are so not tottering! You are strong and smart. And what your sister does is her business. You can't help her. 'Cept maybe to pray for her, I guess."

"Yes, and I do. But life is sort of ironic like that, you know?" Then she thought about it and answered herself, "No, of course you don't know; you aren't old enough to know. But while you are young, you can do things. You have energy. Your body is strong, and you can get around. Trouble is, when you're young, you don't know for sure what it is you should do most of the time. So, you live out your years, you have your successes and your failures, you grow older and hopefully wiser, and the years pile up. Then you get nearer the end, like me. And now I know what should be done, but I can't do a thing about it. It's a farce! It would be laughable if it weren't so tragic."

"Miss Schutte, I swear sometimes I have no idea what you are sayin', but it always makes me feel better hearin' you say it." Marta smiled and patted Loretta's mahogany-brown hand. "I like you, too, dear. But you had better be on your way. Don't worry about me; I'm fine."

Loretta smiled and headed out to the community room. Marta turned back to her table to finish her coffee, read through the obituaries, and contemplate matters of life and of death.

✳✳✳

Cecelia found the lecture to be lucid, persuasive, and erudite. Senator Schutte was a powerful and provocative public speaker. And it became obvious to even the casual observer that the importance of her topic was only amplified by the attempt to silence her voice. Rather than stifle her, the man's violence had the direct opposite effect; Gretel spoke more firmly and with a greater resolve than ever. There was a three-minute standing ovation after her remarks, and some of the young women were so moved that they were seen leaving with tears in their eyes.

"You know," Cecelia said to Gretel, "I was an admirer of your grandmother, but only of the concept of her. Now that I am beginning to know her, I am beginning to see the wisdom of my dissertation chair's idea; I think writing this biography has the potential to be significant far beyond merely completing my doctorate. I think your grandma might very well be an historic figure, someone on the order of Ghandi or Mother Theresa. She deserves to be remembered. And I feel extremely fortunate to be able to share her story."

Gretel took in Cecelia's words thoughtfully. "I never thought of her that way. She is just Grandma to me. But yeah, me too, I guess. She really is amazing. Let's go to the after-party. Maybe we'll get to stand next to the goddess," she said, sardonically. They both laughed and headed for the reception.

They walked into the University's reception hall to find it filled with people, most holding some form of libation. They could not even see Gretel at first, but they followed the most boisterous clamor to its source, and there she was, holding court. Cecelia said, "Follow me." Being small of stature, Cecelia had learned a while ago how to maneuver through gatherings of people. She picked and chose her opportunities, moving this way and that, pausing just enough here and there, and before long she and Gretel were on the periphery of the Senator's group of admirers.

"You are good!" Gretel said. "I am always waiting, waiting. I never would have gotten through that crowd."

"It's all about strategic determination. Being size 3 doesn't hurt either," Cecelia said with a smile.

Gretel was engaged in an energetic repartee with an academic-looking woman with close-cropped, pink-frosted hair and reading glasses dangling from a lanyard around her neck. The woman said, "Yes, yes, I always say, 'men are like copiers; you need them for reproduction, but that's about it.'" There was a rouse of laughter in response, including Gretel, but she didn't take long to bring a more rational tone to the discussion.

"It's fun to laugh at men now and then; after all, they are such easy targets sometimes." More laughter ensued. "But overall, I am growing tired of the many ways we human beings keep trashing one another. Right-wing vs. Left-wing. Wall Street vs. Main Street. Pro-life vs. Pro-choice. Antifa. Neo-Nazis. Attack ads filling up our media space when we should be receiving information about platforms and positions and ideas for helpful problem-solving. It begins to feel like an expectation that we must all be at one another's throats. And the same is true about the relationship between men and women."

The crowd hushed a bit and began to focus in on Gretel's words. "I am, as you know, a strong advocate for the rights of each woman to pursue her own dreams. This applies to work, education, civic pursuits, romantic relationships and the right to bear or to not bear children. But if, in pursuit of these laudable goals, we stoop to the tactics of dismissing and denigrating our male counterparts, we risk continuing the errors that have subjugated women for centuries, and thereby, hurting our own cause. I am a feminist, yes, but I am also and equally a dedicated humanist. It is high time we all learn to treat one another with respect. And this applies just as much to women as it does to men."

The group of observers—which had grown larger as Gretel spoke— broke into applause, to which Gretel responded, "Oh dear, I've done it again. I am standing on my bully pulpit. Please, everyone, forgive my digression and enjoy your drinks and good conversation. At this, the group broke up enough for Cecelia and Gretel to approach.

"That was quite a speech, Grandma," Gretel said. "Good thing you dispersed them, or they may have demanded your elevation to the court of Venus!" The Senator laughed.

"Yes, I'm afraid it has become something of an occupational hazard. I have always felt passionately about certain things, but now when I talk, people tend to listen. So, I can't resist."

"You are still a professor at heart," Cecelia said. "You just have a much bigger classroom now."

"Quite so, my dear," the Senator responded. A fresh group of solicitors was beginning to clamor around Gretel again, hoping for some conversation or a photo op or an autograph. "I think your adoring public is moving in again. Gretel, what do you think?" Cecelia asked, looking at the Ambassador.

"I think we should go somewhere and have a proper drink." She moved in to kiss her grandmother on the cheek. "Great job this evening, Grandma. Especially the not getting assassinated part. I love you. See you soon." Gretel responded in kind and turned toward a young woman who was asking for her attention.

Gretel and Cecelia wormed their way through the now thinning gathering and found their way outside. With the setting of the sun, the heat had abated slightly, but not enough to make much difference. "Cab?" Gretel asked.

"Definitely," came the response. Cecelia raised her hand and made a loud whistle through her fingers with the other. "Taxi!" she yelled.

"You do take charge, don't you!" Gretel laughed.

"It's hot out here," Cecelia said. "Besides, you can blame your grandma. She inspired me."

They got in the cab and headed over to Le Faubourg where Cecelia was staying. After some small talk and two glasses of wine each at the hotel bar, the evening ended early.

Chapter Forty-six

THE train departed Gare de Lyon train station precisely on time at 10:07am on Thursday morning. The Ambassador's staff booked three first class tickets, which afforded them some degree of privacy for the nearly 5-hour trip.

Cecelia had not experienced French rail travel prior to this trip, and she was amazed. "The train left exactly on time!" she said. "And it is quiet and fast and so clean! We could really learn a thing or two from the French when it comes to traveling."

Gretel responded cynically, "Yeah, try to get any form of public transportation bill past the UAW. We are all about selling individual transport in the U.S.A., and as many as we can. It's a battle no one is willing to fight."

"So, Senator, are you ready to begin?" Cecelia asked, placing her tape recorder between them.

"Yes, let's do. Beyond my emergence from the depths of abuse and patricide, what else would you like to know?" she said, smiling.

Cecelia laughed. "Well, I have already done a good deal of research on your academic and professional accomplishments. I interviewed all your Princeton colleagues that I could find, and I spoke to two of your classmates from your years as a grad student at Princeton. I even found someone from your undergraduate years at Lehigh, a Joshua Morgan."

"Josh Morgan! Oh, my goodness, I'll bet you got an earful from him! He was the first young man who got to third base with me."

"Grandma!" the younger Gretel shrieked.

"What?" the older Gretel responded, apparently offended. "He was a really good kisser!" Cecelia laughed out loud.

Gretel sort of whined, "I know, but . . ."

"But what? You think I was never young? That I never had sexual experiences? What do you think? That you emerged from some dream I had?"

"No, of course not, but . . ."

"But, but, but . . . But me no buts!"

"That's Shakespeare, isn't it?" Cecelia asked.

"No, actually, it is from a play called, 'The Busie Body'. It was written in the early 1700's by a woman named Susanna Centlivre. No surprise though that history ascribed it to someone named William instead of someone with the name of my mother. But . . ." Gretel laughed at the irony, "that is beside the point. The point, my dear, is that I am now nearing eighty years old, but I had a rather audacious sex life for the times in which I came up. I even had a lesbian experience once."

"You did? Seriously?" Gretel said, her eyes wide as she covered her mouth with her hand.

"Yes, I did. It was an experiment, of sorts. As I recall, some illicit substances were involved. I have no regrets, but I would not repeat the experience."

"Grandma, you are killing me here," Gretel said. Cecelia was scribbling and giggling. "You are enjoying this way too much," Gretel scowled at Cecelia. Cecelia nodded and kept snickering as she jotted down her notes.

"And your grandfather and I made each other incredibly happy, too" the elder Gretel continued. "It's just a damned shame that our life together was cut so short by that stupid drunk driver. But at least I had your father. Your father kind of saved my life, I think. If I didn't have him to care about, I'm not sure I would have kept going."

Cecelia sensed the emotions being touched at this point; she also sensed Gretel's discomfort with having such feelings displayed. She turned off the tape recorder and excused herself to use the bathroom.

When she returned, Cecelia could see through a crack in the door that grandmother and granddaughter were embracing, holding one another tenderly. Cecelia continued down the walkway and entered the next car. She found an unoccupied seat and sat there, looking out the window. She began thinking of her own parents and of her mother's mother, Grammy Jayne. Somehow, the idea of her Grammy being young and enjoying a sex life had never occurred to her and thinking of it now seemed repugnant to her. *"Why should it bother me so much? Why does it bother Gretel?"* She decided to put those questions away for another time. But she promised herself she would return to them.

Cecelia came back to find both Gretels recomposed, so she sat down and continued with her questions. She proceeded to move through the stages and milestones of Gretel's life, beginning with her early signs of leadership in elementary school. They discussed her family life, her relationship with her grandmother/mother and her sister/mother, and the things she recalled most vividly about her adoptive father. The remainder of the interview was less emotional and was generally enjoyable for all three women. Before they knew it, the time had flown by, and they heard the announcement: "Nous arrivons à Draguignan."

The transit station was about 11 km. south of Draguignan at a place called Des Arcs. The Ambassador's staff had arranged for a driver to deliver the group to the Hôtel Chabran, which was a brief walk away from the Rhone American Cemetery and Memorial.

On arrival, the immediate impression of the Hôtel Chabran was less than favorable. The façade appeared overgrown with vines and shrubs, with a small. arched entryway so enclosed by greenery that it could easily have been missed by the casual observer. Once inside, however, the place exuded a calm, friendly charm which was immediately inviting. The three guests were warmly greeted and escorted to their respective rooms. After getting settled, they reconvened in the small eatery to share some wine and cheese.

"If you don't mind," the Senator said, "I'd like to visit the cemetery alone first. I want to get the lay of the land for tomorrow, and I also want to find my brother's grave." Cecelia and Gretel both agreed, and after she asked for directions to the cemetery, the elder Gretel walked there accompanied only by her security detail at a respectful distance.

It was a short walk, just a few minutes. The cemetery itself was park-like, with a fountain pool at the center and four quadrants of crosses in straight rows, all starkly white against the green, manicured lawn. There was much activity in preparation for the next day's commemoration ceremony. A newly constructed, raised dais was nearly finished, and technicians were stringing video and audio and power cables in many places.

At the visitors' center, Gretel found a staff member sitting at a desk near the entrance. "I believe my brother is buried here. May I know the location of his grave?"

The staff member opened a registry book. "What is his name, please?"

"Johnny—or perhaps Johann—Neuenschwander," she said. The man looked up at her above the reading glasses perched on his nose. "You do know this is an American cemetery, don't you Madame?" Gretel was perplexed at the question. The man repeated the name, quizzically, "First name Johann? Last name Neuen . . ."

"Neuenschwander. Yes, that is the name." Suddenly, the light bulb went on. The very German name seemed incongruent in this very American World War II place. "Oh! Yes, we were German Americans from Pennsylvania. But I assure you, my brother died fighting the Nazis."

The man returned to his registry and found the name. "Here he is, Johann Neuenschwander, died August 15th at Le Muy. I meant no disrespect, ma'am," the man apologized.

"None taken," Gretel replied. "Can you direct me to the location of his grave?"

"I will take you there myself," the man answered. He rose and offered his arm for Gretel to take, and they walked slowly through the lines of headstones for about 50 yards before arriving at Johnny's burial site. "Here we are, ma'am. Are you okay walking back on your own?"

Gretel appreciated the care the man was showing her. "I will be fine, young man, and thank you for your help. You have been very kind." The man tipped his hat and retreated to the visitor's center. Gretel fixed her gaze on the headstone. "Neuenschwander, Johann." She looked up and out, taking in the whole scene. All these young men! And this a mere tiny fraction of the total of Americans lost in just this one war. She began to expand her vision of the losses. *"Forty million dead in World War I. The war to end all wars . . . Eighty-five million dead in World War II. Nearly all of them young men who had not even begun to live their lives,"* she thought to herself. She shook her head, sadly, looking down once again at her brother's resting place. "Such a waste," she said aloud. "Such a monumentally stupid waste."

Gretel spent a few more minutes honoring the sacrifice of the brother she never knew before heading back to the hotel. She needed to make a few changes to the speech she would be giving tomorrow.

Chapter Forty-seven

ESTIVITIES were scheduled to take place throughout the day on the 14th, the day on which, 75 years earlier, Operation Dragoon and the liberation of southern France had begun. There were connections for visitors to tour the nearby Artillery Museum and the Le Musée des Arts et Traditions Populaires. Those looking for vistas could ascend Malmont a few kilometers north. There was a picnic planned at Parc Haussman with activities and watersports available for children and young adults, and plenty of shady spots and benches for the elderly to enjoy.

The commemoration ceremony itself was scheduled for 10am, the centerpiece of which was to be Gretel's speech. Gretel was up revising parts of her remarks until nearly midnight, and when Cecelia came down for breakfast, she found her studiously engaged with her laptop, going over her final changes.

"Good morning, Senator," Cecelia said. "Ready for your big speech?"

"Good morning, Cecelia. I made a few changes last night, but I'm satisfied with it. Just trying to memorize a few transitions."

Cecelia sat quietly with her coffee and a croissant that was so soft and flaky it needed neither butter nor marmalade. After a few moments, Gretel Eberhart appeared. "Coffee!" she said, with earnest yearning. "I need coffee!" The barista laughed, "Oui, oui, mademoiselle, je me dépêche!" The sound of the milk steaming roared amidst the otherwise tranquil setting. Soon, she produced a steaming cup of café latté.

"Merci beaucoup!" Gretel said, and she sat with the others, enjoying her wake-up brew. "All set, Grandma?"

The Senator closed her laptop and said, "I am."

"Did you find your brother's gravesite?" Gretel asked.

"I did. His grave is marked with a white cross inscribed with his name. It is amidst 860 other white crosses, marking the graves of the American soldiers who died during Operation Dragoon."

Cecelia spoke up. "Was it hard for you, being there?"

Gretel paused before responding. "If you mean, was I sad for my brother being dead, I can't say I was. I never even knew him. What I found myself feeling sad and mystified and angry about was the over-arching absurdity of it all. All those young men, Johnny among them. All gone. And why?"

Cecelia said, "They died fighting fascism, right?"

"Yes, of course, they did. They were brave and filled with the vigor of youth, and they were engaged in a noble cause. But what really happened is what always has happened; the young men died because of the stupid, stubborn bravado and incompetence of the old men who created the mess."

"It *is* absurd, isn't it?" Gretel said. "And tragic."

"Well, the experience of being there had a profound effect on me. I went back to the hotel and made some changes to my remarks. I am going to talk about some of these things this morning. But right now, I want to enjoy one of those lovely croissants and another cup of coffee. Madame?" she motioned by holding her cup aloft. "Un autre, s'il vous plait."

✽ ✽ ✽

At around 9:15 the three women walked over to the cemetery. Many were already seated and many more were arriving. There was an air of solemnity but also of expectation.

The mayor and a regional government official welcomed Gretel and her party. "We are honored to have you here, Senator Schutte and Mademoiselle Ambassador. Please come with us and we will show you what has been prepared for you." The three followed their hosts up onto the dais, where they reviewed the order of events on the program brochure and located the seats that had been reserved for them.

Gretel turned toward Cecelia and said, "I guess you'll have to find yourself a seat somewhere. My granddaughter will be up on the platform with me. Apparently, she gets the honor of introducing her old, sex maniac granny." She grinned at Gretel, who shuffled a bit and said, "Come on, give me a break, Grandma!" Cecelia giggled again and departed to find a place to sit.

The minutes seemingly raced by, and suddenly it was time for the commemoration ceremony to begin. After a few words of welcome by the local French officials, all rose as the American anthem was played by a military band, and a color guard affixed and raised the American flag. Many of the visitors were veterans, and they stood solemnly saluting their flag.

After the audience was seated, several military leaders from the U.S. and from France spoke in turn about the importance of Operation Dragoon, and of the resulting liberation of southern France, a liberation enabled by the sacrifices of those laid to rest in this place. After each speaker, the attendees responded with polite applause.

About 30 minutes into the ceremony, the mayor stood at the podium. "It is my honor to introduce the United States Ambassador to France, the Honorable Gretel Eberhart." Applause greeted Gretel as she approached the lectern.

"Thank you. I have the honor today of introducing a great woman. As you all know, she is the ranking Senator from the State of Pennsylvania, having served in the U.S. Congress for nearly 20 years. She is also a Professor of Humanities and Women's Studies at Princeton University, where she remains on emerita status, and where there exists an endowed chair in Women's Studies in her name. Her persistent, courageous, and unflinching efforts to lift up, educate, and empower women across the globe have resulted in the World Women's Initiative, a global movement and call to action which continues to challenge oppressive and misogynistic attitudes and policies everywhere, and for which she was awarded the Nobel Peace Prize. And if all that were not enough, she is also my namesake and my grandmother." The audience laughed quietly. "Ladies and gentlemen, Mesdames et Messsieurs, the Honorable Gretel Schutte."

The applause was warm and sincere as the people welcomed Gretel to the lectern. She embraced her granddaughter warmly and whispered in her ear, "Nicely done. By the way, you know I love you, right?" The younger Gretel stepped back and grinned. "I know, Grandma, I know. Me, too." The Ambassador took her seat, and as the Senator centered herself behind the lectern, the applause courteously ended. Gretel had her laptop open in front of her, but she didn't need it. She knew what she wanted to say.

"I want to thank the people of Draguignan and of France for welcoming me so warmly. Let me begin my remarks by bringing to your awareness that we are in an historic place of battle. Yes, because of what occurred here 75 years ago. But also, long before that.

"Many of us can trace our genealogical history to one place or another in central and Western Europe. We call ourselves French or German or Belgian or a variety of other titles. But long before the current nation states existed, the entire continent was under assault by warring tribes who wandered southward from the Nordic countries, plundering the land and possessions of those they encountered. One of the largest of those tribes was the Teutons, who, along with another large and successful group called the Cimbri, had been harassing and even defeating Roman outposts in what is now Tuscany and into the foothills west of the Alps.

"In 102 B.C., Rome sent an experienced general with an entire legion to defeat the Teutons, whom they called barbarians. One of the most definitive battles took place just a few kilometers from here, near what is now Aix en Provence. In the end, ninety thousand Teutons were killed and several more thousands were captured and brought back to Rome as slaves. Afterward, the Romans built a fortified battlement right here. It all happened right here. This is blood-soaked land.

"The tools and trade of war have been developed and memorialized here, as well. After Napoleon and the French Revolution, a military infantry industry developed here, followed by the establishment of a school of infantry and an infantry museum which still exists. War has long been a part of this area.

"Seventy-five years ago, the battle raged again, and this time my own family's blood was shed. My earliest memory is attending a memorial service back in Pennsylvania for my brother, Johnny. I was not yet five years old. Johnny had enlisted in the Army to join the fight against fascism when I was just a toddler. He was killed not far from here on the second day of Operation Dragoon. His is one of the 861 graves here at the Rhone Memorial.

"Of course, I was too young to understand what was happening. I remember my mother and sisters crying. I recall seeing and feeling the sadness all around. I knew something was wrong, but I didn't know what it was. And yet, of all the things I recall from that early childhood experience, it is the image of a group of uniformed veterans that stands out in my mind. There were four of them, all elderly, all very kind, who stood smartly beside the memorial marker that had been placed on an empty gravesite, honoring the sacrifice of my brother, Johnny. After the service was completed and the people were leaving, those soldiers, all veterans of World War I, continued to stand at attention, maintaining a stiff salute. And I didn't know why at the time, but I felt compelled to join them.

"I know now, of course, that it was a matter of respect. Those men had survived some terrible experiences during the first World War, and they all knew men who served with them who did not survive. They stood and saluted not only my brother, but all those who, like him, were willing to give their own lives for the sake of others.

"Today, it is our solemn duty to join in that ongoing salute to bravery and courage, and to the willingness to resist aggression in service of the greater good. Today, we gather in their final resting place to honor them. But how shall we do that? How shall we best honor them?

"I suggest that the way to honor such an ultimate sacrifice is by seeking an ultimate goal, and that ultimate goal is peace. It is sobering to realize that these 861 gravesites join a myriad of others over the past century alone. An estimated 40 million dead in World War I, the war to end all wars. An estimated 85 million more killed in World War II. What must change to prevent the need for such sacrifices in the future?

"The answer to that question is to develop better leadership. The way we honor the sacrifices of the young men and women who died fighting aggression is to fashion a sort of leadership which will reject the notion of aggression in all its forms. And I believe this refashioning leadership will be enhanced by the ongoing education and empowerment of qualified women, and by elevating them to the seats of power.

"Now, I do not propose to divide us further. I am not proposing that the problem of aggression in the history of the world can be explained solely by the fact that men have held sway throughout the centuries. There have been leaders who were great and visionary men, to be sure. But I do propose that where aggression has surfaced, it has often been for the lack of any contribution by women to the decision-making process. Not every male leader is an aggressor, and not every female is qualified to lead. But dismissing the potential contributions of half the world's population has not helped, and their exclusion may in fact have been a contributing factor in the worst of our conflicts.

"My World Women's Initiative has been working to achieve this ultimate goal of peace through the empowerment of women. In cultures around the globe, the initiative has pushed for educational, economic, social, and professional development policies which will identify and encourage talented young girls and women, and will help them achieve positions of greater authority and responsibility.

"The goals of this initiative and its message have not always been welcomed. In those quarters where traditional systems of domination are firmly entrenched, and among those adherents to patriarchal social structures, the World Women's Initiative has been ridiculed and sometimes, actively resisted. I have been the recipient of thousands of hateful tweets and emails and social media attacks threatening my security. As you all no doubt have heard, a member of a neo-Nazi group attempted to ambush and kill me as I prepared to give a lecture in Paris just two days ago. Thankfully, no one was hurt. But the use of such tactics as threat or violence to stifle a call for feminine empowerment simply emphasizes the point: we need new models of leadership.

"I had not planned to include the topic of women's empowerment in my remarks today. As important as I believe the topic to be, I had no wish to detract from focusing on the purpose of our gathering, which is to honor those who gave their lives here. But as I stood by the grave of my brother yesterday afternoon, I looked out across this beautifully maintained memorial garden and all the perfectly aligned gravestones. I then extended my thoughts beyond this location to the many other memorial spaces throughout Europe. I considered the huge numbers of those killed in both World Wars. And I finally decided that the only way to truly honor all those sacrifices will be to seek remedial action. We must move beyond a somber remembrance to a hopeful and transformative vision. We must seek to build improved leadership.

"This commune of Draguignan takes its name from an ancient story concerning a hermit named Hermanaire, who allegedly killed a dragon that was attacking travelers and threatening the local growers of grapes and olives. The Latin motto of the town is *Alios nutrio, meos devoro*, which means 'I nourish others, I devour my own'. Let us honor our noble dead by promising them that we will find ways to nourish others *without* devouring our own. Let us work hard to change the focus of this commemoration from sacrifice to upbuilding. Let us develop leaders who will help us to do that. Thank you for the opportunity to honor my brother and all the others who are here remembered."

The applause began with the women but was soon joined by nearly all the men. Even many members of the military stood and applauded Gretel's remarks. The applause continued for several minutes.

Chapter Forty-eight

I N the two weeks that had elapsed since Gretel's trip to Paris and Draguignan, she had accepted and completed interview requests from all the major news outlets. Most of the questions centered on the events in Paris, but her remarks at the commemoration event were also making news. There were attacks and derogatory remarks from the usual conservative quarters, which she had by now come to expect and largely dismissed. But having completed all the interviews she chose to accept, Gretel planned to spend this last free weekend before the Senate reconvened at her *sanctum sanctorum*, her family's farm.

Her security detail met her at Philadelphia International, and not even three hours later they arrived in Shenandoah. As they drove up to the farmhouse, Gretel was delighted to see that Marta was there, seated on a lawn chair beneath one of the great elm trees, reading a book. Gretel got out of the car and shouted to Marta, "Hey! What are you doing here? Don't you know you're an old lady and can't be trusted out on your own?"

Marta stood and laughed. "Watch out. I might go looking for a carving knife."

Greta walked right up to her and embraced her lovingly. "You don't scare me," she said. "I know who you are. You are my big sister. You are my hero."

Marta returned the embrace just as warmly. "It is good to see you back safely. Those news reports gave me more than a little pause."

They stepped back and sat down together. "How did you get here?" Gretel asked. "And how did you know I was coming?"

"Well, I saw all the interviews on the morning shows, so I figured that was out of the way. And I read that the Senate was convening next week. I just thought you would certainly want to spend your last weekend of freedom here at the farm. I hired one of the aides to taxi me."

"Smart big sis," Gretel said with an admiring smile. "You are 90 years old, and you haven't lost a step."

"Well, let's just say that I take my steps more slowly and carefully these days."

Gretel laughed. "Yeah, me too. Just for different reasons." She glanced over at her security detail; another new young agent named Denver something.

"I was able to see and hear your speech at Draguignan. It was very moving. I actually cried."

"I changed a bunch of it from what I had written earlier. I meant what I said about visiting Johnny's grave. Oh! I have pictures." She pulled out her iPhone and shared the many photos she took of the Rhone site with Marta.

"It looks lovely there," Marta said. "It seems like there were quite a lot of people."

"There were. Lots of military. Lots of descendants. It was good to be there. It felt sort of like the closing of a circle for me."

"So, what's next?" Marta asked. "The biography? How is that coming?"

"Cecelia has become a friend. She has an honesty about her that is refreshing. I think she could almost be like another granddaughter. She and young Gretel got along very well. And I believe she will write a very thorough, accurate, and probably too adulatory account of my life and accomplishments. But it will be the truth."

Marta looked off into the cornfields, now beginning to ripen and droop. "The whole truth."

Gretel patted her sister's hand. "Yes, my dear, heroic sister. The whole truth. As it should be. We have nothing to apologize for. We have done our work."

Marta looked over at her and placed her other hand on top of Gretel's. "And all is well." They both smiled. She paused for a moment, remembering. "Our mother was so strong," she said.

"Yes, she was," Gretel said. "And so are we. Let's fix some supper."

"Good idea!" Marta said. And so, they did.

www.ingramcontent.com/pod-product-compliance
Lightning Source LLC
Chambersburg PA
CBHW070221030726
47505CB00006B/1769